But the beginning of things, of a world especially, is necessarily vague, tangled, chaotic, and exceedingly disturbing. How few of us ever emerge from such beginning! How many souls perish in its tumult! (page 17)

There were days when she was happy without knowing why. She was happy to be alive and breathing, when her whole being seemed to be one with the sunlight, the color, the odors, the luxuriant warmth of some perfect Southern day. She liked then to wander alone into strange and unfamiliar places. She discovered many a sunny, sleepy corner, fashioned to dream in. And she found it good to dream and to be alone and unmolested.

There were days when she was unhappy, she did not know why—when it did not seem worth while to be glad or sorry, to be alive or dead; when life appeared to her like a grotesque pandemonium and humanity like worms struggling blindly toward inevitable annihilation. She could not work on such a day, nor weave fancies to stir her pulses and warm her blood. (page 77)

She felt as if a mist had been lifted from her eyes, enabling her to look upon and comprehend the significance of life, that monster made up of beauty and brutality. But among the conflicting sensations which assailed her, there was neither shame nor remorse. There was a dull pang of regret because it was not the kiss of love which had inflamed her, because it was not love which had held this cup of life to her lips. (page 112)

She went on and on. She remembered the night she swam far out, and recalled the terror that seized her at the fear of being unable to regain the shore. She did not look back now, but went on and on, thinking of the blue-grass meadow that she had traversed when a little child, believing that it had no beginning and no end. (page 155)

She looked into the distance, and the old terror flamed up for an instant, then sank again. Edna heard her father's voice and her sister Margaret's. She heard the barking of an old dog that was chained to the sycamore tree. The spurs of the cavalry officer clanged as he walked across the porch. There was the hum of bees, and the musky odor of pinks filled the air. (page 155)

THE AWAKENING
AND SELECTED
SHORT FICTION

Kate Chopin

With an Introduction and
Notes by Rachel Adams

George Stade
Consulting Editorial Director

β

BARNES & NOBLE CLASSICS
NEW YORK

℔

BARNES & NOBLE CLASSICS
NEW YORK

The Awakening was first published in 1899.

"Emancipation," "Elizabeth Stock's One Story," "The Storm," and "A Little Country Girl" are reprinted by permission of Louisiana State University Press from *The Complete Works of Kate Chopin*, edited by Per Seyersted. Copyright © 1997 by Louisiana State University Press.

Introduction, Notes, and For Further Reading Copyright © 2003 by Rachel Adams. Note on Kate Chopin, The World of Kate Chopin and *The Awakening*, Inspired by *The Awakening*, and Comments & Questions Copyright © 2003 by Fine Creative Media, Inc.

The Awakening
ISBN 1-59308-001-8
LC Control Number 2003100460

Produced by:
Fine Creative Media, Inc.
322 Eighth Avenue
New York, NY 10001

President & Publisher: Michael J. Fine
Consulting Editorial Director: George Stade
Editor: Jeffrey Broesche
Editorial Research: Jason Baker
Vice-President Production: Stan Last
Senior Production Manager: Mark A. Jordan
Production Editor: Kerriebeth Mello

Printed in the United States of America
QB
3 5 7 9 10 8 6 4

KATE CHOPIN

❧

KATE CHOPIN was born Catherine O'Flaherty on February 8, 1850, in St. Louis, Missouri, to Thomas O'Flaherty, an Irish immigrant, and Eliza Faris O'Flaherty, a Creole (that is, a descendant of the original French settlers of Louisiana). Chopin's sense of womanhood derived largely from the influences of her Creole great-grandmother and her own mother, who was left widowed in charge of a considerable estate at age twenty-seven. Chopin lived for many years in Louisiana following her marriage in 1870 to Oscar Chopin, with whom she had six children.

As a student at the St. Louis Academy of the Sacred Heart, Chopin kept a "commonplace book," a diary of her daily life, and wrote poetry. After the death of her husband in 1882, she became more serious about her writing; since she wrote about the people and culture of New Orleans, Chopin was first known as a Creole writer. She composed more than 100 short stories, which were compiled in *Bayou Folk* (1894) and *A Night in Acadie* (1897).

Chopin developed a reputation for flamboyance. A woman of independent thought, she belonged to a group of liberal intellectuals who wore eccentric clothing. She disliked social functions but attended them to fulfill her "commercial instinct." Although she never considered herself a women's suffragist or a feminist, she associated with women's rights activists who were part of the St. Louis literary circle. During this period, Chopin's stories focused on taboo subjects, such as interracial relationships, women's infidelity, and sexuality. The most notable of these stories, "Désirée's Baby," was published in *Vogue* magazine in 1893.

Chopin transcended her local status with the publication of *The Awakening* (1899). Influenced by the urbane stories of Guy de Maupassant, Chopin boldly questioned and defied the constraints on a woman's freedom and individuality, but not without paying a price. Conservative literary critics relentlessly condemned the novel as immoral, and Chopin found it increasingly difficult to find a publisher. *The Awakening* was never banned, but the scandal surrounding it placed Chopin on the literary "blacklist" for years. It would take almost a century for *The Awakening* to receive due credit as an important work of art; it was revived as a feminist classic in the 1970s.

Kate Chopin died of a cerebral hemorrhage at her St. Louis home on August 22, 1904. In 1992 Chopin's missing manuscripts were discovered in an old warehouse in Worcester, Massachusetts. Known as the Rankin-Marhefka Fragments, these papers are now at the Missouri Historical Society in St. Louis.

TABLE OF CONTENTS

∽

THE WORLD OF KATE CHOPIN
AND *THE AWAKENING*

1820– 1830	Fanny Wright publicly advocates women's suffrage, the abolition of slavery, birth control, and liberal divorce laws in her book *Course of Popular Lectures* and in the *Free Enquirer*, a radical journal on civil rights.
1848	The Seneca Falls Convention for Women's Rights takes place in Seneca Falls, New York.
1850	Catherine (Kate) O'Flaherty is born on February 8 in St. Louis.
1855	In September Kate enrolls at the St. Louis Academy of the Sacred Heart, a boarding school. She becomes a friend of Kitty Garesché, a classmate who shares her love for reading and writing. On November 1, Kate's father, Thomas, dies in a railroad accident. She leaves school for the next two years.
1859	Charles Darwin publishes *On the Origin of Species by Means of Natural Selection*.
1861	On April 12 the American Civil War begins at Fort Sumter, South Carolina. The Garesché family is marginalized for their Confederate sympathies.
1863	In January Kate's great-grandmother and teacher, Victoire Verdon Charleville, dies. In February, George O'Flaherty, Kate's half-brother and a Confederate soldier, dies from typhoid fever.
1865	The Civil War ends. The Thirteenth Amendment to the U.S. Constitution outlaws slavery.
1866	Susan B. Anthony and Elizabeth Cady Stanton found the American Equal Rights Association to promote women's suffrage.

1867	Kate's teachers at the Academy of the Sacred Heart assign her to keep a commonplace book, which becomes a diary of her intellectual and social life.
1868	In June Kate graduates from the Academy. The Fourteenth Amendment grants African Americans equal protection of the law.
1869	Kate writes "Emancipation: A Life Fable." Anthony and Stanton form the National Woman Suffrage Association to advocate easier divorce and to end gender inequity in employment and pay. The American Woman Suffrage Association (AWSA) is formed in Boston.
1870	Kate marries Oscar Chopin in St. Louis; the couple spends the summer in Europe, then settles in New Orleans. Kate writes her last diary entry during her three-month honeymoon. The AWSA founds the *Women's Journal*, edited by Lucy Stone. Women's journals emerge across the nation, including *The Woman Voter* (New York City) and *Western Woman Voter*. The Fifteenth Amendment grants African-American males the right to vote.
1871	On May 22, Kate Chopin's first son, Jean Baptiste, is born in New Orleans. She spends the summer months at Grand Isle, a resort for wealthy Creole women, which she will later use as the setting of *The Awakening*.
1873	Chopin's brother Thomas dies in a buggy accident. The Comstock Law prohibits the use and prescription of contraceptives. Over the next six years Chopin's sons Oscar, George, Frederick, and Felix and her daughter, Lelia, are born.
1879	When Oscar's cotton business nearly fails, the family moves to Cloutierville, in Natchitoches Parish, Louisiana, to the plantation of Oscar's

family, where Kate becomes acquainted with the Creole community.

1882   In December Oscar dies of a severe malarial fever. The family physician, Frederick Kolbenheyer, suggests that Kate use writing as an outlet for her anger and depression.

1883   Chopin embarks upon a year-long affair with Albert Sampite, a married man.

1884   She moves back to St. Louis.

1885   Chopin's mother, Eliza, dies in June. Kate begins reading Guy de Maupassant, who has published *Une Vie* (1883), followed by *Bel-Ami* (1885). His works inspire her to write "life, not fiction."

1889   Chopin's first poem, "If It Might Be," is published in January in *America*, a political and literary journal. In April she brings Oscar's body back from Cloutierville to St. Louis.

1890   Chopin's first novel, *At Fault*, is published at her expense and meets unfavorable reviews. She discovers the "amoral" stories of Guy de Maupassant, whose influence is evident in *The Awakening*. She becomes involved with the St. Louis literary and publishing circle and socializes with feminists. On December 1, Chopin is inaugurated into the Wednesday Club, an organization whose purpose is to "create and maintain an organized center of thought and action among the women of St. Louis." Many of the club's members also belong to the Woman Suffrage Association of Missouri. Chopin travels to Boston in search of a publisher for her "collection of Creole stories." Her novel *Young Dr. Gosse* is rejected by publishers.

1892   On April 4 Chopin resigns from the Wednesday Club after writing "Miss McEnders," a short story satirizing the society women of St. Louis.

1893   Chopin publishes "Désirée's Baby," one of her
            most notable short stories, in *Vogue* magazine.
            "Mrs. Mobry's Reason," a story hinting at vene-
            real disease that had been rejected more than a
            dozen times, is accepted by the *New Orleans
            Times-Democrat*. New Zealand women win the
            right to vote.

1894   In March Houghton Mifflin (New York) pub-
            lishes *Bayou Folk*, the first collection of
            Chopin's short stories.

1896   Kate destroys the manuscript of *Young Dr.
            Gosse*.

1897   Way and Williams (Chicago) publishes a second
            collection of stories, *A Night In Acadie*. Chopin
            begins work on *The Awakening*.

1899   *The Awakening* is published to mixed reviews,
            some of them scathing. The Wednesday Club
            invites Chopin to give a reading of the novel to
            300 women.

1900   Due to the notoriety of *The Awakening*, the pub-
            lication of Chopin's third collection of short sto-
            ries, *A Vocation and a Voice*, is canceled by the
            publisher who had signed a contract to issue the
            volume. Chopin appears in *Who's Who in
            America*.

1904   On August 20 Chopin dies from a cerebral hem-
            orrhage, two days after she visits the St. Louis
            World's Fair.

1916   Margaret Sanger opens the country's first birth-
            control clinic in Brooklyn, New York. She is ar-
            rested and imprisoned for thirty days.

1920   U.S. women win the right to vote when
            Congress passes the Nineteenth Amendment.

1929   Father Daniel Rankin, a Marist priest, asks Lelia
            Chopin Hattersley for her mother's manuscripts.
            When he receives the papers, Rankin places
            them "on loan" at the University of Pennsylvania

library. Virginia Woolf's *A Room of One's Own* is published in England.

1932   Rankin writes the first Chopin biography, *Kate Chopin and Her Creole Stories*, as his doctoral dissertation at the University of Pennsylvania. The book is later criticized by Chopin's descendants for its inaccuracies.

1955   Chopin's manuscripts are transferred from the University of Pennsylvania library to the Missouri Historical Society.

1960s–1970s   Chopin's works undergo a revival. *The Awakening* is hailed as a feminist classic.

1991   *A Vocation and a Voice* is published.

1992   Linda and Robert Marhefka discover Chopin's manuscripts in an old warehouse in Worcester, Massachusetts. They turn out to be part of the body of work that Rankin had received from Lelia Chopin Hattersley in 1929. Today the Rankin-Marhefka Papers are located at the Missouri Historical Society in St. Louis.

INTRODUCTION

❧

On August 20, 1904, Kate Chopin spent the day at the St. Louis World's Fair. That evening she collapsed of a cerebral hemorrhage and died on August 22. An author with a flair for the coincidental, Chopin probably would have appreciated the ironic overlap between the end of her own life and the arrival of the world's largest international exposition in her hometown.

The greatest event in the city's history, the fair brought some 20,000,000 visitors from around the world to commemorate the hundred-year anniversary of the Louisiana Purchase. Designed to showcase the accomplishments of American civilization, it comprised a miniature city of its own, with a vast expanse of white buildings, lagoons, and carefully landscaped vistas that covered 1,272 acres of Forest Park. Among its many attractions were the Department of Physical Culture, exhibits of the newest artistic, architectural, and technological innovations, the world's largest Ferris wheel, and a presentation by Helen Keller and her teacher, Annie Sullivan. Visitors could drink iced tea and sample their first ice cream cone, a treat invented by one of the exposition's concessionaires. Responsibility for representing the world's cultures fell to the anthropological division, the most elaborate of any World's Fair. Two of its exhibits were especially popular: the massive Philippine Reservation, which educated visitors about America's newest colony, and the Pygmy Village populated with authentic African tribespeople. Photographs of the ethnographic attractions, in which primly costumed white ladies and gentlemen peer at scantily clad natives, are a reminder of the jarring encounters that took place in St. Louis. A complex portrait of modernity in the new century, the fair was the site of dizzying juxtapositions of the exotic and the familiar, the traditional and the innovative.

Like the fair, which bore witness to the birth of modernity

in the United States, Chopin's life spanned a tumultuous period in the nation's history. Born in 1850, when St. Louis was still largely a frontier city, Chopin lived to see it become a bustling, cosmopolitan metropolis. Living in a region divided by Union and Confederate sympathies, she experienced the Civil War firsthand. Raised in a family of slave owners and nurtured by a black mammy, she saw the abolition of slavery and the enfranchisement of African Americans. A devoted daughter, wife, and mother who typified the feminine virtues of the Victorian era, she also shared the strength and independence of the controversial New Woman who strode onto the American scene in the 1890s.

Kate Chopin, née Catherine O'Flaherty, was the second of three children born to Thomas and Eliza Faris O'Flaherty. Her parents' disparate backgrounds are representative of the many intersecting histories that made up the population of nineteenth-century St. Louis. Thomas was an Irish immigrant, who rose from manual laborer to become a successful local businessman. Following the death of his first wife, the thirty-nine-year-old Thomas quickly became engaged to Eliza Faris, twenty-three years his junior, who came from a respectable but impoverished Creole family. If Thomas was living the American dream of new arrivals from Europe, Eliza belonged to the St. Louis establishment, such as it was. With roots that extended back well before the city was an American territory, she descended from the French-speaking Charlevilles, who had moved from Montreal to Louisiana in the 1700s. In this, she is a true Creole of the kind who frequently appear in Chopin's fiction. Eleven years after the marriage of Thomas and Eliza, Thomas suffered a fatal accident, ironically brought about by the very success he had sought since his arrival on American soil. One of a group of important local figures invited to dedicate the new Gasconade Bridge to Jefferson City, he died when the structure collapsed as they crossed it by train.

Only five years old at the time of her father's death, Kate was raised in a household dominated by women. She became a favorite of her great grandmother, Victoire Verdon

Charleville, who taught her French, nurtured her musical talents, and entertained her with stories about her tough and resourceful female ancestors. Kate also found a lifelong friend in Kitty Garesché, her classmate at the St. Louis Academy of the Sacred Heart. The close-knit female community that surrounded Chopin left its mark on her fiction, which often dwells on the struggles of women protagonists to reconcile the demands of marriage, family, and social obligations.

Kate's early adolescence was punctuated by separation and death. The Civil War, which forced the closure of her school and divided the city, brought an end to a comfortable, sheltered childhood. Although St. Louis was officially allied with the Union, many of Kate's family and friends sympathized with the Confederacy. Her half-brother, George O'Flaherty, fought for the South and died of typhoid fever before the War's end. She lost her best friend when the Garesché family was expelled from the city because of its patriarch's aid to the Confederacy (they would be reunited upon Kitty's return in 1868). And thirteen-year-old Kate was most directly touched by the conflict when she was arrested for tearing down a Union flag hung on the porch of the family home, a crime punishable by death. A Confederate partisan raised in an atmosphere where slavery was tolerated, Chopin's racial politics remain ambiguous, and critics seeking resolution have found her fiction rife with contradictions. The same cannot be said of her husband, Oscar Chopin, an avowed racial supremacist and member of the Crescent City White League, a New Orleans group dedicated to preserving white Southern rule.

Oscar Chopin entered Kate's life in 1869, another year of ironic coincidences. She wrote her first story, "Emancipation," a fable about an animal who, having been raised in a cage, discovers the sublime joy of freedom. It is possible to read this story as an allegory for the author's yearning to cast off all social bonds. But at the same time she found herself entangled in new relationships of her own, including her engagement to Oscar, whom she would marry in 1870. Of French descent, Oscar had been raised on the family plantation in Natchitoches (pronounced "nak-e-tosh") Parish in northwestern Louisiana. After a honeymoon in Europe, the couple settled in the American quarter of New Orleans, where Oscar returned to work as a cotton factor, a potentially lucrative position as middleman between growers and traders. Intolerant of outsiders, Kate's new relatives were scandalized by her frank manner and her habits of smoking cigarettes and strolling the city by herself. However, while Chopin would frequently depict fictional women who feel restricted by their husbands, there is little evidence that she was dissatisfied with her own marriage. The Chopins had six children, and they often left the oppressive heat of New Orleans in the summer to vacation in Grand Isle, the Creole resort that is the setting of the first half of *The Awakening*.

When Oscar's business failed, the Chopins moved to the family plantation in Cloutierville (pronounced "cloochy-ville"). There, Kate gave birth to her only daughter, Lelia, and helped Oscar run a general store until his death. Despite Oscar's popularity, his wife's outspokenness and independence marked her as a city dweller, and she was never fully accepted into the provincial society of his hometown. After Oscar died of malaria in 1882, rumors of an affair with Albert Sampite, a married man, did nothing to improve matters. She would write about these experiences in her first novel, *At Fault* (1890), a tale of love between a divorced man and a widow. Out of respect for the marital bond, the widow urges him to return to his alcoholic wife, whose convenient death in a flood allows the two lovers to be united.

Chopin may have begun her serious efforts as a writer out of grief. As a young widow, she contended with the provincialism of Cloutierville for two more years before returning to St. Louis to live with her mother, Eliza. When Eliza died of cancer just one year later, Chopin was heartbroken. But she also began to participate in the intellectual life of the city and to make serious efforts to establish herself as a professional author. Although she moved in literary circles, she resisted alliance with any particular group. A brief membership in the Wednesday Club, a select coterie of women intellectuals who gathered for conversation and debate, only strengthened her distaste for such organized activities. More than once, her fiction depicts women reformers or intellectuals in unflattering terms. Concerned about his wife's erratic behavior in *The Awakening*, Léonce consults the family doctor, who asks him if she has "been associating of late with a circle of pseudo-intellectual women—super-spiritual superior beings" (p. 88). These words drip with a disdain that is unrelieved by authorial commentary.

Struggling to find venues for her work, Chopin wrote regularly and kept careful records of submissions and rejections. At first, she was most successful with regional publications, placing her poem "If It Might Be" in a Chicago magazine called *America* and short stories in the *Philadelphia Music Journal* and *St. Louis Post-Dispatch*. It proved more difficult to access national periodicals like *The Atlantic Monthly*, *Harper's*, and *Century*. At a time when the social conservatism of the Victorian era still prevailed, Chopin's treatment of such controversial topics as extramarital affairs, venereal disease, murder, and miscegenation often made her work unpalatable to the major literary magazines. Eventually she would break into this market by publishing stories in nationally circulating periodicals such as *Vogue*, *Century*, and *Youth's Companion*.

Among Chopin's literary influences was the French writer Guy de Maupassant, whose realism and formal sophistication she admired. Her respect for his frank treatment of taboo subjects inspired her to translate a number of his stories, but their controversial nature made publication difficult. A more conventional early model was the eminent realist author and magazine editor William Dean Howells, who sent her a brief note of praise for her short story "Boulot and Boulotte." For the depiction of strong, independent female characters, Chopin looked to Sarah Orne Jewett and Mary Wilkins Freeman. She has frequently been grouped with these women as a writer of local color fiction, a genre unjustly dismissed by several generations of critics. More recently, scholars have seen her use of local color techniques as a strategy to gain a foothold in the literary marketplace and to stake a claim in contemporary debates about gender, race, and region. From this perspective, her short story "A Gentleman of Bayou Têche," in which an artist from the city attempts to exploit a humble fisherman for his "local color," reads like an allegory for the regional writer's confrontation with the literary establishment.

Reviewers of Chopin's first collection, *Bayou Folk* (1894), failed to notice such instances of understated social commentary. While generally positive, contemporary responses hailed her depiction of charming local details, rather than her treatment of social issues. Reviewers found a more complicated outlook and maturity of authorial voice in her second collection, *A Night in Acadie* (1897). An essay in the *St. Louis Post-Dispatch* praising Chopin's artistry and psychological insight urged readers to think beyond the associations with local color, to recognize "gifts . . . that go deeper than mere patois and local description." A second review demurred, describing Chopin as a specialist in the "childlike southern people who are the subject of her brief romances" and expressing regret that some of the stories were "marred by one or two slight and unnecessary coarseness [sic]."

Despite considerable appreciation by her contemporaries, Chopin would have remained neglected by literary history if it were not for the recovery of *The Awakening* in the 1960s. Its renewed popularity also brought attention to the whole corpus of her work, which includes numerous poems, essays, and short stories, as well as her first novel, *At Fault*. These texts illuminate many of the concerns of *The Awakening* but are also of considerable interest in their own right. Read in its entirety, Chopin's fiction introduces a broad swath of personalities, from impoverished blacks and Acadians of the Bayou to plantation elites and urban intellectuals. Whereas some stories turn seemingly trivial events—the shopping spree of an abstemious middle-aged woman, a country girl's visit to the circus—into dramatic interior conflicts, others deal with more overtly controversial issues such as miscegenation, venereal disease, murder, and extramarital sex. The relatively circumscribed geographical parameters of Chopin's fiction extend from lively, cosmopolitan New Orleans to the insular, rural byways of nineteenth-century Louisiana. Unlike the minutely detailed, inclusive catalogues of realist fiction, her preference is for the sketch, which conveys an impression rather than a sharply delineated picture. Frequently, Chopin writes as an insider whose intimacy with her subjects is conveyed through the use of local dialect and allusions. As a result, whereas the human dramas are readily accessible, contemporary readers may struggle to gain a precise understanding of character and locale.

Chopin's first story, "Emancipation: A Life Fable," is an exception to this rule since it is set in no particular time or place. It is significant largely because it anticipates Edna Pontellier's metamorphosis in *The Awakening*. A male creature is raised in a cage where his physical needs are satisfied by an invisible provider. When the cage is left open one day, he escapes and learns that freedom is far better than comfort. In later stories, the issue of awakening more often centers on female desire, which is sometimes at odds with marriage and social obligations. Chopin's female characters often seem motivated by the same creaturely drives that stirred the animal protagonist of "Emancipation." For married women, husbands are like the invisible master whose care made the beast passive and complacent. Often wives find sexual interest or satisfaction in illicit affairs, which are closely associated with the freedom to choose the objects of their desire. In "A Respectable Woman," Mrs. Baroda is attracted, against her will, to her husband's close friend, Gouvernail. By the story's end, without ceasing to love her husband, she has come to terms with her desires and plans to consummate the affair upon her next meeting with Gouvernail. This theme is carried one step further in "The Storm," a sequel to "At the 'Cadian Ball," an earlier story in which the dashing Alcée Laballière gives up Calixta, the woman he desires, in exchange for a respectable marriage. Years later, when the former lovers are thrown together by bad weather, the violence of the natural world is echoed in their illicit passion. The description emphasizes the deep, irrational needs that drive them against their good intentions: "The generous abundance of her passion, without guile or trickery, was like a white flame which penetrated and found response in depths of his own sensuous nature that had never yet been reached" (p. 255). When the sun comes out, so do prudence and social responsibility; they each return, satisfied, to their respective familial obligations. A somewhat different take on the pleasures of escaping one's commitments is found in "A Pair of Silk Stockings," where a middle-aged widow, who has persistently denied her own material needs in order to provide for others, uses a windfall to indulge in a few hours of shopping, eating, and entertainment. Overcome with the sensual feel of expensive department store clothing, the taste of fine food and wine, and the luxuriant pleasures of a matinee, she briefly allows desire to prevail over her reason or sense of responsibility.

From plantation elites to slaves and humble laborers, Chopin's characters cross the spectrum of economic class and social standing. In some cases, her focus on middle- or upper-class white women relegates others to the background. For example, many have observed that Edna Pontellier's freedom of mobility is enabled by numerous servants, nannies, cooks, and workmen who lurk at the periphery of *The Awakening* without ever being given full realization. Chopin's characteristic understatement makes it difficult to determine whether this is her own perception of an underclass or a criticism of her protagonist's insensitivity. Stories such as "Désirée's Baby," "Athénaïse," and "A Respectable Woman" concern the problems of economically privileged characters. But at times she deals more explicitly with interactions among members of different classes. Set on a farm, "A Shameful Affair" is about a young woman visiting from the city whose lust is inflamed after she is kissed by a particularly handsome field hand. Consumed by desirous but condescending thoughts, she is deeply ashamed to learn that he is a man of her own social status who is masquerading as a laborer for the sake of adventure. Although her desire has not transgressed the lines of class, as it initially appeared, the story suggests that proximity to the land and the rugged bodies that work it is an ideal setting for a woman to discover her own sexuality. "A Gentleman of Bayou Têche" is about an artist from the city who learns a hard lesson about the need to respect rural dwellers. When Mr. Sublet visits a plantation, he persuades Evariste, a humble Acadian fisherman, to pose for a portrait in his work clothes, despite the man's desire to be pictured in his finest. Having compromised Evariste's dignity, Sublet must reevaluate his behavior when Evariste saves his son from drowning. In this story, the lowly Acadians are endowed with more courage and self-respect than the refined urban tourists.

It is equally difficult to pin Chopin down on matters of race, since her fiction often appears to express contradictory views. Whereas some have argued that her advocacy of women's autonomy is compromised by formulaic and sometimes condescending representations of nonwhite characters, others point to stories in which African Americans play important and sympathetic roles. Black characters are entirely marginal in *The Awakening*, seemingly existing only to do the work of cooking, cleaning, and childcare. But why mention them at all? Does Chopin do so as a subtle condemnation of her protagonist's self-absorption? Or is their purpose to provide simple background detail? Evidence for both theories can be found in her writing. The protagonist of "A Country Girl" is taunted by a thoughtless black girl after her grandparents forbid her to go to the circus. Unredeemed during the course of the story, Black Gal's meanness simply adds to the child's sense of tragedy at being left behind. Tante Elodie, the protagonist of "The Godmother" "consider[ed] the emancipation of slaves a great mistake" (p. 260). At the same time, Tante Elodie herself is a woman of questionable morality, whose efforts to conceal a murder committed by her godson ruins their relationship and her own health. There is little evidence that Chopin shares the views of such a character.

There are also instances in which she writes with sensitivity about racial conflict. Her most well-known story, "Désirée's Baby," deals unblinkingly with the problem of miscegenation. Désirée, a woman of unknown parentage, gives birth to a dark-skinned child. After her husband's cruelty drives her to commit suicide, the story ends with the revelation that he is the source of the baby's black blood, a secret he knowingly concealed from his wife. Its conclusion, which implies that miscegenation is a dirty secret at the heart of the most elite Southern families, underscores the tragic consequences of insistence on racial purity.

However, the unexpected revelation at the close of "Désirée's Baby" turns it into the story of a white woman's abuse by a black man, making it less racially progressive than it may seem on first reading. If its position on race remains unresolved, its concern with a woman's victimization is indisputable. Indeed, "Désirée's Baby" represents Chopin's most pessimistic view of marriage as an arrangement that often begins to the mutual satisfaction of both parties but later dissolves into conflict and unhappiness. Although she is aware that marriage can be constraining for both husbands and wives, she returns repeatedly to the particular frustrations of married women, who have far less freedom to escape into work and travel than their spouses. As Edna frets and paces around her home in New Orleans, Léonce retreats to his club and disappears on business trips to New York. But it is rare for Chopin to depict a husband as unforgivably cruel as Armand Aubigny, whose abuse and hypocrisy drives Désirée to suicide.

More commonly, husbands are mildly boring and insensitive, flaws that become increasingly intolerable when their wives encounter more desirable romantic prospects. In both "A Respectable Woman" and "The Storm," functional marriages are temporarily disrupted by sexual desire. The end of "The Storm" sees order restored without harm to any of the parties involved, whereas "A Respectable Woman" concludes with the awakening of a wife's desire for another man. In "The Story of an Hour," a happily married woman with a weak heart is devastated by the news of her husband's death. In a cruel twist of fate, just as she recognizes the potential of her newfound freedom, he walks in the door, having been nowhere near the accident reported to have killed him. The shock of his sudden reappearance causes her to collapse and die of cardiac arrest. Laden with irony, the story's final line— "When the doctors came they said she had died of heart disease—of joy that kills" (p. 201)—pairs extreme happiness with fatal affliction.

If Chopin could represent marriage as both lethal and joyful, a more lengthy exploration of her ambivalence is found in "Athénaïse," the story of an unhappy wife who flees her well-meaning husband, Cazeau. After he tracks her down, their homeward journey takes them past a spot that reminds him of a slave who had escaped his father's plantation when he was a boy. This unsettling memory implies that for women, marriage is tantamount to slavery. But when Athénaïse runs away again and Cazeau declines to pursue her, it is clear that he sees her as more than a piece of property. Nonetheless, the slave metaphor hangs over the conclusion of the story, which sees the wife's willing return after several weeks of exile in New Orleans. The decisive factor is the discovery that she is pregnant, which brings her the first sparks of passion for her husband, along with the desire for home. Although the conclusion relegates Athénaïse to her role as wife and mother, its meaning is ambiguous. On the one hand, it seems to propose that learning to accept one's proper place in the social order is a sign of maturity; on the other, it suggests more affirmatively that a woman must have the freedom to choose when and with whom she will assume that place. So, too, Cazeau has come to recognize his wife's autonomy, rather than taking her presence for granted.

Although many of Chopin's stories concern the problems of married women, she also writes perceptively about middle-aged single women. "A Pair of Silk Stockings" and "Elizabeth Stock's One Story" both deal with the struggles of women forced to support themselves. Mrs. Sommers of "A Pair of Silk Stockings" is a generous and self-sacrificing woman who, for once in her life, puts her own desires above those of others. The sympathetic description of her afternoon shopping spree suggests Chopin's understanding of the loneliness and hardship of life as a single mother. Elizabeth Stock is another working woman, who loses her job at the post office after breaking the rules by reading the mail. Ironically, her transgression comes about because of her excessive dedication, which inspired her to deliver a postcard during a snowstorm when she happened to notice that it bore information crucial to a man's career. After being fired, Elizabeth Stock lacks a sense of purpose and her health gradually declines. However, her sad demise also leads to the discovery of her abilities as a writer by the story's unnamed narrator, who has been assigned the task of sorting through the dead woman's papers. Although most are filled with "bad prose and impossible verse," the ensuing narrative is the one piece that "bore any semblance to a connected or consecutive narration" (p. 245). While no undiscovered genius, Elizabeth Stock is a figure for the woman writer who finds a voice to tell the most important story of her life. Both she and Mrs. Sommers demonstrate the costs of excessive self-sacrifice. So, too, "The Godmother" is about a woman whose best interests are eclipsed by her fierce love for her godson. When he accidentally kills a man, she goes to such lengths to conceal the crime that she destroys their relationship, her friendships, and her own health.

Chopin's stories often depict the pain of betrayal, disappointment, or loss of an intimate friend or relative. A woman with few close friends who avoided association with organized groups, she wrote of women who suffer the burden of unwanted social and emotional bonds. *The Awakening* directly confronts the paradox of being surrounded by loving friends and family but longing for freedom. Like the animal protagonist of "Emancipation," Edna Pontellier is oppressed by the easy satisfaction of her material needs. A prosperous and agreeable husband, generous friends, and a bevy of cooks, maids, and nannies attend to her every whim and desire. Nonetheless, during a summer vacation at Grand Isle, she is stirred by a vague dissatisfaction that she finds both unpleasant and stimulating. Her unexciting marriage gradually begins to feel claustrophobic as she recognizes the more proprietary aspects of her husband's behavior. Confronting the demands of marriage, children, and social life, Edna is stricken with a growing desire to escape it all but has limited resources for exploring the alternatives. Back home in New Orleans, she wanders the city by herself, neglects her responsibilities in the home, dabbles at becoming an artist, and engages in an extramarital affair. When none of these outlets proves satisfactory, she wades out into the sea, presumably to her death.

What Chopin's contemporaries found particularly objectionable about *The Awakening* was the author's apparent unwillingness to condemn her protagonist's unconventional choices. Indeed, many reviews expressed concern with the moral constitution of its central character. "If the author had secured our sympathy for this unpleasant person it would not have been a small victory," wrote a reviewer for *Public Opinion* in June 1899, "but we are well satisfied when Mrs. Pontellier deliberately swims out to her death in the waters of the gulf." Others concurred, finding little grounds for identification with Edna's plight. A piece in *The Nation* dismissively summarized the novel's plot, "'The Awakening' is a sad story of a Southern lady who wanted to do what she wanted to. From wanting to, she did, with disastrous consequences; but as she swims out to sea in the end, it is to be hoped that her example may lie for ever undredged. It is with high expectation that we open the volume, remembering the author's agreeable short stories, and with real disappointment that we close it." Given such evidence, it is not surprising that *The Awakening* has been mythologized as a scandal in its own time. It is certainly true that many of Chopin's contemporaries decried the actions of her independently minded protagonist, and that others expressed disappointment at the novel's departure from the charming local color of her previous fiction. However, these facts have led critics to exaggerate the negativity of reactions to *The Awakening*, and their consequences for Chopin herself.

Indeed, a number of reviews recognized the novel's artistic accomplishment. Charles Deyo, exchange editor for the *St. Louis Post-Dispatch*, enthused: "There may be many opinions touching other aspects of Mrs. Chopin's novel 'The

Awakening,' but all must concede its flawless art." Compared with her previous publications, he detected a newfound confidence in its pages: "There is no uncertainty in the lines, so surely and firmly drawn. Complete mastery is apparent on every page. Nothing is wanting to make a complete artistic whole. In delicious English, quick with life, never a word too much, simple and pure, the story proceeds with classic severity through a labyrinth of doubt and temptation to dumb despair." The *New York Times Saturday Review of Books and Art* concurred, praising Chopin for her bold approach to controversial topics: "The author has a clever way of managing a difficult subject, and wisely tempers the emotional elements found in the situation."

Nancy Walker has observed that emphasis on *The Awakening*'s scandalous reception is linked to several other myths about the end of Chopin's life. The first is that Chopin was ostracized by St. Louis society and that her book was banned from libraries. In truth, her most recent biographer, Emily Toth, notes that "the Mercantile Library and the St. Louis Public Library both bought multiple copies and kept them on the shelves until they wore out." Nor is it the case, as a second myth suggests, that negative reactions to *The Awakening* drove Chopin into authorial paralysis. She lived only four years after its publication and, although she struggled to find venues for publishing her work, she continued to write and circulate short stories until her death.

It is true, however, that *The Awakening* was not fully appreciated until its rediscovery half a century later by a new generation of readers, who acknowledged its considerable formal sophistication and the complexity of its characterization. The publication of two major works by Norwegian scholar Per Seyersted—*Kate Chopin: A Critical Biography* and *The Complete Works of Kate Chopin*—inaugurated the reassessment of Chopin's career that would establish her firmly within the annals of American literary history. It is no accident that surging interest in Chopin in the early 1970s coincided with the emergence of feminist criticism, which sought to bring overlooked authors into the literary canon and to

reevaluate themes and locations trivialized by earlier generations of critics because of their association with women writers. While controversial to her contemporaries, Chopin's
frank treatment of female desire and autonomy, the dissatisfactions of marriage and motherhood, and the importance of
artistic expression intersected perfectly with the concerns of
the women's movement. Influential members of the first generation of feminist scholars such as Elaine Showalter, Cynthia
Griffin Wolff, Elizabeth Fox-Genovese, and Sandra Gilbert
would use Chopin as a paradigmatic instance of the work of
feminist literary recovery. But once the struggle to establish
Chopin as an important American author was won, it was
possible to see that her significance extends beyond the bold
thematization of women's concerns. Her fiction's considerable technical accomplishment and complex treatment of diverse characters and topics makes her a subject of ongoing
scholarly interest. As critical tastes change and novels go in
and out of fashion, Chopin's work has consistently remained
in print and become a staple of course syllabi.

The durability of *The Awakening* is due, in part, to the fact
that, as with so much of Chopin's previous writing, it refuses
to provide simple answers to the difficult questions it raises. Its
conclusion has proved especially resistant to definitive inter-
pretation. Is Edna's suicide a victory over the many demands
her society has made of her? Or is it an easy way out of the
otherwise messy and inevitable compromises of modern existence? Has she reclaimed control by asserting the right to end
her own life? Or has she passively acquiesced to her fate? Is
wading into the sea a liberating alternative to the confines of a
male-dominated culture? Or is it a pessimistic admission that
women cannot find a space of their own within the existing
social order?

How various readers have answered these questions has
much to do with their assessment of Edna's character—
whether they take her to be a feminist heroine, selfish woman,
victim, or bold iconoclast—as well as their understanding of
the novel's place within literary tradition. In certain respects,
The Awakening borrows the concerns and settings of nine-

teenth-century sentimental fiction. As Elaine Showalter has
argued, its emphasis on domestic space and relationships between women locates it in the company of novels by such sentimentalist precursors as Harriet Beecher Stowe, Louisa May
Alcott, Susan Warner, and Maria Cummins. However,
Chopin avoids the rhetorical excesses and moralizing tenden-
cies of these earlier authors. Her attention to the specifics of
place, depiction of everyday life, and concern with women's
artistic autonomy aligns her with the somewhat later generation of female regionalists like Sarah Orne Jewett and Mary
Wilkins Freeman.

There is also a case to be made for *The Awakening* as a
work of naturalist fiction, despite the fact that this category
has typically been associated with such aggressively masculine authors as Jack London and Frank Norris. Influenced by
Darwinian theory, the naturalists depicted a world governed
by powerful, amoral forces that would ultimately defeat the
exertion of human agency and will. Bert Bender has suggested that Chopin was provoked by Darwin's theory of sexual
selection, which emphasized the competitive aspects of the
species' struggle for reproduction. Though compelled by the
notion of an innate physical attraction that could not be regulated by social institutions, Chopin objected to Darwin's
Victorian characterization of the female as passive and modest. A robust woman with strong appetites and a well-propor-
tioned physique, Edna is determined to take an active role in
the ritual of sexual selection. In a Darwinian universe, the social conventions of marriage are irrelevant to the sexual drive,
which demands variety over constancy in choice of partners.
In Bender's analysis, Edna's suicide results from the realization that her life is governed by forces outside her control.
Her desire for autonomy is at odds with the species' necessity
to reproduce, which—after the exhilarating process of sexual
conquest—inevitably relegates women to the role of motherhood.

In its emphasis on interior psychology at the expense of external description, and in its formal experimentation with
time and perception, *The Awakening* also anticipates many of

the strategies of modernist fiction. In contrast to the realist commitment to mundane surface detail, Chopin seems relatively unconcerned with mimetic representation. Michael Gilmore has described this quality as a privileging of subjective responses and expressions over the replication of external reality. He attributes Chopin's interest in music to the fact that it is "an imageless art . . . neither mirroring nor duplicating an external form, and it shakes Edna to the depths because it provides immediate entrance to the subjective world of feelings." *The Awakening* seems propelled more by impulse than measured narrative progression. While individual chapters are temporally coherent, the time that passes between one chapter and the next is highly varied, sometimes spanning a few hours and sometimes making a bigger or less clearly delineated leap forward. Memories, particularly of Edna's childhood in the Kentucky blue-grass country, surface at unpredictable moments like a musical refrain that ties past and present together.

Just as time does not move in a predictable pattern, narrative perspective in *The Awakening* is constantly shifting. At some points the third-person narrator seems to echo Edna's point of view. For example, in the final moments of her life, the narrative voice channels the protagonist's own subjectivity: "How strange and awful it seemed to stand naked under the sky! how delicious! She felt like some new-born creature, opening its eyes in a familiar world that it had never known" (p. 154). At other points, it hovers at a remove that allows for ironic commentary. This is the case in an account of an evening at Grand Isle. When a tedious interlude by the Farival twins is interrupted by the parrot's shrieks, the narrator observes wryly, "He was the only being present who possessed sufficient candor to admit that he was not listening to these gracious performances for the first time that summer" (p. 31). We are to understand that these are not Edna's observations, but the products of a more detached narrative consciousness. So, too, on the night of Edna's first swim, the narrator checks Edna's perceptions against reality. Believing herself to be far from shore, "a quick vision of death smote her soul, and for a

second of time appalled and enfeebled her senses" (p. 37).
The sublimity of Edna's experience—in which she genuinely
believes she has confronted the possibility of her own death—
is put into perspective with a more measured description of
the same event: "She had not gone any great distance—that
is, what would have been a great distance for an experienced
swimmer" (p. 37). This tonal disparity distinguishes Edna's
own melodramatic sensibility from a more reasoned narrative
voice. Such experiments with narrative and point of view lo-
cate *The Awakening* somewhere between the realist commitment to external detail and the modernist interest in
individual subjectivity.

Such varied cadences of tone and perspective are well
suited to this story of desire and sexual awakening. Although
the actual consummation of Edna's affair with Alcée Arobin
takes place in the space between chapters XXXI and XXXII,
the novel is suffused with sensual images, from the illicit
books that circulate at Grand Isle to the luxuriant feel of expensive clothes and possessions, the gustatory pleasures of
fine food and drink, the romantic intonations of the piano,
and the caressing waves of the sea. Experiencing a heightened
perception that engages all of her senses, Edna's awakening is
not reducible to heterosexual contact. And although the flir-
tations of Robert Lebrun are most commonly credited for
prompting Edna's desire, Showalter has rightly observed that
her sensuality is actually ignited by intimate relationships
with two women, Adèle Ratignolle and Mademoiselle Reisz.
Sitting with Adèle and Robert, Edna's gaze is drawn not to
Robert but to the "excessive physical charm" (p. 18) of her female companion. Seeking words to describe the intense bond
between Edna and Adèle, the narrator concludes that "we
might as well call [it] love" (p. 18). Edna develops a very different but equally intense attachment to the dour
Mademoiselle Reisz. Hearing her at the piano arouses Edna's
passions to an orgasmic intensity that resonates "within her
soul, swaying it, lashing it, as the waves daily beat upon her
splendid body" (p. 35). As this passage suggests, when it
comes to women, love and physical desire are closely aligned.

In Edna's relationships with men, the two are more often at odds. With a history of romantic attachments to unattainable male figures—"a sad-eyed cavalry officer who visited her father in Kentucky" (p. 23), her neighbor's fiancée, a great tragedian—it is not clear that Edna is actually seeking to consummate a heterosexual relationship. Although she loves Robert, she has sex with Arobin because his kiss awakens her desire. The regret she feels afterward is "neither shame nor remorse" (p. 112), but more a dawning awareness that she is "assailed" by emotions more powerful than reason or affection.

The seeming paradox that a greater knowledge of self comes through the suppression of rationality is at the heart of Edna's development. In spite of its title and the many references to awakening that appear throughout the novel, readers are often surprised at how often Edna is either sleeping or overcome with a drowsiness that obstructs clarity of thought. For every image of a stirring, emergent consciousness there is another of narcotic stupor. As a "light was beginning to dawn dimly within her" (p. 17), Edna is moved not to wakefulness but to dreams; learning to swim gives her new power "to control the working of her body and her soul" (p. 37), but it also inspires her to reach "for the unlimited in which to lose herself" (p. 37). Whereas Adèle is a figure of bustling, productive maternity, Edna is listless and disengaged. Whereas Mademoiselle Reisz turns her artistic talents into a career, Edna is satisfied to dabble at her painting "in an unprofessional way" (p. 15). Ironically, then, the awakening intimated by the novel's title is not an initiation into any of the recognizable social roles modeled by its characters, but rather an escape from them.

This conclusion troubled Chopin's contemporaries because it seemed to endorse a destructive self-absorption at the expense of social responsibility. It has provoked more recent readers because they see the extent to which Edna's freedom is bought through the labor of others. She is surrounded by people who work, either in the home, like the resourceful Adèle, or in professions, like her husband. At the same time, the anonymous and rather disagreeable quadroon who cares for her children, the servants who shop, cook, and clean, and the Mexicans, Acadians, and African Americans who exist on the narrative periphery, create an environment in which Edna has no productive function. It is no wonder that early in the novel Léonce regards his sunburned wife as a piece of damaged property. Her crisis has been described by Michelle Birnbaum as that of the "colonial subject," who cannot consciously recognize the racial and class inequities around her and consequently internalizes those conflicts as divisions within herself. Instead of acknowledging the disparities in her social environment, she experiences an imbalance within her own psychic landscape.

That Edna accepts the racial and class hierarchies of her culture is unsurprising. She lives in a sheltered and highly regulated environment that is rarely interrupted by the surrounding world. This insularity explains why the party at Grand Isle is so dismayed to learn of Robert's imminent departure for Vera Cruz. It also explains the striking ignorance of their observations about Mexico: The pious lady in black asks him to investigate whether the power of her Mexican prayer beads extends beyond the border; Madame Ratignolle remarks that Mexicans are "a treacherous people, unscrupulous and revengeful" (p. 57), and Victor relays a trite story about "a Mexican girl who served chocolate one winter in a restaurant in Dauphine Street" (p. 57). Not only do they know nothing of Mexico, but lacking resources to understand genuine cultural or geographic difference, they can relate to the foreign only though the lens of their own limited experiences. Even less worldly than her companions, Edna remains silent during this conversation because she can "think of nothing to say about Mexico or the Mexicans" (p. 57). Nor, for that matter, can Robert, whose exact reasons for going, aside from an obscure business prospect, remain murky. Critics have noted that the character of Mariequita and an unnamed "Mexican girl" who gives Robert an embroidered tobacco pouch serve to associate travel south of the border with sexual adventure. But they have differed over the meanings of that association, some seeing it as a place of homosexual license, a reading that explains the unconsummated romance between Edna and Robert as well as "the gentleman whom he intend[ed] to join at Vera Cruz" (p. 56), others as a place of heterosexual opportunity.

While the narrative provides little means to resolve these questions, it is possible to remark on Mexico's significance to Edna and her fate. She has nothing to say about it because she cannot conceive of places beyond the bounds of her own limited world. Having led a protected and uneventful life, she is unable to imagine that the solution to her problems lies in going elsewhere. Whereas men move to expand the horizon of experience—Léonce leaves his family behind for business trips to New York, and Robert leaves the country altogether— Edna's only movement (other than circular wanderings in the city) is toward greater confinement, as she relocates from her spacious home into the more enclosed "pigeon house" around the corner. While it might be possible to see the new house as a cozy version of Virginia Woolf's longed-for "room of one's own," it is also, more ominously, akin to the cage in "Emancipation." Facing an increasing claustrophobia, which is inescapable through either imaginative or literal movement, Edna comes to believe that death is the only possible solution.

The profound ignorance of the characters in *The Awakening* about the rest of the world returns us to Chopin's own last activity, her visit to the St. Louis World's Fair. The Fair spoke to Americans' thirst for knowledge about the rest of the world. At the same time, its allegedly wide-angle vision was actually a telescope that used other nations as a reference point to establish American superiority. As much as it addressed the desire to learn about and collaborate with a global community, it was also designed to parade the nation's cultural advancement and growing economic and military might on a world stage. The sad irony that with supremacy come loneliness and isolation is crystallized in the image of Edna's favored musical composition, "Solitude," which evokes a man standing desolate and despairing before the sea. In addition to its many other accomplishments, *The Awakening* succeeds in illustrating the alienation that results from having the best that the world can offer, but existing under conditions that make it impossible to give of oneself in return. Chopin, who read widely, traveled to Europe, and witnessed pivotal events of her time, should not be confused with her protagonist. A widow, single mother, and professional writer, she lived her life fully and to its end. Such experience grants the far more worldly author the insight to depict a character whose lack of reciprocity is less an individual flaw than a flaw of a culture that treated women as property and maintained rigid racial and class structures. Although Chopin herself is often able to see around such obstacles, she also blames them for preventing Edna from finding other opportunities for self-realization on the rich and seething margins of her own empty, white world.

Rachel Adams teaches nineteenth- and twentieth-century American literature at Columbia University. She is the author of *Sideshow U.S.A.: Freaks and the American Cultural Imagination* (Chicago: University of Chicago Press, 2001) and the co-editor of *The Masculinity Studies Reader* (Malden, MA: Blackwell Publishers, 2002). She has also published articles on American literature, film, disability, race, and gender studies.

THE AWAKENING

I

*

A GREEN AND YELLOW parrot, which hung in a cage outside the door, kept repeating over and over:

"*Allez vous-en! Allez vous-en! Sapristi!*° That's all right!"

He could speak a little Spanish, and also a language which nobody understood, unless it was the mocking-bird that hung on the other side of the door, whistling his fluty notes out upon the breeze with maddening persistence.

Mr. Pontellier, unable to read his newspaper with any degree of comfort, arose with an expression and an exclamation of disgust. He walked down the gallery and across the narrow "bridges" which connected the Lebrun cottages one with the other. He had been seated before the door of the main house. The parrot and the mocking-bird were the property of Madame Lebrun, and they had the right to make all the noise they wished. Mr. Pontellier had the privilege of quitting their society when they ceased to be entertaining.

He stopped before the door of his own cottage, which was the fourth one from the main building and next to the last. Seating himself in a wicker rocker which was there, he once more applied himself to the task of reading the newspaper. The day was Sunday; the paper was a day old. The Sunday papers had not yet reached Grand Isle.† He was already acquainted with the market reports, and he glanced restlessly over the editorials and bits of news which he had not had time to read before quitting New Orleans the day before.

Mr. Pontellier wore eye-glasses. He was a man of forty, of medium height and rather slender build; he stooped a little.

---

* Go away! Go away! For God's sake! (French [henceforth, Fr.]).

† An island located in southeastern Louisiana, about 50 miles south of New Orleans, between the Gulf of Mexico and Caminada Bay. In the early 19th century it was the headquarters of pirate Jean Lafitte's smuggling operations.

His hair was brown and straight, parted on one side. His beard was neatly and closely trimmed.

Once in a while he withdrew his glance from the newspaper and looked about him. There was more noise than ever over at the house. The main building was called "the house," to distinguish it from the cottages. The chattering and whistling birds were still at it. Two young girls, the Farival twins, were playing a duet from *Zampa** upon the piano. Madame Lebrun was bustling in and out, giving orders in a high key to a yard-boy whenever she got inside the house, and directions in an equally high voice to a dining-room servant whenever she got outside. She was a fresh, pretty woman, clad always in white with elbow sleeves. Her starched skirts crinkled as she came and went. Farther down, before one of the cottages, a lady in black was walking demurely up and down, telling her beads. A good many persons of the *pension* had gone over to the *Chênière Caminada*† in Beaudelet's lugger‡ to hear mass. Some young people were out under the wateroaks playing croquet. Mr. Pontellier's two children were there—sturdy little fellows of four and five. A quadroon§ nurse followed them about with a far-away, meditative air.

Mr. Pontellier finally lit a cigar and began to smoke, letting the paper drag idly from his hand. He fixed his gaze upon a white sunshade that was advancing at snail's pace from the beach. He could see it plainly between the gaunt trunks of the water-oaks and across the stretch of yellow camomile. The gulf looked far away, melting hazily into the blue of the horizon. The sunshade continued to approach slowly. Beneath its pink-lined shelter were his wife, Mrs. Pontellier, and young Robert Lebrun. When they reached the cottage, the two

---

* A romantic opera about love and betrayal by the French composer Ferdinand Hérold (1791–1833); it was first performed in 1831.

† A popular vacation resort located on the Louisiana coast of the Gulf of Mexico.

‡ A small sailboat.

§ A person with one-quarter black ancestry.

seated themselves with some appearance of fatigue upon the upper step of the porch, facing each other, each leaning against a supporting post.

"What folly! to bathe at such an hour in such heat!" exclaimed Mr. Pontellier. He himself had taken a plunge at daylight. That was why the morning seemed long to him.

"You are burnt beyond recognition," he added, looking at his wife as one looks at a valuable piece of personal property which has suffered some damage. She held up her hands, strong, shapely hands, and surveyed them critically, drawing up her lawn* sleeves above the wrists. Looking at them reminded her of her rings, which she had given to her husband before leaving for the beach. She silently reached out to him, and he, understanding, took the rings from his vest pocket and dropped them into her open palm. She slipped them upon her fingers; then clasping her knees, she looked across at Robert and began to laugh. The rings sparkled upon her fingers. He sent back an answering smile.

"What is it?" asked Pontellier, looking lazily and amused from one to the other. It was some utter nonsense; some adventure out there in the water, and they both tried to relate it at once. It did not seem half so amusing when told. They realized this, and so did Mr. Pontellier. He yawned and stretched himself. Then he got up, saying he had half a mind to go over to Klein's hotel and play a game of billiards.

"Come go along, Lebrun," he proposed to Robert. But Robert admitted quite frankly that he preferred to stay where he was and talk to Mrs. Pontellier.

"Well, send him about his business when he bores you, Edna," instructed her husband as he prepared to leave.

"Here, take the umbrella," she exclaimed, holding it out to him. He accepted the sunshade, and lifting it over his head descended the steps and walked away.

"Coming back to dinner?" his wife called after him. He halted a moment and shrugged his shoulders. He felt in his

---

* Delicate fabric of cotton or linen.

vest pocket; there was a ten-dollar bill there. He did not know; perhaps he would return for the early dinner and perhaps he would not. It all depended upon the company which he found over at Klein's and the size of "the game." He did not say this, but she understood it, and laughed, nodding good-by to him.

Both children wanted to follow their father when they saw him starting out. He kissed them and promised to bring them back bonbons and peanuts.

II

MRS. PONTELLIER'S EYES WERE quick and bright; they were a yellowish brown, about the color of her hair. She had a way of turning them swiftly upon an object and holding them there as if lost in some inward maze of contemplation or thought.

Her eyebrows were a shade darker than her hair. They were thick and almost horizontal, emphasizing the depth of her eyes. She was rather handsome than beautiful. Her face was captivating by reason of a certain frankness of expression and a contradictory subtle play of features. Her manner was engaging.

Robert rolled a cigarette. He smoked cigarettes because he could not afford cigars, he said. He had a cigar in his pocket which Mr. Pontellier had presented him with, and he was saving it for his after-dinner smoke.

This seemed quite proper and natural on his part. In coloring he was not unlike his companion. A clean-shaved face made the resemblance more pronounced than it would otherwise have been. There rested no shadow of care upon his open countenance. His eyes gathered in and reflected the light and languor of the summer day.

Mrs. Pontellier reached over for a palm-leaf fan that lay on the porch and began to fan herself, while Robert sent between his lips light puffs from his cigarette. They chatted incessantly: about the things around them; their amusing adventure out in the water—it had again assumed its entertaining aspect; about the wind, the trees, the people who had gone to the *Chênière*; about the children playing croquet under the oaks, and the Farival twins, who were now performing the overture to "The Poet and the Peasant."*

Robert talked a good deal about himself. He was very young, and did not know any better. Mrs. Pontellier talked a little about herself for the same reason. Each was interested in what the other said. Robert spoke of his intention to go to Mexico in the autumn, where fortune awaited him. He was always intending to go to Mexico, but some way never got there. Meanwhile he held on to his modest position in a mercantile house† in New Orleans, where an equal familiarity with English, French and Spanish gave him no small value as a clerk and correspondent.

He was spending his summer vacation, as he always did, with his mother at Grand Isle. In former times, before Robert could remember, "the house" had been a summer luxury of the Lebruns. Now, flanked by its dozen or more cottages, which were always filled with exclusive visitors from the *"Quartier Français,"*‡ it enabled Madame Lebrun to maintain the easy and comfortable existence which appeared to be her birthright.

Mrs. Pontellier talked about her father's Mississippi plantation and her girlhood home in the old Kentucky blue-grass country. She was an American woman, with a small infusion of French which seemed to have been lost in dilution. She read a letter from her sister, who was away in the East, and

---

* A musical composition by the Austrian Franz Suppé (1819–1895), known as a composer of operettas.

† A commercial institution involving finance or trading.

‡ The French Quarter (Fr.), the oldest part of New Orleans, settled in the 1700s.

who had engaged herself to be married. Robert was interested, and wanted to know what manner of girls the sisters were, what the father was like, and how long the mother had been dead.

When Mrs. Pontellier folded the letter it was time for her to dress for the early dinner.

"I see Léonce isn't coming back," she said, with a glance in the direction whence her husband had disappeared. Robert supposed he was not, as there were a good many New Orleans club men over at Klein's.

When Mrs. Pontellier left him to enter her room, the young man descended the steps and strolled over toward the croquet players, where, during the half-hour before dinner, he amused himself with the little Pontellier children, who were very fond of him.

III

IT WAS ELEVEN O'CLOCK that night when Mr. Pontellier returned from Klein's hotel. He was in an excellent humor, in high spirits, and very talkative. His entrance awoke his wife, who was in bed and fast asleep when he came in. He talked to her while he undressed, telling her anecdotes and bits of news and gossip that he had gathered during the day. From his trousers pockets he took a fistful of crumpled bank notes and a good deal of silver coin, which he piled on the bureau indiscriminately with keys, knife, handkerchief, and whatever else happened to be in his pockets. She was overcome with sleep, and answered him with little half utterances.

He thought it very discouraging that his wife, who was the sole object of his existence, evinced so little interest in things which concerned him, and valued so little his conversation.

Mr. Pontellier had forgotten the bonbons and peanuts for

the boys. Notwithstanding he loved them very much, and went into the adjoining room where they slept to take a look at them and make sure that they were resting comfortably. The result of his investigation was far from satisfactory. He turned and shifted the youngsters about in bed. One of them began to kick and talk about a basket full of crabs.

Mr. Pontellier returned to his wife with the information that Raoul had a high fever and needed looking after. Then he lit a cigar and went and sat near the open door to smoke it.

Mrs. Pontellier was quite sure Raoul had no fever. He had gone to bed perfectly well, she said, and nothing had ailed him all day. Mr. Pontellier was too well acquainted with fever symptoms to be mistaken. He assured her the child was consuming at that moment in the next room.

He reproached his wife with her inattention, her habitual neglect of the children. If it was not a mother's place to look after children, whose on earth was it? He himself had his hands full with his brokerage business. He could not be in two places at once; making a living for his family on the street, and staying at home to see that no harm befell them. He talked in a monotonous, insistent way.

Mrs. Pontellier sprang out of bed and went into the next room. She soon came back and sat on the edge of the bed, leaning her head down on the pillow. She said nothing, and refused to answer her husband when he questioned her. When his cigar was smoked out he went to bed, and in half a minute he was fast asleep.

Mrs. Pontellier was by that time thoroughly awake. She began to cry a little, and wiped her eyes on the sleeve of her *peignoir.** Blowing out the candle, which her husband had left burning, she slipped her bare feet into a pair of satin *mules*† at the foot of the bed and went out on the porch, where she sat down in the wicker chair and began to rock gently to and fro.

---

* Robe (Fr.).

† Slippers (Fr.).

It was then past midnight. The cottages were all dark. A single faint light gleamed out from the hallway of the house. There was no sound abroad except the hooting of an old owl in the top of a water-oak, and the everlasting voice of the sea, that was not uplifted at that soft hour. It broke like a mournful lullaby upon the night.

The tears came so fast to Mrs. Pontellier's eyes that the damp sleeve of her *peignoir* no longer served to dry them. She was holding the back of her chair with one hand; her loose sleeve had slipped almost to the shoulder of her uplifted arm. Turning, she thrust her face, steaming and wet, into the bend of her arm, and she went on crying there, not caring any longer to dry her face, her eyes, her arms. She could not have told why she was crying. Such experiences as the foregoing were not uncommon in her married life. They seemed never before to have weighed much against the abundance of her husband's kindness and a uniform devotion which had come to be tacit and self-understood.

An indescribable oppression, which seemed to generate in some unfamiliar part of her consciousness, filled her whole being with a vague anguish. It was like a shadow, like a mist passing across her soul's summer day. It was strange and unfamiliar; it was a mood. She did not sit there inwardly upbraiding her husband, lamenting at Fate, which had directed her footsteps to the path which they had taken. She was just having a good cry all to herself. The mosquitoes made merry over her, biting her firm, round arms and nipping at her bare insteps.

The little stinging, buzzing imps succeeded in dispelling a mood which might have held her there in the darkness half a night longer.

The following morning Mr. Pontellier was up in good time to take the rockaway* which was to convey him to the steamer at the wharf. He was returning to the city to his business, and they would not see him again at the Island till the coming Saturday. He had regained his composure, which seemed to

---

* A light, low, four-wheeled, horse-drawn carriage.

have been somewhat impaired the night before. He was eager to be gone, as he looked forward to a lively week in Carondelet Street.*

Mr. Pontellier gave his wife half of the money which he had brought away from Klein's hotel the evening before. She liked money as well as most women, and accepted it with no little satisfaction.

"It will buy a handsome wedding present for Sister Janet!" she exclaimed, smoothing out the bills as she counted them one by one.

"Oh! we'll treat Sister Janet better than that, my dear," he laughed, as he prepared to kiss her good-by.

The boys were tumbling about, clinging to his legs, imploring that numerous things be brought back to them. Mr. Pontellier was a great favorite, and ladies, men, children, even nurses, were always on hand to say good-by to him. His wife stood smiling and waving, the boys shouting, as he disappeared in the old rockaway down the sandy road.

A few days later a box arrived for Mrs. Pontellier from New Orleans. It was from her husband. It was filled with *friandises*,† with luscious and toothsome bits—the finest of fruits, *pâtes*,‡ a rare bottle or two, delicious syrups, and bonbons in abundance.

Mrs. Pontellier was always very generous with the contents of such a box; she was quite used to receiving them when away from home. The *pâtes* and fruit were brought to the dining-room; the bonbons were passed around. And the ladies, selecting with dainty and discriminating fingers and a little greedily, all declared that Mr. Pontellier was the best husband in the world. Mrs. Pontellier was forced to admit that she knew of none better.

---

* The financial and commercial center of New Orleans. Chopin's husband, Oscar, who worked as a cotton broker, moved his office to this prime location.

† Delicacies (Fr.).

‡ Filled pastries (Fr.).

IV

❧

IT WOULD HAVE BEEN a difficult matter for Mr. Pontellier to define to his own satisfaction or any one else's wherein his wife failed in her duty toward their children. It was something which he felt rather than perceived, and he never voiced the feeling without subsequent regret and ample atonement.

If one of the little Pontellier boys took a tumble whilst at play, he was not apt to rush crying to his mother's arms for comfort; he would more likely pick himself up, wipe the water out of his eyes and the sand out of his mouth, and go on playing. Tots as they were, they pulled together and stood their ground in childish battles with doubled fists and uplifted voices, which usually prevailed against the other mother-tots. The quadroon nurse was looked upon as a huge encumbrance, only good to button up waists and panties and to brush and part hair; since it seemed to be a law of society that hair must be parted and brushed.

In short, Mrs. Pontellier was not a mother-woman. The mother-women seemed to prevail that summer at Grand Isle. It was easy to know them, fluttering about with extended, protecting wings when any harm, real or imaginary, threatened their precious brood. They were women who idolized their children, worshiped their husbands, and esteemed it a holy privilege to efface themselves as individuals and grow wings as ministering angels.

Many of them were delicious in the rôle; one of them was the embodiment of every womanly grace and charm. If her husband did not adore her, he was a brute, deserving of death by slow torture. Her name was Adèle Ratignolle. There are no words to describe her save the old ones that have served so often to picture the bygone heroine of romance and the fair lady of our dreams. There was nothing subtle or hidden about her charms; her beauty was all there, flaming and apparent: the spun-gold hair that comb nor confining pin could re-

10

strain; the blue eyes that were like nothing but sapphires; two lips that pouted, that were so red one could only think of cherries or some other delicious crimson fruit in looking at them. She was growing a little stout, but it did not seem to detract an iota from the grace of every step, pose, gesture. One would not have wanted her white neck a mite less full or her beautiful arms more slender. Never were hands more exquisite than hers, and it was a joy to look at them when she threaded her needle or adjusted her gold thimble to her taper middle finger as she sewed away on the little night-drawers or fashioned a bodice or a bib.

Madame Ratignolle was very fond of Mrs. Pontellier, and often she took her sewing and went over to sit with her in the afternoons. She was sitting there the afternoon of the day the box arrived from New Orleans. She had possession of the rocker, and she was busily engaged in sewing upon a diminutive pair of night-drawers.

She had brought the pattern of the drawers for Mrs. Pontellier to cut out—a marvel of construction, fashioned to enclose a baby's body so effectually that only two small eyes might look out from the garment, like an Eskimo's. They were designed for winter wear, when treacherous drafts came down chimneys and insidious currents of deadly cold found their way through key-holes.

Mrs. Pontellier's mind was quite at rest concerning the present material needs of her children, and she could not see the use of anticipating and making winter night garments the subject of her summer meditations. But she did not want to appear unamiable and uninterested, so she had brought forth newspapers, which she spread upon the floor of the gallery, and under Madame Ratignolle's directions she had cut a pattern of the impervious garment.

Robert was there, seated as he had been the Sunday before, and Mrs. Pontellier also occupied her former position on the upper step, leaning listlessly against the post. Beside her was a box of bonbons, which she held out at intervals to Madame Ratignolle.

That lady seemed at a loss to make a selection, but finally settled upon a stick of nugat,* wondering if it were not too rich; whether it could possibly hurt her. Madame Ratignolle had been married seven years. About every two years she had a baby. At that time she had three babies, and was beginning to think of a fourth one. She was always talking about her "condition." Her "condition" was in no way apparent, and no one would have known a thing about it but for her persistence in making it the subject of conversation.

Robert started to reassure her, asserting that he had known a lady who had subsisted upon nugat during the entire—but seeing the color mount into Mrs. Pontellier's face he checked himself and changed the subject.

Mrs. Pontellier, though she had married a Creole,† was not thoroughly at home in the society of Creoles; never before had she been thrown so intimately among them. There were only Creoles that summer at Lebrun's. They all knew each other, and felt like one large family, among whom existed the most amicable relations. A characteristic which distinguished them and which impressed Mrs. Pontellier most forcibly was their entire absence of prudery. Their freedom of expression was at first incomprehensible to her, though she had no difficulty in reconciling it with a lofty chastity which in the Creole woman seems to be inborn and unmistakable.

Never would Edna Pontellier forget the shock with which she heard Madame Ratignolle relating to old Monsieur Farival the harrowing story of one of her *accouchements,*‡ withholding no intimate detail. She was growing accustomed to like shocks, but she could not keep the mounting color back from her cheeks. Oftener than once her coming had in-

---

* Nougat; a chewy candy traditionally flavored with pistachios or almonds.

† French-speaking descendants of the early French settlers in Louisiana.

‡ Childbirths (Fr.).

terrupted the droll story with which Robert was entertaining some amused group of married women.

A book had gone the rounds of the *pension*. When it came her turn to read it, she did so with profound astonishment. She felt moved to read the book in secret and solitude, though none of the others had done so—to hide it from view at the sound of approaching footsteps. It was openly criticised and freely discussed at table. Mrs. Pontellier gave over being astonished, and concluded that wonders would never cease.

V

THEY FORMED A CONGENIAL group sitting there that summer afternoon—Madame Ratignolle sewing away, often stopping to relate a story or incident with much expressive gesture of her perfect hands; Robert and Mrs. Pontellier sitting idle, exchanging occasional words, glances or smiles which indicated a certain advanced stage of intimacy and *camaraderie*.

He had lived in her shadow during the past month. No one thought anything of it. Many had predicted that Robert would devote himself to Mrs. Pontellier when he arrived. Since the age of fifteen, which was eleven years before, Robert each summer at Grand Isle had constituted himself the devoted attendant of some fair dame or damsel. Sometimes it was a young girl, again a widow; but as often as not it was some interesting married woman.

For two consecutive seasons he lived in the sunlight of Mademoiselle Duvigné's presence. But she died between summers; then Robert posed as an inconsolable, prostrating himself at the feet of Madame Ratignolle for whatever crumbs of sympathy and comfort she might be pleased to vouchsafe.

Mrs. Pontellier liked to sit and gaze at her fair companion as she might look upon a faultless Madonna.

"Could any one fathom the cruelty beneath that fair exterior?" murmured Robert. "She knew that I adored her once, and she let me adore her. It was 'Robert, come; go; stand up; sit down; do this; do that; see if the baby sleeps; my thimble, please, that I left God knows where. Come and read Daudet* to me while I sew.' "

"*Par exemple!*† I never had to ask. You were always there under my feet, like a troublesome cat."

"You mean like an adoring dog. And just as soon as Ratignolle appeared on the scene, then it *was* like a dog. '*Passez! Adieu! Allez vous-en!*' "‡

"Perhaps I feared to make Alphonse jealous," she interjoined, with excessive naïveté. That made them all laugh. The right hand jealous of the left! The heart jealous of the soul! But for that matter, the Creole husband is never jealous; with him the gangrene passion is one which has become dwarfed by disuse.

Meanwhile Robert, addressing Mrs. Pontellier, continued to tell of his one time hopeless passion for Madame Ratignolle; of sleepless nights, of consuming flames till the very sea sizzled when he took his daily plunge. While the lady at the needle kept up a little running, contemptuous comment:

"*Blagueur—farceur—gros bête, va!*"§

He never assumed this serio-comic tone when alone with Mrs. Pontellier. She never knew precisely what to make of it; at that moment it was impossible for her to guess how much of it was jest and what proportion was earnest. It was understood that he had often spoken words of love to Madame

---

* Alphonse Daudet (1840–1897), a French novelist whom Chopin admired.

† For goodness' sake! (Fr.).

‡ Go on! Good-bye! Go away! (Fr.).

§ Joker—comedian—silly, come off it! (Fr.).

Ratignolle, without any thought of being taken seriously. Mrs. Pontellier was glad he had not assumed a similar rôle toward herself. It would have been unacceptable and annoying.

Mrs. Pontellier had brought her sketching materials, which she sometimes dabbled with in an unprofessional way. She liked the dabbling. She felt in it satisfaction of a kind which no other employment afforded her.

She had long wished to try herself on Madame Ratignolle. Never had that lady seemed a more tempting subject than at that moment, seated there like some sensuous Madonna, with the gleam of the fading day enriching her splendid color.

Robert crossed over and seated himself upon the step below Mrs. Pontellier, that he might watch her work. She handled her brushes with a certain ease and freedom which came, not from long and close acquaintance with them, but from a natural aptitude. Robert followed her work with close attention, giving forth little ejaculatory expressions of appreciation in French, which he addressed to Madame Ratignolle.

"*Mais ce n'est pas mal! Elle s'y connait, elle a de la force, oui.*"*

During his oblivious attention he once quietly rested his head against Mrs. Pontellier's arm. As gently she repulsed him. Once again he repeated the offense. She could not but believe it to be thoughtlessness on his part; yet that was no reason she should submit to it. She did not remonstrate, except again to repulse him quietly but firmly. He offered no apology.

The picture completed bore no resemblance to Madame Ratignolle. She was greatly disappointed to find that it did not look like her. But it was a fair enough piece of work, and in many respects satisfying.

Mrs. Pontellier evidently did not think so. After surveying the sketch critically she drew a broad smudge of paint across its surface, and crumpled the paper between her hands.

---

* Not bad at all! Not bad at all! She knows what she's doing, she has talent (Fr.).

The youngsters came tumbling up the steps, the quadroon following at the respectful distance which they required her to observe. Mrs. Pontellier made them carry her paints and things into the house. She sought to detain them for a little talk and some pleasantry. But they were greatly in earnest. They had only come to investigate the contents of the bonbon box. They accepted without murmuring what she chose to give them, each holding out two chubby hands scoop-like in the vain hope that they might be filled; and then away they went.

The sun was low in the west, and the breeze soft and lan-guorous that came up from the south, charged with the se-ductive odor of the sea. Children, freshly befur-belowed,* were gathering for their games under the oaks. Their voices were high and penetrating.

Madame Ratignolle folded her sewing, placing thimble, scissors and thread all neatly together in the roll, which she pinned securely. She complained of faintness. Mrs. Pontellier flew for the cologne water and a fan. She bathed Madame Ratignolle's face with cologne, while Robert plied the fan with unnecessary vigor.

The spell was soon over, and Mrs. Pontellier could not help wondering if there were not a little imagination responsi-ble for its origin, for the rose tint had never faded from her friend's face.

She stood watching the fair woman walk down the long line of galleries with the grace and majesty which queens are sometimes supposed to possess. Her little ones ran to meet her. Two of them clung about her white skirts, the third she took from its nurse and with a thousand endearments bore it along in her own fond, encircling arms. Though, as every-body well knew, the doctor had forbidden her to lift so much as a pin!

"Are you going bathing?" asked Robert of Mrs. Pontellier. It was not so much a question as a reminder.

---

* Dressed.

"Oh, no," she answered, with a tone of indecision. "I'm tired; I think not." Her glance wandered from his face away toward the Gulf, whose sonorous murmur reached her like a loving but imperative entreaty.

"Oh, come!" he insisted. "You mustn't miss your bath. Come on. The water must be delicious; it will not hurt you. Come."

He reached up for her big, rough straw hat that hung on a peg outside the door, and put it on her head. They descended the steps, and walked away together toward the beach. The sun was low in the west and the breeze was soft and warm.

VI

ᕲ

EDNA PONTELLIER COULD NOT have told why, wishing to go to the beach with Robert, she should in the first place have declined, and in the second place have followed in obedience to one of the two contradictory impulses which impelled her.

A certain light was beginning to dawn dimly within her—the light which, showing the way, forbids it.

At that early period it served but to bewilder her. It moved her to dreams, to thoughtfulness, to the shadowy anguish which had overcome her the midnight when she had abandoned herself to tears.

In short, Mrs. Pontellier was beginning to realize her position in the universe as a human being, and to recognize her relations as an individual to the world within and about her. This may seem like a ponderous weight of wisdom to descend upon the soul of a young woman of twenty-eight—perhaps more wisdom than the Holy Ghost is usually pleased to vouchsafe to any woman.

But the beginning of things, of a world especially, is necessarily vague, tangled, chaotic, and exceedingly disturbing.

How few of us ever emerge from such beginning! How many
souls perish in its tumult!

The voice of the sea is seductive; never ceasing, whispering, clamoring, murmuring, inviting the soul to wander for a
spell in abysses of solitude; to lose itself in mazes of inward
contemplation.

The voice of the sea speaks to the soul. The touch of the
sea is sensuous, enfolding the body in its soft, close embrace.

VII

MRS. PONTELLIER WAS NOT a woman given to confidences, a
characteristic hitherto contrary to her nature. Even as a child
she had lived her own small life all within herself. At a very
early period she had apprehended instinctively the dual life—
that outward existence which conforms, the inward life which
questions.

That summer at Grand Isle she began to loosen a little the
mantle of reserve that had always enveloped her. There may
have been—there must have been—influences, both subtle
and apparent, working in their several ways to induce her to
do this; but the most obvious was the influence of Adèle
Ratignolle. The excessive physical charm of the Creole had
first attracted her, for Edna had a sensuous susceptibility to
beauty. Then the candor of the woman's whole existence,
which every one might read, and which formed so striking a
contrast to her own habitual reserve—this might have furnished a link. Who can tell what metals the gods use in forg-
ing the subtle bond which we call sympathy, which we might
as well call love.

The two women went away one morning to the beach together, arm in arm, under the huge white sunshade. Edna
had prevailed upon Madame Ratignolle to leave the children

behind, though she could not induce her to relinquish a diminutive roll of needlework, which Adèle begged to be allowed to slip into the depths of her pocket. In some unaccountable way they had escaped from Robert.

The walk to the beach was no inconsiderable one, consisting as it did of a long, sandy path, upon which a sporadic and tangled growth that bordered it on either side made frequent and unexpected inroads. There were acres of yellow camomile reaching out on either hand. Further away still, vegetable gardens abounded, with frequent small plantations of orange or lemon trees intervening. The dark green clusters glistened from afar in the sun.

The women were both of goodly height, Madame Ratignolle possessing the more feminine and matronly figure. The charm of Edna Pontellier's physique stole insensibly upon you. The lines of her body were long, clean and symmetrical; it was a body which occasionally fell into splendid poses; there was no suggestion of the trim, stereotyped fashion-plate about it. A casual and indiscriminating observer, in passing, might not cast a second glance upon the figure. But with more feeling and discernment he would have recognized the noble beauty of its modeling, and the graceful severity of poise and movement, which made Edna Pontellier different from the crowd.

She wore a cool muslin that morning—white, with a waving vertical line of brown running through it; also a white linen collar and the big straw hat which she had taken from the peg outside the door. The hat rested any way on her yellow-brown hair, that waved a little, was heavy, and clung close to her head.

Madame Ratignolle, more careful of her complexion, had twined a gauze veil about her head. She wore dogskin gloves, with gauntlets that protected her wrists. She was dressed in pure white, with a fluffiness of ruffles that became her. The draperies and fluttering things which she wore suited her rich, luxuriant beauty as a greater severity of line could not have done.

There were a number of bath-houses along the beach, of rough but solid construction, built with small, protecting galleries facing the water. Each house consisted of two compartments, and each family at Lebrun's possessed a compartment for itself, fitted out with all the essential paraphernalia of the bath and whatever other conveniences the owners might desire. The two women had no intention of bathing; they had just strolled down to the beach for a walk and to be alone and near the water. The Pontellier and Ratignolle compartments adjoined one another under the same roof.

Mrs. Pontellier had brought down her key through force of habit. Unlocking the door of her bath-room she went inside, and soon emerged, bringing a rug, which she spread upon the floor of the gallery, and two huge hair pillows covered with crash,* which she placed against the front of the building.

The two seated themselves there in the shade of the porch, side by side, with their backs against the pillows and their feet extended. Madame Ratignolle removed her veil, wiped her face with a rather delicate handkerchief, and fanned herself with the fan which she always carried suspended somewhere about her person by a long, narrow ribbon. Edna removed her collar and opened her dress at the throat. She took the fan from Madame Ratignolle and began to fan both herself and her companion. It was very warm, and for a while they did nothing but exchange remarks about the heat, the sun, the glare. But there was a breeze blowing, a choppy, stiff wind that whipped the water into froth. It fluttered the skirts of the two women and kept them for a while engaged in adjusting, readjusting, tucking in, securing hair-pins and hat-pins. A few persons were sporting some distance away in the water. The beach was very still of human sound at that hour. The lady in black was reading her morning devotions on the porch of a neighboring bath-house. Two young lovers were exchanging their hearts' yearnings beneath the children's tent, which they had found unoccupied.

---

* Coarse linen fabric.

Edna Pontellier, casting her eyes about, had finally kept them at rest upon the sea. The day was clear and carried the gaze out as far as the blue sky went; there were a few white clouds suspended idly over the horizon. A lateen sail* was visible in the direction of Cat Island,† and others to the south seemed almost motionless in the far distance.

"Of whom—of what are you thinking?" asked Adèle of her companion, whose countenance she had been watching with a little amused attention, arrested by the absorbed expression which seemed to have seized and fixed every feature into a statuesque repose.

"Nothing," returned Mrs. Pontellier, with a start, adding at once: "How stupid! But it seems to me it is the reply we make instinctively to such a question. Let me see," she went on, throwing back her head and narrowing her fine eyes till they shone like two vivid points of light. "Let me see. I was really not conscious of thinking of anything; but perhaps I can retrace my thoughts."

"Oh! never mind!" laughed Madame Ratignolle. "I am not quite so exacting. I will let you off this time. It is really too hot to think, especially to think about thinking."

"But for the fun of it," persisted Edna. "First of all, the sight of the water stretching so far away, those motionless sails against the blue sky, made a delicious picture that I just wanted to sit and look at. The hot wind beating in my face made me think—without any connection that I can trace—of a summer day in Kentucky, of a meadow that seemed as big as the ocean to the very little girl walking through the grass, which was higher than her waist. She threw out her arms as if swimming when she walked, beating the tall grass as one strikes out in the water. Oh, I see the connection now!"

"Where were you going that day in Kentucky, walking through the grass?"

---

* A triangular sail.

† A peninsula near where the Mississippi River empties into the Gulf of Mexico.

"I don't remember now. I was just walking diagonally across a big field. My sun-bonnet obstructed the view. I could see only the stretch of green before me, and I felt as if I must walk on forever, without coming to the end of it. I don't remember whether I was frightened or pleased. I must have been entertained.

"Likely as not it was Sunday," she laughed; "and I was running away from prayers, from the Presbyterian service, read in a spirit of gloom by my father that chills me yet to think of."

"And have you been running away from prayers ever since, *ma chère?*"* asked Madame Ratignolle, amused.

"No! oh, no!" Edna hastened to say. "I was a little unthinking child in those days, just following a misleading impulse without question. On the contrary, during one period of my life religion took a firm hold upon me; after I was twelve and until—until—why, I suppose until now, though I never thought much about it—just driven along by habit. But do you know," she broke off, turning her quick eyes upon Madame Ratignolle and leaning forward a little so as to bring her face quite close to that of her companion, "sometimes I feel this summer as if I were walking through the green meadow again; idly, aimlessly, unthinking and unguided."

Madame Ratignolle laid her hand over that of Mrs. Pontellier, which was near her. Seeing that the hand was not withdrawn, she clasped it firmly and warmly. She even stroked it a little, fondly, with the other hand, murmuring in an undertone, "*Pauvre chérie.*"†

The action was at first a little confusing to Edna, but she soon lent herself readily to the Creole's gentle caress. She was not accustomed to an outward and spoken expression of affection, either in herself or in others. She and her younger sister, Janet, had quarreled a good deal through force of unfortunate habit. Her older sister, Margaret, was matronly and dignified, probably from having assumed matronly and house-wifely re-

---

* My dear (Fr.).

† Poor dear (Fr.).

sponsibilities too early in life, their mother having died when they were quite young. Margaret was not effusive; she was practical. Edna had had an occasional girl friend, but whether accidentally or not, they seemed to have been all of one type—the self-contained. She never realized that the reserve of her own character had much, perhaps everything, to do with this. Her most intimate friend at school had been one of rather exceptional intellectual gifts, who wrote fine-sounding essays, which Edna admired and strove to imitate; and with her she talked and glowed over the English classics, and sometimes held religious and political controversies.

Edna often wondered at one propensity which sometimes had inwardly disturbed her without causing any outward show or manifestation on her part. At a very early age—perhaps it was when she traversed the ocean of waving grass—she remembered that she had been passionately enamored of a dignified and sad-eyed cavalry officer who visited her father in Kentucky. She could not leave his presence when he was there, nor remove her eyes from his face, which was something like Napoleon's, with a lock of black hair falling across the forehead. But the cavalry officer melted imperceptibly out of her existence.

At another time her affections were deeply engaged by a young gentleman who visited a lady on a neighboring plantation. It was after they went to Mississippi to live. The young man was engaged to be married to the young lady, and they sometimes called upon Margaret, driving over of afternoons in a buggy. Edna was a little miss, just merging into her teens; and the realization that she herself was nothing, nothing, nothing to the engaged young man was a bitter affliction to her. But he, too, went the way of dreams.

She was a grown young woman when she was overtaken by what she supposed to be the climax of her fate. It was when the face and figure of a great tragedian began to haunt her imagination and stir her senses. The persistence of the infatuation lent it an aspect of genuineness. The hopelessness of it colored it with the lofty tones of great passion.

The picture of the tragedian stood enframed upon her desk. Any one may possess the portrait of a tragedian without exciting suspicion or comment. (This was a sinister reflection which she cherished.) In the presence of others she expressed admiration for his exalted gifts, as she handed the photograph around and dwelt upon the fidelity of the likeness. When alone she sometimes picked it up and kissed the cold glass passionately.

Her marriage to Léonce Pontellier was purely an accident, in this respect resembling many other marriages which masquerade as the decrees of Fate. It was in the midst of her secret great passion that she met him. He fell in love, as men are in the habit of doing, and pressed his suit with an earnestness and an ardor which left nothing to be desired. He pleased her; his absolute devotion flattered her. She fancied there was a sympathy of thought and taste between them, in which fancy she was mistaken. Add to this the violent opposition of her father and her sister Margaret to her marriage with a Catholic, and we need seek no further for the motives which led her to accept Monsieur Pontellier for her husband.

The acme of bliss, which would have been a marriage with the tragedian, was not for her in this world. As the devoted wife of a man who worshiped her, she felt she would take her place with a certain dignity in the world of reality, closing the portals forever behind her upon the realm of romance and dreams.

But it was not long before the tragedian had gone to join the cavalry officer and the engaged young man and a few others; and Edna found herself face to face with the realities. She grew fond of her husband, realizing with some unaccountable satisfaction that no trace of passion or excessive and fictitious warmth colored her affection, thereby threatening its dissolution.

She was fond of her children in an uneven, impulsive way. She would sometimes gather them passionately to her heart; she would sometimes forget them. The year before they had spent part of the summer with their grandmother Pontellier in

Iberville.* Feeling secure regarding their happiness and welfare, she did not miss them except with an occasional intense longing. Their absence was a sort of relief, though she did not admit this, even to herself. It seemed to free her of a responsibility which she had blindly assumed and for which Fate had not fitted her.

Edna did not reveal so much as all this to Madame Ratignolle that summer day when they sat with faces turned to the sea. But a good part of it escaped her. She had put her head down on Madame Ratignolle's shoulder. She was flushed and felt intoxicated with the sound of her own voice and the unaccustomed taste of candor. It muddled her like wine, or like a first breath of freedom.

There was the sound of approaching voices. It was Robert, surrounded by a troop of children, searching for them. The two little Pontelliers were with him, and he carried Madame Ratignolle's little girl in his arms. There were other children beside, and two nurse-maids followed, looking disagreeable and resigned.

The women at once rose and began to shake out their draperies and relax their muscles. Mrs. Pontellier threw the cushions and rug into the bath-house. The children all scampered off to the awning, and they stood there in a line, gazing upon the intruding lovers, still exchanging their vows and sighs. The lovers got up, with only a silent protest, and walked slowly away somewhere else.

The children possessed themselves of the tent, and Mrs. Pontellier went over to join them.

Madame Ratignolle begged Robert to accompany her to the house; she complained of cramp in her limbs and stiffness of the joints. She leaned draggingly upon his arm as they walked.

---

* Either a parish near Baton Rouge at the border between Louisiana and Mississippi, or a village with the same name.

VIII

❧

"Do me a favor, Robert," spoke the pretty woman at his side, almost as soon as she and Robert had started on their slow, homeward way. She looked up in his face, leaning on his arm beneath the encircling shadow of the umbrella which he had lifted.

"Granted; as many as you like," he returned, glancing down into her eyes that were full of thoughtfulness and some speculation.

"I only ask for one; let Mrs. Pontellier alone."

"Tiens!" he exclaimed, with a sudden, boyish laugh. *"Voilà que Madame Ratignolles est jalouse!"**

"Nonsense! I'm in earnest; I mean what I say. Let Mrs. Pontellier alone."

"Why?" he asked; himself growing serious at his companion's solicitation.

"She is not one of us; she is not like us. She might make the unfortunate blunder of taking you seriously."

His face flushed with annoyance, and taking off his soft hat he began to beat it impatiently against his leg as he walked. "Why shouldn't she take me seriously?" he demanded sharply. "Am I a comedian, a clown, a jack-in-the-box? Why shouldn't she? You Creoles! I have no patience with you! Am I always to be regarded as a feature of an amusing programme? I hope Mrs. Pontellier does take me seriously. I hope she has discernment enough to find in me something besides the *blagueur.*† If I thought there was any doubt—"

"Oh, enough, Robert!" she broke into his heated outburst. "You are not thinking of what you are saying. You speak with about as little reflection as we might expect from one of those

---

* So Madame Ratignolle is jealous! (Fr.).

† Joker (Fr.).

children down there playing in the sand. If your attentions to any married women here were ever offered with any intention of being convincing, you would not be the gentleman we all know you to be, and you would be unfit to associate with the wives and daughters of the people who trust you."

Madame Ratignolle had spoken what she believed to be the law and the gospel. The young man shrugged his shoulders impatiently.

"Oh! well! That isn't it," slamming his hat down vehemently upon his head. "You ought to feel that such things are not flattering to say to a fellow."

"Should our whole intercourse consist of an exchange of compliments? *Ma foi!*"*

"It isn't pleasant to have a woman tell you—" he went on, unheedingly, but breaking off suddenly: "Now if I were like Arobin—you remember Alcée Arobin and that story of the consul's wife at Biloxi?" And he related the story of Alcée Arobin and the consul's wife; and another about the tenor of the French Opera, who received letters which should never have been written; and still other stories, grave and gay, till Mrs. Pontellier and her possible propensity for taking young men seriously was apparently forgotten.

Madame Ratignolle, when they had regained her cottage, went in to take the hour's rest which she considered helpful. Before leaving her, Robert begged her pardon for the impatience—he called it rudeness—with which he had received her well-meant caution.

"You made one mistake, Adèle," he said, with a light smile; "there is no earthly possibility of Mrs. Pontellier ever taking me seriously. You should have warned me against taking myself seriously. Your advice might then have carried some weight and given me subject for some reflection. *Au revoir.*† But you look tired," he added, solicitously. "Would you like a

---

* For heaven's sake! (Fr.).

† Good-bye, until later (Fr.).

cup of bouillon? Shall I stir you a toddy?* Let me mix you a toddy with a drop of Angostura."[†]

She acceded to the suggestion of bouillon, which was grateful and acceptable. He went himself to the kitchen, which was a building apart from the cottages and lying to the rear of the house. And he himself brought her the golden-brown bouillon, in a dainty Sèvres[‡] cup, with a flaky cracker or two on the saucer.

She thrust a bare, white arm from the curtain which shielded her open door, and received the cup from his hands. She told him he was a *bon garçon*,[§] and she meant it. Robert thanked her and turned away toward "the house."

The lovers were just entering the grounds of the *pension*. They were leaning toward each other as the water-oaks bent from the sea. There was not a particle of earth beneath their feet. Their heads might have been turned upside-down, so absolutely did they tread upon blue ether. The lady in black, creeping behind them, looked a trifle paler and more jaded than usual. There was no sign of Mrs. Pontellier and the children. Robert scanned the distance for any such apparition. They would doubtless remain away till the dinner hour. The young man ascended to his mother's room. It was situated at the top of the house, made up of odd angles and a queer, sloping ceiling. Two broad dormer windows looked out toward the Gulf, and as far across it as a man's eye might reach. The furnishings of the room were light, cool, and practical.

Madame Lebrun was busily engaged at the sewing-machine. A little black girl sat on the floor, and with her hands worked the treadle of the machine. The Creole woman does not take any chances which may be avoided of imperiling her health.

---

* A hot drink consisting of liquor (such as rum), water, sugar, and spices.

† A rum-based liquor from Trinidad.

‡ High-quality French porcelain.

§ A nice fellow (Fr.).

Robert went over and seated himself on the broad sill of one of the dormer windows. He took a book from his pocket and began energetically to read it, judging by the precision and frequency with which he turned the leaves. The sewing-machine made a resounding clatter in the room; it was of a ponderous, by-gone make. In the lulls, Robert and his mother exchanged bits of desultory conversation.

"Where is Mrs. Pontellier?"

"Down at the beach with the children."

"I promised to lend her the Goncourt.* Don't forget to take it down when you go; it's there on the bookshelf over the small table." Clatter, clatter, clatter, bang! for the next five or eight minutes.

"Where is Victor going with the rockaway?"

"The rockaway? Victor?"

"Yes; down there in front. He seems to be getting ready to drive away somewhere."

"Call him." Clatter, clatter!

Robert uttered a shrill, piercing whistle which might have been heard back at the wharf.

"He won't look up."

Madame Lebrun flew to the window. She called "Victor!" She waved a handkerchief and called again. The young fellow below got into the vehicle and started the horse off at a gallop.

Madame Lebrun went back to the machine, crimson with annoyance. Victor was the younger son and brother—a *tête montée*,† with a temper which invited violence and a will which no ax could break.

"Whenever you say the word I'm ready to thrash any amount of reason into him that he's able to hold."

---

* The reference is to a book by the French brothers and literary collaborators Edmond (1822–1896) and Jules (1830–1870) Goncourt, who wrote social histories, art criticism, and novels in the style of literary naturalism.

† An impulsive character (Fr.).

"If your father had only lived!" Clatter, clatter, clatter, clatter, bang! It was a fixed belief with Madame Lebrun that the conduct of the universe and all things pertaining thereto would have been manifestly of a more intelligent and higher order had not Monsieur Lebrun been removed to other spheres during the early years of their married life.

"What do you hear from Montel?" Montel was a middle-aged gentleman whose vain ambition and desire for the past twenty years had been to fill the void which Monsieur Lebrun's taking off had left in the Lebrun household. Clatter, clatter, bang, clatter!

"I have a letter somewhere," looking in the machine drawer and finding the letter in the bottom of the work-basket. "He says to tell you he will be in Vera Cruz the beginning of next month"—clatter, clatter!—"and if you still have the intention of joining him"—bang! clatter, clatter, bang!

"Why didn't you tell me so before, mother? You know I wanted—" Clatter, clatter, clatter!

"Do you see Mrs. Pontellier starting back with the children? She will be in late to luncheon again. She never starts to get ready for luncheon till the last minute." Clatter, clatter! "Where are you going?"

"Where did you say the Goncourt was?"

IX

Every light in the hall was ablaze; every lamp turned as high as it could be without smoking the chimney or threatening explosion. The lamps were fixed at intervals against the wall, encircling the whole room. Some one had gathered orange and lemon branches, and with these fashioned graceful festoons between. The dark green of the branches stood out and glistened against the white muslin curtains which draped the windows, and which puffed, floated, and flapped at the capricious will of a stiff breeze that swept up from the Gulf.

It was Saturday night a few weeks after the intimate conversation held between Robert and Madame Ratignolle on their way from the beach. An unusual number of husbands, fathers, and friends had come down to stay over Sunday; and they were being suitably entertained by their families, with the material help of Madame Lebrun. The dining tables had all been removed to one end of the hall, and the chairs ranged about in rows and in clusters. Each little family group had had its say and exchanged its domestic gossip earlier in the evening. There was now an apparent disposition to relax; to widen the circle of confidences and give a more general tone to the conversation.

Many of the children had been permitted to sit up beyond their usual bedtime. A small band of them were lying on their stomachs on the floor looking at the colored sheets of the comic papers which Mr. Pontellier had brought down. The little Pontellier boys were permitting them to do so, and making their authority felt.

Music, dancing, and a recitation or two were the entertainments furnished, or rather, offered. But there was nothing systematic about the programme, no appearance of pre-arrangement nor even premeditation.

At an early hour in the evening the Farival twins were prevailed upon to play the piano. They were girls of fourteen, always clad in the Virgin's colors, blue and white, having been dedicated to the Blessed Virgin at their baptism. They played a duet from *Zampa*, and at the earnest solicitation of every one present followed it with the overture to "The Poet and the Peasant."

"*Allez vous-en! Sapristi!*" shrieked the parrot outside the door. He was the only being present who possessed sufficient candor to admit that he was not listening to these gracious performances for the first time that summer. Old Monsieur Farival, grandfather of the twins, grew indignant over the interruption, and insisted upon having the bird removed and consigned to regions of darkness. Victor Lebrun objected; and his decrees were as immutable as those of Fate. The parrot fortunately offered no further interruption to the entertainment, the whole venom of his nature apparently having been cherished up and hurled against the twins in that one impetuous outburst.

Later a young brother and sister gave recitations, which every one present had heard many times at winter evening entertainments in the city.

A little girl performed a skirt dance in the center of the floor. The mother played her accompaniments and at the same time watched her daughter with greedy admiration and nervous apprehension. She need have had no apprehension. The child was mistress of the situation. She had been properly dressed for the occasion in black tulle and black silk tights. Her little neck and arms were bare, and her hair, artificially crimped, stood out like fluffy black plumes over her head. Her poses were full of grace, and her little black-shod toes twinkled as they shot out and upward with a rapidity and suddenness which were bewildering.

But there was no reason why every one should not dance. Madame Ratignolle could not, so it was she who gaily consented to play for the others. She played very well, keeping excellent waltz time and infusing an expression into the strains which was indeed inspiring. She was keeping up her music on account of the children, she said; because she and her husband both considered it a means of brightening the home and making it attractive.

Almost every one danced but the twins, who could not be induced to separate during the brief period when one or the other should be whirling around the room in the arms of a man. They might have danced together, but they did not think of it.

The children were sent to bed. Some went submissively; others with shrieks and protests as they were dragged away. They had been permitted to sit up till after the ice-cream, which naturally marked the limit of human indulgence.

The ice-cream was passed around with cake—gold and silver cake arranged on platters in alternate slices; it had been made and frozen during the afternoon back of the kitchen by two black women, under the supervision of Victor. It was pronounced a great success—excellent if it had only contained a little less vanilla or a little more sugar, if it had been frozen a degree harder, and if the salt might have been kept out of portions of it. Victor was proud of his achievement, and went about recommending it and urging every one to partake of it to excess.

After Mrs. Pontellier had danced twice with her husband, once with Robert, and once with Monsieur Ratignolle, who was thin and tall and swayed like a reed in the wind when he danced, she went out on the gallery and seated herself on the low window-sill, where she commanded a view of all that went on in the hall and could look out toward the Gulf. There was a soft effulgence in the east. The moon was coming up, and its mystic shimmer was casting a million lights across the distant, restless water.

"Would you like to hear Mademoiselle Reisz play?" asked Robert, coming out on the porch where she was. Of course Edna would like to hear Mademoiselle Reisz play; but she feared it would be useless to entreat her.

"I'll ask her," he said. "I'll tell her that you want to hear her. She likes you. She will come." He turned and hurried away to one of the far cottages, where Mademoiselle Reisz was shuffling away. She was dragging a chair in and out of her room, and at intervals objecting to the crying of a baby, which a nurse in the adjoining cottage was endeavoring to put to sleep. She was a disagreeable little woman, no longer young, who had quarreled with almost every one, owing to a temper which was self-assertive and a disposition to trample upon the rights of others. Robert prevailed upon her without any too great difficulty.

She entered the hall with him during a lull in the dance. She made an awkward, imperious little bow as she went in. She was a homely woman, with a small weazened face and body and eyes that glowed. She had absolutely no taste in dress, and wore a batch of rusty black lace with a bunch of artificial violets pinned to the side of her hair.

"Ask Mrs. Pontellier what she would like to hear me play," she requested of Robert. She sat perfectly still before the piano, not touching the keys, while Robert carried her message to Edna at the window. A general air of surprise and genuine satisfaction fell upon every one as they saw the pianist enter. There was a settling down, and a prevailing air of expectancy everywhere. Edna was a trifle embarrassed at being thus signaled out for the imperious little woman's favor. She would not dare to choose, and begged that Mademoiselle Reisz would please herself in her selections.

Edna was what she herself called very fond of music. Musical strains, well rendered, had a way of evoking pictures in her mind. She sometimes liked to sit in the room of mornings when Madame Ratignolle played or practiced. One piece which that lady played Edna had entitled "Solitude." It was a short, plaintive, minor strain. The name of the piece was something else, but she called it "Solitude." When she heard it there came before her imagination the figure of a man standing beside a desolate rock on the seashore. He was naked. His attitude was one of hopeless resignation as he looked toward a distant bird winging its flight away from him.

Another piece called to her mind a dainty young woman clad in an Empire gown,* taking mincing dancing steps as she came down a long avenue between tall hedges. Again, another reminded her of children at play, and still another of nothing on earth but a demure lady stroking a cat.

The very first chords which Mademoiselle Reisz struck upon the piano sent a keen tremor down Mrs. Pontellier's spinal column. It was not the first time she had heard an artist at the piano. Perhaps it was the first time she was ready, perhaps the first time her being was tempered to take an impress of the abiding truth.

---

* A dress made from rich fabric with a high neckline and waist beginning just below the bosom.

She waited for the material pictures which she thought would gather and blaze before her imagination. She waited in vain. She saw no pictures of solitude, of hope, of longing, or of despair. But the very passions themselves were aroused within her soul, swaying it, lashing it, as the waves daily beat upon her splendid body. She trembled, she was choking, and the tears blinded her.

Mademoiselle had finished. She arose, and bowing her stiff, lofty bow, she went away, stopping for neither thanks nor applause. As she passed along the gallery she patted Edna upon the shoulder.

"Well, how did you like my music?" she asked. The young woman was unable to answer; she pressed the hand of the pianist convulsively. Mademoiselle Reisz perceived her agitation and even her tears. She patted her again upon the shoulder as she said:

"You are the only one worth playing for. Those others? Bah!" and she went shuffling and sidling on down the gallery toward her room.

But she was mistaken about "those others." Her playing had aroused a fever of enthusiasm. "What passion!" "What an artist!" "I have always said no one could play Chopin like Mademoiselle Reisz!" "That last prelude! Bon Dieu! It shakes a man!"

It was growing late, and there was a general disposition to disband. But some one, perhaps it was Robert, thought of a bath at that mystic hour and under that mystic moon.

X

AT ALL EVENTS ROBERT proposed it, and there was not a dissenting voice. There was not one but was ready to follow when he led the way. He did not lead the way, however, he directed the way; and he himself loitered behind with the lovers, who had betrayed a disposition to linger and hold themselves apart. He walked between them, whether with malicious or mischievous intent was not wholly clear, even to himself.

The Pontelliers and Ratignolles walked ahead; the women leaning upon the arms of their husbands. Edna could hear Robert's voice behind them, and could sometimes hear what he said. She wondered why he did not join them. It was unlike him not to. Of late he had sometimes held away from her for an entire day, redoubling his devotion upon the next and the next, as though to make up for hours that had been lost. She missed him the days when some pretext served to take him away from her, just as one misses the sun on a cloudy day without having thought much about the sun when it was shining.

The people walked in little groups toward the beach. They talked and laughed; some of them sang. There was a band playing down at Klein's hotel, and the strains reached them faintly, tempered by the distance. There were strange, rare odors abroad—a tangle of the sea smell and of weeds and damp, new-plowed earth, mingled with the heavy perfume of a field of white blossoms somewhere near. But the night sat lightly upon the sea and the land. There was no weight of darkness; there were no shadows. The white light of the moon had fallen upon the world like the mystery and the softness of sleep.

Most of them walked into the water as though into a native element. The sea was quiet now, and swelled lazily in broad billows that melted into one another and did not break except upon the beach in little foamy crests that coiled back like slow, white serpents.

Edna had attempted all summer to learn to swim. She had received instructions from both the men and women; in some instances from the children. Robert had pursued a system of lessons almost daily; and he was nearly at the point of discouragement in realizing the futility of his efforts. A certain ungovernable dread hung about her when in the water, unless there was a hand near by that might reach out and reassure her.

But that night she was like the little tottering, stumbling, clutching child, who of a sudden realizes its powers, and walks for the first time alone, boldly and with over-confidence. She could have shouted for joy. She did shout for joy, as with a sweeping stroke or two she lifted her body to the surface of the water.

A feeling of exultation overtook her, as if some power of significant import had been given her to control the working of her body and her soul. She grew daring and reckless, over-estimating her strength. She wanted to swim far out, where no woman had swum before.

Her unlooked-for achievement was the subject of wonder, applause, and admiration. Each one congratulated himself that his special teachings had accomplished this desired end.

"How easy it is!" she thought. "It is nothing," she said aloud; "why did I not discover before that it was nothing. Think of the time I have lost splashing about like a baby!" She would not join the groups in their sports and bouts, but intoxicated with her newly conquered power, she swam out alone.

She turned her face seaward to gather in an impression of space and solitude, which the vast expanse of water, meeting and melting with the moonlit sky, conveyed to her excited fancy. As she swam she seemed to be reaching out for the unlimited in which to lose herself.

Once she turned and looked toward the shore, toward the people she had left there. She had not gone any great distance—that is, what would have been a great distance for an experienced swimmer. But to her unaccustomed vision the stretch of water behind her assumed the aspect of a barrier which her unaided strength would never be able to overcome.

A quick vision of death smote her soul, and for a second of time appalled and enfeebled her senses. But by an effort she rallied her staggering faculties and managed to regain the land.

She made no mention of her encounter with death and

her flash of terror, except to say to her husband, "I thought I should have perished out there alone."

"You were not so very far, my dear; I was watching you," he told her.

Edna went at once to the bath-house, and she had put on her dry clothes and was ready to return home before the others had left the water. She started to walk away alone. They all called to her and shouted to her. She waved a dissenting hand, and went on, paying no further heed to their renewed cries which sought to detain her.

"Sometimes I am tempted to think that Mrs. Pontellier is capricious," said Madame Lebrun, who was amusing herself immensely and feared that Edna's abrupt departure might put an end to the pleasure.

"I know she is," assented Mr. Pontellier; "sometimes, not often."

Edna had not traversed a quarter of the distance on her way home before she was overtaken by Robert.

"Did you think I was afraid?" she asked him, without a shade of annoyance.

"No; I knew you weren't afraid."

"Then why did you come? Why didn't you stay out there with the others?"

"I never thought of it."

"Thought of what?"

"Of anything. What difference does it make?"

"I'm very tired," she uttered, complainingly.

"I know you are."

"You don't know anything about it. Why should you know? I never was so exhausted in my life. But it isn't unpleasant. A thousand emotions have swept through me to-night. I don't comprehend half of them. Don't mind what I'm saying; I am just thinking aloud. I wonder if I shall ever be stirred again as Mademoiselle Reisz's playing moved me to-night. I wonder if any night on earth will ever again be like this one. It is like a night in a dream. The people about me are like some uncanny, half-human beings. There must be spirits abroad to-night."

"There are," whispered Robert. "Didn't you know this was the twenty-eighth of August?"

"The twenty-eighth of August?"

"Yes. On the twenty-eighth of August, at the hour of midnight, and if the moon is shining—the moon must be shining—a spirit that has haunted these shores for ages rises up from the Gulf. With its own penetrating vision the spirit seeks some one mortal worthy to hold him company, worthy of being exalted for a few hours into realms of the semi-celestials. His search has always hitherto been fruitless, and he has sunk back, disheartened, into the sea. But to-night he found Mrs. Pontellier. Perhaps he will never wholly release her from the spell. Perhaps she will never again suffer a poor, unworthy earthling to walk in the shadow of her divine presence."

"Don't banter me," she said, wounded at what appeared to be his flippancy. He did not mind the entreaty, but the tone with its delicate note of pathos was like a reproach. He could not explain; he could not tell her that he had penetrated her mood and understood. He said nothing except to offer her his arm, for, by her own admission, she was exhausted. She had been walking alone with her arms hanging limp, letting her white skirts trail along the dewy path. She took his arm, but she did not lean upon it. She let her hand lie listlessly, as though her thoughts were elsewhere—somewhere in advance of her body, and she was striving to overtake them.

Robert assisted her into the hammock which swung from the post before her door out to the trunk of a tree.

"Will you stay out here and wait for Mr. Pontellier?" he asked.

"I'll stay out here. Good-night."

"Shall I get you a pillow?"

"There's one here," she said, feeling about, for they were in the shadow.

"It must be soiled; the children have been tumbling it about."

"No matter." And having discovered the pillow, she adjusted it beneath her head. She extended herself in the hammock with a deep breath of relief. She was not a supercilious or an over-dainty woman. She was not much given to reclining in the hammock, and when she did so it was with no cat-like suggestion of voluptuous ease, but with a beneficent repose which seemed to invade her whole body.

"Shall I stay with you till Mr. Pontellier comes?" asked Robert, seating himself on the outer edge of one of the steps and taking hold of the hammock rope which was fastened to the post.

"If you wish. Don't swing the hammock. Will you get my white shawl which I left on the window-sill over at the house?"

"Are you chilly?"

"No; but I shall be presently."

"Presently?" he laughed. "Do you know what time it is? How long are you going to stay out here?"

"I don't know. Will you get the shawl?"

"Of course I will," he said, rising. He went over to the house, walking along the grass. She watched his figure pass in and out of the strips of moonlight. It was past midnight. It was very quiet.

When he returned with the shawl she took it and kept it in her hand. She did not put it around her.

"Did you say I should stay till Mr. Pontellier came back?"

"I said you might if you wished to."

He seated himself again and rolled a cigarette, which he smoked in silence. Neither did Mrs. Pontellier speak. No multitude of words could have been more significant than those moments of silence, or more pregnant with the first-felt throbbings of desire.

When the voices of the bathers were heard approaching, Robert said good-night. She did not answer him. He thought she was asleep. Again she watched his figure pass in and out of the strips of moonlight as he walked away.

XI

❧

"WHAT ARE YOU DOING out here, Edna? I thought I should find you in bed," said her husband, when he discovered her lying there. He had walked up with Madame Lebrun and left her at the house. His wife did not reply.

"Are you asleep?" he asked, bending down close to look at her.

"No." Her eyes gleamed bright and intense, with no sleepy shadows, as they looked into his.

"Do you know it is past one o'clock? Come on," and he mounted the steps and went into their room.

"Edna!" called Mr. Pontellier from within, after a few moments had gone by.

"Don't wait for me," she answered. He thrust his head through the door.

"You will take cold out there," he said, irritably. "What folly is this? Why don't you come in?"

"It isn't cold; I have my shawl."

"The mosquitoes will devour you."

"There are no mosquitoes."

She heard him moving about the room, every sound indicating impatience and irritation. Another time she would have gone in at his request. She would, through habit, have yielded to his desire; not with any sense of submission or obedience to his compelling wishes, but unthinkingly, as we walk, move, sit, stand, go through the daily treadmill of the life which has been portioned out to us.

"Edna, dear, are you not coming in soon?" he asked again, this time fondly, with a note of entreaty.

"No; I am going to stay out here."

"This is more than folly," he blurted out. "I can't permit you to stay out there all night. You must come in the house instantly."

With a writhing motion she settled herself more securely in the hammock. She perceived that her will had blazed up, stubborn and resistant. She could not at that moment have done other than denied and resisted. She wondered if her husband had ever spoken to her like that before, and if she had submitted to his command. Of course she had; she remembered that she had. But she could not realize why or how she should have yielded, feeling as she then did.

"Léonce, go to bed," she said. "I mean to stay out here. I don't wish to go in, and I don't intend to. Don't speak to me like that again; I shall not answer you."

Mr. Pontellier had prepared for bed, but he slipped on an extra garment. He opened a bottle of wine, of which he kept a small and select supply in a buffet of his own. He drank a glass of the wine and went out on the gallery and offered a glass to his wife. She did not wish any. He drew up the rocker, hoisted his slippered feet on the rail, and proceeded to smoke a cigar. He smoked two cigars; then he went inside and drank another glass of wine. Mrs. Pontellier again declined to accept a glass when it was offered to her. Mr. Pontellier once more seated himself with elevated feet, and after a reasonable interval of time smoked some more cigars.

Edna began to feel like one who awakens gradually out of a dream, a delicious, grotesque, impossible dream, to feel again the realities pressing into her soul. The physical need for sleep began to overtake her; the exuberance which had sustained and exalted her spirit left her helpless and yielding to the conditions which crowded her in.

The stillest hour of the night had come, the hour before dawn, when the world seems to hold its breath. The moon hung low, and had turned from silver to copper in the sleeping sky. The old owl no longer hooted, and the water-oaks had ceased to moan as they bent their heads.

Edna arose, cramped from lying so long and still in the hammock. She tottered up the steps, clutching feebly at the post before passing into the house.

"Are you coming in, Léonce?" she asked, turning her face toward her husband.

"Yes, dear," he answered, with a glance following a misty puff of smoke. "Just as soon as I have finished my cigar."

XII

∽

SHE SLEPT BUT A few hours. They were troubled and feverish hours, disturbed with dreams that were intangible, that eluded her, leaving only an impression upon her half-awakened senses of something unattainable. She was up and dressed in the cool of the early morning. The air was invigorating and steadied somewhat her faculties. However, she was not seeking refreshment or help from any source, either external or from within. She was blindly following whatever impulse moved her, as if she had placed herself in alien hands for direction, and freed her soul of responsibility.

Most of the people at that early hour were still in bed and asleep. A few, who intended to go over to the *Chênière* for mass, were moving about. The lovers, who had laid their plans the night before, were already strolling toward the wharf. The lady in black, with her Sunday prayer-book, velvet and gold-clasped, and her Sunday silver beads, was following them at no great distance. Old Monsieur Farival was up, and was more than half inclined to do anything that suggested itself. He put on his big straw hat, and taking his umbrella from the stand in the hall, followed the lady in black, never overtaking her.

The little negro girl who worked Madame Lebrun's sewing-machine was sweeping the galleries with long, absent-minded strokes of the broom. Edna sent her up into the house to awaken Robert.

"Tell him I am going to the *Chênière*. The boat is ready; tell him to hurry."

He had soon joined her. She had never sent for him before. She had never asked for him. She had never seemed to want him before. She did not appear conscious that she had done anything unusual in commanding his presence. He was apparently equally unconscious of anything extraordinary in the situation. But his face was suffused with a quiet glow when he met her.

They went together back to the kitchen to drink coffee. There was no time to wait for any nicety of service. They stood outside the window and the cook passed them their coffee and a roll, which they drank and ate from the window-sill. Edna said it tasted good. She had not thought of coffee nor of anything. He told her he had often noticed that she lacked forethought.

"Wasn't it enough to think of going to the *Chênière* and waking you up?" she laughed. "Do I have to think of everything?—as Léonce says when he's in a bad humor. I don't blame him; he'd never be in a bad humor if it weren't for me."

They took a short cut across the sands. At a distance they could see the curious procession moving toward the wharf— the lovers, shoulder to shoulder, creeping; the lady in black, gaining steadily upon them; old Monsieur Farival, losing ground inch by inch, and a young barefooted Spanish girl, with a red kerchief on her head and a basket on her arm, bringing up the rear.

Robert knew the girl, and he talked to her a little in the boat. No one present understood what they said. Her name was Mariequita. She had a round, sly, piquant face and pretty black eyes. Her hands were small, and she kept them folded over the handle of her basket. Her feet were broad and coarse. She did not strive to hide them. Edna looked at her feet, and noticed the sand and slime between her brown toes.

Beaudelet grumbled because Mariequita was there, taking up so much room. In reality he was annoyed at having old Monsieur Farival, who considered himself the better sailor of the two. But he would not quarrel with so old a man as Monsieur Farival, so he quarreled with Mariequita. The girl was deprecatory at one moment, appealing to Robert. She was saucy the next, moving her head up and down, making "eyes" at Robert and making "mouths" at Beaudelet.

The lovers were all alone. They saw nothing, they heard nothing. The lady in black was counting her beads for the third time. Old Monsieur Farival talked incessantly of what he knew about handling a boat, and of what Beaudelet did not know on the same subject.

Edna liked it all. She looked Mariequita up and down, from her ugly brown toes to her pretty black eyes, and back again.

"Why does she look at me like that?" inquired the girl of Robert.

"Maybe she thinks you are pretty. Shall I ask her?"

"No. Is she your sweetheart?"

"She's a married lady, and has two children."

"Oh! well! Francisco ran away with Sylvano's wife, who had four children. They took all his money and one of the children and stole his boat."

"Shut up!"

"Does she understand?"

"Oh, hush!"

"Are those two married over there—leaning on each other?"

"Of course not," laughed Robert.

"Of course not," echoed Mariequita, with a serious, confirmatory bob of the head.

The sun was high up and beginning to bite. The swift breeze seemed to Edna to bury the sting of it into the pores of her face and hands. Robert held his umbrella over her.

As they went cutting sidewise through the water, the sails bellied taut, with the wind filling and overflowing them. Old Monsieur Farival laughed sardonically at something as he looked at the sails, and Beaudelet swore at the old man under his breath.

Sailing across the bay to the *Chênière Caminada*, Edna felt as if she were being borne away from some anchorage

which had held her fast, whose chains had been loosening—
had snapped the night before when the mystic spirit was
abroad, leaving her free to drift whithersoever she chose to set
her sails. Robert spoke to her incessantly; he no longer noticed Mariequita. The girl had shrimps in her bamboo basket.
They were covered with Spanish moss. She beat the moss
down impatiently, and muttered to herself sullenly.

"Let us go to Grande Terre* to-morrow?" said Robert in a
low voice.

"What shall we do there?"

"Climb up the hill to the old fort and look at the little wriggling gold snakes, and watch the lizards sun themselves."

She gazed away toward Grande Terre and thought she
would like to be alone there with Robert, in the sun, listening
to the ocean's roar and watching the slimy lizards writhe in
and out among the ruins of the old fort.

"And the next day or the next we can sail to the Bayou
Brulow,"† he went on.

"What shall we do there?"

"Anything—cast bait for fish."

"No; we'll go back to Grande Terre. Let the fish alone."

"We'll go wherever you like," he said. "I'll have Tonie
come over and help me patch and trim my boat. We shall
not need Beaudelet nor any one. Are you afraid of the
pirogue?"‡

"Oh, no."

"Then I'll take you some night in the pirogue when the
moon shines. Maybe your Gulf spirit will whisper to you in
which of these islands the treasures are hidden—direct you to
the very spot, perhaps."

"And in a day we should be rich!" she laughed. "I'd give it
all to you, the pirate gold and every bit of treasure we could

---

* An island adjacent to Grand Isle.

† Located near Grand Isle, a small settlement for shrimping and
fishing constructed on platforms raised above the water by stilts.

‡ Canoe; widely used for fishing in the Gulf of Mexico.

dig up. I think you would know how to spend it. Pirate gold isn't a thing to be hoarded or utilized. It is something to squander and throw to the four winds, for the fun of seeing the golden specks fly."

"We'd share it, and scatter it together," he said. His face flushed.

They all went together up to the quaint little Gothic church of Our Lady of Lourdes, gleaming all brown and yellow with paint in the sun's glare.

Only Beaudelet remained behind, tinkering at his boat, and Mariequita walked away with her basket of shrimps, casting a look of childish ill-humor and reproach at Robert from the corner of her eye.

XIII

∾

A FEELING OF OPPRESSION and drowsiness overcame Edna during the service. Her head began to ache, and the lights on the altar swayed before her eyes. Another time she might have made an effort to regain her composure; but her one thought was to quit the stifling atmosphere of the church and reach the open air. She arose, climbing over Robert's feet with a muttered apology. Old Monsieur Farival, flurried, curious, stood up, but upon seeing that Robert had followed Mrs. Pontellier, he sank back into his seat. He whispered an anxious inquiry of the lady in black, who did not notice him or reply, but kept her eyes fastened upon the pages of her velvet prayer-book.

"I felt giddy and almost overcome," Edna said, lifting her hands instinctively to her head and pushing her straw hat up from her forehead. "I couldn't have stayed through the service." They were outside in the shadow of the church. Robert was full of solicitude.

"It was folly to have thought of going in the first place, let alone staying. Come over to Madame Antoine's; you can rest there." He took her arm and led her away, looking anxiously and continuously down into her face.

How still it was, with only the voice of the sea whispering through the reeds that grew in the salt-water pools! The long line of little gray, weather-beaten houses nestled peacefully among the orange trees. It must always have been God's day on that low, drowsy island, Edna thought. They stopped, leaning over a jagged fence made of sea-drift, to ask for water. A youth, a mild-faced Acadian,* was drawing water from the cistern, which was nothing more than a rusty buoy, with an opening on one side, sunk in the ground. The water which the youth handed to them in a tin pail was not cold to taste, but it was cool to her heated face, and it greatly revived and refreshed her.

Madame Antoine's cot was at the far end of the village. She welcomed them with all the native hospitality, as she would have opened her door to let the sunlight in. She was fat, and walked heavily and clumsily across the floor. She could speak no English, but when Robert made her understand that the lady who accompanied him was ill and desired to rest, she was all eagerness to make Edna feel at home and to dispose of her comfortably.

The whole place was immaculately clean, and the big, four-posted bed, snow-white, invited one to repose. It stood in a small side room which looked out across a narrow grass plot toward the shed, where there was a disabled boat lying keel upward.

Madame Antoine had not gone to mass. Her son Tonie had, but she supposed he would soon be back, and she invited Robert to be seated and wait for him. But he went and sat out-

---

* A descendant of French Canadians whom the British, in the 18th century, drove from the captured French colony of Acadia (now Nova Scotia and adjacent areas) and who settled in the bayou lands of southern Louisiana.

side the door and smoked. Madame Antoine busied herself in the large front room preparing dinner. She was boiling mullets[*] over a few red coals in the huge fireplace.

Edna, left alone in the little side room, loosened her clothes, removing the greater part of them. She bathed her face, her neck and arms in the basin that stood between the windows. She took off her shoes and stockings and stretched herself in the very center of the high, white bed. How luxurious it felt to rest thus in a strange, quaint bed, with its sweet country odor of laurel lingering about the sheets and mattress! She stretched her strong limbs that ached a little. She ran her fingers through her loosened hair for a while. She looked at her round arms as she held them straight up and rubbed them one after the other, observing closely, as if it were something she saw for the first time, the fine, firm quality and texture of her flesh. She clasped her hands easily above her head, and it was thus she fell asleep.

She slept lightly at first, half awake and drowsily attentive to the things about her. She could hear Madame Antoine's heavy, scraping tread as she walked back and forth on the sanded floor. Some chickens were clucking outside the windows, scratching for bits of gravel in the grass. Later she half heard the voices of Robert and Tonie talking under the shed. She did not stir. Even her eyelids rested numb and heavily over her sleepy eyes. The voices went on—Tonie's slow, Acadian drawl, Robert's quick, soft, smooth French. She understood French imperfectly unless directly addressed, and the voices were only part of the other drowsy, muffled sounds lulling her senses.

When Edna awoke it was with the conviction that she had slept long and soundly. The voices were hushed under the shed. Madame Antoine's step was no longer to be heard in the adjoining room. Even the chickens had gone elsewhere to scratch and cluck. The mosquito bar was drawn over her; the old woman had come in while she slept and let down the bar.

---

[*] A type of fish.

Edna arose quietly from the bed, and looking between the curtains of the window, she saw by the slanting rays of the sun that the afternoon was far advanced. Robert was out there under the shed, reclining in the shade against the sloping keel of the overturned boat. He was reading from a book. Tonie was no longer with him. She wondered what had become of the rest of the party. She peeped out at him two or three times as she stood washing herself in the little basin between the windows.

Madame Antoine had laid some coarse, clean towels upon a chair, and had placed a box of *poudre de riz** within easy reach. Edna dabbed the powder upon her nose and cheeks as she looked at herself closely in the little distorted mirror which hung on the wall above the basin. Her eyes were bright and wide awake and her face glowed.

When she had completed her toilet she walked into the adjoining room. She was very hungry. No one was there. But there was a cloth spread upon the table that stood against the wall, and a cover was laid for one, with a crusty brown loaf and a bottle of wine beside the plate. Edna bit a piece from the brown loaf, tearing it with her strong, white teeth. She poured some of the wine into the glass and drank it down. Then she went softly out of doors, and plucking an orange from the low-hanging bough of a tree, threw it at Robert, who did not know she was awake and up.

An illumination broke over his whole face when he saw her and joined her under the orange tree.

"How many years have I slept?" she inquired. "The whole island seems changed. A new race of beings must have sprung up, leaving only you and me as past relics. How many ages ago did Madame Antonie and Tonie die? and when did our people from Grand Isle disappear from the earth?"

He familiarly adjusted a ruffle upon her shoulder.

"You have slept precisely one hundred years. I was left here to guard your slumbers; and for one hundred years I

---

* Rice powder; for dusting the face and chest (Fr.).

have been out under the shed reading a book. The only evil I couldn't prevent was to keep a broiled fowl from drying up."

"If it has turned to stone, still will I eat it," said Edna, moving with him into the house. "But really, what has become of Monsieur Farival and the others?"

"Gone hours ago. When they found that you were sleeping they thought it best not to awake you. Any way, I wouldn't have let them. What was I here for?"

"I wonder if Léonce will be uneasy!" she speculated, as she seated herself at table.

"Of course not; he knows you are with me," Robert replied, as he busied himself among sundry pans and covered dishes which had been left standing on the hearth.

"Where are Madame Antoine and her son?" asked Edna.

"Gone to Vespers, and to visit some friends, I believe. I am to take you back in Tonie's boat whenever you are ready to go."

He stirred the smoldering ashes till the broiled fowl began to sizzle afresh. He served her with no mean repast, dripping the coffee anew and sharing it with her. Madame Antoine had cooked little else than the mullets, but while Edna slept Robert had foraged the island. He was childishly gratified to discover her appetite, and to see the relish with which she ate the food which he had procured for her.

"Shall we go right away?" she asked, after draining her glass and brushing together the crumbs of the crusty loaf.

"The sun isn't as low as it will be in two hours," he answered.

"The sun will be gone in two hours."

"Well, let it go; who cares!"

They waited a good while under the orange trees, till Madame Antoine came back, panting, waddling, with a thousand apologies to explain her absence. Tonie did not dare to return. He was shy, and would not willingly face any woman except his mother.

It was very pleasant to stay there under the orange trees, while the sun dipped lower and lower, turning the western sky to flaming copper and gold. The shadows lengthened and crept out like stealthy, grotesque monsters across the grass.

Edna and Robert both sat upon the ground—that is, he lay upon the ground beside her, occasionally picking at the hem of her muslin gown.

Madame Antoine seated her fat body, broad and squat, upon a bench beside the door. She had been talking all the afternoon, and had wound herself up to the story-telling pitch.

And what stories she told them! But twice in her life she had left the *Chênière Caminada*, and then for the briefest span. All her years she had squatted and waddled there upon the island, gathering legends of the Baratarians* and the sea. The night came on, with the moon to lighten it. Edna could hear the whispering voices of dead men and the click of muffled gold.

When she and Robert stepped into Tonie's boat, with the red lateen sail, misty spirit forms were prowling in the shadows and among the reeds, and upon the water were phantom ships, speeding to cover.

XIV

⟋⟍

THE YOUNGEST BOY, ÉTIENNE, had been very naughty, Madame Ratignolle said, as she delivered him into the hands of his mother. He had been unwilling to go to bed and had made a scene; whereupon she had taken charge of him and pacified him as well as she could. Raoul had been in bed and asleep for two hours.

---

* Jean Lafitte and his brother Pierre, who between 1810 and 1814 organized a colony of pirates and smugglers around the coast of Barataria Bay, an inlet of the Gulf of Mexico. The name Barataria is derived from the Spanish word meaning "to deceive."

The youngster was in his long white nightgown, that kept tripping him up as Madame Ratignolle led him along by the hand. With the other chubby fist he rubbed his eyes, which were heavy with sleep and ill-humor. Edna took him in her arms, and seating herself in the rocker, began to coddle and caress him, calling him all manner of tender names, soothing him to sleep.

It was not more than nine o'clock. No one had yet gone to bed but the children.

Léonce had been very uneasy at first, Madame Ratignolle said, and had wanted to start at once for the *Chênière*. But Monsieur Farival had assured him that his wife was only overcome with sleep and fatigue, that Tonie would bring her safely back later in the day; and he had thus been dissuaded from crossing the bay. He had gone over to Klein's, looking up some cotton broker whom he wished to see in regard to securities, exchanges, stocks, bonds, or something of the sort, Madame Ratignolle did not remember what. He said he would not remain away late. She herself was suffering from heat and oppression, she said. She carried a bottle of salts and a large fan. She would not consent to remain with Edna, for Monsieur Ratignolle was alone, and he detested above all things to be left alone.

When Étienne had fallen asleep Edna bore him into the back room, and Robert went and lifted the mosquito bar that she might lay the child comfortably in his bed. The quadroon had vanished. When they emerged from the cottage Robert bade Edna good-night.

"Do you know we have been together the whole livelong day, Robert—since early this morning?" she said at parting.

"All but the hundred years when you were sleeping. Goodnight."

He pressed her hand and went away in the direction of the beach. He did not join any of the others, but walked alone toward the Gulf.

Edna stayed outside, awaiting her husband's return. She had no desire to sleep or to retire; nor did she feel like going over to sit with the Ratignolles, or to join Madame Lebrun and a group whose animated voices reached her as they sat in conversation before the house. She let her mind wander back over her stay at Grand Isle; and she tried to discover wherein this summer had been different from any and every other summer of her life. She could only realize that she herself— her present self—was in some way different from the other self. That she was seeing with different eyes and making the acquaintance of new conditions in herself that colored and changed her environment, she did not yet suspect.

She wondered why Robert had gone away and left her. It did not occur to her to think he might have grown tired of being with her the livelong day. She was not tired, and she felt that he was not. She regretted that he had gone. It was so much more natural to have him stay, when he was not absolutely required to leave her.

As Edna waited for her husband she sang low a little song that Robert had sung as they crossed the bay. It began with *"Ah! si tu savais!"** and every verse ended with *"si tu savais!"*

Robert's voice was not pretentious. It was musical and true. The voice, the notes, the whole refrain haunted her memory.

XV

∽

WHEN EDNA ENTERED THE dining-room one evening a little late, as was her habit, an unusually animated conversation seemed to be going on. Several persons were talking at once, and Victor's voice was predominating, even over that of his mother. Edna had returned late from her bath, had dressed in some haste, and her face was flushed. Her head, set off by her dainty white gown, suggested a rich, rare blossom. She took

---

* If only you could know! (Fr.).

her seat at table between old Monsieur Farival and Madame Ratignolle.

As she seated herself and was about to begin to eat her soup, which had been served when she entered the room, several persons informed her simultaneously that Robert was going to Mexico. She laid her spoon down and looked about her bewildered. He had been with her, reading to her all the morning, and had never even mentioned such a place as Mexico. She had not seen him during the afternoon; she had heard some one say he was at the house, upstairs with his mother. This she had thought nothing of, though she was surprised when he did not join her later in the afternoon, when she went down to the beach.

She looked across at him, where he sat beside Madame Lebrun, who presided. Edna's face was a blank picture of bewilderment, which she never thought of disguising. He lifted his eyebrows with the pretext of a smile as he returned her glance. He looked embarrassed and uneasy.

"When is he going?" she asked of everybody in general, as if Robert were not there to answer for himself.

"To-night!" "This very evening!" "Did you ever!" "What possesses him!" were some of the replies she gathered, uttered simultaneously in French and English.

"Impossible!" she exclaimed. "How can a person start off from Grand Isle to Mexico at a moment's notice, as if he were going over to Klein's or to the wharf or down to the beach?"

"I said all along I was going to Mexico; I've been saying so for years!" cried Robert, in an excited and irritable tone, with the air of a man defending himself against a swarm of stinging insects.

Madame Lebrun knocked on the table with her knife handle.

"Please let Robert explain why he is going, and why he is going to-night," she called out. "Really, this table is getting to be more and more like Bedlam every day, with everybody talking at once. Sometimes—I hope God will forgive me—

but positively, sometimes I wish Victor would lose the power of speech."

Victor laughed sardonically as he thanked his mother for her holy wish, of which he failed to see the benefit to anybody, except that it might afford her a more ample opportunity and license to talk herself.

Monsieur Farival thought that Victor should have been taken out in mid-ocean in his earliest youth and drowned. Victor thought there would be more logic in thus disposing of old people with an established claim for making themselves universally obnoxious. Madame Lebrun grew a trifle hysterical; Robert called his brother some sharp, hard names.

"There's nothing much to explain, mother," he said; though he explained, nevertheless—looking chiefly at Edna—that he could only meet the gentleman whom he intended to join at Vera Cruz by taking such and such a steamer, which left New Orleans on such a day; that Beaudelet was going out with his lugger-load of vegetables that night, which gave him an opportunity of reaching the city and making his vessel in time.

"But when did you make up your mind to all this?" demanded Monsieur Farival.

"This afternoon," returned Robert, with a shade of annoyance.

"At what time this afternoon?" persisted the old gentleman, with nagging determination, as if he were cross-questioning a criminal in a court of justice.

"At four o'clock this afternoon, Monsieur Farival," Robert replied, in a high voice and with a lofty air, which reminded Edna of some gentleman on the stage.

She had forced herself to eat most of her soup, and now she was picking the flaky bits of a *court bouillon*° with her fork.

The lovers were profiting by the general conversation on Mexico to speak in whispers of matters which they rightly

---

° Stewed fish (Fr.).

considered were interesting to no one but themselves. The lady in black had once received a pair of prayer-beads of curious workmanship from Mexico, with very special indulgence attached to them, but she had never been able to ascertain whether the indulgence extended outside the Mexican border. Father Fochel of the Cathedral had attempted to explain it; but he had not done so to her satisfaction. And she begged that Robert would interest himself, and discover, if possible, whether she was entitled to the indulgence accompanying the remarkably curious Mexican prayer-beads.

Madame Ratignolle hoped that Robert would exercise extreme caution in dealing with the Mexicans, who, she considered, were a treacherous people, unscrupulous and revengeful. She trusted she did them no injustice in thus condemning them as a race. She had known personally but one Mexican, who made and sold excellent tamales, and whom she would have trusted implicitly, so soft-spoken was he. One day he was arrested for stabbing his wife. She never knew whether he had been hanged or not.

Victor had grown hilarious, and was attempting to tell an anecdote about a Mexican girl who served chocolate one winter in a restaurant in Dauphine Street. No one would listen to him but old Monsieur Farival, who went into convulsions over the droll story.

Edna wondered if they had all gone mad, to be talking and clamoring at that rate. She herself could think of nothing to say about Mexico or the Mexicans.

"At what time do you leave?" she asked Robert.

"At ten," he told her. "Beaudelet wants to wait for the moon."

"Are you all ready to go?"

"Quite ready. I shall only take a hand-bag, and shall pack my trunk in the city."

He turned to answer some question put to him by his mother, and Edna, having finished her black coffee, left the table.

She went directly to her room. The little cottage was close

and stuffy after leaving the outer air. But she did not mind; there appeared to be a hundred different things demanding her attention indoors. She began to set the toilet-stand to rights, grumbling at the negligence of the quadroon, who was in the adjoining room putting the children to bed. She gathered together stray garments that were hanging on the backs of chairs, and put each where it belonged in closet or bureau drawer. She changed her gown for a more comfortable and commodious wrapper. She rearranged her hair, combing and brushing it with unusual energy. Then she went in and assisted the quadroon in getting the boys to bed.

They were very playful and inclined to talk—to do anything but lie quiet and go to sleep. Edna sent the quadroon away to her supper and told her she need not return. Then she sat and told the children a story. Instead of soothing it excited them, and added to their wakefulness. She left them in heated argument, speculating about the conclusion of the tale which their mother promised to finish the following night.

The little black girl came in to say that Madame Lebrun would like to have Mrs. Pontellier go and sit with them over at the house till Mr. Robert went away. Edna returned answer that she had already undressed, that she did not feel quite well, but perhaps she would go over to the house later. She started to dress again, and got as far advanced as to remove her *peignoir*. But changing her mind once more she resumed the *peignoir*, and went outside and sat down before her door. She was overheated and irritable, and fanned herself energetically for a while. Madame Ratignolle came down to discover what was the matter.

"All that noise and confusion at the table must have upset me," replied Edna, "and moreover, I hate shocks and surprises. The idea of Robert starting off in such a ridiculously sudden and dramatic way! As if it were a matter of life and death! Never saying a word about it all morning when he was with me."

"Yes," agreed Madame Ratignolle. "I think it was showing

us all—you especially—very little consideration. It wouldn't have surprised me in any of the others; those Lebruns are all given to heroics. But I must say I should never have expected such a thing from Robert. Are you not coming down? Come on, dear; it doesn't look friendly."

"No," said Edna, a little sullenly. "I can't go to the trouble of dressing again; I don't feel like it."

"You needn't dress; you look all right; fasten a belt around your waist. Just look at me!"

"No," persisted Edna; "but you go on. Madame Lebrun might be offended if we both stayed away."

Madame Ratignolle kissed Edna good-night, and went away, being in truth rather desirous of joining in the general and animated conversation which was still in progress concerning Mexico and the Mexicans.

Somewhat later Robert came up, carrying his hand-bag.

"Aren't you feeling well?" he asked.

"Oh, well enough. Are you going right away?"

He lit a match and looked at his watch. "In twenty minutes," he said. The sudden and brief flare of the match emphasized the darkness for a while. He sat down upon a stool which the children had left out on the porch.

"Get a chair," said Edna.

"This will do," he replied. He put on his soft hat and nervously took it off again, and wiping his face with his handkerchief, complained of the heat.

"Take the fan," said Edna, offering it to him.

"Oh, no! Thank you. It does no good; you have to stop fanning some time, and feel all the more uncomfortable afterward."

"That's one of the ridiculous things which men always say. I have never known one to speak otherwise of fanning. How long will you be gone?"

"Forever, perhaps. I don't know. It depends upon a good many things."

"Well, in case it shouldn't be forever, how long will it be?"

"I don't know."

"This seems to me perfectly preposterous and uncalled for. I don't like it. I don't understand your motive for silence and mystery, never saying a word to me about it this morning." He remained silent, not offering to defend himself. He only said, after a moment:

"Don't part from me in an ill-humor. I never knew you to be out of patience with me before."

"I don't want to part in any ill-humor," she said. "But can't you understand? I've grown used to seeing you, to having you with me all the time, and your action seems unfriendly, even unkind. You don't even offer an excuse for it. Why, I was planning to be together, thinking of how pleasant it would be to see you in the city next winter."

"So was I," he blurted. "Perhaps that's the—" He stood up suddenly and held out his hand. "Good-by, my dear Mrs. Pontellier; good-by. You won't—I hope you won't completely forget me." She clung to his hand, striving to detain him.

"Write to me when you get there, won't you, Robert?" she entreated.

"I will, thank you. Good-by."

How unlike Robert! The merest acquaintance would have said something more emphatic than "I will, thank you; good-by," to such a request.

He had evidently already taken leave of the people over at the house, for he descended the steps and went to join Beaudelet, who was out there with an oar across his shoulder waiting for Robert. They walked away in the darkness. She could only hear Beaudelet's voice; Robert had apparently not even spoken a word of greeting to his companion.

Edna bit her handkerchief convulsively, striving to hold back and to hide, even from herself as she would have hidden from another, the emotion which was troubling—tearing—her. Her eyes were brimming with tears.

For the first time she recognized anew the symptoms of infatuation which she had felt incipiently as a child, as a girl in her earliest teens, and later as a young woman. The recognition did not lessen the reality, the poignancy of the revelation by any suggestion or promise of instability. The past was nothing to her; offered no lesson which she was willing to heed. The future was a mystery which she never attempted to penetrate. The present alone was significant; was hers, to torture her as it was doing then with the biting conviction that she had lost that which she had held, that she had been denied that which her impassioned, newly awakened being demanded.

XVI

∞

"Do you miss your friend greatly?" asked Mademoiselle Reisz one morning as she came creeping up behind Edna, who had just left her cottage on her way to the beach. She spent much of her time in the water since she had acquired finally the art of swimming. As their stay at Grand Isle drew near its close, she felt that she could not give too much time to a diversion which afforded her the only real pleasurable moments that she knew. When Mademoiselle Reisz came and touched her upon the shoulder and spoke to her, the woman seemed to echo the thought which was ever in Edna's mind; or, better, the feeling which constantly possessed her.

Robert's going had some way taken the brightness, the color, the meaning out of everything. The conditions of her life were in no way changed, but her whole existence was dulled, like a faded garment which seems to be no longer worth wearing. She sought him everywhere—in others whom she induced to talk about him. She went up in the mornings to Madame Lebrun's room, braving the clatter of the old sewing-machine. She sat there and chatted at intervals as Robert had done. She gazed around the room at the pictures and photographs hanging upon the wall, and discovered in some corner an old family album, which she examined with the keenest interest, appealing to Madame Lebrun for enlightenment concerning the many figures and faces which she discovered between its pages.

There was a picture of Madame Lebrun with Robert as a baby, seated in her lap, a round-faced infant with a fist in his mouth. The eyes alone in the baby suggested the man. And that was he also in kilts, at the age of five, wearing long curls and holding a whip in his hand. It made Edna laugh, and she laughed, too, at the portrait in his first long trousers; while another interested her, taken when he left for college, looking thin, long-faced, with eyes full of fire, ambition and great intentions. But there was no recent picture, none which suggested the Robert who had gone away five days ago, leaving a void and wilderness behind him.

"Oh, Robert stopped having his pictures taken when he had to pay for them himself! He found wiser use for his money, he says," explained Madame Lebrun. She had a letter from him, written before he left New Orleans. Edna wished to see the letter, and Madame Lebrun told her to look for it either on the table or the dresser, or perhaps it was on the mantelpiece.

The letter was on the bookshelf. It possessed the greatest interest and attraction for Edna; the envelope, its size and shape, the post-mark, the handwriting. She examined every detail of the outside before opening it. There were only a few lines, setting forth that he would leave the city that afternoon, that he had packed his trunk in good shape, that he was well, and sent her his love and begged to be affectionately remembered to all. There was no special message to Edna except a postscript saying that if Mrs. Pontellier desired to finish the book which he had been reading to her, his mother would find it in his room, among other books there on the table. Edna experienced a pang of jealousy because he had written to his mother rather than to her.

Every one seemed to take for granted that she missed him. Even her husband, when he came down the Saturday following Robert's departure, expressed regret that he had gone.

"How do you get on without him, Edna?" he asked.

"It's very dull without him," she admitted. Mr. Pontellier had seen Robert in the city, and Edna asked him a dozen questions or more. Where had they met? On Carondelet Street, in the morning. They had gone "in" and had a drink and a cigar together. What had they talked about? Chiefly about his prospects in Mexico, which Mr. Pontellier thought were promising. How did he look? How did he seem—grave, or gay, or how? Quite cheerful, and wholly taken up with the idea of his trip, which Mr. Pontellier found altogether natural in a young fellow about to seek fortune and adventure in a strange, queer country.

Edna tapped her foot impatiently, and wondered why the children persisted in playing in the sun when they might be under the trees. She went down and led them out of the sun, scolding the quadroon for not being more attentive.

It did not strike her as in the least grotesque that she should be making of Robert the object of conversation and leading her husband to speak of him. The sentiment which she entertained for Robert in no way resembled that which she felt for her husband, or had ever felt, or ever expected to feel. She had all her life long been accustomed to harbor thoughts and emotions which never voiced themselves. They had never taken the form of struggles. They belonged to her and were her own, and she entertained the conviction that she had a right to them and that they concerned no one but herself. Edna had once told Madame Ratignolle that she would never sacrifice herself for her children, or for any one. Then had followed a rather heated argument; the two women did not appear to understand each other or to be talking the same language. Edna tried to appease her friend, to explain.

"I would give up the unessential; I would give my money, I would give my life for my children; but I wouldn't give myself. I can't make it more clear; it's only something which I am beginning to comprehend, which is revealing itself to me."

"I don't know what you would call the essential, or what you mean by the unessential," said Madame Ratignolle, cheerfully; "but a woman who would give her life for her children could do no more than that—your Bible tells you so. I'm sure I couldn't do more than that."

"Oh, yes you could!" laughed Edna.

She was not surprised at Mademoiselle Reisz's question the morning that lady, following her to the beach, tapped her on the shoulder and asked if she did not greatly miss her young friend.

"Oh, good morning, Mademoiselle; is it you? Why, of course I miss Robert. Are you going down to bathe?"

"Why should I go down to bathe at the very end of the season when I haven't been in the surf all summer," replied the woman, disagreeably.

"I beg your pardon," offered Edna, in some embarrassment, for she should have remembered that Mademoiselle Reisz's avoidance of the water had furnished a theme for much pleasantry. Some among them thought it was on account of her false hair, or the dread of getting the violets wet, while others attributed it to the natural aversion for water sometimes believed to accompany the artistic temperament. Mademoiselle offered Edna some chocolates in a paper bag, which she took from her pocket, by way of showing that she bore no ill feeling. She habitually ate chocolates for their sustaining quality; they contained much nutriment in small compass, she said. They saved her from starvation, as Madame Lebrun's table was utterly impossible; and no one save so impertinent a woman as Madame Lebrun could think of offering such food to people and requiring them to pay for it.

"She must feel very lonely without her son," said Edna, desiring to change the subject. "Her favorite son, too. It must have been quite hard to let him go."

Mademoiselle laughed maliciously.

"Her favorite son! Oh, dear! Who could have been imposing such a tale upon you? Aline Lebrun lives for Victor, and for Victor alone. She has spoiled him into the worthless creature he is. She worships him and the ground he walks on.

Robert is very well in a way, to give up all the money he can earn to the family, and keep the barest pittance for himself. Favorite son, indeed! I miss the poor fellow myself, my dear. I liked to see him and to hear him about the place—the only Lebrun who is worth a pinch of salt. He comes to see me often in the city. I like to play to him. That Victor! hanging would be too good for him. It's a wonder Robert hasn't beaten him to death long ago."

"I thought he had great patience with his brother," offered Edna, glad to be talking about Robert, no matter what was said.

"Oh! he thrashed him well enough a year or two ago," said Mademoiselle. "It was about a Spanish girl, whom Victor considered that he had some sort of claim upon. He met Robert one day talking to the girl, or walking with her, or bathing with her, or carrying her basket—I don't remember what—and he became so insulting and abusive that Robert gave him a thrashing on the spot that has kept him comparatively in order for a good while. It's about time he was getting another."

"Was her name Mariequita?" asked Edna.

"Mariequita—yes, that was it; Mariequita. I had forgotten. Oh, she's a sly one, and a bad one, that Mariequita!"

Edna looked down at Mademoiselle Reisz and wondered how she could have listened to her venom so long. For some reason she felt depressed, almost unhappy. She had not intended to go into the water; but she donned her bathing suit, and left Mademoiselle alone, seated under the shade of the children's tent. The water was growing cooler as the season advanced. Edna plunged and swam about with an abandon that thrilled and invigorated her. She remained a long time in the water, half hoping that Mademoiselle Reisz would not wait for her.

But Mademoiselle waited. She was very amiable during the walk back, and raved much over Edna's appearance in her bathing suit. She talked about music. She hoped that Edna would go to see her in the city, and wrote her address with the stub of a pencil on a piece of card which she found in her pocket.

"When do you leave?" asked Edna.

"Next Monday; and you?"

"The following week," answered Edna, adding, "It has been a pleasant summer, hasn't it, Mademoiselle?"

"Well," agreed Mademoiselle Reisz, with a shrug, "rather pleasant, if it hadn't been for the mosquitoes and the Farival twins."

XVII

∽

THE PONTELLIERS POSSESSED A very charming home on Esplanade Street* in New Orleans. It was a large, double cottage, with a broad front veranda, whose round, fluted columns supported the sloping roof. The house was painted a dazzling white; the outside shutters, or jalousies, were green. In the yard, which was kept scrupulously neat, were flowers and plants of every description which flourishes in South Louisiana. Within doors the appointments were perfect after the conventional type. The softest carpets and rugs covered the floors; rich and tasteful draperies hung at doors and windows. There were paintings, selected with judgment and discrimination, upon the walls. The cut glass, the silver, the heavy damask† which daily appeared upon the table were the envy of many women whose husbands were less generous than Mr. Pontellier.

---

* A broad, tree-lined avenue that parallels Canal Street on the downriver side of the French Quarter; a prestigious location, the street was lined by large, affluent homes and gardens belonging to the Creole elite.

† A firm, lustrous fabric used for drapes, napkins, and tablecloths.

Mr. Pontellier was very fond of walking about his house examining its various appointments and details, to see that nothing was amiss. He greatly valued his possessions, chiefly because they were his, and derived genuine pleasure from contemplating a painting, a statuette, a rare lace curtain—no matter what—after he had bought it and placed it among his household gods.

On Tuesday afternoons—Tuesday being Mrs. Pontellier's reception day—there was a constant stream of callers—women who came in carriages or in the street cars, or walked when the air was soft and distance permitted. A light-colored mulatto boy, in dress coat and bearing a diminutive silver tray for the reception of cards, admitted them. A maid, in white fluted cap, offered the callers liqueur, coffee, or chocolate, as they might desire. Mrs. Pontellier, attired in a handsome reception gown, remained in the drawing-room the entire afternoon receiving her visitors. Men sometimes called in the evening with their wives.

This had been the programme which Mrs. Pontellier had religiously followed since her marriage, six years before. Certain evenings during the week she and her husband attended the opera or sometimes the play.

Mr. Pontellier left his home in the mornings between nine and ten o'clock, and rarely returned before half-past six or seven in the evening—dinner being served at half-past seven.

He and his wife seated themselves at table one Tuesday evening, a few weeks after their return from Grand Isle. They were alone together. The boys were being put to bed; the patter of their bare, escaping feet could be heard occasionally, as well as the pursuing voice of the quadroon, lifted in mild protest and entreaty. Mrs. Pontellier did not wear her usual Tuesday reception gown; she was in ordinary house dress. Mr. Pontellier, who was observant about such things, noticed it, as he served the soup and handed it to the boy in waiting.

"Tired out, Edna? Whom did you have? Many callers?" he asked. He tasted his soup and began to season it with pepper, salt, vinegar, mustard—everything within reach.

"There were a good many," replied Edna, who was eating her soup with evident satisfaction. "I found their cards when I got home; I was out."

"Out!" exclaimed her husband, with something like genuine consternation in his voice as he laid down the vinegar cruet and looked at her through his glasses. "Why, what could have taken you out on Tuesday? What did you have to do?"

"Nothing. I simply felt like going out, and I went out."

"Well, I hope you left some suitable excuse," said her husband, somewhat appeased, as he added a dash of cayenne pepper to the soup.

"No, I left no excuse. I told Joe to say I was out, that was all."

"Why, my dear, I should think you'd understand by this time that people don't do such things; we've got to observe *les convenances*[*] if we ever expect to get on and keep up with the procession. If you felt that you had to leave home this afternoon, you should have left some suitable explanation for your absence.

"This soup is really impossible; it's strange that woman hasn't learned yet to make a decent soup. Any free-lunch stand in town serves a better one. Was Mrs. Belthrop here?"

"Bring the tray with the cards, Joe. I don't remember who was here."

The boy retired and returned after a moment, bringing the tiny silver tray, which was covered with ladies' visiting cards. He handed it to Mrs. Pontellier.

"Give it to Mr. Pontellier," she said.

Joe offered the tray to Mr. Pontellier, and removed the soup.

Mr. Pontellier scanned the names of his wife's callers, reading some of them aloud, with comments as he read.

" 'The Misses Delasidas.' I worked a big deal in futures for their father this morning; nice girls; it's time they were getting married. 'Mrs. Belthrop.' I tell you what it is, Edna; you can't

---

[*] Proprieties; social conventions (Fr.).

afford to snub Mrs. Belthrop. Why, Belthrop could buy and sell us ten times over. His business is worth a good, round sum to me. You'd better write her a note. 'Mrs. James Highcamp.' Hugh! the less you have to do with Mrs. Highcamp, the better. 'Madame Laforcé.' Came all the way from Carrolton, too, poor old soul. 'Miss Wiggs,' 'Mrs. Eleanor Boltons.' " He pushed the cards aside.

"Mercy!" exclaimed Edna, who had been fuming. "Why are you taking the thing so seriously and making such a fuss over it?"

"I'm not making any fuss over it. But it's just such seeming trifles that we've got to take seriously; such things count."

The fish was scorched. Mr. Pontellier would not touch it. Edna said she did not mind a little scorched taste. The roast was in some way not to his fancy, and he did not like the manner in which the vegetables were served.

"It seems to me," he said, "we spend money enough in this house to procure at least one meal a day which a man could eat and retain his self-respect."

"You used to think the cook was a treasure," returned Edna, indifferently.

"Perhaps she was when she first came; but cooks are only human. They need looking after, like any other class of persons that you employ. Suppose I didn't look after the clerks in my office, just let them run things their own way; they'd soon make a nice mess of me and my business."

"Where are you going?" asked Edna, seeing that her husband arose from table without having eaten a morsel except a taste of the highly-seasoned soup.

"I'm going to get my dinner at the club. Good-night." He went into the hall, took his hat and stick from the stand, and left the house.

She was somewhat familiar with such scenes. They had often made her very unhappy. On a few previous occasions she had been completely deprived of any desire to finish her dinner. Sometimes she had gone into the kitchen to administer a tardy rebuke to the cook. Once she went to her room and studied the cookbook during an entire evening, finally writing out a menu for the week, which left her harassed with a feeling that, after all, she had accomplished no good that was worth the name.

But that evening Edna finished her dinner alone, with forced deliberation. Her face was flushed and her eyes flamed with some inward fire that lighted them. After finishing her dinner she went to her room, having instructed the boy to tell any other callers that she was indisposed.

It was a large, beautiful room, rich and picturesque in the soft, dim light which the maid had turned low. She went and stood at an open window and looked out upon the deep tangle of the garden below. All the mystery and witchery of the night seemed to have gathered there amid the perfumes and the dusky and tortuous outlines of flowers and foliage. She was seeking herself and finding herself in just such sweet, half-darkness which met her moods. But the voices were not soothing that came to her from the darkness and the sky above and the stars. They jeered and sounded mournful notes without promise, devoid even of hope. She turned back into the room and began to walk to and fro down its whole length, without stopping, without resting. She carried in her hands a thin handkerchief, which she tore into ribbons, rolled into a ball, and flung from her. Once she stopped, and taking off her wedding ring, flung it upon the carpet. When she saw it lying there, she stamped her heel upon it, striving to crush it. But her small boot heel did not make an indenture, not a mark upon the little glittering circlet.

In a sweeping passion she seized a glass vase from the table and flung it upon the tiles of the hearth. She wanted to destroy something. The crash and clatter were what she wanted to hear.

A maid, alarmed at the din of breaking glass, entered the room to discover what was the matter.

"A vase fell upon the hearth," said Edna. "Never mind; leave it till morning."

"Oh! you might get some of the glass in your feet, ma'am,"

insisted the young woman, picking up bits of the broken vase that were scattered upon the carpet. "And here's your ring, ma'am, under the chair."

Edna held out her hand, and taking the ring, slipped it upon her finger.

XVIII

∽

THE FOLLOWING MORNING MR. Pontellier, upon leaving for his office, asked Edna if she would not meet him in town in order to look at some new fixtures for the library.

"I hardly think we need new fixtures, Léonce. Don't let us get anything new; you are too extravagant. I don't believe you ever think of saving or putting by."

"The way to become rich is to make money, my dear Edna, not to save it," he said. He regretted that she did not feel inclined to go with him and select new fixtures. He kissed her good-by, and told her she was not looking well and must take care of herself. She was unusually pale and very quiet.

She stood on the front veranda as he quitted the house, and absently picked a few sprays of jessamine* that grew upon a trellis near by. She inhaled the odor of the blossoms and thrust them into the bosom of her white morning gown. The boys were dragging along the banquette a small "express wagon," which they had filled with blocks and sticks. The quadroon was following them with little quick steps, having assumed a fictitious animation and alacrity for the occasion. A fruit vender was crying his wares in the street.

Edna looked straight before her with a self-absorbed expression upon her face. She felt no interest in anything about her. The street, the children, the fruit vender, the flowers

---

* Jasmine; a fragrant flower.

growing there under her eyes, were all part and parcel of an alien world which had suddenly become antagonistic.

She went back into the house. She had thought of speaking to the cook concerning her blunders of the previous night; but Mr. Pontellier had saved her that disagreeable mission, for which she was so poorly fitted. Mr. Pontellier's arguments were usually convincing with those whom he employed. He left home feeling quite sure that he and Edna would sit down that evening, and possibly a few subsequent evenings, to a dinner deserving of the name.

Edna spent an hour or two in looking over some of her old sketches. She could see their shortcomings and defects, which were glaring in her eyes. She tried to work a little, but found she was not in the humor. Finally she gathered together a few of the sketches—those which she considered the least discreditable; and she carried them with her when, a little later, she dressed and left the house. She looked handsome and distinguished in her street gown. The tan of the seashore had left her face, and her forehead was smooth, white, and polished beneath her heavy, yellow-brown hair. There were a few freckles on her face, and a small, dark mole near the under lip and one on the temple, half-hidden in her hair.

As Edna walked along the street she was thinking of Robert. She was still under the spell of her infatuation. She had tried to forget him, realizing the inutility of remembering. But the thought of him was like an obsession, ever pressing itself upon her. It was not that she dwelt upon details of their acquaintance, or recalled in any special or peculiar way his personality; it was his being, his existence, which dominated her thought, fading sometimes as if it would melt into the mist of the forgotten, reviving again with an intensity which filled her with an incomprehensible longing.

Edna was on her way to Madame Ratignolle's. Their intimacy, begun at Grand Isle, had not declined, and they had seen each other with some frequency since their return to the city. The Ratignolles lived at no great distance from Edna's home, on the corner of a side street, where Monsieur

Ratignolle owned and conducted a drug store which enjoyed
a steady and prosperous trade. His father had been in the business before him, and Monsieur Ratignolle stood well in the
community and bore an enviable reputation for integrity and
clear-headedness. His family lived in commodious apartments over the store, having an entrance on the side within
the *porte cochère*.* There was something which Edna thought
very French, very foreign, about their whole manner of living.
In the large and pleasant salon which extended across the
width of the house, the Ratignolles entertained their friends
once a fortnight with a *soirée musicale*,† sometimes diversified
by card-playing. There was a friend who played upon the
'cello. One brought his flute and another his violin, while
there were some who sang and a number who performed
upon the piano with various degrees of taste and agility. The
Ratignolles' *soirées musicales* were widely known, and it was
considered a privilege to be invited to them.

Edna found her friend engaged in assorting the clothes
which had returned that morning from the laundry. She at
once abandoned her occupation upon seeing Edna, who had
been ushered without ceremony into her presence.

" 'Cité can do it as well as I; it is really her business," she
explained to Edna, who apologized for interrupting her. And
she summoned a young black woman, whom she instructed,
in French, to be very careful in checking off the list which she
handed her. She told her to notice particularly if a fine linen
handkerchief of Monsieur Ratignolle's, which was missing
last week, had been returned; and to be sure to set to one side
such pieces as required mending and darning.

Then placing an arm around Edna's waist, she led her to
the front of the house, to the salon, where it was cool and
sweet with the odor of great roses that stood upon the hearth
in jars.

---

* A covered porch to shelter passengers as they enter and exit a carriage (Fr.).

† An evening of music (Fr.).

Madame Ratignolle looked more beautiful than ever there at home, in a negligé which left her arms almost wholly bare and exposed the rich, melting curves of her white throat.

"Perhaps I shall be able to paint your picture some day," said Edna with a smile when they were seated. She produced the roll of sketches and started to unfold them. "I believe I ought to work again. I feel as if I wanted to be doing something. What do you think of them? Do you think it worth while to take it up again and study some more? I might study for a while with Laidpore."

She knew that Madame Ratignolle's opinion in such a matter would be next to valueless, that she herself had not alone decided, but determined; but she sought the words of praise and encouragement that would help her to put heart into her venture.

"Your talent is immense, dear!"

"Nonsense!" protested Edna, well pleased.

"Immense, I tell you," persisted Madame Ratignolle, surveying the sketches one by one, at close range, then holding them at arm's length, narrowing her eyes, and dropping her head on one side. "Surely, this Bavarian peasant is worthy of framing; and this basket of apples! never have I seen anything more lifelike. One might almost be tempted to reach out a hand and take one."

Edna could not control a feeling which bordered upon complacency at her friend's praise, even realizing, as she did, its true worth. She retained a few of the sketches, and gave all the rest to Madame Ratignolle, who appreciated the gift far beyond its value and proudly exhibited the pictures to her husband when he came up from the store a little later for his midday dinner.

Mr. Ratignolle was one of those men who are called the salt of the earth. His cheerfulness was unbounded, and it was matched by his goodness of heart, his broad charity, and common sense. He and his wife spoke English with an accent which was only discernible through its un-English emphasis and a certain carefulness and deliberation. Edna's husband spoke English with no accent whatever. The Ratignolles understood each other perfectly. If ever the fusion of two human beings into one has been accomplished on this sphere it was surely in their union.

As Edna seated herself at table with them she thought, "Better a dinner of herbs," though it did not take her long to discover that [here] was no dinner of herbs, but a delicious repast, simple, choice, and in every way satisfying.

Monsieur Ratignolle was delighted to see her, though he found her looking not so well as at Grand Isle, and he advised a tonic. He talked a good deal on various topics, a little politics, some city news and neighborhood gossip. He spoke with an animation and earnestness that gave an exaggerated importance to every syllable he uttered. His wife was keenly interested in everything he said, laying down her fork the better to listen, chiming in, taking the words out of his mouth.

Edna felt depressed rather than soothed after leaving them. The little glimpse of domestic harmony which had been offered her gave her no regret, no longing. It was not a condition of life which fitted her, and she could see in it but an appalling and hopeless ennui.* She was moved by a kind of commiseration for Madame Ratignolle—a pity for that colorless existence which never uplifted its possessor beyond the region of blind contentment, in which no moment of anguish ever visited her soul, in which she would never have the taste of life's delirium. Edna vaguely wondered what she meant by "life's delirium." It had crossed her thought like some unsought, extraneous impression.

---

* Weariness and dissatisfaction.

XIX

❧

EDNA COULD NOT HELP but think that it was very foolish, very childish, to have stamped upon her wedding ring and smashed the crystal vase upon the tiles. She was visited by no more outbursts, moving her to such futile expedients. She began to do as she liked and to feel as she liked. She completely abandoned her Tuesdays at home, and did not return the visits of those who had called upon her. She made no ineffectual efforts to conduct her household *en bonne ménagère,*˚ going and coming as it suited her fancy, and, so far as she was able, lending herself to any passing caprice.

Mr. Pontellier had been a rather courteous husband so long as he met a certain tacit submissiveness in his wife. But her new and unexpected line of conduct completely bewildered him. It shocked him. Then her absolute disregard for her duties as a wife angered him. When Mr. Pontellier became rude, Edna grew insolent. She had resolved never to take another step backward.

"It seems to me the utmost folly for a woman at the head of a household, and the mother of children, to spend in an atelier[†] days which would be better employed contriving for the comfort of her family."

"I feel like painting," answered Edna. "Perhaps I shan't always feel like it."

"Then in God's name paint! but don't let the family go to the devil. There's Madame Ratignolle; because she keeps up her music, she doesn't let everything else go to chaos. And she's more of a musician than you are a painter."

"She isn't a musician, and I'm not a painter. It isn't on account of painting that I let things go."

"On account of what, then?"

˚ As a good housewife (Fr.).

† An artist's studio.

"Oh! I don't know. Let me alone; you bother me."

It sometimes entered Mr. Pontellier's mind to wonder if his wife were not growing a little unbalanced mentally. He could see plainly that she was not herself. That is, he could not see that she was becoming herself and daily casting aside that fictitious self which we assume like a garment with which to appear before the world.

Her husband let her alone as she requested, and went away to his office. Edna went up to her atelier—a bright room in the top of the house. She was working with great energy and interest, without accomplishing anything, however, which satisfied her even in the smallest degree. For a time she had the whole household enrolled in the service of art. The boys posed for her. They thought it amusing at first, but the occupation soon lost its attractiveness when they discovered that it was not a game arranged especially for their entertainment. The quadroon sat for hours before Edna's palette, patient as a savage, while the house-maid took charge of the children, and the drawing-room went undusted. But the house-maid, too, served her term as model when Edna perceived that the young woman's back and shoulders were molded on classic lines, and that her hair, loosened from its confining cap, became an inspiration. While Edna worked she sometimes sang low the little air, "*Ah! si tu savais!*"

It moved her with recollections. She could hear again the ripple of the water, the flapping sail. She could see the glint of the moon upon the bay, and could feel the soft, gusty beating of the hot south wind. A subtle current of desire passed through her body, weakening her hold upon the brushes and making her eyes burn.

There were days when she was very happy without knowing why. She was happy to be alive and breathing, when her whole being seemed to be one with the sunlight, the color, the odors, the luxuriant warmth of some perfect Southern day. She liked then to wander alone into strange and unfamiliar places. She discovered many a sunny, sleepy corner, fash-

ioned to dream in. And she found it good to dream and to be
alone and unmolested.

There were days when she was unhappy, she did not know
why—when it did not seem worth while to be glad or sorry, to
be alive or dead; when life appeared to her like a grotesque
pandemonium and humanity like worms struggling blindly
toward inevitable annihilation. She could not work on such a
day, nor weave fancies to stir her pulses and warm her blood.

XX

∾

IT WAS DURING SUCH a mood that Edna hunted up
Mademoiselle Reisz. She had not forgotten the rather disagreeable impression left upon her by their last interview; but
she nevertheless felt a desire to see her—above all, to listen
while she played upon the piano. Quite early in the afternoon
she started upon her quest for the pianist. Unfortunately she
had mislaid or lost Mademoiselle Reisz's card, and looking up
her address in the city directory, she found that the woman
lived on Bienville Street,* some distance away. The directory
which fell into her hands was a year or more old, however,
and upon reaching the number indicated, Edna discovered
that the house was occupied by a respectable family of mulat-
toes who had *chambres garnies*† to let. They had been living
there for six months, and knew absolutely nothing of a
Mademoiselle Reisz. In fact, they knew nothing of any of
their neighbors; their lodgers were all people of the highest
distinction, they assured Edna. She did not linger to discuss
class distinctions with Madame Pouponne, but hastened to a

---

* Located across the French Quarter from the Pontellier home, a
street that ended in a waterfront wharf.

† Furnished rooms (Fr.).

neighboring grocery store, feeling sure that Mademoiselle would have left her address with the proprietor.

He knew Mademoiselle Reisz a good deal better than he wanted to know her, he informed his questioner. In truth, he did not want to know her at all, or anything concerning her—the most disagreeable and unpopular woman who ever lived in Bienville Street. He thanked heaven she had left the neighborhood, and was equally thankful that he did not know where she had gone.

Edna's desire to see Mademoiselle Reisz had increased tenfold since these unlooked-for obstacles had arisen to thwart it. She was wondering who could give her the information she sought, when it suddenly occurred to her that Madame Lebrun would be the one most likely to do so. She knew it was useless to ask Madame Ratignolle, who was on the most distant terms with the musician, and preferred to know nothing concerning her. She had once been almost as emphatic in expressing herself upon the subject as the corner grocer.

Edna knew that Madame Lebrun had returned to the city, for it was the middle of November. And she also knew where the Lebruns lived, on Chartres Street.*

Their home from the outside looked like a prison, with iron bars before the door and lower windows. The iron bars were a relic of the old *régime*,† and no one had ever thought of dislodging them. At the side was a high fence enclosing the garden. A gate or door opening upon the street was locked. Edna rang the bell at this side garden gate, and stood upon the banquette, waiting to be admitted.

It was Victor who opened the gate for her. A black woman, wiping her hands upon her apron, was close at his heels. Before she saw them Edna could hear them in altercation, the woman—plainly an anomaly—claiming the right to be al-

---

* A street at the center of the French Quarter.

† An architectural style belonging to the period when New Orleans was under Spanish rule (1762–1803).

lowed to perform her duties, one of which was to answer the bell.

Victor was surprised and delighted to see Mrs. Pontellier, and he made no attempt to conceal either his astonishment or his delight. He was a dark-browed, good-looking youngster of nineteen, greatly resembling his mother, but with ten times her impetuosity. He instructed the black woman to go at once and inform Madame Lebrun that Mrs. Pontellier desired to see her. The woman grumbled a refusal to do part of her duty when she had not been permitted to do it all, and started back to her interrupted task of weeding the garden. Whereupon Victor administered a rebuke in the form of a volley of abuse, which, owing to its rapidity and incoherence, was all but incomprehensible to Edna. Whatever it was, the rebuke was convincing, for the woman dropped her hoe and went mumbling into the house.

Edna did not wish to enter. It was very pleasant there on the side porch, where there were chairs, a wicker lounge, and a small table. She seated herself, for she was tired from her long tramp; and she began to rock gently and smooth out the folds of her silk parasol. Victor drew up his chair beside her. He at once explained that the black woman's offensive conduct was all due to imperfect training, as he was not there to take her in hand. He had only come up from the island the morning before, and expected to return next day. He stayed all winter at the island; he lived there, and kept the place in order and got things ready for the summer visitors.

But a man needed occasional relaxation, he informed Mrs. Pontellier, and every now and again he drummed up a pretext to bring him to the city. My! but he had had a time of it the evening before! He wouldn't want his mother to know, and he began to talk in a whisper. He was scintillant* with recollections. Of course, he couldn't think of telling Mrs. Pontellier all about it, she being a woman and not comprehending such things. But it all began with a girl peeping and

---

* Sparkling, brimming enthusiastically.

smiling at him through the shutters as he passed by. Oh! but she was a beauty! Certainly he smiled back, and went up and talked to her. Mrs. Pontellier did not know him if she supposed he was one to let an opportunity like that escape him. Despite herself, the youngster amused her. She must have betrayed in her look some degree of interest or entertainment. The boy grew more daring, and Mrs. Pontellier might have found herself, in a little while, listening to a highly colored story but for the timely appearance of Madame Lebrun.

That lady was still clad in white, according to her custom of the summer. Her eyes beamed an effusive welcome. Would not Mrs. Pontellier go inside? Would she partake of some refreshment? Why had she not been there before? How was that dear Mr. Pontellier and how were those sweet children? Had Mrs. Pontellier ever known such a warm November?

Victor went and reclined on the wicker lounge behind his mother's chair, where he commanded a view of Edna's face. He had taken her parasol from her hands while he spoke to her, and he now lifted it and twirled it above him as he lay on his back. When Madame Lebrun complained that it was *so* dull coming back to the city; that she saw *so* few people now; that even Victor, when he came up from the island for a day or two, had *so* much to occupy him and engage his time; then it was that the youth went into contortions on the lounge and winked mischievously at Edna. She somehow felt like a confederate in crime, and tried to look severe and disapproving.

There had been but two letters from Robert, with little in them, they told her. Victor said it was really not worth while to go inside for the letters, when his mother entreated him to go in search of them. He remembered the contents, which in truth he rattled off very glibly when put to the test.

One letter was written from Vera Cruz and the other from the City of Mexico. He had met Montel, who was doing everything toward his advancement. So far, the financial situation was no improvement over the one he had left in New Orleans, but of course the prospects were vastly better. He wrote of the City of Mexico, the buildings, the people and their habits, the conditions of life which he found there. He sent his love to the family. He inclosed a check to his mother, and hoped she would affectionately remember him to all his friends. That was about the substance of the two letters. Edna felt that if there had been a message for her, she would have received it. The despondent frame of mind in which she had left home began again to overtake her, and she remembered that she wished to find Mademoiselle Reisz.

Madame Lebrun knew where Mademoiselle Reisz lived. She gave Edna the address, regretting that she would not consent to stay and spend the remainder of the afternoon, and pay a visit to Mademoiselle Reisz some other day. The afternoon was already well advanced.

Victor escorted her out upon the banquette, lifted her parasol, and held it over her while he walked to the car with her. He entreated her to bear in mind that the disclosures of the afternoon were strictly confidential. She laughed and bantered him a little, remembering too late that she should have been dignified and reserved.

"How handsome Mrs. Pontellier looked!" said Madame Lebrun to her son.

"Ravishing!" he admitted. "The city atmosphere has improved her. Some way she doesn't seem like the same woman."

XXI

ॐ

SOME PEOPLE CONTENDED THAT the reason Mademoiselle Reisz always chose apartments up under the roof was to discourage the approach of beggars, peddlars and callers. There were plenty of windows in her little front room. They were for the most part dingy, but as they were nearly always open it did not make so much difference. They often admitted into the room a good deal of smoke and soot; but at the same time all the light and air that there was came through them. From her windows could be seen the crescent of the river, the masts of ships and the big chimneys of the Mississippi steamers. A magnificent piano crowded the apartment. In the next room she slept, and in the third and last she harbored a gasoline stove on which she cooked her meals when disinclined to descend to the neighboring restaurant. It was there also that she ate, keeping her belongings in a rare old buffet, dingy and battered from a hundred years of use.

When Edna knocked at Mademoiselle Reisz's front room door and entered, she discovered that person standing beside the window, engaged in mending or patching an old prunella gaiter.* The little musician laughed all over when she saw Edna. Her laugh consisted of a contortion of the face and all the muscles of the body. She seemed strikingly homely, standing there in the afternoon light. She still wore the shabby lace and the artificial bunch of violets on the side of her head.

"So you remembered me at last," said Mademoiselle. "I had said to myself, 'Ah, bah! she will never come.' "

"Did you want me to come?" asked Edna with a smile.

"I had not thought much about it," answered Mademoiselle. The two had seated themselves on a little bumpy sofa which stood against the wall. "I am glad, however, that you came. I have the water boiling back there, and was just about to make some coffee. You will drink a cup with me. And how is *la belle dame?*† Always handsome! always healthy! always contented!" She took Edna's hand between her strong wiry fingers, holding it loosely without warmth, and executing a sort of double theme upon the back and palm.

"Yes," she went on; "I sometimes thought: 'She will never come. She promised as those women in society always do,

---

* A foot or leg covering made from heavy woolen fabric.

† The beautiful woman (Fr.).

without meaning it. She will not come.' For I really don't believe you like me, Mrs. Pontellier."

"I don't know whether I like you or not," replied Edna, gazing down at the little woman with a quizzical look.

The candor of Mrs. Pontellier's admission greatly pleased Mademoiselle Reisz. She expressed her gratification by repairing forthwith to the region of the gasoline stove and rewarding her guest with the promised cup of coffee. The coffee and the biscuit accompanying it proved very acceptable to Edna, who had declined refreshment at Madame Lebrun's and was now beginning to feel hungry. Mademoiselle set the tray which she brought in upon a small table near at hand, and seated herself once again on the lumpy sofa.

"I have had a letter from your friend," she remarked, as she poured a little cream into Edna's cup and handed it to her.

"My friend?"

"Yes, your friend Robert. He wrote to me from the City of Mexico."

"Wrote to *you?*" repeated Edna in amazement, stirring her coffee absently.

"Yes, to me. Why not? Don't stir all the warmth out of your coffee; drink it. Though the letter might as well have been sent to you; it was nothing but Mrs. Pontellier from beginning to end."

"Let me see it," requested the young woman, entreatingly.

"No; a letter concerns no one but the person who writes it and the one to whom it is written."

"Haven't you just said it concerned me from beginning to end?"

"It was written about you, not to you. 'Have you seen Mrs. Pontellier? How is she looking?' he asks. 'As Mrs. Pontellier says,' or 'as Mrs. Pontellier once said.' 'If Mrs. Pontellier should call upon you, play for her that Impromptu of Chopin's, my favorite. I heard it here a day or two ago, but not as you play it. I should like to know how it affects her,' and so on, as if he supposed we were constantly in each other's society."

"Let me see the letter."

"Oh, no."

"Have you answered it?"

"No."

"Let me see the letter."

"No, and again, no."

"Then play the Impromptu for me."

"It is growing late; what time do you have to be home?"

"Time doesn't concern me. Your question seems a little rude. Play the Impromptu."

"But you have told me nothing of yourself. What are you doing?"

"Painting!" laughed Edna. "I am becoming an artist. Think of it!"

"Ah! an artist! You have pretensions, Madame."

"Why pretensions? Do you think I could not become an artist?"

"I do not know you well enough to say. I do not know your talent or your temperament. To be an artist includes much; one must possess many gifts—absolute gifts—which have not been acquired by one's own effort. And, moreover, to succeed, the artist must possess the courageous soul."

"What do you mean by the courageous soul?"

"Courageous, *ma foi!*[*] The brave soul. The soul that dares and defies."

"Show me the letter and play for me the Impromptu. You see that I have persistence. Does that quality count for anything in art?"

"It counts with a foolish old woman whom you have captivated," replied Mademoiselle, with her wriggling laugh.

The letter was right there at hand in the drawer of the little table upon which Edna had just placed her coffee cup. Mademoiselle opened the drawer and drew forth the letter, the topmost one. She placed it in Edna's hands, and without further comment arose and went to the piano.

---

* Indeed! (Fr.).

Mademoiselle played a soft interlude. It was an improvisation. She sat low at the instrument, and the lines of her body settled into ungraceful curves and angles that gave it an appearance of deformity. Gradually and imperceptibly the interlude melted into the soft opening minor chords of the Chopin Impromptu.

Edna did not know when the Impromptu began or ended. She sat in the sofa corner reading Robert's letter by the fading light. Mademoiselle had glided from the Chopin into the quivering love-notes of Isolde's song, and back again to the Impromptu with its soulful and poignant longing.

The shadows deepened in the little room. The music grew strange and fantastic—turbulent, insistent, plaintive and soft with entreaty. The shadows grew deeper. The music filled the room. It floated out upon the night, over the housetops, the crescent of the river, losing itself in the silence of the upper air.

Edna was sobbing, just as she had wept one midnight at Grand Isle when strange, new voices awoke in her. She arose in some agitation to take her departure. "May I come again, Mademoiselle?" she asked at the threshold.

"Come whenever you feel like it. Be careful; the stairs and landings are dark; don't stumble."

Mademoiselle reëntered and lit a candle. Robert's letter was on the floor. She stooped and picked it up. It was crumpled and damp with tears. Mademoiselle smoothed the letter out, restored it to the envelope, and replaced it in the table drawer.

XXII

ONE MORNING ON HIS way into town Mr. Pontellier stopped at the house of his old friend and family physician, Doctor

Mandelet. The Doctor was a semi-retired physician, resting, as the saying is, upon his laurels. He bore a reputation for wisdom rather than skill—leaving the active practice of medicine to his assistants and younger contemporaries—and was much sought for in matters of consultation. A few families, united to him by bonds of friendship, he still attended when they required the services of a physician. The Pontelliers were among these.

Mr. Pontellier found the Doctor reading at the open window of his study. His house stood rather far back from the street, in the center of a delightful garden, so that it was quiet and peaceful at the old gentleman's study window. He was a great reader. He stared up disapprovingly over his eye-glasses as Mr. Pontellier entered, wondering who had the temerity to disturb him at that hour of the morning.

"Ah, Pontellier! Not sick, I hope. Come and have a seat. What news do you bring this morning?" He was quite portly, with a profusion of gray hair, and small blue eyes which age had robbed of much of their brightness but none of their penetration.

"Oh! I'm never sick, Doctor. You know that I come of tough fiber—of that old Creole race of Pontelliers that dry up and finally blow away. I came to consult—no, not precisely to consult—to talk to you about Edna. I don't know what ails her."

"Madame Pontellier not well?" marveled the Doctor. "Why, I saw her—I think it was a week ago—walking along Canal Street,* the picture of health, it seemed to me."

"Yes, yes; she seems quite well," said Mr. Pontellier, leaning forward and whirling his stick between his two hands; "but she doesn't act well. She's odd, she's not like herself. I can't make her out, and I thought perhaps you'd help me."

"How does she act?" inquired the doctor.

"Well, it isn't easy to explain," said Mr. Pontellier, throw-

---

* A wide street in New Orleans that formed a dividing line between the French and American districts.

ing himself back in his chair. "She lets the housekeeping go to the dickens."

"Well, well; women are not all alike, my dear Pontellier. We've got to consider—"

"I know that; I told you I couldn't explain. Her whole attitude—toward me and everybody and everything—has changed. You know I have a quick temper, but I don't want to quarrel or be rude to a woman, especially my wife; yet I'm driven to it, and feel like ten thousand devils after I've made a fool of myself. She's making it devilishly uncomfortable for me," he went on nervously. "She's got some sort of notion in her head concerning the eternal rights of women; and—you understand—we meet in the morning at the breakfast table."

The old gentleman lifted his shaggy eyebrows, protruded his thick nether lip, and tapped the arms of his chair with his cushioned finger-tips.

"What have you been doing to her, Pontellier?"

"Doing! *Parbleu!*"*

"Has she," asked the Doctor, with a smile, "has she been associating of late with a circle of pseudo-intellectual women—super-spiritual superior beings?† My wife has been telling me about them."

"That's the trouble," broke in Mr. Pontellier, "she hasn't been associating with any one. She has abandoned her Tuesdays at home, has thrown over all her acquaintances, and goes tramping about by herself, moping in the street-cars, getting in after dark. I tell you she's peculiar. I don't like it; I feel a little worried over it."

This was a new aspect for the Doctor. "Nothing hereditary?" he asked, seriously. "Nothing peculiar about her family antecedents, is there?"

"Oh, no, indeed! She comes of sound old Presbyterian Kentucky stock. The old gentleman, her father, I have heard,

* My goodness! (Fr.).

† A disparaging reference to women's clubs popular during the late 19th century.

used to atone for his week-day sins with his Sunday devotions. I know for a fact, that his race horses literally ran away with the prettiest bit of Kentucky farming land I ever laid eyes upon. Margaret—you know Margaret—she has all the Presbyterianism undiluted. And the youngest is something of a vixen. By the way, she gets married in a couple of weeks from now."

"Send your wife up to the wedding," exclaimed the Doctor, foreseeing a happy solution. "Let her stay among her own people for a while; it will do her good."

"That's what I want her to do. She won't go to the marriage. She says a wedding is one of the most lamentable spectacles on earth. Nice thing for a woman to say to her husband!" exclaimed Mr. Pontellier, fuming anew at the recollection.

"Pontellier," said the Doctor, after a moment's reflection, "let your wife alone for a while. Don't bother her, and don't let her bother you. Woman, my dear friend, is a very peculiar and delicate organism—a sensitive and highly organized woman, such as I know Mrs. Pontellier to be, is especially peculiar. It would require an inspired psychologist to deal successfully with them. And when ordinary fellows like you and me attempt to cope with their idiosyncrasies the result is bungling. Most women are moody and whimsical. This is some passing whim of your wife, due to some cause or causes which you and I needn't try to fathom. But it will pass happily over, especially if you let her alone. Send her around to see me."

"Oh! I couldn't do that; there'd be no reason for it," objected Mr. Pontellier.

"Then I'll go around and see her," said the Doctor. "I'll drop in to dinner some evening *en bon ami*."*

"Do! by all means," urged Mr. Pontellier. "What evening will you come? Say Thursday. Will you come Thursday?" he asked, rising to take his leave.

---

* As a friend (Fr.).

"Very well; Thursday. My wife may possibly have some engagement for me Thursday. In case she has, I shall let you know. Otherwise, you may expect me."

Mr. Pontellier turned before leaving to say:

"I am going to New York on business very soon. I have a big scheme on hand, and want to be on the field proper to pull the ropes and handle the ribbons. We'll let you in on the inside if you say so, Doctor," he laughed.

"No, I thank you, my dear sir," returned the Doctor. "I leave such ventures to you younger men with the fever of life still in your blood."

"What I wanted to say," continued Mr. Pontellier, with his hand on the knob; "I may have to be absent a good while. Would you advise me to take Edna along?"

"By all means, if she wishes to go. If not, leave her here. Don't contradict her. The mood will pass, I assure you. It may take a month, two, three months—possibly longer, but it will pass; have patience."

"Well, good-by, *à jeudi*,"* said Mr. Pontellier, as he let himself out.

The Doctor would have liked during the course of conversation to ask, "Is there any man in the case?" but he knew his Creole too well to make such a blunder as that.

He did not resume his book immediately, but sat for a while meditatively looking out into the garden.

XXIII

∽

EDNA'S FATHER WAS IN the city, and had been with them several days. She was not very warmly or deeply attached to him, but they had certain tastes in common, and when together

---

* Until Thursday (Fr.).

they were companionable. His coming was in the nature of a welcome disturbance; it seemed to furnish a new direction for her emotions.

He had come to purchase a wedding gift for his daughter, Janet, and an outfit for himself in which he might make a creditable appearance at her marriage. Mr. Pontellier had selected the bridal gift, as every one immediately connected with him always deferred to his taste in such matters. And his suggestions on the question of dress—which too often assumes the nature of a problem—were of inestimable value to his father-in-law. But for the past few days the old gentleman had been upon Edna's hands, and in his society she was becoming acquainted with a new set of sensations. He had been a colonel in the Confederate army, and still maintained, with the title, the military bearing which had always accompanied it. His hair and mustache were white and silky; emphasizing the rugged bronze of his face. He was tall and thin, and wore his coats padded, which gave a fictitious breadth and depth to his shoulders and chest. Edna and her father looked very distinguished together, and excited a good deal of notice during their perambulations. Upon his arrival she began by introducing him to her atelier and making a sketch of him. He took the whole matter very seriously. If her talent had been tenfold greater than it was, it would not have surprised him, convinced as he was that he had bequeathed to all of his daughters the germs of a masterful capability, which only depended upon their own efforts to be directed toward successful achievement.

Before her pencil he sat rigid and unflinching, as he had faced the cannon's mouth in days gone by. He resented the intrusion of the children, who gaped with wondering eyes at him, sitting so stiff up there in their mother's bright atelier. When they drew near he motioned them away with an expressive action of the foot, loath to disturb the fixed lines of his countenance, his arms, or his rigid shoulders.

Edna, anxious to entertain him, invited Mademoiselle Reisz to meet him, having promised him a treat in her piano playing; but Mademoiselle declined the invitation. So together they attended a *soirée musicale* at the Ratignolle's. Monsieur and Madame Ratignolle made much of the Colonel, installing him as the guest of honor and engaging him at once to dine with them the following Sunday, or any day which he might select. Madame coquetted with him in the most captivating and naïve manner, with eyes, gestures, and a profusion of compliments, till the Colonel's old head felt thirty years younger on his padded shoulders. Edna marveled, not comprehending. She herself was almost devoid of coquetry.

There were one or two men whom she observed at the *soirée musicale*; but she would never have felt moved to any kittenish display to attract their notice—to any feline or feminine wiles to express herself toward them. Their personality attracted her in an agreeable way. Her fancy selected them, and she was glad when a lull in the music gave them an opportunity to meet her and talk with her. Often on the street the glance of strange eyes had lingered in her memory, and sometimes had disturbed her.

Mr. Pontellier did not attend these *soirées musicales*. He considered them *bourgeois,** and found more diversion at the club. To Madame Ratignolle he said the music dispensed at her *soirées* was too "heavy," too far beyond his untrained comprehension. His excuse flattered her. But she disapproved of Mr. Pontellier's club, and she was frank enough to tell Edna so.

"It's a pity Mr. Pontellier doesn't stay home more in the evenings. I think you would be more—well, if you don't mind my saying it—more united, if he did."

"Oh! dear no!" said Edna, with a blank look in her eyes. "What should I do if he stayed home? We wouldn't have anything to say to each other."

She had not much of anything to say to her father, for that matter; but he did not antagonize her. She discovered that he

---

* Middle class, common.

interested her, though she realized that he might not interest her long; and for the first time in her life she felt as if she were thoroughly acquainted with him. He kept her busy serving him and ministering to his wants. It amused her to do so. She would not permit a servant or one of the children to do anything for him which she might do herself. Her husband noticed, and thought it was the expression of a deep filial attachment which he had never suspected.

The Colonel drank numerous "toddies" during the course of the day, which left him, however, imperturbed. He was an expert at concocting strong drinks. He had even invented some, to which he had given fantastic names, and for whose manufacture he required diverse ingredients that it devolved upon Edna to procure for him.

When Doctor Mandelet dined with the Pontelliers on Thursday he could discern in Mrs. Pontellier no trace of that morbid condition which her husband had reported to him. She was excited and in a manner radiant. She and her father had been to the race course, and their thoughts when they seated themselves at table were still occupied with the events of the afternoon, and their talk was still of the track. The Doctor had not kept pace with turf affairs. He had certain recollections of racing in what he called "the good old times" when the Lecompte stables flourished, and he drew upon this fund of memories so that he might not be left out and seem wholly devoid of the modern spirit. But he failed to impose upon the Colonel, and was even far from impressing him with this trumped-up knowledge of bygone days. Edna had staked her father on his last venture, with the most gratifying results to both of them. Besides, they had met some very charming people, according to the Colonel's impressions. Mrs. Mortimer Merriman and Mrs. James Highcamp, who were there with Alcée Arobin, had joined them and had enlivened the hours in a fashion that warmed him to think of.

Mr. Pontellier himself had no particular leaning toward horse-racing, and was even rather inclined to discourage it as a pastime, especially when he considered the fate of that blue-grass farm in Kentucky. He endeavored, in a general way, to express a particular disapproval, and only succeeded in arousing the ire and opposition of his father-in-law. A pretty dispute followed, in which Edna warmly espoused her father's cause and the Doctor remained neutral.

He observed his hostess attentively from under his shaggy brows, and noted a subtle change which had transformed her from the listless woman he had known into a being who, for the moment, seemed palpitant with the forces of life. Her speech was warm and energetic. There was no repression in her glance or gesture. She reminded him of some beautiful, sleek animal waking up in the sun.

The dinner was excellent. The claret was warm and the champagne was cold, and under their beneficent influence the threatened unpleasantness melted and vanished with the fumes of the wine.

Mr. Pontellier warmed up and grew reminiscent. He told some amusing plantation experiences, recollections of old Iberville and his youth, when he hunted 'possum in company with some friendly darky; thrashed the pecan trees, shot the grosbec,* and roamed the woods and fields in mischievous idleness.

The Colonel, with little sense of humor and of the fitness of things, related a somber episode of those dark and bitter days, in which he had acted a conspicuous part and always formed a central figure. Nor was the Doctor happier in his selection, when he told the old, ever new and curious story of the waning of a woman's love, seeking strange, new channels, only to return to its legitimate source after days of fierce unrest. It was one of the many little human documents which had been unfolded to him during his long career as a physician. The story did not seem especially to impress Edna. She had one of her own to tell, of a woman who paddled away with her lover one night in a pirogue and never came back. They were lost amid the Baratarian Islands, and no one ever heard

---

* Grosbeak, a species of bird.

of them or found trace of them from that day to this. It was a pure invention. She said that Madame Antoine had related it to her. That, also, was an invention. Perhaps it was a dream she had had. But every glowing word seemed real to those who listened. They could feel the hot breath of the Southern night; they could hear the long sweep of the pirogue through the glistening moonlit water, the beating of birds' wings, rising startled from among the reeds in the salt-water pools; they could see the faces of the lovers, pale, close together, rapt in oblivious forgetfulness, drifting into the unknown.

The champagne was cold, and its subtle fumes played fantastic tricks with Edna's memory that night.

Outside, away from the glow of the fire and the soft lamplight, the night was chill and murky. The Doctor doubled his old-fashioned cloak across his breast as he strode home through the darkness. He knew his fellow-creatures better than most men; knew that inner life which so seldom unfolds itself to unanointed eyes. He was sorry he had accepted Pontellier's invitation. He was growing old, and beginning to need rest and an imperturbed spirit. He did not want the secrets of other lives thrust upon him.

"I hope it isn't Arobin," he muttered to himself as he walked. "I hope to heaven it isn't Alcée Arobin."

XXIV

⁂

EDNA AND HER FATHER had a warm, and almost violent dispute upon the subject of her refusal to attend her sister's wedding. Mr. Pontellier declined to interfere, to interpose either his influence or his authority. He was following Doctor Mandelet's advice, and letting her do as she liked. The Colonel reproached his daughter for her lack of filial kindness and respect, her want of sisterly affection and womanly consideration. His arguments were labored and unconvincing. He doubted if Janet would accept any excuse—forgetting that Edna had offered none. He doubted if Janet would ever speak to her again, and he was sure Margaret would not.

Edna was glad to be rid of her father when he finally took himself off with his wedding garments and his bridal gifts, with his padded shoulders, his Bible reading, his "toddies" and ponderous oaths.

Mr. Pontellier followed him closely. He meant to stop at the wedding on his way to New York and endeavor by every means which money and love could devise to atone somewhat for Edna's incomprehensible action.

"You are too lenient, too lenient by far, Léonce," asserted the Colonel. "Authority, coercion are what is needed. Put your foot down good and hard; the only way to manage a wife. Take my word for it."

The Colonel was perhaps unaware that he had coerced his own wife into her grave. Mr. Pontellier had a vague suspicion of it which he thought it needless to mention at that late day.

Edna was not so consciously gratified at her husband's leaving home as she had been over the departure of her father. As the day approached when he was to leave her for a comparatively long stay, she grew melting and affectionate, remembering his many acts of consideration and his repeated expressions of an ardent attachment. She was solicitous about his health and his welfare. She bustled around, looking after his clothing, thinking about heavy underwear, quite as Madame Ratignolle would have done under similar circumstances. She cried when he went away, calling him her dear, good friend, and she was quite certain she would grow lonely before very long and go to join him in New York.

But after all, a radiant peace settled upon her when she at last found herself alone. Even the children were gone. Old Madame Pontellier had come herself and carried them off to Iberville with their quadroon. The old madame did not venture to say she was afraid they would be neglected during Léonce's absence; she hardly ventured to think so. She was hungry for them—even a little fierce in her attachment. She did not want them to be wholly "children of the pavement," she always said when begging to have them for a space. She wished them to know the country, with its streams, its fields, its woods, its freedom, so delicious to the young. She wished them to taste something of the life their father had lived and known and loved when he, too, was a little child.

When Edna was at last alone, she breathed a big, genuine sigh of relief. A feeling that was unfamiliar but very delicious came over her. She walked all through the house, from one room to another, as if inspecting it for the first time. She tried the various chairs and lounges, as if she had never sat and reclined upon them before. And she perambulated around the outside of the house, investigating, looking to see if windows and shutters were secure and in order. The flowers were like new acquaintances; she approached them in a familiar spirit, and made herself at home among them. The garden walks were damp, and Edna called to the maid to bring out her rubber sandals. And there she stayed, and stooped, digging around the plants, trimming, picking dead, dry leaves. The children's little dog came out, interfering, getting in her way. She scolded him, laughed at him, played with him. The garden smelled so good and looked so pretty in the afternoon sunlight. Edna plucked all the bright flowers she could find, and went into the house with them, she and the little dog.

Even the kitchen assumed a sudden interesting character which she had never before perceived. She went in to give directions to the cook, to say that the butcher would have to bring much less meat, that they would require only half their usual quantity of bread, of milk and groceries. She told the cook that she herself would be greatly occupied during Mr. Pontellier's absence, and she begged her to take all thought and responsibility of the larder upon her own shoulders.

That night Edna dined alone. The candelabra, with a few candles in the center of the table, gave all the light she needed. Outside the circle of light in which she sat, the large dining-room looked solemn and shadowy. The cook, placed

upon her mettle, served a delicious repast—a luscious tender-loin broiled à point.* The wine tasted good; the marron glacé†
seemed to be just what she wanted. It was so pleasant, too, to
dine in a comfortable peignoir.

She thought a little sentimentally about Léonce and the
children, and wondered what they were doing. As she gave a
dainty scrap or two to the doggie, she talked intimately to him
about Étienne and Raoul. He was beside himself with astonishment and delight over these companionable advances, and
showed his appreciation by his little quick, snappy barks and a
lively agitation.

Then Edna sat in the library after dinner and read
Emerson until she grew sleepy. She realized that she had neglected her reading, and determined to start anew upon a
course of improving studies, now that her time was completely her own to do with as she liked.

After a refreshing bath, Edna went to bed. And as she snug-
gled comfortably beneath the eiderdown a sense of restfulness
invaded her, such as she had not known before.

XXV

* confront*

WHEN THE WEATHER WAS dark and cloudy Edna could not
work. She needed the sun to mellow and temper her mood to
the sticking point. She had reached a stage when she seemed
to be no longer feeling her way, working, when in the humor,
with sureness and ease. And being devoid of ambition, and
striving not toward accomplishment, she drew satisfaction
from the work in itself.

---

* Rare.

† A French confection made from whole chestnuts preserved in
sugar solution.

On rainy or melancholy days Edna went out and sought the society of the friends she had made at Grand Isle. Or else she stayed indoors and nursed a mood with which she was becoming too familiar for her own comfort and peace of mind. It was not despair; but it seemed to her as if life were passing by, leaving its promise broken and unfulfilled. Yet there were other days when she listened, was led on and deceived by fresh promises which her youth held out to her.

She went again to the races, and again. Alcée Arobin and Mrs. Highcamp called for her one bright afternoon in Arobin's drag.* Mrs. Highcamp was a worldly but unaffected, intelligent, slim, tall blonde woman in the forties, with an indifferent manner and blue eyes that stared. She had a daughter who served her as a pretext for cultivating the society of young men of fashion. Alcée Arobin was one of them. He was a familiar figure at the race course, the opera, the fashionable clubs. There was a perpetual smile in his eyes, which seldom failed to awaken a corresponding cheerfulness in any one who looked into them and listened to his good-humored voice. His manner was quiet, and at times a little insolent. He possessed a good figure, a pleasing face, not overburdened with depth of thought or feeling; and his dress was that of the conventional man of fashion.

He admired Edna extravagantly, after meeting her at the races with her father. He had met her before on other occasions, but she had seemed to him unapproachable until that day. It was at his instigation that Mrs. Highcamp called to ask her to go with them to the Jockey Club to witness the turf event of the season.

There were possibly a few track men out there who knew the race horse as well as Edna, but there was certainly none who knew it better. She sat between her two companions as one having authority to speak. She laughed at Arobin's pretensions, and deplored Mrs. Highcamp's ignorance. The race horse was a friend and intimate associate of her childhood.

---

* A horse-drawn vehicle.

The atmosphere of the stables and the breath of the blue-grass paddock revived in her memory and lingered in her nostrils. She did not perceive that she was talking like her father as the sleek geldings ambled in review before them. She played for very high stakes, and fortune favored her. The fever of the game flamed in her cheeks and eyes, and it got into her blood and into her brain like an intoxicant. People turned their heads to look at her, and more than one lent an attentive ear to her utterances, hoping thereby to secure the elusive but ever-desired "tip." Arobin caught the contagion of excitement which drew him to Edna like a magnet. Mrs. Highcamp remained, as usual, unmoved, with her indifferent stare and uplifted eyebrows.

Edna stayed and dined with Mrs. Highcamp upon being urged to do so. Arobin also remained and sent away his drag.

The dinner was quiet and uninteresting, save for the cheerful efforts of Arobin to enliven things. Mrs. Highcamp deplored the absence of her daughter from the races, and tried to convey to her what she had missed by going to the "Dante reading" instead of joining them. The girl held a geranium leaf up to her nose and said nothing, but looked knowing and noncommittal. Mr. Highcamp was a plain, bald-headed man, who only talked under compulsion. He was unresponsive. Mrs. Highcamp was full of delicate courtesy and consideration toward her husband. She addressed most of her conversation to him at table. They sat in the library after dinner and read the evening papers together under the drop-light, while the younger people went into the drawing-room near by and talked. Miss Highcamp played some selections from Grieg* upon the piano. She seemed to have apprehended all of the composer's coldness and none of his poetry. While Edna listened she could not help wondering if she had lost her taste for music.

When the time came for her to go home, Mr. Highcamp

---

* The Norwegian composer Edvard Grieg (1843–1907), whose music is noted for a refined lyrical sense.

grunted a lame offer to escort her, looking down at his slippered feet with tactless concern. It was Arobin who took her home. The car ride was long, and it was late when they reached Esplanade Street. Arobin asked permission to enter for a second to light his cigarette—his match safe was empty. He filled his match safe, but did not light his cigarette until he left her, after she had expressed her willingness to go to the races with him again.

Edna was neither tired nor sleepy. She was hungry again, for the Highcamp dinner, though of excellent quality, had lacked abundance. She rummaged in the larder and brought forth a slice of "Gruyère"* and some crackers. She opened a bottle of beer which she found in the ice-box. Edna felt extremely restless and excited. She vacantly hummed a fantastic tune as she poked at the wood embers on the hearth and munched a cracker.

She wanted something to happen—something, anything; she did not know what. She regretted that she had not made Arobin stay a half hour to talk over the horses with her. She counted the money she had won. But there was nothing else to do, so she went to bed, and tossed there for hours in a sort of monotonous agitation.

In the middle of the night she remembered that she had forgotten to write her regular letter to her husband; and she decided to do so next day and tell him about her afternoon at the Jockey Club. She lay wide awake composing a letter which was nothing like the one which she wrote next day. When the maid awoke her in the morning Edna was dreaming of Mr. Highcamp playing the piano at the entrance of a music store on Canal Street, while his wife was saying to Alcée Arobin, as they boarded an Esplanade Street car:

"What a pity that so much talent has been neglected! but I must go."

When, a few days later, Alcée Arobin again called for Edna in his drag, Mrs. Highcamp was not with him. He said

---

* A firm cheese from France or Switzerland.

they would pick her up. But as that lady had not been apprised of his intention of picking her up, she was not at home. The daughter was just leaving the house to attend the meeting of a branch Folk Lore Society, and regretted that she could not accompany them. Arobin appeared non plused, and asked Edna if there were any one else she cared to ask.

She did not deem it worth while to go in search of any of the fashionable acquaintances from whom she had withdrawn herself. She thought of Madame Ratignolle, but knew that her fair friend did not leave the house, except to take a languid walk around the block with her husband after nightfall. Mademoiselle Reisz would have laughed at such a request from Edna. Madame Lebrun might have enjoyed the outing, but for some reason Edna did not want her. So they went alone, she and Arobin.

The afternoon was intensely interesting to her. The excitement came back upon her like a remittent fever. Her talk grew familiar and confidential. It was no labor to become intimate with Arobin. His manner invited easy confidence. The preliminary stage of becoming acquainted was one which he always endeavored to ignore when a pretty and engaging woman was concerned.

He stayed and dined with Edna. He stayed and sat beside the wood fire. They laughed and talked; and before it was time to go he was telling her how different life might have been if he had known her years before. With ingenuous frankness he spoke of what a wicked, ill-disciplined boy he had been, and impulsively drew up his cuff to exhibit upon his wrist the scar from a saber cut which he had received in a duel outside of Paris when he was nineteen. She touched his hand as she scanned the red cicatrice* on the inside of his white wrist. A quick impulse that was somewhat spasmodic impelled her fingers to close in a sort of clutch upon his hand. He felt the pressure of her pointed nails in the flesh of his palm.

---

* Scar (Fr.).

She arose hastily and walked toward the mantel.

"The sight of a wound or scar always agitates and sickens me," she said. "I shouldn't have looked at it."

"I beg your pardon," he entreated, following her; "it never occurred to me that it might be repulsive."

He stood close to her, and the effrontery in his eyes repelled the old, vanishing self in her, yet drew all her awakening sensuousness. He saw enough in her face to impel him to take her hand and hold it while he said his lingering good night.

"Will you go to the races again?" he asked.

"No," she said. "I've had enough of the races. I don't want to lose all the money I've won, and I've got to work when the weather is bright, instead of—"

"Yes; work; to be sure. You promised to show me your work. What morning may I come up to your atelier? To-morrow?"

"No!"

"Day after?"

"No, no."

"Oh, please don't refuse me! I know something of such things. I might help you with a stray suggestion or two."

"No. Good-night. Why don't you go after you have said good-night? I don't like you," she went on in a high, excited pitch, attempting to draw away her hand. She felt that her words lacked dignity and sincerity, and she knew that he felt it.

"I'm sorry you don't like me. I'm sorry I offended you. How have I offended you? What have I done? Can't you forgive me?" And he bent and pressed his lips upon her hand as if he wished never more to withdraw them.

"Mr. Arobin," she complained, "I'm greatly upset by the excitement of the afternoon; I'm not myself. My manner must have misled you in some way. I wish you to go, please." She spoke in a monotonous, dull tone. He took his hat from the table, and stood with eyes turned from her, looking into the dying fire. For a moment or two he kept an impressive silence.

"Your manner has not misled me, Mrs. Pontellier," he said finally. "My own emotions have done that. I couldn't help it. When I'm near you, how could I help it? Don't think anything of it, don't bother, please. You see, I go when you command me. If you wish me to stay away, I shall do so. If you let me come back, I—oh! you will let me come back?"

He cast one appealing glance at her, to which she made no response. Alcée Arobin's manner was so genuine that it often deceived even himself.

Edna did not care or think whether it were genuine or not. When she was alone she looked mechanically at the back of her hand which he had kissed so warmly. Then she leaned her head down on the mantelpiece. She felt somewhat like a woman who in a moment of passion is betrayed into an act of infidelity, and realizes the significance of the act without being wholly awakened from its glamour. The thought was passing vaguely through her mind, "What would he think?"

She did not mean her husband; she was thinking of Robert Lebrun. Her husband seemed to her now like a person whom she had married without love as an excuse.

She lit a candle and went up to her room. Alcée Arobin was absolutely nothing to her. Yet his presence, his manners, the warmth of his glances, and above all the touch of his lips upon her hand had acted like a narcotic upon her.

She slept a languorous sleep, interwoven with vanishing dreams.

XXVI

∽

ALCÉE AROBIN WROTE EDNA an elaborate note of apology, palpitant with sincerity. It embarrassed her; for in a cooler, quieter moment it appeared to her absurd that she should have taken his action so seriously, so dramatically. She felt sure that the significance of the whole occurrence had lain in her own self-consciousness. If she ignored his note it would give undue importance to a trivial affair. If she replied to it in a serious spirit it would still leave in his mind the impression that she had in a susceptible moment yielded to his influence. After all, it was no great matter to have one's hand kissed. She was provoked at his having written the apology. She answered in as light and bantering a spirit as she fancied it deserved, and said she would be glad to have him look in upon her at work whenever he felt the inclination and his business gave him the opportunity.

He responded at once by presenting himself at her home with all his disarming naïveté. And then there was scarcely a day which followed that she did not see him or was not reminded of him. He was prolific in pretexts. His attitude became one of good-humored subservience and tacit adoration. He was ready at all times to submit to her moods, which were as often kind as they were cold. She grew accustomed to him. They became intimate and friendly by imperceptible degrees, and then by leaps. He sometimes talked in a way that astonished her at first and brought the crimson into her face; in a way that pleased her at last, appealing to the animalism that stirred impatiently within her.

There was nothing which so quieted the turmoil of Edna's senses as a visit to Mademoiselle Reisz. It was then, in the presence of that personality which was offensive to her, that the woman, by her divine art, seemed to reach Edna's spirit and set it free.

It was misty, with heavy, lowering atmosphere, one afternoon, when Edna climbed the stairs to the pianist's apartments under the roof. Her clothes were dripping with moisture. She felt chilled and pinched as she entered the room. Mademoiselle was poking at a rusty stove that smoked a little and warmed the room indifferently. She was endeavoring to heat a pot of chocolate on the stove. The room looked cheerless and dingy to Edna as she entered. A bust of Beethoven, covered with a hood of dust, scowled at her from the mantelpiece.

"Ah! here comes the sunlight!" exclaimed Mademoiselle, rising from her knees before the stove. "Now it will be warm and bright enough; I can let the fire alone."

She closed the stove door with a bang, and approaching, assisted in removing Edna's dripping mackintosh.

"You are cold; you look miserable. The chocolate will soon be hot. But would you rather have a taste of brandy? I have scarcely touched the bottle which you brought me for my cold." A piece of red flannel was wrapped around Mademoiselle's throat; a stiff neck compelled her to hold her head on one side.

"I will take some brandy," said Edna, shivering as she removed her gloves and overshoes. She drank the liquor from the glass as a man would have done. Then flinging herself upon the uncomfortable sofa she said, "Mademoiselle, I am going to move away from my house on Esplanade Street."

"Ah!" ejaculated the musician, neither surprised nor especially interested. Nothing ever seemed to astonish her very much. She was endeavoring to adjust the bunch of violets which had become loose from its fastening in her hair. Edna drew her down upon the sofa, and taking a pin from her own hair, secured the shabby artificial flowers in their accustomed place.

"Aren't you astonished?"

"Passably. Where are you going? to New York? to Iberville? to your father in Mississippi? where?"

"Just two steps away," laughed Edna, "in a little four-room house around the corner. It looks so cozy, so inviting and restful, whenever I pass by; and it's for rent. I'm tired looking after that big house. It never seemed like mine, anyway—like home. It's too much trouble. I have to keep too many servants. I am tired bothering with them."

"That is not your true reason, *ma belle*. There is no use in telling me lies. I don't know your reason, but you have not told me the truth." Edna did not protest or endeavor to justify herself.

"The house, the money that provides for it, are not mine. Isn't that enough reason?"

"They are your husband's," returned Mademoiselle, with a shrug and a malicious elevation of the eyebrows.

"Oh! I see there is no deceiving you. Then let me tell you: It is a caprice. I have a little money of my own from my mother's estate, which my father sends me by driblets. I won a large sum this winter on the races, and I am beginning to sell my sketches. Laidpore is more and more pleased with my work; he says it grows in force and individuality. I cannot judge of that myself, but I feel that I have gained in ease and confidence. However, as I said, I have sold a good many through Laidpore. I can live in the tiny house for little or nothing, with one servant. Old Celestine, who works occasionally for me, says she will come stay with me and do my work. I know I shall like it, like the feeling of freedom and independence."

"What does your husband say?"

"I have not told him yet. I only thought of it this morning. He will think I am demented, no doubt. Perhaps you think so."

Mademoiselle shook her head slowly. "Your reason is not yet clear to me," she said.

Neither was it quite clear to Edna herself; but it unfolded itself as she sat for a while in silence. Instinct had prompted her to put away her husband's bounty in casting off her allegiance. She did not know how it would be when he returned. There would have to be an understanding, an explanation. Conditions would some way adjust themselves, she felt; but whatever came, she had resolved never again to belong to another than herself.

"I shall give a grand dinner before I leave the old house!" Edna exclaimed. "You will have to come to it, Mademoiselle. I will give you everything that you like to eat and to drink. We shall sing and laugh and be merry for once." And she uttered a sigh that came from the very depths of her being.

If Mademoiselle happened to have received a letter from

Robert during the interval of Edna's visits, she would give her
the letter unsolicited. And she would seat herself at the piano
and play as her humor prompted her while the young woman
read the letter.

The little stove was roaring; it was red-hot, and the chocolate in the tin sizzled and sputtered. Edna went forward and
opened the stove door, and Mademoiselle, rising, took a letter
from under the bust of Beethoven and handed it to Edna.

"Another! so soon!" she exclaimed, her eyes filled with
delight. "Tell me, Mademoiselle, does he know that I see his
letters?"

"Never in the world! He would be angry and would never
write to me again if he thought so. Does he write to you?
Never a line. Does he send you a message? Never a word. It is
because he loves you, poor fool, and is trying to forget you,
since you are not free to listen to him or to belong to him."

"Why do you show me his letters, then?"

"Haven't you begged for them? Can I refuse you anything?
Oh! you cannot deceive me," and Mademoiselle approached
her beloved instrument and began to play. Edna did not at
once read the letter. She sat holding it in her hand, while the
music penetrated her whole being like an effulgence, warm-
ing and brightening the dark places of her soul. It prepared
her for joy and exultation.

"Oh!" she exclaimed, letting the letter fall to the floor.
"Why did you not tell me?" She went and grasped
Mademoiselle's hands up from the keys. "Oh! unkind! mali-
cious! Why did you not tell me?"

"That he was coming back? No great news, *ma foi*. I wonder he did not come long ago."

"But when, when?" cried Edna, impatiently. "He does not
say when."

"He says 'very soon.' You know as much about it as I do; it
is all in the letter."

"But why? Why is he coming? Oh, if I thought—" and she
snatched the letter from the floor and turned the pages this

way and that way, looking for the reason, which was left untold.

"If I were young and in love with a man," said Mademoiselle, turning on the stool and pressing her wiry hands between her knees as she looked down at Edna, who sat on the floor holding the letter, "it seems to me he would have to be some *grand esprit;*[*] a man with lofty aims and ability to reach them; one who stood high enough to attract the notice of his fellow-men. It seems to me if I were young and in love I should never deem a man of ordinary caliber worthy of my devotion."

"Now it is you who are telling lies and seeking to deceive me, Mademoiselle; or else you have never been in love, and know nothing about it. Why," went on Edna, clasping her knees and looking up into Mademoiselle's twisted face, "do you suppose a woman knows why she loves? Does she select? Does she say to herself: 'Go to! Here is a distinguished statesman with presidential possibilities; I shall proceed to fall in love with him.' Or, 'I shall set my heart upon this musician, whose fame is on every tongue?' Or, 'This financier, who controls the world's money markets?' "

"You are purposely misunderstanding me, *ma reine.*[†] Are you in love with Robert?"

"Yes," said Edna. It was the first time she had admitted it, and a glow overspread her face, blotching it with red spots.

"Why?" asked her companion. "Why do you love him when you ought not to?"

Edna, with a motion or two, dragged herself on her knees before Mademoiselle Reisz, who took the glowing face between her two hands.

"Why? Because his hair is brown and grows away from his temples; because he opens and shuts his eyes, and his nose is a little out of drawing; because he has two lips and a square

---

* Great spirit (Fr.).

† My queen; my love (Fr.).

chin, and a little finger which he can't straighten from having played baseball too energetically in his youth. Because—"

"Because you do, in short," laughed Mademoiselle. "What will you do when he comes back?" she asked.

"Do? Nothing, except feel glad and happy to be alive."

She was already glad and happy to be alive at the mere thought of his return. The murky, lowering sky, which had depressed her a few hours before, seemed bracing and invigorating as she splashed through the streets on her way home.

She stopped at a confectioner's and ordered a huge box of bonbons for the children in Iberville. She slipped a card in the box, on which she scribbled a tender message and sent an abundance of kisses.

Before dinner in the evening Edna wrote a charming letter to her husband, telling him of her intention to move for a while into the little house around the block, and to give a farewell dinner before leaving, regretting that he was not there to share it, to help her out with the menu and assist her in entertaining the guests. Her letter was brilliant and brimming with cheerfulness.

XXVII

⁓

"What is the matter with you?" asked Arobin that evening. "I never found you in such a happy mood." Edna was tired by that time, and was reclining on the lounge before the fire.

"Don't you know the weather prophet has told us we shall see the sun pretty soon?"

"Well, that ought to be reason enough," he acquiesced. "You wouldn't give me another if I sat here all night imploring you." He sat close to her on a low tabouret,* and as he

---

* A cylindrical seat or stool without arms or back.

spoke his fingers lightly touched the hair that fell a little over her forehead. She liked the touch of his fingers through her hair, and closed her eyes sensitively.

"One of these days," she said, "I'm going to pull myself together for a while and think—try to determine what character of a woman I am; for, candidly, I don't know. By all the codes which I am acquainted with, I am a devilishly wicked specimen of the sex. But some way I can't convince myself that I am. I must think about it."

"Don't. What's the use? Why should you bother thinking about it when I can tell you what manner of woman you are." His fingers strayed occasionally down to her warm, smooth cheeks and firm chin, which was growing a little full and double.

"Oh, yes! You will tell me that I am adorable; everything that is captivating. Spare yourself the effort."

"No; I shan't tell you anything of the sort, though I shouldn't be lying if I did."

"Do you know Mademoiselle Reisz?" she asked irrelevantly.

"The pianist? I know her by sight. I've heard her play."

"She says queer things sometimes in a bantering way that you don't notice at the time and you find yourself thinking about afterward."

"For instance?"

"Well, for instance, when I left her today, she put her arms around me and felt my shoulder blades, to see if my wings were strong, she said. 'The bird that would soar above the level plain of tradition and prejudice must have strong wings. It is a sad spectacle to see the weaklings bruised, exhausted, fluttering back to earth.'"

"Whither would you soar?"

"I'm not thinking of any extraordinary flights. I only half comprehend her."

"I've heard she's partially demented," said Arobin.

"She seems to me wonderfully sane," Edna replied.

"I'm told she's extremely disagreeable and unpleasant.

Why have you introduced her at a moment when I desired to talk of you?"

"Oh! talk of me if you like," cried Edna, clasping her hands beneath her head; "but let me think of something else while you do."

"I'm jealous of your thoughts to-night. They're making you a little kinder than usual; but some way I feel as if they were wandering, as if they were not here with me." She only looked at him and smiled. His eyes were very near. He leaned upon the lounge with an arm extended across her, while the other hand still rested upon her hair. They continued silently to look into each other's eyes. When he leaned forward and kissed her, she clasped his head, holding his lips to hers.

It was the first kiss of her life to which her nature had really responded. It was a flaming torch that kindled desire.

XXVIII

ᘓ

EDNA CRIED A LITTLE that night after Arobin left her. It was only one phase of the multitudinous emotions which had assailed her. There was with her an overwhelming feeling of irresponsibility. There was the shock of the unexpected and the unaccustomed. There was her husband's reproach looking at her from the external things around her which he had provided for her external existence. There was Robert's reproach making itself felt by a quicker, fiercer, more overpowering love, which had awakened within her toward him. Above all, there was understanding. She felt as if a mist had been lifted from her eyes, enabling her to look upon and comprehend the significance of life, that monster made up of beauty and brutality. But among the conflicting sensations which assailed her, there was neither shame nor remorse. There was a dull

pang of regret because it was not the kiss of love which had inflamed her, because it was not love which had held this cup
of life to her lips.

XXIX

⚜

WITHOUT EVEN WAITING FOR an answer from her husband regarding his opinion or wishes in the matter, Edna hastened
her preparations for quitting her home on Esplanade Street
and moving into the little house around the block. A feverish
anxiety attended her every action in that direction. There was
no moment of deliberation, no interval of repose between the
thought and its fulfillment. Early upon the morning following
those hours passed in Arobin's society, Edna set about securing her new abode and hurrying her arrangements for occupying it. Within the precincts of her home she felt like one
who has entered and lingered within the portals of some forbidden temple in which a thousand muffled voices bade her
begone.

Whatever was her own in the house, everything which she
had acquired aside from her husband's bounty, she caused to
be transported to the other house, supplying simple and meager deficiencies from her own resources.

Arobin found her with rolled sleeves, working in company
with the house-maid when he looked in during the afternoon.
She was splendid and robust, and had never appeared hand-
somer than in the old blue gown, with a red silk handkerchief
knotted at random around her head to protect her hair from
the dust. She was mounted upon a high step-ladder, unhooking a picture from the wall when he entered. He had found
the front door open, and had followed his ring by walking in
unceremoniously.

"Come down!" he said. "Do you want to kill yourself?"

She greeted him with affected carelessness, and appeared absorbed in her occupation.

If he had expected to find her languishing, reproachful, or indulging in sentimental tears, he must have been greatly surprised.

He was no doubt prepared for any emergency, ready for any one of the foregoing attitudes, just as he bent himself easily and naturally to the situation which confronted him.

"Please come down," he insisted, holding the ladder and looking up at her.

"No," she answered; "Ellen is afraid to mount the ladder. Joe is working over at the 'pigeon house'—that's the name Ellen gives it, because it's so small and looks like a pigeon house—and some one has to do this."

Arobin pulled off his coat, and expressed himself ready and willing to tempt fate in her place. Ellen brought him one of her dust-caps, and went into contortions of mirth, which she found it impossible to control, when she saw him put it on before the mirror as grotesquely as he could. Edna herself could not refrain from smiling when she fastened it at his request. So it was he who in turn mounted the ladder, unhooking pictures and curtains, and dislodging ornaments as Edna directed. When he had finished he took off his dust-cap and went out to wash his hands.

Edna was sitting on the tabouret, idly brushing the tips of a feather duster along the carpet when he came in again.

"Is there anything more you will let me do?" he asked.

"That is all," she answered. "Ellen can manage the rest." She kept the young woman occupied in the drawing-room, unwilling to be left alone with Arobin.

"What about the dinner?" he asked; "the grand event, the *coup d'état?*"*

"It will be day after to-morrow. Why do you call it the *'coup d'état?'* Oh! it will be very fine; all my best of everything—crystal, silver and gold, Sèvres, flowers, music, and

_____

* A sudden and unexpected overthrow of power (Fr.).

champagne to swim in. I'll let Léonce pay the bills. I wonder what he'll say when he sees the bills."

"And you ask me why I call it a *coup d'état?*" Arobin had put on his coat, and he stood before her and asked if his cravat was plumb.* She told him it was, looking no higher than the tip of his collar.

"When do you go to the 'pigeon house?'—with all due acknowledgment to Ellen."

"Day after to-morrow, after the dinner. I shall sleep there."

"Ellen, will you very kindly get me a glass of water?" asked Arobin. "The dust in the curtains, if you will pardon me for hinting such a thing, has parched my throat to a crisp."

"While Ellen gets the water," said Edna, rising, "I will say good-by and let you go. I must get rid of this grime, and I have a million things to do and think of."

"When shall I see you?" asked Arobin, seeking to detain her, the maid having left the room.

"At the dinner, of course. You are invited."

"Not before?—not to-night or to-morrow morning or to-morrow noon or night? or the day after morning or noon? Can't you see yourself, without my telling you, what an eternity it is?"

He had followed her into the hall and to the foot of the stairway, looking up at her as she mounted with her face half turned to him.

"Not an instant sooner," she said. But she laughed and looked at him with eyes that at once gave him courage to wait and made it torture to wait.

---

* If his necktie was straight.

XXX

❧

THOUGH EDNA HAD SPOKEN of the dinner as a very grand affair, it was in truth a very small affair and very select, in so
much as the guests invited were few and were selected with
discrimination. She had counted upon an even dozen seating
themselves at her round mahogany board, forgetting for the
moment that Madame Ratignolle was to the last degree *souffrante** and unpresentable, and not foreseeing that Madame
Lebrun would send a thousand regrets at the last moment. So
there were only ten, after all, which made a cozy, comfortable
number.

There were Mr. and Mrs. Merriman, a pretty, vivacious little woman in the thirties; her husband, a jovial fellow, something of a shallow-pate,† who laughed a good deal at other
people's witticisms, and had thereby made himself extremely
popular. Mrs. Highcamp had accompanied them. Of course,
there was Alcée Arobin; and Mademoiselle Reisz had consented to come. Edna had sent her a fresh bunch of violets
with black lace trimmings for her hair. Monsieur Ratignolle
brought himself and his wife's excuses. Victor Lebrun, who
happened to be in the city, bent upon relaxation, had accepted with alacrity. There was a Miss Mayblunt, no longer in
her teens, who looked at the world through lorgnettes‡ and
with the keenest interest. It was thought and said that she was
intellectual; it was suspected of her that she wrote under a
nom de guerre.§ She had come with a gentleman by the name
of Gouvernail, connected with one of the daily papers, of
whom nothing special could be said, except that he was observant and seemed quiet and inoffensive. Edna herself made

---

* In the late stages of pregnancy (Fr.).

† A dim-witted person.

‡ A pair of eyeglasses with a handle.

§ Pseudonym; pen name (Fr.).

the tenth, and at half-past eight they seated themselves at table, Arobin and Monsieur Ratignolle on either side of their hostess.

Mrs. Highcamp sat between Arobin and Victor Lebrun. Then came Mrs. Merriman, Mr. Gouvernail, Miss Mayblunt, Mr. Merriman, and Mademoiselle Reisz next to Monsieur Ratignolle.

There was something extremely gorgeous about the appearance of the table, an effect of splendor conveyed by a cover of pale yellow satin under strips of lace-work. There were wax candles in massive brass candelabra, burning softly under yellow silk shades; full, fragrant roses, yellow and red, abounded. There were silver and gold, as she had said there would be, and crystal which glittered like the gems which the women wore.

The ordinary stiff dining chairs had been discarded for the occasion and replaced by the most commodious and luxurious which could be collected throughout the house. Mademoiselle Reisz, being exceedingly diminutive, was elevated upon cushions, as small children are sometimes hoisted at table upon bulky volumes.

"Something new, Edna?" exclaimed Miss Mayblunt, with lorgnette directed toward a magnificent cluster of diamonds that sparkled, that almost sputtered, in Edna's hair, just over the center of her forehead.

"Quite new; 'brand' new, in fact; a present from my husband. It arrived this morning from New York. I may as well admit that this is my birthday, and that I am twenty-nine. In good time I expect you to drink to my health. Meanwhile, I shall ask you to begin with this cocktail, composed—would you say 'composed?'" with an appeal to Miss Mayblunt—"composed by my father in honor of Sister Janet's wedding."

Before each guest stood a tiny glass that looked and sparkled like a garnet gem.

"Then, all things considered," spoke Arobin, "it might not be amiss to start out by drinking the Colonel's health in the cocktail which he composed, on the birthday of the most charming of women—the daughter whom he invented."

Mr. Merriman's laugh at this sally was such a genuine outburst and so contagious that it started the dinner with an agreeable swing that never slackened.

Miss Mayblunt begged to be allowed to keep her cocktail untouched before her, just to look at. The color was marvelous! She could compare it to nothing she had ever seen, and the garnet lights which it emitted were unspeakably rare. She pronounced the Colonel an artist, and stuck to it.

Monsieur Ratignolle was prepared to take things seriously: the *mets*, the *entre-mets*,* the service, the decorations, even the people. He looked up from his pompono† and inquired of Arobin if he were related to the gentleman of that name who formed one of the firm of Laitner and Arobin, lawyers. The young man admitted that Laitner was a warm personal friend, who permitted Arobin's name to decorate the firm's letterheads and to appear upon a shingle that graced Perdido Street.‡

"There are so many inquisitive people and institutions abounding," said Arobin, "that one is really forced as a matter of convenience these days to assume the virtue of an occupation if he has it not."

Monsieur Ratignolle stared a little, and turned to ask Mademoiselle Reisz if she considered the symphony concerts up to the standard which had been set the previous winter. Mademoiselle Reisz anwered Monsieur Ratignolle in French, which Edna thought a little rude, under the circumstances, but characteristic. Mademoiselle had only disagreeable things to say of the symphony concerts, and insulting

---

* Main courses and side dishes (Fr.).

† Pompano, a fish from Florida or the West Indies. In New Orleans it is typically cooked in parchment.

‡ A street in the American Quarter running parallel to Canal Street; according to legend, it was once lost in a cypress swamp, and was thus named for the Spanish word meaning "lost."

remarks to make of all the musicians of New Orleans, singly and collectively. All her interest seemed to be centered upon the delicacies placed before her.

Mr. Merriman said that Mr. Arobin's remark about inquisitive people reminded him of a man from Waco the other day at the St. Charles Hotel—but as Mr. Merriman's stories were always lame and lacking point, his wife seldom permitted him to complete them. She interrupted him to ask if he remembered the name of the author whose book she had bought the week before to send to a friend in Geneva. She was talking "books" with Mr. Gouvernail and trying to draw from him his opinion upon current literary topics. Her husband told the story of the Waco man privately to Miss Mayblunt, who pretended to be greatly amused and to think it extremely clever.

Mrs. Highcamp hung with languid but unaffected interest upon the warm and impetuous volubility of her left-hand neighbor, Victor Lebrun. Her attention was never for a moment withdrawn from him after seating herself at table; and when he turned to Mrs. Merriman, who was prettier and more vivacious than Mrs. Highcamp, she waited with easy indifference for an opportunity to reclaim his attention. There was the occasional sound of music, of mandolins, sufficiently removed to be an agreeable accompaniment rather than an interruption to the conversation. Outside the soft, monotonous splash of a fountain could be heard; the sound penetrated into the room with the heavy odor of jessamine that came through the open windows.

The golden shimmer of Edna's satin gown spread in rich folds on either side of her. There was a soft fall of lace encircling her shoulders. It was the color of her skin, without the glow, the myriad living tints that one may sometimes discover in vibrant flesh. There was something in her attitude, in her whole appearance when she leaned her head against the high-backed chair and spread her arms, which suggested the regal woman, the one who rules, who looks on, who stands alone.

But as she sat there amid her guests, she felt the old ennui overtaking her; the hopelessness which so often assailed her, which came upon her like an obsession, like something extraneous, independent of volition. It was something which announced itself; a chill breath that seemed to issue from some vast cavern wherein discords wailed. There came over her the acute longing which always summoned into her spiritual vision the presence of the beloved one, overpowering her at once with a sense of the unattainable.

The moments glided on, while a feeling of good fellowship passed around the circle like a mystic cord, holding and binding these people together with jest and laughter. Monsieur Ratignolle was the first to break the pleasant charm. At ten o'clock he excused himself. Madame Ratignolle was waiting for him at home. She was *bien souffrante*,* and she was filled with vague dread, which only her husband's presence could allay.

Mademoiselle Reisz arose with Monsieur Ratignolle, who offered to escort her to the car. She had eaten well; she had tasted the good, rich wines, and they must have turned her head, for she bowed pleasantly to all as she withdrew from table. She kissed Edna upon the shoulder, and whispered: "*Bonne nuit, ma reine; soyez sage.*"† She had been a little bewildered upon rising, or rather, descending from her cushions, and Monsieur Ratignolle gallantly took her arm and led her away.

Mrs. Highcamp was weaving a garland of roses, yellow and red. When she had finished the garland, she laid it lightly upon Victor's black curls. He was reclining far back in the luxurious chair, holding a glass of champagne to the light.

As if a magician's wand had touched him, the garland of roses transformed him into a vision of Oriental beauty. His cheeks were the color of crushed grapes, and his dusky eyes glowed with a languishing fire.

---

* Awaiting delivery; ill (Fr.).

† Good night, my love; be good (Fr.).

"*Sapristi!*"* exclaimed Arobin.

But Mrs. Highcamp had one more touch to add to the picture. She took from the back of her chair a white silken scarf, with which she had covered her shoulders in the early part of the evening. She draped it across the boy in graceful folds, and in a way to conceal his black, conventional evening dress. He did not seem to mind what she did to him, only smiled, showing a faint gleam of white teeth, while he continued to gaze with narrowing eyes at the light through his glass of champagne.

"Oh! to be able to paint in color rather than in words!" exclaimed Miss Mayblunt, losing herself in a rhapsodic dream as she looked at him.

> " 'There was a graven image of Desire
>   Painted with red blood on a ground of gold' "†

murmured Gouvernail, under his breath.

The effect of the wine upon Victor was, to change his accustomed volubility into silence. He seemed to have abandoned himself to a reverie, and to be seeing pleasing visions in the amber bead.

"Sing," entreated Mrs. Highcamp. "Won't you sing to us?"

"Let him alone," said Arobin.

"He's posing," offered Mr. Merriman; "let him have it out."

"I believe he's paralyzed," laughed Mrs. Merriman. And leaning over the youth's chair, she took the glass from his hand and held it to his lips. He sipped the wine slowly, and when he had drained the glass she laid it upon the table and wiped his lips with her little filmy handkerchief.

"Yes, I'll sing for you," he said, turning in his chair toward

---

* Good Lord! (Fr.).

† The lines are from "A Cameo," a sonnet about insatiable desire and the inevitability of death, by the English poet Algernon Charles Swinburne (1837–1909).

Mrs. Highcamp: He clasped his hands behind his head, and looking up at the ceiling began to hum a little, trying his voice like a musician tuning an instrument. Then, looking at Edna, he began to sing:

> "Ah! si tu savais!"*

"Stop!" she cried, "don't sing that. I don't want you to sing it," and she laid her glass so impetuously and blindly upon the table as to shatter it against a carafe. The wine spilled over Arobin's legs and some of it trickled down upon Mrs. Highcamp's black gauze gown. Victor had lost all idea of courtesy, or else he thought his hostess was not in earnest, for he laughed and went on:

> "Ah! si tu savais
> Ce que tes yeux me disent" — †

"Oh! you mustn't! you mustn't," exclaimed Edna, and pushing back her chair she got up, and going behind him placed her hand over his mouth. He kissed the soft palm that pressed upon his lips.

"No, no, I won't, Mrs. Pontellier. I didn't know you meant it," looking up at her with caressing eyes. The touch of his lips was like a pleasing sting to her hand. She lifted the garland of roses from his head and flung it across the room.

"Come, Victor; you've posed long enough. Give Mrs. Highcamp her scarf."

Mrs. Highcamp undraped the scarf from about him with her own hands. Miss Mayblunt and Mr. Gouvernail suddenly conceived the notion that it was time to say good-night. And Mr. and Mrs. Merriman wondered how it could be so late.

Before parting from Victor, Mrs. Highcamp invited him to call upon her daughter, who she knew would be charmed to

---

* See chap. XIV, p. 54.

† What your eyes are saying to me now (Fr.).

meet him and talk French and sing French songs with him. Victor expressed his desire and intention to call upon Miss Highcamp at the first opportunity which presented itself. He asked if Arobin were going his way. Arobin was not.

The mandolin players had long since stolen away. A profound stillness had fallen upon the broad, beautiful street. The voices of Edna's disbanding guests jarred like a discordant note upon the quiet harmony of the night.

XXXI

∽

"WELL?" QUESTIONED AROBIN, WHO had remained with Edna after the others had departed.

"Well," she reiterated, and stood up, stretching her arms, and feeling the need to relax her muscles after having been so long seated.

"What next?" he asked.

"The servants are all gone. They left when the musicians did. I have dismissed them. The house has to be closed and locked, and I shall trot around to the pigeon house, and shall send Celestine over in the morning to straighten things up."

He looked around, and began to turn out some of the lights.

"What about upstairs?" he inquired.

"I think it is all right; but there may be a window or two unlatched. We had better look; you might take a candle and see. And bring me my wrap and hat on the foot of the bed in the middle room."

He went up with the light, and Edna began closing doors and windows. She hated to shut in the smoke and the fumes of the wine. Arobin found her cape and hat, which he brought down and helped her to put on.

When everything was secured and the lights put out, they

left through the front door, Arobin locking it and taking the key, which he carried for Edna. He helped her down the steps.

"Will you have a spray of jessamine?" he asked, breaking off a few blossoms as he passed.

"No; I don't want anything."

She seemed disheartened, and had nothing to say. She took his arm, which he offered her, holding up the weight of her satin train with the other hand. She looked down, noticing the black line of his leg moving in and out so close to her against the yellow shimmer of her gown. There was the whistle of a railway train somewhere in the distance, and the midnight bells were ringing. They met no one in their short walk.

The "pigeon-house" stood behind a locked gate, and a shallow *parterre*° that had been somewhat neglected. There was a small front porch, upon which a long window and the front door opened. The door opened directly into the parlor; there was no side entry. Back in the yard was a room for servants, in which old Celestine had been ensconced.

Edna had left a lamp burning low upon the table. She had succeeded in making the room look habitable and home-like. There were some books on the table and a lounge near at hand. On the floor was a fresh matting, covered with a rug or two; and on the walls hung a few tasteful pictures. But the room was filled with flowers. These were a surprise to her. Arobin had sent them, and had had Celestine distribute them during Edna's absence. Her bedroom was adjoining, and across a small passage were the dining-room and kitchen.

Edna seated herself with every appearance of discomfort.

"Are you tired?" he asked.

"Yes, and chilled, and miserable. I feel as if I had been wound up to a certain pitch—too tight—and something inside of me had snapped." She rested her head against the table upon her bare arm.

° Garden; flower-bed (Fr.).

"You want to rest," he said, "and to be quiet. I'll go; I'll leave you and let you rest."

"Yes," she replied.

He stood up beside her and smoothed her hair with his soft, magnetic hand. His touch conveyed to her a certain physical comfort. She could have fallen quietly asleep there if he had continued to pass his hand over her hair. He brushed the hair upward from the nape of her neck.

"I hope you will feel better and happier in the morning," he said. "You have tried to do too much in the past few days. The dinner was the last straw; you might have dispensed with it."

"Yes," she admitted; "it was stupid."

"No, it was delightful; but it has worn you out." His hand had strayed to her beautiful shoulders, and he could feel the response of her flesh to his touch. He seated himself beside her and kissed her lightly upon the shoulder.

"I thought you were going away," she said, in an uneven voice.

"I am, after I have said good-night."

"Good-night," she murmured.

He did not answer, except to continue to caress her. He did not say good-night until she had become supple to his gentle, seductive entreaties.

XXXII

&

WHEN MR. PONTELLIER LEARNED of his wife's intention to abandon her home and take up her residence elsewhere, he immediately wrote her a letter of unqualified disapproval and remonstrance. She had given reasons which he was unwilling to acknowledge as adequate. He hoped she had not acted upon her rash impulse; and he begged her to consider first, foremost, and above all else, what people would say. He was not dreaming of scandal when he uttered this warning; that was a thing which would never have entered into his mind to consider in connection with his wife's name or his own. He was simply thinking of his financial integrity. It might get noised about that the Pontelliers had met with reverses, and were forced to conduct their *ménage*° on a humbler scale than heretofore. It might do incalculable mischief to his business prospects.

But remembering Edna's whimsical turn of mind of late, and foreseeing that she had immediately acted upon her impetuous determination, he grasped the situation with his usual promptness and handled it with his well-known business tact and cleverness.

The same mail which brought to Edna his letter of disapproval carried instructions—the most minute instructions—to a well-known architect concerning the remodeling of his home, changes which he had long contemplated, and which he desired carried forward during his temporary absence.

Expert and reliable packers and movers were engaged to convey the furniture, carpets, pictures—everything movable, in short—to places of security. And in an incredibly short time the Pontellier house was turned over to the artisans. There was to be an addition—a small snuggery;† there was to be frescoing, and hardwood flooring was to be put into such rooms as had not yet been subjected to this improvement.

Furthermore, in one of the daily papers appeared a brief notice to the effect that Mr. and Mrs. Pontellier were contemplating a summer sojourn abroad, and that their handsome residence on Esplanade Street was undergoing sumptuous alterations, and would not be ready for occupancy until their return. Mr. Pontellier had saved appearances!

Edna admired the skill of his maneuver, and avoided any occasion to balk his intentions. When the situation as set forth

---

* Household (Fr.).

† Cozy room.

by Mr. Pontellier was accepted and taken for granted, she was apparently satisfied that it should be so.

The pigeon-house pleased her. It at once assumed the intimate character of a home, while she herself invested it with a charm which it reflected like a warm glow. There was with her a feeling of having descended in the social scale, with a corresponding sense of having risen in the spiritual. Every step which she took toward relieving herself from obligations added to her strength and expansion as an individual. She began to look with her own eyes; to see and to apprehend the deeper undercurrents of life. No longer was she content to "feed upon opinion" when her own soul had invited her.

After a little while, a few days, in fact, Edna went up and spent a week with her children in Iberville. They were delicious February days, with all the summer's promise hovering in the air.

How glad she was to see the children! She wept for very pleasure when she felt their little arms clasping her; their hard, ruddy cheeks pressed against her own glowing cheeks. She looked into their faces with hungry eyes that could not be satisfied with looking. And what stories they had to tell their mother! About the pigs, the cows, the mules! About riding to the mill behind Gluglu; fishing back in the lake with their Uncle Jasper; picking pecans with Lidie's little black brood, and hauling chips in their express wagon. It was a thousand times more fun to haul real chips for old lame Susie's real fire than to drag painted blocks along the banquette on Esplanade Street!

She went with them herself to see the pigs and the cows, to look at the darkies laying the cane, to thrash the pecan trees, and catch fish in the back lake. She lived with them a whole week long, giving them all of herself, and gathering and filling herself with their young existence. They listened, breathless, when she told them the house in Esplanade Street was crowded with workmen, hammering, nailing, sawing, and filling the place with clatter. They wanted to know where their bed was; what had been done with their rocking-horse; and where did Joe sleep, and where had Ellen gone, and the cook? But, above all, they were fired with a desire to see the little house around the block. Was there any place to play? Were there any boys next door? Raoul, with pessimistic foreboding, was convinced that there were only girls next door. Where would they sleep, and where would papa sleep? She told them the fairies would fix it all right.

The old Madame was charmed with Edna's visit, and showered all manner of delicate attentions upon her. She was delighted to know that the Esplanade Street house was in a dismantled condition. It gave her the promise and pretext to keep the children indefinitely.

It was with a wrench and a pang that Edna left her children. She carried away with her the sound of their voices and the touch of their cheeks. All along the journey homeward their presence lingered with her like the memory of a delicious song. But by the time she had regained the city the song no longer echoed in her soul. She was again alone.

XXXIII

∾

IT HAPPENED SOMETIMES WHEN Edna went to see Mademoiselle Reisz that the little musician was absent, giving a lesson or making some small necessary household purchase. The key was always left in a secret hiding-place in the entry, which Edna knew. If Mademoiselle happened to be away, Edna would usually enter and wait for her return.

When she knocked at Mademoiselle Reisz's door one afternoon there was no response; so unlocking the door, as usual, she entered and found the apartment deserted, as she had expected. Her day had been quite filled up, and it was for a rest, for a refuge, and to talk about Robert, that she sought out her friend.

She had worked at her canvas—a young Italian character study—all the morning, completing the work without the model; but there had been many interruptions, some incident to her modest housekeeping, and others of a social nature.

Madame Ratignolle had dragged herself over, avoiding the too public thorough fares, she said. She complained that Edna had neglected her much of late. Besides, she was consumed with curiosity to see the little house and the manner in which it was conducted. She wanted to hear all about the dinner party; Monsieur Ratignolle had left *so* early. What had happened after he left? The champagne and grapes which Edna sent over were *too* delicious. She had so little appetite; they had refreshed and toned her stomach. Where on earth was she going to put Mr. Pontellier in that little house, and the boys? And then she made Edna promise to go to her when her hour of trial overtook her.

"At any time—any time of the day or night, dear," Edna assured her.

Before leaving Madame Ratignolle said:

"In some way you seem to me like a child, Edna. You seem to act without a certain amount of reflection which is necessary in this life. That is the reason I want to say you mustn't mind if I advise you to be a little careful while you are living here alone. Why don't you have some one come and stay with you? Wouldn't Mademoiselle Reisz come?"

"No; she wouldn't wish to come, and I shouldn't want her always with me."

"Well, the reason—you know how evil-minded the world is—some one was talking of Alcée Arobin visiting you. Of course, it wouldn't matter if Mr. Arobin had not such a dreadful reputation. Monsieur Ratignolle was telling me that his attentions alone are considered enough to ruin a woman's name."

"Does he boast of his successes?" asked Edna, indifferently, squinting at her picture.

"No, I think not. I believe he is a decent fellow as far as that goes. But his character is so well known among the men.

I shan't be able to come back and see you; it was very, very imprudent to-day."

"Mind the step!" cried Edna.

"Don't neglect me," entreated Madame Ratignolle; "and
don't mind what I said about Arobin, or having some one to
stay with you."

"Of course not," Edna laughed. "You may say anything
you like to me." They kissed each other good-by. Madame
Ratignolle had not far to go, and Edna stood on the porch a
while watching her walk down the street.

Then in the afternoon Mrs. Merriman and Mrs.
Highcamp had made their "party call." Edna felt that they
might have dispensed with the formality. They had also come
to invite her to play *vingt-et-un*[*] one evening at Mrs.
Merriman's. She was asked to go early, to dinner, and Mr.
Merriman or Mr. Arobin would take her home. Edna ac-
cepted in a half-hearted way. She sometimes felt very tired of
Mrs. Highcamp and Mrs. Merriman.

Late in the afternoon she sought refuge with
Mademoiselle Reisz, and stayed there alone, waiting for her,
feeling a kind of repose invade her with the very atmosphere
of the shabby, unpretentious little room.

Edna sat at the window, which looked out over the housetops and across the river. The window frame was filled with
pots of flowers, and she sat and picked the dry leaves from a
rose geranium. The day was warm, and the breeze which
blew from the river was very pleasant. She removed her hat
and laid it on the piano. She went on picking the leaves and
digging around the plants with her hat pin. Once she thought
she heard Mademoiselle Reisz approaching. But it was a
young black girl, who came in, bringing a small bundle of
laundry, which she deposited in the adjoining room, and
went away.

Edna seated herself at the piano, and softly picked out with
one hand the bars of a piece of music which lay open before

---

[*] Twenty-one (Fr.), or blackjack, a card game.

her. A half-hour went by. There was the occasional sound of people going and coming in the lower hall. She was growing interested in her occupation of picking out the aria, when there was a second rap at the door. She vaguely wondered what these people did when they found Mademoiselle's door locked.

"Come in," she called, turning her face toward the door. And this time it was Robert Lebrun who presented himself. She attempted to rise; she could not have done so without betraying the agitation which mastered her at sight of him, so she fell back upon the stool, only exclaiming, "Why, Robert!"

He came and clasped her hand, seemingly without knowing what he was saying or doing.

"Mrs. Pontellier! How do you happen—oh! how well you look! Is Mademoiselle Reisz not here? I never expected to see you."

"When did you come back?" asked Edna in an unsteady voice, wiping her face with her handkerchief. She seemed ill at ease on the piano stool, and he begged her to take the chair by the window. She did so, mechanically, while he seated himself on the stool.

"I returned day before yesterday," he answered, while he leaned his arm on the keys, bringing forth a crash of discordant sound.

"Day before yesterday!" she repeated, aloud; and went on thinking to herself, "day before yesterday," in a sort of an uncomprehending way. She had pictured him seeking her at the very first hour, and he had lived under the same sky since day before yesterday; while only by accident had he stumbled upon her. Mademoiselle must have lied when she said, "Poor fool, he loves you."

"Day before yesterday," she repeated, breaking off a spray of Mademoiselle's geranium; "then if you had not met me here to-day you wouldn't—when—that is, didn't you mean to come and see me?"

"Of course, I should have gone to see you. There have been so many things—" he turned the leaves of Mademoiselle's music nervously. "I started in at once yesterday with the old firm. After all there is as much chance for me here as there was there—that is, I might find it profitable some day. The Mexicans were not very congenial."

So he had come back because the Mexicans were not congenial; because business was as profitable here as there; because of any reason, and not because he cared to be near her. She remembered the day she sat on the floor, turning the pages of his letter, seeking the reason which was left untold.

She had not noticed how he looked—only feeling his presence; but she turned deliberately and observed him. After all, he had been absent but a few months, and was not changed. His hair—the color of hers—waved back from his temples in the same way as before. His skin was not more burned than it had been at Grand Isle. She found in his eyes, when he looked at her for one silent moment, the same tender caress, with an added warmth and entreaty which had not been there before—the same glance which had penetrated to the sleeping places of her soul and awakened them.

A hundred times Edna had pictured Robert's return, and imagined their first meeting. It was usually at her home, whither he had sought her out at once. She always fancied him expressing or betraying in some way his love for her. And here, the reality was that they sat ten feet apart, she at the window, crushing geranium leaves in her hand and smelling them, he twirling around on the piano stool, saying:

"I was very much surprised to hear of Mr. Pontellier's absence; it's a wonder Mademoiselle Reisz did not tell me; and your moving—mother told me yesterday. I should think you would have gone to New York with him, or to Iberville with the children, rather than be bothered here with housekeeping. And you are going abroad, too, I hear. We shan't have you at Grand Isle next summer; it won't seem—do you see much of Mademoiselle Reisz? She often spoke of you in the few letters she wrote."

"Do you remember that you promised to write to me when you went away?" A flush overspread his whole face.

"I couldn't believe that my letters would be of any interest to you."

"That is an excuse; it isn't the truth." Edna reached for her hat on the piano. She adjusted it, sticking the hat pin through the heavy coil of hair with some deliberation.

"Are you not going to wait for Mademoiselle Reisz?" asked Robert.

"No; I have found when she is absent this long, she is liable not to come back till late." She drew on her gloves, and Robert picked up his hat.

"Won't you wait for her?" asked Edna.

"Not if you think she will not be back till late," adding, as if suddenly aware of some discourtesy in his speech, "and I should miss the pleasure of walking home with you." Edna locked the door and put the key back in its hiding-place.

They went together, picking their way across muddy streets and sidewalks encumbered with the cheap display of small tradesmen. Part of the distance they rode in the car, and after disembarking, passed the Pontellier mansion, which looked broken and half torn asunder. Robert had never known the house, and looked at it with interest.

"I never knew you in your home," he remarked.

"I am glad you did not."

"Why?" She did not answer. They went on around the corner, and it seemed as if her dreams were coming true after all, when he followed her into the little house.

"You must stay and dine with me, Robert. You see I am all alone, and it is so long since I have seen you. There is so much I want to ask you."

She took off her hat and gloves. He stood irresolute, making some excuse about his mother who expected him; he even muttered something about an engagement. She struck a match and lit the lamp on the table; it was growing dusk. When he saw her face in the lamp-light, looking pained, with all the soft lines gone out of it, he threw his hat aside and seated himself.

"Oh! you know I want to stay if you will let me!" he exclaimed. All the softness came back. She laughed, and went and put her hand on his shoulder.

"This is the first moment you have seemed like the old Robert. I'll go tell Celestine." She hurried away to tell Celestine to set an extra place. She even sent her off in search of some added delicacy which she had not thought of for herself. And she recommended great care in dripping the coffee and having the omelet done to a proper turn.

When she reëntered, Robert was turning over magazines, sketches, and things that lay upon the table in great disorder. He picked up a photograph, and exclaimed:

"Alcée Arobin! What on earth is his picture doing here?"

"I tried to make a sketch of his head one day," answered Edna, "and he thought the photograph might help me. It was at the other house. I thought it had been left there. I must have packed it up with my drawing materials."

"I should think you would give it back to him if you have finished with it."

"Oh! I have a great many such photographs. I never think of returning them. They don't amount to anything." Robert kept on looking at the picture.

"It seems to me—do you think his head worth drawing? Is he a friend of Mr. Pontellier's? You never said you knew him."

"He isn't a friend of Mr. Pontellier's; he's a friend of mine. I always knew him—that is, it is only of late that I know him pretty well. But I'd rather talk about you, and know what you have been seeing and doing and feeling out there in Mexico." Robert threw aside the picture.

"I've been seeing the waves and the white beach of Grand Isle; the quiet, grassy street of the *Chênière*; the old fort at Grande Terre. I've been working like a machine, and feeling like a lost soul. There was nothing interesting."

She leaned her head upon her hand to shade her eyes from the light.

"And what have you been seeing and doing and feeling all these days?" he asked.

"I've been seeing the waves and the white beach of Grand

Isle; the quiet, grassy street of the *Chênière Caminada*; the old sunny fort at Grande Terre. I've been working with a little more comprehension than a machine, and still feeling like a lost soul. There was nothing interesting."

"Mrs. Pontellier, you are cruel," he said, with feeling, closing his eyes and resting his head back in his chair. They remained in silence till old Celestine announced dinner.

XXXIV

∽

THE DINING-ROOM WAS VERY small. Edna's round mahogany would have almost filled it. As it was there was but a step or two from the little table to the kitchen, to the mantel, the small buffet, and the side door that opened out on the narrow brick-paved yard.

A certain degree of ceremony settled upon them with the announcement of dinner. There was no return to personalities. Robert related incidents of his sojourn in Mexico, and Edna talked of events likely to interest him, which had occurred during his absence. The dinner was of ordinary quality, except for the few delicacies which she had sent out to purchase. Old Celestine, with a bandana *tignon** twisted about her head, hobbled in and out, taking a personal interest in everything; and she lingered occasionally to talk patois† with Robert, whom she had known as a boy.

He went out to a neighboring cigar stand to purchase cigarette papers, and when he came back he found that Celestine had served the black coffee in the parlor.

---

* A scarf used to tie back the hair (Fr.).

† Regional dialect; here specifically, an Acadian dialect combining archaic French with English, Spanish, German, and Native American words.

"Perhaps I shouldn't have come back," he said. "When you are tired of me, tell me to go."

"You never tire me. You must have forgotten the hours and hours at Grand Isle in which we grew accustomed to each other and used to being together."

"I have forgotten nothing at Grand Isle," he said, not looking at her, but rolling a cigarette. His tobacco pouch, which he laid upon the table, was a fantastic embroidered silk affair, evidently the handiwork of a woman.

"You used to carry your tobacco in a rubber pouch," said Edna, picking up the pouch and examining the needlework.

"Yes; it was lost."

"Where did you buy this one? In Mexico?"

"It was given to me by a Vera Cruz girl; they are very generous," he replied, striking a match and lighting his cigarette.

"They are very handsome, I suppose, those Mexican women; very picturesque, with their black eyes and their lace scarfs."

"Some are; others are hideous. Just as you find women everywhere."

"What was she like—the one who gave you the pouch? You must have known her very well."

"She was very ordinary. She wasn't of the slightest importance. I knew her well enough."

"Did you visit at her house? Was it interesting? I should like to know and hear about the people you met, and the impressions they made on you."

"There are some people who leave impressions not so lasting as the imprint of an oar upon the water."

"Was she such a one?"

"It would be ungenerous for me to admit that she was of that order and kind." He thrust the pouch back in his pocket, as if to put away the subject with the trifle which had brought it up.

Arobin dropped in with a message from Mrs. Merriman, to say that the card party was postponed on account of the illness of one of her children.

"How do you do, Arobin?" said Robert, rising from the obscurity.

"Oh! Lebrun. To be sure! I heard yesterday you were back. How did they treat you down in Mexique?"

"Fairly well."

"But not well enough to keep you there. Stunning girls, though, in Mexico. I thought I should never get away from Vera Cruz when I was down there a couple of years ago."

"Did they embroider slippers and tobacco pouches and hat-bands and things for you?" asked Edna.

"Oh! my! no! I didn't get so deep in their regard. I fear they made more impression on me than I made on them."

"You were less fortunate than Robert, then."

"I am always less fortunate than Robert. Has he been imparting tender confidences?"

"I've been imposing myself long enough," said Robert, rising, and shaking hands with Edna. "Please convey my regards to Mr. Pontellier when you write."

He shook hands with Arobin and went away.

"Fine fellow, that Lebrun," said Arobin when Robert had gone. "I never heard you speak of him."

"I knew him last summer at Grand Isle," she replied. "Here is that photograph of yours. Don't you want it?"

"What do I want with it? Throw it away." She threw it back on the table.

"I'm not going to Mrs. Merriman's," she said. "If you see her, tell her so. But perhaps I had better write. I think I shall write now, and say that I am sorry her child is sick, and tell her not to count on me."

"It would be a good scheme," acquiesced Arobin. "I don't blame you; stupid lot!"

Edna opened the blotter, and having procured paper and pen, began to write the note. Arobin lit a cigar and read the evening paper, which he had in his pocket.

"What is the date?" she asked. He told her.

"Will you mail this for me when you go out?"

"Certainly." He read to her little bits out of the newspaper, while she straightened things on the table.

"What do you want to do?" he asked, throwing aside the paper. "Do you want to go out for a walk or a drive or anything? It would be a fine night to drive."

"No; I don't want to do anything but just be quiet. You go away and amuse yourself. Don't stay."

"I'll go away if I must; but I shan't amuse myself. You know that I only live when I am near you."

He stood up to bid her good-night.

"Is that one of the things you always say to women?"

"I have said it before, but I don't think I ever came so near meaning it," he answered with a smile. There were no warm lights in her eyes; only a dreamy, absent look.

"Good-night. I adore you. Sleep well," he said, and he kissed her hand and went away.

She stayed alone in a kind of reverie—a sort of stupor. Step by step she lived over every instant of the time she had been with Robert after he had entered Mademoiselle Reisz's door. She recalled his words, his looks. How few and meager they had been for her hungry heart! A vision—a transcendently seductive vision of a Mexican girl arose before her. She writhed with a jealous pang. She wondered when he would come back. He had not said he would come back. She had been with him, had heard his voice and touched his hand. But some way he had seemed nearer to her off there in Mexico.

XXXV

∽

THE MORNING WAS FULL of sunlight and hope. Edna could see before her no denial—only the promise of excessive joy. She lay in bed awake, with bright eyes full of speculation. "He loves you, poor fool." If she could but get that conviction firmly fixed in her mind, what mattered about the rest? She felt she had been childish and unwise the night before in giving herself over to despondency. She recapitulated the motives which no doubt explained Robert's reserve. They were not insurmountable; they would not hold if he really loved her; they could not hold against her own passion, which he must come to realize in time. She pictured him going to his business that morning. She even saw how he was dressed; how he walked down one street, and turned the corner of another; saw him bending over his desk, talking to people who entered the office, going to his lunch, and perhaps watching for her on the street. He would come to her in the afternoon or evening, sit and roll his cigarette, talk a little, and go away as he had done the night before. But how delicious it would be to have him there with her! She would have no regrets, nor seek to penetrate his reserve if he still chose to wear it.

Edna ate her breakfast only half dressed. The maid brought her a delicious printed scrawl from Raoul, expressing his love, asking her to send him some bonbons, and telling her they had found that morning ten tiny white pigs all lying in a row beside Lidie's big white pig.

A letter also came from her husband, saying he hoped to be back early in March, and then they would get ready for that journey abroad which he had promised her so long, which he felt now fully able to afford; he felt able to travel as people should, without any thought of small economies—thanks to his recent speculations in Wall Street.

Much to her surprise she received a note from Arobin, written at midnight from the club. It was to say good morning to her, to hope that she had slept well, to assure her of his devotion, which he trusted she in some faintest manner returned.

All these letters were pleasing to her. She answered the children in a cheerful frame of mind, promising them bonbons, and congratulating them upon their happy find of the little pigs.

She answered her husband with friendly evasiveness—not

with any fixed design to mislead him, only because all sense of reality had gone out of her life; she had abandoned herself to Fate, and awaited the consequences with indifference.

To Arobin's note she made no reply. She put it under Celestine's stove-lid.

Edna worked several hours with much spirit. She saw no one but a picture dealer, who asked her if it were true that she was going abroad to study in Paris.

She said possibly she might, and he negotiated with her for some Parisian studies to reach him in time for the holiday trade in December.

Robert did not come that day. She was keenly disappointed. He did not come the following day, nor the next. Each morning she awoke with hope, and each night she was a prey to despondency. She was tempted to seek him out. But far from yielding to the impulse, she avoided any occasion which might throw her in his way. She did not go to Mademoiselle Reisz's nor pass by Madame Lebrun's, as she might have done if he had still been in Mexico.

When Arobin, one night, urged her to drive with him, she went—out to the lake, on the Shell Road.* His horses were full of mettle, and even a little unmanageable. She liked the rapid gait at which they spun along, and the quick, sharp sound of the horses' hoofs on the hard road. They did not stop anywhere to eat or to drink. Arobin was not needlessly imprudent. But they ate and they drank when they regained Edna's little dining-room—which was comparatively early in the evening.

It was late when he left her. It was getting to be more than a passing whim with Arobin to see her and be with her. He had detected the latent sensuality, which unfolded under his delicate sense of her nature's requirements like a torpid, torrid, sensitive blossom.

---

* A smooth, level white road paved with shells leading to Lake Pontchartrain.

There was no despondency when she fell asleep that night; nor was there hope when she awoke in the morning.

XXXVI

∽

THERE WAS A GARDEN out in the suburbs; a small, leafy corner, with a few green tables under the orange trees. An old cat slept all day on the stone step in the sun, and an old *mulatresse** slept her idle hours away in her chair at the open window, till some one happened to knock on one of the green tables. She had milk and cream cheese to sell, and bread and butter. There was no one who could make such excellent coffee or fry a chicken so golden brown as she.

The place was too modest to attract the attention of people of fashion, and so quiet as to have escaped the notice of those in search of pleasure and dissipation. Edna had discovered it accidentally one day when the high-board gate stood ajar. She caught sight of a little green table, blotched with the checkered sunlight that filtered through the quivering leaves overhead. Within she had found the slumbering mulatresse, the drowsy cat, and a glass of milk which reminded her of the milk she had tasted in Iberville.

She often stopped there during her perambulations; sometimes taking a book with her, and sitting an hour or two under the trees when she found the place deserted. Once or twice she took a quiet dinner there alone, having instructed Celestine beforehand to prepare no dinner at home. It was the last place in the city where she would have expected to meet any one she knew.

Still she was not astonished when, as she was partaking of a

---

* A mulatto woman (Fr.); that is, one of mixed black and white heritage.

modest dinner late in the afternoon, looking into an open book, stroking the cat, which had made friends with her—she was not greatly astonished to see Robert come in at the tall garden gate.

"I am destined to see you only by accident," she said, shoving the cat off the chair beside her. He was surprised, ill at ease, almost embarrassed at meeting her thus so unexpectedly.

"Do you come here often?" he asked.

"I almost live here," she said.

"I used to drop in very often for a cup of Catiche's good coffee. This is the first time since I came back."

"She'll bring you a plate, and you will share my dinner. There's always enough for two—even three." Edna had intended to be indifferent and as reserved as he when she met him; she had reached the determination by a laborious train of reasoning, incident to one of her despondent moods. But her resolve melted when she saw him before her, seated there beside her in the little garden, as if a designing Providence had led him into her path.

"Why have you kept away from me, Robert?" she asked, closing the book that lay open upon the table.

"Why are you so personal, Mrs. Pontellier? Why do you force me to idiotic subterfuges?" he exclaimed with sudden warmth. "I suppose there's no use telling you I've been very busy, or that I've been sick, or that I've been to see you and not found you at home. Please let me off with any one of these excuses."

"You are the embodiment of selfishness," she said. "You save yourself something—I don't know what—but there is some selfish motive, and in sparing yourself you never consider for a moment what I think, or how I feel your neglect and indifference. I suppose this is what you would call unwomanly; but I have got into a habit of expressing myself. It doesn't matter to me, and you may think me unwomanly if you like."

"No; I only think you cruel, as I said the other day. Maybe

not intentionally cruel; but you seem to be forcing me into disclosures which can result in nothing; as if you would have me bare a wound for the pleasure of looking at it, without the intention or power of healing it."

"I'm spoiling your dinner, Robert; never mind what I say. You haven't eaten a morsel."

"I only came in for a cup of coffee." His sensitive face was all disfigured with excitement.

"Isn't this a delightful place?" she remarked. "I am so glad it has never actually been discovered. It is so quiet, so sweet, here. Do you notice there is scarcely a sound to be heard? It's so out of the way; and a good walk from the car. However, I don't mind walking. I always feel so sorry for women who don't like to walk; they miss so much—so many rare little glimpses of life; and we women learn so little of life on the whole."

"Catiche's coffee is always hot. I don't know how she manages it, here in the open air. Celestine's coffee gets cold bringing it from the kitchen to the dining-room. Three lumps! How can you drink it so sweet? Take some of the cress with your chop; it's so biting and crisp. Then there's the advantage of being able to smoke with your coffee out here. Now, in the city—aren't you going to smoke?"

"After a while," he said, laying a cigar on the table.

"Who gave it to you?" she laughed.

"I bought it. I suppose I'm getting reckless; I bought a whole box." She was determined not to be personal again and make him uncomfortable.

The cat made friends with him, and climbed into his lap when he smoked his cigar. He stroked her silky fur, and talked a little about her. He looked at Edna's book, which he had read; and he told her the end, to save her the trouble of wading through it, he said.

Again he accompanied her back to her home; and it was after dusk when they reached the little "pigeon-house." She did not ask him to remain, which he was grateful for, as it permitted him to stay without the discomfort of blundering through an excuse which he had no intention of considering. He helped her to light the lamp; then she went into her room to take off her hat and to bathe her face and hands.

When she came back Robert was not examining the pictures and magazines as before; he sat off in the shadow, leaning his head back on the chair as if in a reverie. Edna lingered a moment beside the table, arranging the books there. Then she went across the room to where he sat. She bent over the arm of his chair and called his name.

"Robert," she said, "are you asleep?"

"No," he answered, looking up at her.

She leaned over and kissed him—a soft, cool, delicate kiss, whose voluptuous sting penetrated his whole being—then she moved away from him. He followed, and took her in his arms, just holding her close to him. She put her hand up to his face and pressed his cheek against her own. The action was full of love and tenderness. He sought her lips again. Then he drew her down upon the sofa beside him and held her hand in both of his.

"Now you know," he said, "now you know what I have been fighting against since last summer at Grand Isle; what drove me away and drove me back again."

"Why have you been fighting against it?" she asked. Her face glowed with soft lights.

"Why? Because you were not free; you were Léonce Pontellier's wife. I couldn't help loving you if you were ten times his wife; but so long as I went away from you and kept away I could help telling you so." She put her free hand up to his shoulder, and then against his cheek, rubbing it softly. He kissed her again. His face was warm and flushed.

"There in Mexico I was thinking of you all the time, and longing for you."

"But not writing to me," she interrupted.

"Something put into my head that you cared for me; and I lost my senses. I forgot everything but a wild dream of your some way becoming my wife."

"Your wife!"

"Religion, loyalty, everything would give way if only you cared."

"Then you must have forgotten that I was Léonce Pontellier's wife."

"Oh! I was demented, dreaming of wild, impossible things, recalling men who had set their wives free, we have heard of such things."

"Yes, we have heard of such things."

"I came back full of vague, mad intentions. And when I got here—"

"When you got here you never came near me!" She was still caressing his cheek.

"I realized what a cur I was to dream of such a thing, even if you had been willing."

She took his face between her hands and looked into it as if she would never withdraw her eyes more. She kissed him on the forehead, the eyes, the cheeks, and the lips.

"You have been a very, very foolish boy, wasting your time dreaming of impossible things when you speak of Mr. Pontellier setting me free! I am no longer one of Mr. Pontellier's possessions to dispose of or not. I give myself where I choose. If he were to say, 'Here, Robert, take her and be happy; she is yours,' I should laugh at you both."

His face grew a little white. "What do you mean?" he asked.

There was a knock at the door. Old Celestine came in to say that Madame Ratignolle's servant had come around the back way with a message that Madame had been taken sick and begged Mrs. Pontellier to go to her immediately.

"Yes, yes," said Edna, rising; "I promised. Tell her yes—to wait for me. I'll go back with her."

"Let me walk over with you," offered Robert.

"No," she said; "I will go with the servant." She went into her room to put on her hat, and when she came in again she sat once more upon the sofa beside him. He had not stirred. She put her arms about his neck.

"Good-by, my sweet Robert. Tell me good-by." He kissed

her with a degree of passion which had not before entered into his caress, and strained her to him.

"I love you," she whispered, "only you; no one but you. It was you who awoke me last summer out of a life-long, stupid dream. Oh! you have made me so unhappy with your indifference. Oh! I have suffered, suffered! Now you are here we shall love each other, my Robert. We shall be everything to each other. Nothing else in the world is of any consequence. I must go to my friend; but you will wait for me? No matter how late; you will wait for me, Robert?"

"Don't go; don't go! Oh! Edna, stay with me," he pleaded. "Why should you go? Stay with me, stay with me."

"I shall come back as soon as I can; I shall find you here." She buried her face in his neck, and said good-by again. Her seductive voice, together with his great love for her, had enthralled his senses, had deprived him of every impulse but the longing to hold her and keep her.

XXXVII

∽

EDNA LOOKED IN AT the drug store. Monsieur Ratignolle was putting up a mixture himself, very carefully, dropping a red liquid into a tiny glass. He was grateful to Edna for having come; her presence would be a comfort to his wife. Madame Ratignolle's sister, who had always been with her at such trying times, had not been able to come up from the plantation, and Adèle had been inconsolable until Mrs. Pontellier so kindly promised to come to her. The nurse had been with them at night for the past week, as she lived a great distance away. And Dr. Mandelet had been coming and going all the afternoon. They were then looking for him any moment.

Edna hastened upstairs by a private stairway that led from the rear of the store to the apartments above. The children were all sleeping in a back room. Madame Ratignolle was in the salon, whither she had strayed in her suffering impatience. She sat on the sofa, clad in an ample white *peignoir*, holding a handkerchief tight in her hand with a nervous clutch. Her face was drawn and pinched, her sweet blue eyes haggard and unnatural. All her beautiful hair had been drawn back and plaited. It lay in a long braid on the sofa pillow, coiled like a golden serpent. The nurse, a comfortable-looking *Griffe** woman in white apron and cap, was urging her to return to her bedroom.

"There is no use, there is no use," she said at once to Edna. "We must get rid of Mandelet; he is getting too old and careless. He said he would be here at half-past seven; now it must be eight. See what time it is, Joséphine."

The woman was possessed of a cheerful nature, and refused to take any situation too seriously, especially a situation with which she was so familiar. She urged Madame to have courage and patience. But Madame only set her teeth hard into her under lip, and Edna saw the sweat gather in beads on her white forehead. After a moment or two she uttered a profound sigh and wiped her face with the handkerchief rolled in a ball. She appeared exhausted. The nurse gave her a fresh handkerchief, sprinkled with cologne water.

"This is too much!" she cried. "Mandelet ought to be killed! Where is Alphonse? Is it possible I am to be abandoned like this—neglected by every one?"

"Neglected, indeed!" exclaimed the nurse. Wasn't she there? And here was Mrs. Pontellier leaving, no doubt, a pleasant evening at home to devote to her? And wasn't Monsieur Ratignolle coming that very instant through the hall? And Joséphine was quite sure she had heard Doctor Mandelet's coupé. Yes, there it was, down at the door.

Adèle consented to go back to her room. She sat on the edge of a little low couch next to her bed.

Doctor Mandelet paid no attention to Madame

---

* The offspring of a black man and a mulatto woman.

Ratignolle's upbraidings. He was accustomed to them at such times, and was too well convinced of her loyalty to doubt it.

He was glad to see Edna, and wanted her to go with him into the salon and entertain him. But Madame Ratignolle would not consent that Edna should leave her for an instant. Between agonizing moments, she chatted a little, and said it took her mind off her sufferings.

Edna began to feel uneasy. She was seized with a vague dread. Her own like experiences seemed far away, unreal, and only half remembered. She recalled faintly an ecstasy of pain, the heavy odor of chloroform, a stupor which had deadened sensation, and an awakening to find a little new life to which she had given being, added to the great unnumbered multitude of souls that come and go.

She began to wish she had not come; her presence was not necessary. She might have invented a pretext for staying away; she might even invent a pretext now for going. But Edna did not go. With an inward agony, with a flaming, outspoken revolt against the ways of Nature, she witnessed the scene [of] torture.

She was still stunned and speechless with emotion when later she leaned over her friend to kiss her and softly say good-by. Adèle, pressing her cheek, whispered in an exhausted voice: "Think of the children, Edna. Oh think of the children! Remember them!"

XXXVIII

✑

EDNA STILL FELT DAZED when she got outside in the open air. The Doctor's coupé had returned for him and stood before the *porte cochère*. She did not wish to enter the coupé, and told Doctor Mandelet she would walk; she was not afraid, and would go alone. He directed his carriage to meet him at Mrs. Pontellier's, and he started to walk home with her.

Up—away up, over the narrow street between the tall houses, the stars were blazing. The air was mild and caressing, but cool with the breath of spring and the night. They walked slowly, the Doctor with a heavy, measured tread and his hands behind him; Edna, in an absent-minded way, as she had walked one night at Grand Isle, as if her thoughts had gone ahead of her and she was striving to overtake them.

"You shouldn't have been there, Mrs. Pontellier," he said. "That was no place for you. Adèle is full of whims at such times. There were a dozen women she might have had with her, unimpressionable women. I felt that it was cruel, cruel. You shouldn't have gone."

"Oh, well!" she answered, indifferently. "I don't know that it matters after all. One has to think of the children some time or other; the sooner the better."

"When is Léonce coming back?"

"Quite soon. Some time in March."

"And you are going abroad?"

"Perhaps—no, I am not going. I'm not going to be forced into doing things. I don't want to go abroad. I want to be let alone. Nobody has any right—except children, perhaps—and even then, it seems to me—or it did seem—" She felt that her speech was voicing the incoherency of her thoughts, and stopped abruptly.

"The trouble is," sighed the Doctor, grasping her meaning intuitively, "that youth is given up to illusions. It seems to be a provision of Nature; a decoy to secure mothers for the race. And Nature takes no account of moral consequences, of arbitrary conditions which we create, and which we feel obliged to maintain at any cost."

"Yes," she said. "The years that are gone seem like dreams—if one might go on sleeping and dreaming—but to wake up and find—oh! well! perhaps it is better to wake up after all, even to suffer, rather than to remain a dupe to illusions all one's life."

"It seems to me, my dear child," said the Doctor at parting, holding her hand, "you seem to me to be in trouble. I am not

going to ask for your confidence. I will only say that if ever
you feel moved to give it to me, perhaps I might help you. I
know I would understand, and I tell you there are not many
who would—not many, my dear."

"Some way I don't feel moved to speak of things that trouble me. Don't think I am ungrateful or that I don't appreciate
your sympathy. There are periods of despondency and suffering which take possession of me. But I don't want anything
but my own way. That is wanting a good deal, of course, when
you have to trample upon the lives, the hearts, the prejudices
of others—but no matter—still, I shouldn't want to trample
upon the little lives. Oh! I don't know what I'm saying,
Doctor. Good-night. Don't blame me for anything."

"Yes, I will blame you if you don't come and see me soon.
We will talk of things you never have dreamt of talking about
before. It will do us both good. I don't want you to blame
yourself, whatever comes. Good-night, my child."

She let herself in at the gate, but instead of entering she sat
upon the step of the porch. The night was quiet and soothing.
All the tearing emotion of the last few hours seemed to fall
away from her like a somber, uncomfortable garment, which
she had but to loosen to be rid of. She went back to that hour
before Adèle had sent for her; and her senses kindled afresh in
thinking of Robert's words, the pressure of his arms, and the
feeling of his lips upon her own. She could picture at that moment no greater bliss on earth than possession of the beloved
one. His expression of love had already given him to her in
part. When she thought that he was there at hand, waiting for
her, she grew numb with the intoxication of expectancy. It
was so late; he would be asleep perhaps. She would awaken
him with a kiss. She hoped he would be asleep that she might
arouse him with her caresses.

Still, she remembered Adèle's voice whispering, "Think of
the children; think of them." She meant to think of them; that
determination had driven into her soul like a death wound—
but not to-night. To-morrow would be time to think of everything.

Robert was not waiting for her in the little parlor. He was nowhere at hand. The house was empty. But he had scrawled on a piece of paper that lay in the lamp-light:

"I love you. Good-by—because I love you."

Edna grew faint when she read the words. She went and sat on the sofa. Then she stretched herself out there, never uttering a sound. She did not sleep. She did not go to bed. The lamp sputtered and went out. She was still awake in the morning, when Celestine unlocked the kitchen door and came in to light the fire.

XXXIX

∽

VICTOR, WITH HAMMER AND nails and scraps of scantling,* was patching a corner of one of the galleries. Mariequita sat near by, dangling her legs, watching him work, and handing him nails from the tool-box. The sun was beating down upon them. The girl had covered her head with her apron folded into a square pad. They had been talking for an hour or more. She was never tired of hearing Victor describe the dinner at Mrs. Pontellier's. He exaggerated every detail, making it appear a veritable Lucillean† feast. The flowers were in tubs, he said. The champagne was quaffed from huge golden goblets. Venus rising from the foam‡ could have presented no more entrancing a spectacle than Mrs. Pontellier, blazing with

---

* Small pieces of lumber used for house framing.

† The reference is to Lucius Licinus Lucullus, a Roman general of the first century A.D. who was famous for his banquets.

‡ Venus, the Roman goddess of love and fertility, known for her romantic intrigues and affairs with both gods and mortals. The daughter of Jupiter and Dione, she is said to have emerged full-grown from the ocean foam.

beauty and diamonds at the head of the board, while the other women were all of them youthful houris,* possessed of incomparable charms.

She got it into her head that Victor was in love with Mrs. Pontellier, and he gave her evasive answers, framed so as to confirm her belief. She grew sullen and cried a little, threatening to go off and leave him to his fine ladies. There were a dozen men crazy about her at the *Chênière*; and since it was the fashion to be in love with married people, why, she could run away any time she liked to New Orleans with Célina's husband.

Célina's husband was a fool, a coward, and a pig, and to prove it to her, Victor intended to hammer his head into a jelly the next time he encountered him. This assurance was very consoling to Mariequita. She dried her eyes, and grew cheerful at the prospect.

They were still talking of the dinner and the allurements of city life when Mrs. Pontellier herself slipped around the corner of the house. The two youngsters stayed dumb with amazement before what they considered to be an apparition. But it was really she in flesh and blood, looking tired and a little travel-stained.

"I walked up from the wharf," she said, "and heard the hammering. I supposed it was you, mending the porch. It's a good thing. I was always tripping over those loose planks last summer. How dreary and deserted everything looks!"

It took Victor some little time to comprehend that she had come in Beaudelet's lugger, that she had come alone, and for no purpose but to rest.

"There's nothing fixed up yet, you see. I'll give you my room; it's the only place."

"Any corner will do," she assured him.

"And if you can stand Philomel's cooking," he went on, "though I might try to get her mother while you are here. Do you think she would come?" turning to Mariequita.

---

* Voluptuously beautiful virgins.

Mariequita thought that perhaps Philomel's mother might come for a few days, and money enough.

Beholding Mrs. Pontellier make her appearance, the girl had at once suspected a lovers' rendezvous. But Victor's astonishment was so genuine, and Mrs. Pontellier's indifference so apparent, that the disturbing notion did not lodge long in her brain. She contemplated with the greatest interest this woman who gave the most sumptuous dinners in America, and who had all the men in New Orleans at her feet.

"What time will you have dinner?" asked Edna. "I'm very hungry; but don't get anything extra."

"I'll have it ready in little or no time," he said, bustling and packing away his tools. "You may go to my room to brush up and rest yourself. Mariequita will show you."

"Thank you," said Edna. "But, do you know, I have a notion to go down to the beach and take a good wash and even a little swim, before dinner?"

"The water is too cold!" they both exclaimed. "Don't think of it."

"Well, I might go down and try—dip my toes in. Why, it seems to me the sun is hot enough to have warmed the very depths of the ocean. Could you get me a couple of towels? I'd better go right away, so as to be back in time. It would be a little too chilly if I waited till this afternoon."

Mariequita ran over to Victor's room, and returned with some towels, which she gave to Edna.

"I hope you have fish for dinner," said Edna, as she started to walk away; "but don't do anything extra if you haven't."

"Run and find Philomel's mother," Victor instructed the girl. "I'll go to the kitchen and see what I can do. By Gimminy! Women have no consideration! She might have sent me word."

Edna walked on down to the beach rather mechanically, not noticing anything special except that the sun was hot. She was not dwelling upon any particular train of thought. She had done all the thinking which was necessary after Robert went away, when she lay awake upon the sofa till morning.

She had said over and over to herself: "To-day it is Arobin; to-morrow it will be some one else. It makes no difference to me, it doesn't matter about Léonce Pontellier—but Raoul and Étienne!" She understood now clearly what she had meant long ago when she said to Adèle Ratignolle that she would give up the unessential, but she would never sacrifice herself for her children.

Despondency had come upon her there in the wakeful night, and had never lifted. There was no one thing in the world that she desired. There was no human being whom she wanted near her except Robert; and she even realized that the day would come when he, too, and the thought of him would melt out of her existence, leaving her alone. The children appeared before her like antagonists who had overcome her; who had overpowered and sought to drag her into the soul's slavery for the rest of her days. But she knew a way to elude them. She was not thinking of these things when she walked down to the beach.

The water of the Gulf stretched out before her, gleaming with the million lights of the sun. The voice of the sea is seductive, never ceasing, whispering, clamoring, murmuring, inviting the soul to wander in abysses of solitude. All along the white beach, up and down, there was no living thing in sight. A bird with a broken wing was beating the air above, reeling, fluttering, circling disabled down, down to the water.

Edna had found her old bathing suit still hanging, faded, upon its accustomed peg.

She put it on, leaving her clothing in the bath-house. But when she was there beside the sea, absolutely alone, she cast the unpleasant, pricking garments from her, and for the first time in her life she stood naked in the open air, at the mercy of the sun, the breeze that beat upon her, and the waves that invited her.

How strange and awful it seemed to stand naked under the sky! how delicious! She felt like some new-born creature, opening its eyes in a familiar world that it had never known.

The foamy wavelets curled up to her white feet, and coiled

like serpents about her ankles. She walked out. The water was chill, but she walked on. The water was deep, but she lifted her white body and reached out with a long, sweeping stroke. The touch of the sea is sensuous, enfolding the body in its soft, close embrace.

She went on and on. She remembered the night she swam far out, and recalled the terror that seized her at the fear of being unable to regain the shore. She did not look back now, but went on and on, thinking of the blue-grass meadow that she had traversed when a little child, believing that it had no beginning and no end.

Her arms and legs were growing tired.

She thought of Léonce and the children. They were a part of her life. But they need not have thought that they could possess her, body and soul. How Mademoiselle Reisz would have laughed, perhaps sneered, if she knew! "And you call yourself an artist! What pretensions, Madame! The artist must possess the courageous soul that dares and defies."

Exhaustion was pressing upon and over-powering her.

"Good-by—because I love you." He did not know; he did not understand. He would never understand. Perhaps Doctor Mandelet would have understood if she had seen him—but it was too late; the shore was far behind her, and her strength was gone.

She looked into the distance, and the old terror flamed up for an instant, then sank again. Edna heard her father's voice and her sister Margaret's. She heard the barking of an old dog that was chained to the sycamore tree. The spurs of the cavalry officer clanged as he walked across the porch. There was the hum of bees, and the musky odor of pinks filled the air.

Selected Short Fiction

EMANCIPATION: A LIFE FABLE

THERE WAS ONCE AN animal born into this world, and opening his eyes upon Life, he saw above and about him confining walls, and before him were bars of iron through which came air and light from without; this animal was born in a cage.

Here he grew, and throve in strength and beauty under care of an invisible protecting hand. Hungering, food was ever at hand. When he thirsted water was brought, and when he felt the need of rest, there was provided a bed of straw upon which to lie: and here he found it good, licking his handsome flanks, to bask in the sun beam that he thought existed but to lighten his home.

Awaking one day from his slothful rest, lo! the door of his cage stood open: accident had opened it. In the corner he crouched, wondering and fearingly. Then slowly did he approach the door, dreading the unaccustomed, and would have closed it, but for such a task his limbs were purposeless. So out the opening he thrust his head, to see the canopy of the sky grow broader, and the world waxing wider.

Back to his corner but not to rest, for the spell of the Unknown was over him, and again and again he goes to the open door, seeing each time more Light.

Then one time standing in the flood of it; a deep in-drawn breath—a bracing of strong limbs, and with a bound he was gone.

On he rushes, in his mad flight, heedless that he is wounding and tearing his sleek sides—seeing, smelling, touching of all things; even stopping to put his lips to the noxious pool, thinking it may be sweet.

Hungering there is no food but such as he must seek and ofttimes fight for; and his limbs are weighted before he reaches the water that is good to his thirsting throat.

So does he live, seeking, finding, joying and suffering. The door which accident had opened is open still, but the cage remains forever empty!

A SHAMEFUL AFFAIR

∽

I

MILDRED ORME, SEATED IN the snuggest corner of the big front porch of the Kraummer farmhouse, was as content as a girl need hope to be.

This was no such farm as one reads about in humorous fiction. Here were swelling acres where the undulating wheat gleamed in the sun like a golden sea. For silver there was the Meramec* — or, better, it was pure crystal, for here and there one might look clean through it down to where the pebbles lay like green and yellow gems. Along the river's edge trees were growing to the very water, and in it, sweeping it when they were willows.

The house itself was big and broad, as country houses should be. The master was big and broad, too. The mistress was small and thin, and it was always she who went out at noon to pull the great clanging bell that called the farmhands in to dinner.

From her agreeable corner where she lounged with her Browning or her Ibsen,† Mildred watched the woman do this every day. Yet when the clumsy farmhands all came tramping up the steps and crossed the porch in going to their meal that was served within, she never looked at them. Why should she?

---

* A river feeding into the Mississippi.

† The reference to Browning and Ibsen distinguishes Mildred as a woman with sophisticated literary tastes from the farmhands who surround her. Robert Browning (1812–1889) was a major English poet noted for his mastery of dramatic monologue and psychological portraiture; Henrik Ibsen (1828–1906) was a Norwegian playwright perhaps best known for his socially realistic plays that addressed and defied the conventions of established 19th-century society.

160

Farmhands are not so very nice to look at, and she was nothing of an anthropologist. But once when the half dozen men came along, a paper which she had laid carelessly upon the railing was blown across their path. One of them picked it up, and when he had mounted the steps restored it to her. He was young, and brown, of course, as the sun had made him. He had nice blue eyes. His fair hair was dishevelled. His shoulders were broad and square and his limbs strong and clean. A not unpicturesque figure in the rough attire that bared his throat to view and gave perfect freedom to his every motion.

Mildred did not make these several observations in the half second that she looked at him in courteous acknowledgment. It took her as many days to note them all. For she signaled him out each time that he passed her, meaning to give him a condescending little smile, as she knew how. But he never looked at her. To be sure, clever young women of twenty, who are handsome, besides, who have refused their half dozen offers and are settling down to the conviction that life is a tedious affair, are not going to care a straw whether farmhands look at them or not. And Mildred did not care, and the thing would not have occupied her a moment if Satan had not intervened, in offering the employment which natural conditions had failed to supply. It was summer time; she was idle; she was piqued, and that was the beginning of the shameful affair.

"Who are these men, Mrs. Kraummer, that work for you? Where do you pick them up?"

"Oh, ve picks 'em up everyvere. Some is neighbors, some is tramps, and so."

"And that broad-shouldered young fellow—is he a neighbor? The one who handed me my paper the other day—you remember?"

"Gott, no! You might yust as well say he vas a tramp. Aber he vorks like a steam ingine."

"Well, he's an extremely disagreeable-looking man. I should think you'd be afraid to have him about, not knowing him."

"Vat you vant to be 'fraid for?" laughed the little woman. "He don't talk no more un ven he vas deef und dumb. I didn't t'ought you vas sooch a baby."

"But, Mrs. Kraummer, I don't want you to think I'm a baby, as you say—a coward, as you mean. Ask the man if he will drive me to church to-morrow. You see, I'm not so very much afraid of him," she added with a smile.

The answer which this unmannerly farmhand returned to Mildred's request was simply a refusal. He could not drive her to church because he was going fishing.

"Aber," offered good Mrs. Kraummer, "Hans Platzfeldt will drive you to church, oder vereever you vants. He vas a goot boy vat you can trust, dat Hans."

"Oh, thank him very much. But I find I have so many letters to write to-morrow, and it promises to be hot, too. I shan't care to go to church after all."

She could have cried for vexation. Snubbed by a farmhand! a tramp, perhaps. She, Mildred Orme, who ought really to have been with the rest of the family at Narragansett*—who had come to seek in this retired spot the repose that would enable her to follow exalted lines of thought. She marveled at the problematic nature of farmhands.

After sending her the uncivil message already recorded, and as he passed beneath the porch where she sat, he did look at her finally, in a way to make her positively gasp at the sudden effrontery of the man.

But the inexplicable look stayed with her. She could not banish it.

II

IT WAS NOT SO very hot after all, the next day, when Mildred walked down the long narrow footpath that led through the bending wheat to the river. High above her waist reached the

---

* A town in southern Rhode Island.

yellow grain. Mildred's brown eyes filled with a reflected golden light as they caught the glint of it, as she heard the trill that it answered to the gentle breeze. Anyone who has walked through the wheat in mid-summer time knows that sound.

In the woods it was sweet and solemn and cool. And there beside the river was the wretch who had annoyed her, first, with his indifference, then with the sudden boldness of his glance.

"Are you fishing?" she asked politely and with kindly dignity, which she supposed would define her position toward him. The inquiry lacked not pertinence, seeing that he sat motionless, with a pole in his hand and his eyes fixed on a cork that bobbed aimlessly on the water.

"Yes, madam," was his brief reply.

"It won't disturb you if I stand here a moment, to see what success you will have?"

"No, madam."

She stood very still, holding tight to the book she had brought with her. Her straw hat had slipped disreputably to one side, over the wavy bronze-brown bang that half covered her forehead. Her cheeks were ripe with color that the sun had coaxed there; so were her lips.

All the other farmhands had gone forth in Sunday attire. Perhaps this one had none better than these working clothes that he wore. A feminine commiseration swept her at the thought. He spoke never a word. She wondered how many hours he could sit there, so patiently waiting for fish to come to his hook. For her part, the situation began to pall, and she wanted to change it at last.

"Let me try a moment, please? I have an idea—"

"Yes, madam."

"The man is surely an idiot, with his monosyllables," she commented inwardly. But she remembered that monosyllables belong to a boor's* equipment.

She laid her book carefully down and took the pole gin-

---

* "Boor" in this context means peasant.

gerly that he came to place in her hands. Then it was his turn to stand back and look respectfully and silently on at the absorbing performance.

"Oh!" cried the girl, suddenly, seized with excitement upon seeing the line dragged deep in the water.

"Wait, wait! Not yet."

He sprang to her side. With his eyes eagerly fastened on the tense line, he grasped the pole to prevent her drawing it, as her intention seemed to be. That is, he meant to grasp the pole, but instead, his brown hand came down upon Mildred's white one.

He started violently at finding himself so close to a bronze-brown tangle that almost swept his chin—to a hot cheek only a few inches away from his shoulder, to a pair of young, dark eyes that gleamed for an instant unconscious things into his own.

Then, why ever it happened, or how ever it happened, his arms were holding Mildred and he kissed her lips. She did not know if it was ten times or only once.

She looked around—her face milk-white—to see him disappear with rapid strides through the path that had brought her there. Then she was alone.

Only the birds had seen, and she could count on their discretion. She was not wildly indignant, as many would have been. Shame stunned her. But through it she gropingly wondered if she should tell the Kraummers that her chaste lips had been rifled of their innocence. Publish her own confusion? No! Once in her room she would give calm thought to the situation, and determine then how to act. The secret must remain her own: a hateful burden to bear alone until she could forget it.

III

AND BECAUSE SHE feared not to forget it, Mildred wept that night. All day long a hideous truth had been thrusting itself upon her that made her ask herself if she could be mad. She feared it. Else why was that kiss the most delicious thing she had known in her twenty years of life? The sting of it had never left her lips since it was pressed into them. The sweet trouble of it banished sleep from her pillow.

But Mildred would not bend the outward conditions of her life to serve any shameful whim that chanced to visit her soul, like an ugly dream. She would avoid nothing. She would go and come as always.

In the morning she found in her chair upon the porch the book she had left by the river. A fresh indignity! But she came and went as she intended to, and sat as usual upon the porch amid her familiar surroundings. When the Offender passed her by she knew it, though her eyes were never lifted. Are there only sight and sound to tell such things? She discerned it by a wave that swept her with confusion and she knew not what besides.

She watched him furtively, one day, when he talked with Farmer Kraummer out in the open. When he walked away she remained like one who has drunk much wine. Then unhesitatingly she turned and began her preparations to leave the Kraummer farmhouse.

When the afternoon was far spent they brought letters to her. One of them read like this:

"My Mildred, deary! I am only now at Narragansett, and so broke up not to find you. So you are down at that Kraummer farm, on the Iron Mountain. Well! What do you think of that delicious crank, Fred Evelyn? For a man must be a crank who does such things. Only fancy! Last year he chose to drive an engine back and forth across the plains. This year he tills the soil with laborers. Next year it will be something else as insane—because he likes to live more lives than one kind, and other Quixotic* reasons. We are great chums. He writes me

---

* Capricious, unpredictable; an allusion to the novel *Don Quixote*, by Miguel de Cervantes (1547–1616), about an idealist who traveled the countryside in pursuit of romantic adventures.

he's grown as strong as an ox. But he hasn't mentioned that you are there. I know you don't get on with him, for he isn't a bit intellectual—detests Ibsen and abuses Tolstoi.* He doesn't read 'in books'—says they are spectacles for the short-sighted to look at life through. Don't snub him, dear, or be too hard on him; he has a heart of gold, if he is the first crank in America."

Mildred tried to think—to feel that the intelligence which this letter brought to her would take somewhat of the sting from the shame that tortured her. But it did not. She knew that it could not.

In the gathering twilight she walked again through the wheat that was heavy and fragrant with dew. The path was very long and very narrow. When she was midway she saw the Offender coming toward her. What could she do? Turn and run, as a little child might? Spring into the wheat, as some frightened four-footed creature would? There was nothing but to pass him with the dignity which the occasion clearly demanded.

But he did not let her pass. He stood squarely in the pathway before her, hat in hand, a perturbed look upon his face.

"Miss Orme," he said, "I have wanted to say to you, every hour of the past week, that I am the most consummate hound that walks the earth."

She made no protest. Her whole bearing seemed to indicate that her opinion coincided with his own.

"If you have a father, or brother, or any one, in short, to whom you may say such things—"

"I think you aggravate the offense, sir, by speaking of it. I shall ask you never to mention it again. I want to forget that it ever happened. Will you kindly let me by."

"Oh," he ventured eagerly, "you want to forget it! Then, maybe, since you are willing to forget, you will be generous enough to forgive the offender some day?"

"Some day," she repeated, almost inaudibly, looking seem-

---

* Leo Tolstoi (1828–1910), great Russian author of realist fiction.

ingly through him, but not at him—"some day—perhaps; when I shall have forgiven myself."

He stood motionless, watching her slim, straight figure lessening by degrees as she walked slowly away from him. He was wondering what she meant. Then a sudden, quick wave came beating into his brown throat and staining it crimson, when he guessed what it might be.

AT THE 'CADIAN* BALL

❧

BOBINÔT, THAT BIG, BROWN, good-natured Bobinôt, had no
intention of going to the ball, even though he knew Calixta
would be there. For what came of those balls but heartache,
and a sickening disinclination for work the whole week
through, till Saturday night came again and his tortures began
afresh? Why could he not love Ozéina, who would marry him
to-morrow; or Fronie, or any one of a dozen others, rather
than that little Spanish vixen? Calixta's slender foot had never
touched Cuban soil; but her mother's had, and the Spanish
was in her blood all the same. For that reason the prairie people forgave her much that they would not have overlooked in
their own daughters or sisters.

Her eyes—Bobinôt thought of her eyes, and weakened—
the bluest, the drowsiest, most tantalizing that ever looked
into a man's; he thought of her flaxen hair that kinked worse
than a mulatto's close to her head; that broad, smiling mouth
and tip-tilted nose, that full figure; that voice like a rich con-
tralto song, with cadences in it that must have been taught by
Satan, for there was no one else to teach her tricks on that
'Cadian prairie. Bobinôt thought of them all as he plowed his
rows of cane.

There had even been a breath of scandal whispered about
her a year ago, when she went to Assumption[†]—but why talk
of it? No one did now. "C'est Espagnol, ça,"[‡] most of them said
with lenient shoulder-shrugs. "Bon chien tient de race,"[§] the
old men mumbled over their pipes, stirred by recollections.

---

* Acadian; see The Awakening, chap. XIII, p. 48.

† A parish in southeastern Louisiana.

‡ That's the Spanish (Fr.). The old men attribute Calixta's wayward
behavior to her Spanish blood.

§ A good dog shows its breeding (Fr.), a version of a French proverb,
"Children take after their parents."

Nothing was made of it, except that Fronie threw it up to Calixta when the two quarreled and fought on the church steps after mass one Sunday, about a lover. Calixta swore roundly in fine 'Cadian French and with true Spanish spirit, and slapped Fronie's face. Fronie had slapped her back; *"Tiens, cocotte, va!"* *"Espèce de lionèse; prends ça, et ça!"** till the curé† himself was obliged to hasten and make peace between them. Bobinôt thought of it all, and would not go to the ball.

But in the afternoon, over at Friedheimer's store, where he was buying a trace-chain, he heard some one say that Alcée Laballière would be there. Then wild horses could not have kept him away. He knew how it would be—or rather he did not know how it would be—if the handsome young planter came over to the ball as he sometimes did. If Alcée happened to be in a serious mood, he might only go to the card-room and play a round or two; or he might stand out on the galleries talking crops and politics with the old people. But there was no telling. A drink or two could put the devil in his head—that was what Bobinôt said to himself, as he wiped the sweat from his brow with his red bandana; a gleam from Calixta's eyes, a flash of her ankle, a twirl of her skirts could do the same. Yes, Bobinôt would go to the ball.

That was the year Alcée Laballière put nine hundred acres in rice. It was putting a good deal of money into the ground, but the returns promised to be glorious. Old Madame Laballière, sailing about the spacious galleries in her white *volante*,‡ figured it all out in her head. Clarisse, her goddaughter, helped her a little, and together they built more air-castles than enough. Alcée worked like a mule that time; and if he did not kill himself, it was because his constitution was an iron one. It was an every-day affair for him to come in from the field well-nigh exhausted, and wet to the waist. He did not

---

* An insult: "Hey, bitch! You lioness, take that and that!" (Fr.).

† Pastor (Fr.).

‡ A billowing robe; Creole term for a loosely hanging garment.

mind if there were visitors; he left them to his mother and Clarisse. There were often guests: young men and women who came up from the city, which was but a few hours away, to visit his beautiful kinswoman. She was worth going a good deal farther than that to see. Dainty as a lily; hardy as a sunflower; slim, tall, graceful, like one of the reeds that grew in the marsh. Cold and kind and cruel by turn, and everything that was aggravating to Alcée.

He would have liked to sweep the place of those visitors, often. Of the men, above all, with their ways and their manners; their swaying of fans like women, and dandling about hammocks. He could have pitched them over the levee into the river, if it hadn't meant murder. That was Alcée. But he must have been crazy the day he came in from the rice-field, and, toil-stained as he was, clasped Clarisse by the arms and panted a volley of hot, blistering love-words into her face. No man had ever spoken love to her like that.

"Monsieur!" she exclaimed, looking him full in the eyes, without a quiver. Alcée's hands dropped and his glance wavered before the chill of her calm, clear eyes.

"*Par exemple!*"* she muttered disdainfully, as she turned from him, deftly adjusting the careful toilet that he had so brutally disarranged.

That happened a day or two before the cyclone came that cut into the rice like fine steel. It was an awful thing, coming so swiftly, without a moment's warning in which to light a holy candle or set a piece of blessed palm burning.† Old madame wept openly and said her beads, just as her son Didier, the New Orleans one, would have done. If such a thing had happened to Alphonse, the Laballière planting cotton up in Natchitoches,‡ he would have raved and stormed

---

* Honestly! (Fr.).

† Roman Catholic rituals to request divine protection.

‡ Pronounced "Nack-e-tosh"; a parish in northwest Louisiana, birthplace of Oscar Chopin (husband of Kate) and home to the Chopin family during the 1880s.

like a second cyclone, and made his surroundings unbearable
for a day or two. But Alcée took the misfortune differently. He
looked ill and gray after it, and said nothing. His speechless-
ness was frightful. Clarisse's heart melted with tenderness; but
when she offered her soft, purring words of condolence, he
accepted them with mute indifference. Then she and her *nénaine** wept afresh in each other's arms.

A night or two later, when Clarisse went to her window to
kneel there in the moonlight and say her prayers before retiring, she saw that Bruce, Alcée's negro servant, had led his
master's saddle-horse noiselessly along the edge of the sward
that bordered the gravel-path, and stood holding him near by.
Presently, she heard Alcée quit his room, which was beneath
her own, and traverse the lower portico. As he emerged from
the shadow and crossed the strip of moonlight, she perceived
that he carried a pair of well-filled saddle-bags which he at
once flung across the animal's back. He then lost no time in
mounting, and after a brief exchange of words with Bruce,
went cantering away, taking no precaution to avoid the noisy
gravel as the negro had done.

Clarisse had never suspected that it might be Alcée's custom to sally forth from the plantation secretly, and at such an
hour; for it was nearly midnight. And had it not been for the
telltale saddle-bags, she would only have crept to bed, to wonder, to fret and dream unpleasant dreams. But her impatience
and anxiety would not be held in check. Hastily unbolting the
shutters of her door that opened upon the gallery, she stepped
outside and called softly to the old negro.

"Gre't Peter! Miss Clarisse. I was n' sho it was a ghos' o'
w'at, stan'in' up dah, plumb in de night, dataway."

He mounted halfway up the long, broad flight of stairs.
She was standing at the top.

"Bruce, w'ere has Monsieur Alcée gone?" she asked.

"W'y, he gone 'bout he business, I reckin," replied Bruce,
striving to be non-committal at the outset.

---

* Godmother (Fr.).

"W'ere has Monsieur Alcée gone?" she reiterated, stamping her bare foot. "I won't stan' any nonsense or any lies; mine, Bruce."

"I don't ric'lic ez I eva tole you lie *yit*, Miss Clarisse. Mista Alcée, he all broke up, sho."

"W'ere—has—he gone? Ah, *Sainte Vierge! faut de la patience! butor, va!*"*

"W'en I was in he room, a-breshin' off he clo'es to-day," the darky began, settling himself against the stair-rail, "he look dat speechless an' down, I say, 'You 'pear to me like some pussun w'at gwine have a spell o' sickness, Mista Alcée.' He say, 'You reckin?' 'I dat he git up, go look hisse'f stiddy in de glass. Den he go to de chimbly an' jerk up de quinine† bottle an' po' a gre't hoss-dose‡ on to he han'. An' he swalla dat mess in a wink, an' wash hit down wid a big dram o' w'iskey w'at he keep in he room, aginst he come all soppin' wet outen de fiel'.

"He 'lows, 'No, I ain' gwine be sick, Bruce.' Den he square off. He say, 'I kin mak out to stan' up an' gi' an' take wid any man I knows, lessen hit's John L. Sulvun. But w'en God A'mighty an' a 'oman jines fo'ces agin me, dat 's one too many fur me.' I tell 'im, 'Jis so,' whils' I 'se makin' out to bresh a spot off w'at ain' dah, on he coat colla. I tell 'im, 'You wants li'le res', suh.' He say, 'No, I wants li'le fling; dat w'at I wants; an' I gwine git it. Pitch me a fis'ful o' clo'es in dem 'ar saddlebags.' Dat w'at he say. Don't you bodda, missy. He jis' gone a-caperin' yonda to de Cajun ball. Uh—uh—de skeeters is fair' a-swarmin' like bees roun' yo' foots!"

The mosquitoes were indeed attacking Clarisse's white feet savagely. She had unconsciously been alternately rubbing one foot over the other during the darky's recital.

"The 'Cadian ball," she repeated contemptuously. "Humph! *Par exemple!* Nice conduc' for a Laballière. An' he

---

* Holy Virgin! Give me patience! Brute, get away! (Fr.).

† A bitter medicine used as an anesthetic and muscle relaxant.

‡ Large quantity, an amount suitable for a horse.

needs a saddle-bag, fill' with clothes, to go to the 'Cadian
ball!"

"Oh, Miss Clarisse; you go on to bed, chile; git yo' soun'
sleep. He 'low he come back in couple weeks o' so. I kiarn be
repeatin' lot o' truck w'at young mans say, out heah face o'
young gal."

Clarisse said no more, but turned and abruptly reëntered
the house.

"You done talk too much wid yo' mouf a'ready, you ole
fool nigga, you," muttered Bruce to himself as he walked
away.

Alcée reached the ball very late, of course—too late for the
chicken gumbo which had been served at midnight.

The big, low-ceiled room—they called it a hall—was
packed with men and women dancing to the music of three
fiddles. There were broad galleries all around it. There was a
room at one side where sober-faced men were playing cards.
Another, in which babies were sleeping, was called *le parc
aux petits.** Any one who is white may go to a 'Cadian ball,
but he must pay for his lemonade, his coffee and chicken
gumbo. And he must behave himself like a 'Cadian.
Grosboeuf was giving this ball. He had been giving them
since he was a young man, and he was a middle-aged one,
now. In that time he could recall but one disturbance, and
that was caused by American railroaders, who were not in
touch with their surroundings and had no business there.
"Ces maudits gens du raiderode,"† Grosboeuf called them.

Alcée Laballière's presence at the ball caused a flutter
even among the men, who could not but admire his "nerve"
after such misfortune befalling him. To be sure, they knew
the Laballières were rich—that there were resources East,
and more again in the city. But they felt it took a *brave
homme*‡ to stand a blow like that philosophically. One old

---

* Children's room (Fr.), a traditional feature of Acadian balls.

† These damn people from the railroad (Fr.).

‡ Good man (Fr.).

gentleman, who was in the habit of reading a Paris newspaper and knew things, chuckled gleefully to everybody that Alcée's conduct was altogether *chic, mais chic*.* That he had more *panache*† than Boulanger.‡ Well, perhaps he had.

But what he did not show outwardly was that he was in a mood for ugly things to-night. Poor Bobinôt alone felt it vaguely. He discerned a gleam of it in Alcée's handsome eyes, as the young planter stood in the doorway, looking with rather feverish glance upon the assembly, while he laughed and talked with a 'Cadian farmer who was beside him.

Bobinôt himself was dull-looking and clumsy. Most of the men were. But the young women were very beautiful. The eyes that glanced into Alcée's as they passed him were big, dark, soft as those of the young heifers standing out in the cool prairie grass.

But the belle was Calixta. Her white dress was not nearly so handsome or well made as Fronie's (she and Fronie had quite forgotten the battle on the church steps, and were friends again), nor were her slippers so stylish as those of Ozéina; and she fanned herself with a handkerchief, since she had broken her red fan at the last ball, and her aunts and uncles were not willing to give her another. But all the men agreed she was at her best to-night. Such animation! and abandon! such flashes of wit!

"*Hé*, Bobinôt! *Mais* w'at 's the matta?§ W'at you standin' *planté là*‖ like ole Ma'ame Tina's cow in the bog, you?"

That was good. That was an excellent thrust at Bobinôt, who had forgotten the figure of the dance with his mind bent on other things, and it started a clamor of laughter at his ex-

---

* Fashionable, how fashionable (Fr.).

† Dash or flamboyance of style (Fr.).

‡ General Georges Boulanger (1837–1891), a charismatic French politician who died romantically by committing suicide when he was charged with treason.

§ But what's the matter? (Fr.).

‖ Planted there (Fr.).

pense. He joined good-naturedly. It was better to receive even such notice as that from Calixta than none at all. But Madame Suzonne, sitting in a corner, whispered to her neighbor that if Ozéina were to conduct herself in a like manner, she should immediately be taken out to the mule-cart and driven home. The women did not always approve of Calixta.

Now and then were short lulls in the dance, when couples flocked out upon the galleries for a brief respite and fresh air. The moon had gone down pale in the west, and in the east was yet no promise of day. After such an interval, when the dancers again assembled to resume the interrupted quadrille, Calixta was not among them.

She was sitting upon a bench out in the shadow, with Alcée beside her. They were acting like fools. He had attempted to take a little gold ring from her finger; just for the fun of it, for there was nothing he could have done with the ring but replace it again. But she clinched her hand tight. He pretended that it was a very difficult matter to open it. Then he kept the hand in his. They seemed to forget about it. He played with her earring, a thin crescent of gold hanging from her small brown ear. He caught a wisp of the kinky hair that had escaped its fastening, and rubbed the ends of it against his shaven cheek.

"You know, last year in Assumption, Calixta?" They belonged to the younger generation, so preferred to speak English.

"Don't come say Assumption to me, M'sieur Alcée. I done yeard Assumption till I'm plumb sick."

"Yes, I know. The idiots! Because you were in Assumption, and I happened to go to Assumption, they must have it that we went together. But it was nice—*hein,*° Calixta?—in Assumption?"

They saw Bobinôt emerge from the hall and stand a moment outside the lighted doorway, peering uneasily and

---

° Eh? (Fr.).

searchingly into the darkness. He did not see them, and went slowly back.

"There is Bobinôt looking for you. You are going to set poor Bobinôt crazy. You'll marry him some day; hein, Calixta?"

"I don't say no, me," she replied, striving to withdraw her hand, which he held more firmly for the attempt.

"But come, Calixta; you know you said you would go back to Assumption, just to spite them."

"No, I neva said that, me. You mus' dreamt that."

"Oh, I thought you did. You know I'm going down to the city."

"W'en?"

"To-night."

"Betta make has'e, then; it's mos' day."

"Well, to-morrow'll do."

"W'at you goin' do, yonda?"

"I don't know. Drown myself in the lake, maybe; unless you go down there to visit your uncle."

Calixta's senses were reeling; and they well-nigh left her when she felt Alcée's lips brush her ear like the touch of a rose.

"Mista Alcée! Is dat Mista Alcée?" the thick voice of a negro was asking; he stood on the ground, holding to the banister-rails near which the couple sat.

"W'at do you want now?" cried Alcée impatiently. "Can't I have a moment of peace?"

"I ben huntin' you high an' low, suh," answered the man. "Dey—dey some one in de road, onda de mulbare-tree, want see you a minute."

"I wouldn't go out to the road to see the Angel Gabriel. And if you come back here with any more talk, I'll have to break your neck." The negro turned mumbling away.

Alcée and Calixta laughed softly about it. Her boisterousness was all gone. They talked low, and laughed softly, as lovers do.

"Alcée! Alcée Laballière!"

It was not the negro's voice this time; but one that went through Alcée's body like an electric shock, bringing him to his feet.

Clarisse was standing there in her riding-habit, where the negro had stood. For an instant confusion reigned in Alcée's thoughts, as with one who awakes suddenly from a dream. But he felt that something of serious import had brought his cousin to the ball in the dead of night.

"W'at does this mean, Clarisse?" he asked.

"It means something has happen' at home. You mus' come."

"Happened to *maman*?" he questioned, in alarm.

"No; *nénaine* is well, and asleep. It is something else. Not to frighten you. But you mus' come. Come with me, Alcée."

There was no need for the imploring note. He would have followed the voice anywhere.

She had now recognized the girl sitting back on the bench.

"Ah, *c'est vous, Calixta? Comment ça va, mon enfant?*"*

"*Tcha va b'en; et vous, mam'zélle?*"†

Alcée swung himself over the low rail and started to follow Clarisse, without a word, without a glance back at the girl. He had forgotten he was leaving her there. But Clarisse whispered something to him, and he turned back to say "Goodnight, Calixta," and offer his hand to press through the railing. She pretended not to see it.

"How come that? You settin' yere by yo'se'f, Calixta?" It was Bobinôt who had found her there alone. The dancers had not yet come out. She looked ghastly in the faint, gray light struggling out of the east.

"Yes, that's me. Go yonda in the *parc aux petits* an' ask Aunt Olisse fu' my hat. She knows w'ere 't is. I want to go home, me."

---

* Oh, is it you, Calixta? How are you doing, my child? (Fr.).

† I'm well; and you, miss? (Fr.).

"How you came?"

"I come afoot, with the Cateaus. But I'm goin' now. I ent goin' wait fu' 'em. I'm plumb wo' out, me."

"Kin I go with you, Calixta?"

"I don' care."

They went together across the open prairie and along the edge of the fields, stumbling in the uncertain light. He told her to lift her dress that was getting wet and bedraggled; for she was pulling at the weeds and grasses with her hands.

"I don' care; it's got to go in the tub, anyway. You been sayin' all along you want to marry me, Bobinôt. Well, if you want, yet, I don' care, me."

The glow of a sudden and overwhelming happiness shone out in the brown, rugged face of the young Acadian. He could not speak, for very joy. It choked him.

"Oh well, if you don' want," snapped Calixta, flippantly, pretending to be piqued at his silence.

"*Bon Dieu!*° You know that makes me crazy, w'at you sayin'. You mean that, Calixta? You ent goin' turn roun' agin?"

"I neva tole you that much *yet*, Bobinôt. I mean that. *Tiens*," and she held out her hand in the business-like manner of a man who clinches a bargain with a hand-clasp. Bobinôt grew bold with happiness and asked Calixta to kiss him. She turned her face, that was almost ugly after the night's dissipation, and looked steadily into his.

"I don' want to kiss you, Bobinôt," she said, turning away again, "not to-day. Some other time. *Bonté divine!*† ent you satisfy, *yet!*"

"Oh, I'm satisfy, Calixta," he said.

Riding through a patch of wood, Clarisse's saddle became ungirted, and she and Alcée dismounted to readjust it.

For the twentieth time he asked her what had happened at home.

---

* Good God! (Fr.).

† Good heavens! (Fr.).

"But, Clarisse, w'at is it? Is it a misfortune?"

"*Ah Dieu sait!** It's only something that happen' to me."

"To you!"

"I saw you go away las' night, Alcée, with those saddle-bags," she said, haltingly, striving to arrange something about the saddle, "an' I made Bruce tell me. He said you had gone to the ball, an' wouldn' be home for weeks an' weeks. I thought, Alcée—maybe you were going to—to Assumption. I got wild. An' then I knew if you didn't come back, *now*, to-night, I couldn't stan' it—again."

She had her face hidden in her arm that she was resting against the saddle when she said that.

He began to wonder if this meant love. But she had to tell him so, before he believed it. And when she told him, he thought the face of the Universe was changed—just like Bobinôt. Was it last week the cyclone had well-nigh ruined him? The cyclone seemed a huge joke, now. It was he, then, who, an hour ago was kissing little Calixta's ear and whispering nonsense into it. Calixta was like a myth, now. The one, only, great reality in the world was Clarisse standing before him, telling him that she loved him.

In the distance they heard the rapid discharge of pistol-shots; but it did not disturb them. They knew it was only the negro musicians who had gone into the yard to fire their pistols into the air, as the custom is, and to announce "*le bal est fini.*"†

---

* Oh God knows! (Fr.).

† The ball is over (Fr.).

DÉSIRÉE'S BABY

As the day was pleasant, Madame Valmondé drove over to L'Abri to see Désirée and the baby.

It made her laugh to think of Désirée with a baby. Why, it seemed but yesterday that Désirée was little more than a baby herself; when Monsieur in riding through the gateway of Valmondé had found her lying asleep in the shadow of the big stone pillar.

The little one awoke in his arms and began to cry for "Dada." That was as much as she could do or say. Some people thought she might have strayed there of her own accord, for she was of the toddling age. The prevailing belief was that she had been purposely left by a party of Texans, whose canvas-covered wagon, late in the day, had crossed the ferry that Coton Maïs kept, just below the plantation. In time Madame Valmondé abandoned every speculation but the one that Désirée had been sent to her by a beneficent Providence to be the child of her affection, seeing that she was without child of the flesh. For the girl grew to be beautiful and gentle, affectionate and sincere—the idol of Valmondé.

It was no wonder, when she stood one day against the stone pillar in whose shadow she had lain asleep, eighteen years before, that Armand Aubigny riding by and seeing her there, had fallen in love with her. That was the way all the Aubignys fell in love, as if struck by a pistol shot. The wonder was that he had not loved her before; for he had known her since his father brought him home from Paris, a boy of eight, after his mother died there. The passion that awoke in him that day, when he saw her at the gate, swept along like an avalanche, or like a prairie fire, or like anything that drives headlong over all obstacles.

Monsieur Valmondé grew practical and wanted things well considered: that is, the girl's obscure origin. Armand looked into her eyes and did not care. He was reminded that she was nameless. What did it matter about a name when he could give her one of the oldest and proudest in Louisiana? He ordered the *corbeille** from Paris, and contained himself with what patience he could until it arrived; then they were married.

Madame Valmondé had not seen Désirée and the baby for four weeks. When she reached L'Abri she shuddered at the first sight of it, as she always did. It was a sad-looking place, which for many years had not known the gentle presence of a mistress, old Monsieur Aubigny having married and buried his wife in France, and she having loved her own land too well ever to leave it. The roof came down steep and black like a cowl, reaching out beyond the wide galleries that encircled the yellow stuccoed house. Big, solemn oaks grew close to it, and their thick-leaved, far-reaching branches shadowed it like a pall. Young Aubigny's rule was a strict one, too, and under it his negroes had forgotten how to be gay, as they had been during the old master's easy-going and indulgent lifetime.

The young mother was recovering slowly, and lay full length, in her soft white muslins and laces, upon a couch. The baby was beside her, upon her arm, where he had fallen asleep, at her breast. The yellow nurse woman sat beside a window fanning herself.

Madame Valmondé bent her portly figure over Désirée and kissed her, holding her an instant tenderly in her arms. Then she turned to the child.

"This is not the baby!" she exclaimed, in startled tones. French was the language spoken at Valmondé in those days.

"I knew you would be astonished," laughed Désirée, "at the way he has grown. The little *cochon de lait!*† Look at his legs, mamma, and his hands and fingernails—real fingernails. Zandrine had to cut them this morning. Isn't it true, Zandrine?"

---

* Wedding presents from the groom to his bride (Fr.).

† Piglet (Fr.); a term of endearment.

The woman bowed her turbaned head majestically, "*Mais si,*° *Madame.*"

"And the way he cries," went on Désirée, "is deafening. Armand heard him the other day as far away as La Blanche's cabin."

Madame Valmondé had never removed her eyes from the child. She lifted it and walked with it over to the window that was lightest. She scanned the baby narrowly, then looked as searchingly at Zandrine, whose face was turned to gaze across the fields.

"Yes, the child has grown, has changed," said Madame Valmondé, slowly, as she replaced it beside its mother. "What does Armand say?"

Désirée's face became suffused with a glow that was happiness itself.

"Oh, Armand is the proudest father in the parish, I believe, chiefly because it is a boy, to bear his name; though he says not—that he would have loved a girl as well. But I know it isn't true. I know he says that to please me. And mamma," she added, drawing Madame Valmondé's head down to her, and speaking in a whisper, "he hasn't punished one of them—not one of them—since baby is born. Even Négrillon, who pretended to have burnt his leg that he might rest from work—he only laughed, and said Négrillon was a great scamp. Oh, mamma, I'm so happy; it frightens me."

What Désirée said was true. Marriage, and later the birth of his son had softened Armand Aubigny's imperious and exacting nature greatly. This was what made the gentle Désirée so happy, for she loved him desperately. When he frowned she trembled, but loved him. When he smiled, she asked no greater blessing of God. But Armand's dark, handsome face had not often been disfigured by frowns since the day he fell in love with her.

When the baby was about three months old, Désirée awoke one day to the conviction that there was something in

---

° But of course (Fr.).

the air menacing her peace. It was at first too subtle to grasp. It had only been a disquieting suggestion; an air of mystery among the blacks; unexpected visits from far-off neighbors who could hardly account for their coming. Then a strange, an awful change in her husband's manner, which she dared not ask him to explain. When he spoke to her, it was with averted eyes, from which the old love-light seemed to have gone out. He absented himself from home; and when there, avoided her presence and that of her child, without excuse. And the very spirit of Satan seemed suddenly to take hold of him in his dealings with the slaves. Désirée was miserable enough to die.

She sat in her room, one hot afternoon, in her *peignoir*; listlessly drawing through her fingers the strands of her long, silky brown hair that hung about her shoulders. The baby, half naked, lay asleep upon her own great mahogany bed, that was like a sumptuous throne, with its satin-lined half-canopy. One of La Blanche's little quadroon boys—half naked too— stood fanning the child slowly with a fan of peacock feathers. Désirée's eyes had been fixed absently and sadly upon the baby, while she was striving to penetrate the threatening mist that she felt closing about her. She looked from her child to the boy who stood beside him, and back again; over and over. "Ah!" It was a cry that she could not help; which she was not conscious of having uttered. The blood turned like ice in her veins, and a clammy moisture gathered upon her face.

She tried to speak to the little quadroon boy; but no sound would come, at first. When he heard his name uttered, he looked up, and his mistress was pointing to the door. He laid aside the great, soft fan, and obediently stole away, over the polished floor, on his bare tiptoes.

She stayed motionless, with gaze riveted upon her child, and her face the picture of fright.

Presently her husband entered the room, and without noticing her, went to a table and began to search among some papers which covered it.

"Armand," she called to him, in a voice which must have

stabbed him, if he was human. But he did not notice. "Armand," she said again. Then she rose and tottered toward him. "Armand," she panted once more, clutching his arm, "look at our child. What does it mean? tell me."

He coldly but gently loosened her fingers from about his arm and thrust the hand away from him. "Tell me what it means!" she cried despairingly.

"It means," he answered lightly, "that the child is not white; it means that you are not white."

A quick conception of all that this accusation meant for her nerved her with unwonted courage to deny it. "It is a lie; it is not true, I am white! Look at my hair, it is brown; and my eyes are gray, Armand, you know they are gray. And my skin is fair," seizing his wrist. "Look at my hand; whiter than yours, Armand," she laughed hysterically.

"As white as La Blanche's," he returned cruelly; and went away leaving her alone with their child.

When she could hold a pen in her hand, she sent a despairing letter to Madame Valmondé.

"My mother, they tell me I am not white. Armand has told me I am not white. For God's sake tell them it is not true. You must know it is not true. I shall die. I must die. I cannot be so unhappy, and live."

The answer that came was as brief:

"My own Désirée: Come home to Valmondé; back to your mother who loves you. Come with your child."

When the letter reached Désirée she went with it to her husband's study, and laid it open upon the desk before which he sat. She was like a stone image: silent, white, motionless after she placed it there.

In silence he ran his cold eyes over the written words. He said nothing. "Shall I go, Armand?" she asked in tones sharp with agonized suspense.

"Yes, go."

"Do you want me to go?"

"Yes, I want you to go."

He thought Almighty God had dealt cruelly and unjustly

with him; and felt, somehow, that he was paying Him back in kind when he stabbed thus into his wife's soul. Moreover he no longer loved her, because of the unconscious injury she had brought upon his home and his name.

She turned away like one stunned by a blow, and walked slowly toward the door, hoping he would call her back.

"Good-by, Armand," she moaned.

He did not answer her. That was his last blow at fate.

Désirée went in search of her child. Zandrine was pacing the sombre gallery with it. She took the little one from the nurse's arms with no word of explanation, and descending the steps, walked away, under the live-oak branches.

It was an October afternoon; the sun was just sinking. Out in the still fields the negroes were picking cotton.

Désirée had not changed the thin white garment nor the slippers which she wore. Her hair was uncovered and the sun's rays brought a golden gleam from its brown meshes. She did not take the broad, beaten road which led to the far-off plantation of Valmondé. She walked across a deserted field, where the stubble bruised her tender feet, so delicately shod, and tore her thin gown to shreds.

She disappeared among the reeds and willows that grew thick along the banks of the deep, sluggish bayou;* and she did not come back again.

Some weeks later there was a curious scene enacted at L'Abri. In the centre of the smoothly swept back yard was a great bonfire. Armand Aubigny sat in the wide hallway that commanded a view of the spectacle; and it was he who dealt out to a half dozen negroes the material which kept this fire ablaze.

A graceful cradle of willow, with all its dainty furbishings, was laid upon the pyre, which had already been fed with the richness of a priceless *layette*.† Then there were silk gowns,

---

* A marshy body of water; Désirée's death by drowning anticipates the fate of Edna Pontellier in *The Awakening*.

† A set of infant clothing and blankets (Fr.).

and velvet and satin ones added to these; laces, too, and embroideries; bonnets and gloves; for the *corbeille* had been of rare quality.

The last thing to go was a tiny bundle of letters; innocent little scribblings that Désirée had sent to him during the days of their espousal. There was the remnant of one back in the drawer from which he took them. But it was not Désirée's; it was part of an old letter from his mother to his father. He read it. She was thanking God for the blessing of her husband's love—

"But, above all," she wrote, "night and day, I thank the good God for having so arranged our lives that our dear Armand will never know that his mother, who adores him, belongs to the race that is cursed with the brand of slavery."

A GENTLEMAN OF BAYOU TÊCHE[*]

〜

IT WAS NO WONDER Mr. Sublet, who was staying at the Hallet plantation, wanted to make a picture of Evariste. The 'Cadian was rather a picturesque subject in his way, and a tempting one to an artist looking for bits of "local color" along the Têche.

Mr. Sublet had seen the man on the back gallery just as he came out of the swamp, trying to sell a wild turkey to the housekeeper. He spoke to him at once, and in the course of conversation engaged him to return to the house the following morning and have his picture drawn. He handed Evariste a couple of silver dollars to show that his intentions were fair, and that he expected the 'Cadian to keep faith with him.

"He tell' me he want' put my picture in one fine '*Mag*'zine,'" said Evariste to his daughter, Martinette, when the two were talking the matter over in the afternoon. "W'at fo' you reckon he want' do dat?" They sat within the low, homely cabin of two rooms, that was not quite so comfortable as Mr. Hallet's negro quarters.

Martinette pursed her red lips that had little sensitive curves to them, and her black eyes took on a reflective expression.

"Mebbe he yeard 'bout that big fish w'at you ketch las' winta in Carancro[†] Lake. You know it was all wrote about in the *Suga Bowl*." Her father set aside the suggestion with a deprecatory wave of the hand.

"Well, anyway, you got to fix yo'se'f up," declared Martinette, dismissing further speculation; "put on yo' otha pant'loon an' yo' good coat; an' you betta ax Mr. Léonce to cut yo' hair, an' yo' w'sker' a li'le bit."

"It's w'at I say," chimed in Evariste. "I tell dat gent'man I'm

---

[*] A body of water in southwest Louisiana.

[†] Carancro means "black vulture" in Acadian.

goin' make myse'f fine. He say', 'No, no,' like he ent please'. He want' me like I come out de swamp. So much betta if my pant'loon' an' coat is tore, he say, an' color' like de mud." They could not understand these eccentric wishes on the part of the strange gentleman, and made no effort to do so.

An hour later Martinette, who was quite puffed up over the affair, trotted across to Aunt Dicey's cabin to communicate the news to her. The negress was ironing; her irons stood in a long row before the fire of logs that burned on the hearth. Martinette seated herself in the chimney corner and held her feet up to the blaze; it was damp and a little chilly out of doors. The girl's shoes were considerably worn and her garments were a little too thin and scant for the winter season. Her father had given her the two dollars he had received from the artist, and Martinette was on her way to the store to invest them as judiciously as she knew how.

"You know, Aunt Dicey," she began a little complacently after listening awhile to Aunt Dicey's unqualified abuse of her own son, Wilkins, who was dining-room boy at Mr. Hallet's, "you know that stranger gentleman up to Mr. Hallet's? he want' to make my popa's picture; an' he say' he goin' put it in one fine *Mag*'zine yonda."

Aunt Dicey spat upon her iron to test its heat. Then she began to snicker. She kept on laughing inwardly, making her whole fat body shake, and saying nothing.

"W'at you laughin' 'bout, Aunt Dice?" inquired Martinette mistrustfully.

"I isn' laughin', chile!"

"Yas, you' laughin'."

"Oh, don't pay no 'tention to me. I jis studyin' how simple you an' yo' pa is. You is bof de simplest somebody I eva come 'crost."

"You got to say plumb out w'at you mean, Aunt Dice," insisted the girl doggedly, suspicious and alert now.

"Well, dat w'y I say you is simple," proclaimed the woman, slamming down her iron on an inverted, battered pie pan, "jis like you says, dey gwine put yo' pa's picture yonda in de picture paper. An' you know w'at readin' dey gwine sot down on'neaf dat picture?" Martinette was intensely attentive. "Dey gwine sot down on'neaf: 'Dis heah is one dem low-down 'Cajuns o' Bayeh Têche!' "

The blood flowed from Martinette's face, leaving it deathly pale; in another instant it came beating back in a quick flood, and her eyes smarted with pain as if the tears that filled them had been fiery hot.

"I knows dem kine o' folks," continued Aunt Dicey, resuming her interrupted ironing. "Dat stranger he got a li'le boy w'at ain't none too big to spank. Dat li'le imp he come a hoppin' in heah yistiddy wid a kine o' box on'neaf his arm. He say' 'Good mo'nin', madam. Will you be so kine an' stan' jis like you is dah at yo' i'onin', an' lef me take yo' picture?' I 'lowed I gwine make a picture outen him wid dis heah flati'on, ef he don' cl'ar hisse'f quick. An' he say he baig my pardon fo' his intrudement. All dat kine o' talk to a ole nigga 'oman! Dat plainly sho' he don' know his place."

"W'at you want 'im to say, Aunt Dice?" asked Martinette, with an effort to conceal her distress.

"I wants 'im to come in heah an' say: 'Howdy, Aunt Dicey! will you be so kine and go put on yo' noo calker* dress an' yo' bonnit w'at you w'ars to meetin', an' stan' 'side f'om dat i'onin'-boa'd w'ilse I gwine take yo' photygraph.' Dat de way fo' a boy to talk w'at had good raisin'."

Martinette had arisen, and began to take slow leave of the woman. She turned at the cabin door to observe tentatively: "I reckon it's Wilkins tells you how the folks they talk, yonda up to Mr. Hallet's."

She did not go to the store as she had intended, but walked with a dragging step back to her home. The silver dollars clicked in her pocket as she walked. She felt like flinging them across the field; they seemed to her somehow the price of shame.

The sun had sunk, and twilight was settling like a silver

---

* Calico.

beam upon the bayou and enveloping the fields in a gray mist. Evariste, slim and slouchy, was waiting for his daughter in the cabin door. He had lighted a fire of sticks and branches, and placed the kettle before it to boil. He met the girl with his slow, serious, questioning eyes, astonished to see her empty-handed.

"How come you did n' bring nuttin' f'om de sto', Martinette?"

She entered and flung her gingham sun-bonnet upon a chair. "No, I did n' go yonda;" and with sudden exasperation: "You got to go take back that money; you mus'n' git no picture took."

"But, Martinette," her father mildly interposed, "I promise' 'im; an' he's goin' give me some mo' money w'en he finish."

"If he give you a ba'el o' money, you mus'n' git no picture took. You know w'at he want to put un'neath that picture, fo' ev'body to read?" She could not tell him the whole hideous truth as she had heard it distorted from Aunt Dicey's lips; she would not hurt him that much. "He 's goin' to write: 'This is one '*Cajun*' o' the Bayou Têche.' " Evariste winced.

"How you know?" he asked.

"I yeard so. I know it's true."

The water in the kettle was boiling. He went and poured a small quantity upon the coffee which he had set there to drip. Then he said to her: "I reckon you jus' as well go care dat two dolla' back, tomo' mo'nin'; me, I'll go yonda ketch a mess o' fish in Carancro Lake."

Mr. Hallet and a few masculine companions were assembled at a rather late breakfast the following morning. The dining-room was a big, bare one, enlivened by a cheerful fire of logs that blazed in the wide chimney on massive andirons. There were guns, fishing tackle, and other implements of sport lying about. A couple of fine dogs strayed unceremoniously in and out behind Wilkins, the negro boy who waited upon the table. The chair beside Mr. Sublet, usually occupied by his little son, was vacant, as the child had gone for an early morning outing and had not yet returned.

When breakfast was about half over, Mr. Hallet noticed Martinette standing outside upon the gallery. The dining-room door had stood open more than half the time.

"Isn't that Martinette out there, Wilkins?" inquired the jovial-faced young planter.

"Dat's who, suh," returned Wilkins. "She ben standin' dah sence mos' sun-up; look like she studyin' to take root to de gal-l'ry."

"What in the name of goodness does she want? Ask her what she wants. Tell her to come in to the fire."

Martinette walked into the room with much hesitancy. Her small, brown face could hardly be seen in the depths of the gingham sun-bonnet. Her blue cottonade skirt scarcely reached the thin ankles that it should have covered.

"Bonjou'," she murmured, with a little comprehensive nod that took in the entire company. Her eyes searched the table for the "stranger gentleman," and she knew him at once, because his hair was parted in the middle and he wore a pointed beard. She went and laid the two silver dollars beside his plate and motioned to retire without a word of explanation.

"Hold on, Martinette!" called out the planter, "what's all this pantomime business? Speak out, little one."

"My popa don't want any picture took," she offered, a little timorously. On her way to the door she had looked back to say this. In that fleeting glance she detected a smile of intelligence pass from one to the other of the group. She turned quickly, facing them all, and spoke out, excitement making her voice bold and shrill: "My popa ent one low-down 'Cajun. He ent goin' to stan' to have that kine o' writin' put down un'neath his picture!"

She almost ran from the room, half blinded by the emotion that had helped her to make so daring a speech.

Descending the gallery steps she ran full against her father who was ascending, bearing in his arms the little boy, Archie Sublet. The child was most grotesquely attired in garments far too large for his diminutive person—the rough jeans clothing of some negro boy. Evariste himself had evidently been taking a bath without the preliminary ceremony of removing his clothes, that were now half dried upon his person by the wind and sun.

"Yere you' li'le boy," he announced, stumbling into the room. "You ought not lef dat li'le chile go by hisse'f *comme ça** in de pirogue." Mr. Sublet darted from his chair, the others following suit almost as hastily. In an instant, quivering with apprehension, he had his little son in his arms. The child was quite unharmed, only somewhat pale and nervous, as the consequence of a recent very serious ducking.

Evariste related in his uncertain, broken English how he had been fishing for an hour or more in Carancro Lake, when he noticed the boy paddling over the deep, black water in a shell-like pirogue. Nearing a clump of cypress-trees that rose from the lake, the pirogue became entangled in the heavy moss that hung from the tree limbs and trailed upon the water. The next thing he knew, the boat had overturned, he heard the child scream, and saw him disappear beneath the still, black surface of the lake.

"W'en I done swim to de sho' wid 'im," continued Evariste, "I hurry yonda to Jake Baptiste's cabin, an' we rub 'im an' warm 'im up, an' dress 'im up dry like you see. He all right now, M'sieur; but you mus'n lef 'im go no mo' by hisse'f in one pirogue."

Martinette had followed into the room behind her father. She was feeling and tapping his wet garments solicitously, and begging him in French to come home. Mr. Hallet at once ordered hot coffee and a warm breakfast for the two; and they sat down at the corner of the table, making no manner of objection in their perfect simplicity. It was with visible reluctance and ill-disguised contempt that Wilkins served them.

When Mr. Sublet had arranged his son comfortably, with tender care, upon the sofa, and had satisfied himself that the child was quite uninjured, he attempted to find words with which to thank Evariste for this service which no treasure of

---

* Like that (Fr.).

words or gold could pay for. These warm and heart-felt expressions seemed to Evariste to exaggerate the importance of his action, and they intimidated him. He attempted shyly to hide his face as well as he could in the depths of his bowl of coffee.

"You will let me make your picture now, I hope, Evariste," begged Mr. Sublet, laying his hand upon the 'Cadian's shoulder. "I want to place it among things I hold most dear, and shall call it 'A hero of Bayou Têche.' " This assurance seemed to distress Evariste greatly.

"No, no," he protested, "it's nuttin' hero' to take a li'le boy out de water. I jus' as easy do dat like I stoop down an' pick up a li'le chile w'at fall down in de road. I ent goin' to 'low dat, me. I don't git no picture took, *va!*"

Mr. Hallet, who now discerned his friend's eagerness in the matter, came to his aid.

"I tell you, Evariste, let Mr. Sublet draw your picture, and you yourself may call it whatever you want. I'm sure he'll let you."

"Most willingly," agreed the artist.

Evariste glanced up at him with shy and child-like pleasure. "It's a bargain?" he asked.

"A bargain," affirmed Mr. Sublet.

"Popa," whispered Martinette, "you betta come home an' put on yo' otha pant'loon' an' yo' good coat."

"And now, what shall we call the much talked-of picture?" cheerily inquired the planter, standing with his back to the blaze.

Evariste in a business-like manner began carefully to trace on the table-cloth imaginary characters with an imaginary pen; he could not have written the real characters with a real pen—he did not know how.

"You will put on'neat' de picture," he said, deliberately, " 'Dis is one picture of Mista Evariste Anatole Bonamour, a gent'man of de Bayou Têche.' "

A RESPECTABLE WOMAN

❧

Mrs. Baroda was a little provoked to learn that her husband expected his friend, Gouvernail, up to spend a week or two on the plantation.

They had entertained a good deal during the winter; much of the time had also been passed in New Orleans in various forms of mild dissipation. She was looking forward to a period of unbroken rest, now, and undisturbed *tête-à-tête** with her husband, when he informed her that Gouvernail was coming up to stay a week or two.

This was a man she had heard much of but never seen. He had been her husband's college friend; was now a journalist, and in no sense a society man or "a man about town," which were, perhaps, some of the reasons she had never met him. But she had unconsciously formed an image of him in her mind. She pictured him tall, slim, cynical; with eye-glasses, and his hands in his pockets; and she did not like him. Gouvernail was slim enough, but he wasn't very tall nor very cynical; neither did he wear eye-glasses nor carry his hands in his pockets. And she rather liked him when he first presented himself.

But why she liked him she could not explain satisfactorily to herself when she partly attempted to do so. She could discover in him none of those brilliant and promising traits which Gaston, her husband, had often assured her that he possessed. On the contrary, he sat rather mute and receptive before her chatty eagerness to make him feel at home and in face of Gaston's frank and wordy hospitality. His manner was as courteous toward her as the most exacting woman could require; but he made no direct appeal to her approval or even esteem.

Once settled at the plantation he seemed to like to sit

---

* Intimate conversation (Fr.).

upon the wide portico* in the shade of one of the big Corinthian† pillars, smoking his cigar lazily and listening attentively to Gaston's experience as a sugar planter.

"This is what I call living," he would utter with deep satisfaction, as the air that swept across the sugar field caressed him with its warm and scented velvety touch. It pleased him also to get on familiar terms with the big dogs that came about him, rubbing themselves sociably against his legs. He did not care to fish, and displayed no eagerness to go out and kill grosbecs when Gaston proposed doing so.

Gouvernail's personality puzzled Mrs. Baroda, but she liked him. Indeed, he was a lovable, inoffensive fellow. After a few days, when she could understand him no better than at first, she gave over being puzzled and remained piqued. In this mood she left her husband and her guest, for the most part, alone together. Then finding that Gouvernail took no manner of exception to her action, she imposed her society upon him, accompanying him in his idle strolls to the mill and walks along the *batture*.‡ She persistently sought to penetrate the reserve in which he had unconsciously enveloped himself.

"When is he going—your friend?" she one day asked her husband. "For my part, he tires me frightfully."

"Not for a week yet, dear. I can't understand; he gives you no trouble."

"No. I should like him better if he did; if he were more like others, and I had to plan somewhat for his comfort and enjoyment."

Gaston took his wife's pretty face between his hands and looked tenderly and laughingly into her troubled eyes. They were making a bit of toilet§ sociably together in Mrs. Baroda's dressing-room.

---

* A covered walkway at the entrance of a building.

† Ornately decorated columns in the Classical Revival style, c. 1835–1850, favored by wealthy American planters.

‡ Land by the river (Fr.).

§ Light grooming.

"You are full of surprises, *ma belle*," he said to her. "Even I can never count upon how you are going to act under given conditions." He kissed her and turned to fasten his cravat before the mirror.

"Here you are," he went on, "taking poor Gouvernail seriously and making a commotion over him, the last thing he would desire or expect."

"Commotion!" she hotly resented. "Nonsense! How can you say such a thing? Commotion, indeed! But, you know, you said he was clever."

"So he is. But the poor fellow is run down by overwork now. That's why I asked him here to take a rest."

"You used to say he was a man of ideas," she retorted, unconciliated. "I expected him to be interesting, at least. I'm going to the city in the morning to have my spring gowns fitted. Let me know when Mr. Gouvernail is gone; I shall be at my Aunt Octavie's."

That night she went and sat alone upon a bench that stood beneath a live-oak tree at the edge of the gravel walk.

She had never known her thoughts or her intentions to be so confused. She could gather nothing from them but the feeling of a distinct necessity to quit her home in the morning.

Mrs. Baroda heard footsteps crunching the gravel, but could discern in the darkness only the approaching red point of a lighted cigar. She knew it was Gouvernail, for her husband did not smoke. She hoped to remain unnoticed, but her white gown revealed her to him. He threw away his cigar and seated himself upon the bench beside her, without a suspicion that she might object to his presence.

"Your husband told me to bring this to you, Mrs. Baroda," he said, handing her a filmy, white scarf with which she sometimes enveloped her head and shoulders. She accepted the scarf from him with a murmur of thanks, and let it lie in her lap.

He made some commonplace observation upon the bane-

ful effect of the night air at that season. Then as his gaze
reached out into the darkness, he murmured, half to himself:

> " 'Night of south winds—night of the large few
>   stars!
> Still nodding night—' "*

She made no reply to this apostrophe to the night, which
indeed, was not addressed to her.

Gouvernail was in no sense a diffident man, for he was not
a self-conscious one. His periods of reserve were not constitutional, but the result of moods. Sitting there beside Mrs.
Baroda, his silence melted for the time.

He talked freely and intimately in a low, hesitating drawl
that was not unpleasant to hear. He talked of the old college
days when he and Gaston had been a good deal to each other;
of the days of keen and blind ambitions and large intentions.
Now there was left with him, at least, a philosophic acquiescence to the existing order—only a desire to be permitted to
exist, with now and then a little whiff of genuine life, such as
he was breathing now.

Her mind only vaguely grasped what he was saying. Her
physical being was for the moment predominant. She was not
thinking of his words, only drinking in the tones of his voice.
She wanted to reach out her hand in the darkness and touch
him with the sensitive tips of her fingers upon the face or the
lips. She wanted to draw close to him and whisper against his
cheek—she did not care what—as she might have done if she
had not been a respectable woman.

The stronger the impulse grew to bring herself near him,
the further, in fact, did she draw away from him. As soon as
she could do so without an appearance of too great rudeness,
she rose and left him there alone.

---

* The lines are from *Song of Myself* (1855) by Walt Whitman
(1819–1892), whom Chopin admired for his celebration of sexual
freedom.

Before she reached the house, Gouvernail had lighted a fresh cigar and ended his apostrophe to the night.

Mrs. Baroda was greatly tempted that night to tell her husband—who was also her friend—of this folly that had seized her. But she did not yield to the temptation. Beside being a respectable woman she was a very sensible one; and she knew there are some battles in life which a human being must fight alone.

When Gaston arose in the morning, his wife had already departed. She had taken an early morning train to the city. She did not return till Gouvernail was gone from under her roof.

There was some talk of having him back during the summer that followed. That is, Gaston greatly desired it; but this desire yielded to his wife's strenuous opposition.

However, before the year ended, she proposed, wholly from herself, to have Gouvernail visit them again. Her husband was surprised and delighted with the suggestion coming from her.

"I am glad, *chère amie,*° to know that you have finally overcome your dislike for him; truly he did not deserve it."

"Oh," she told him, laughingly, after pressing a long, tender kiss upon his lips, "I have overcome everything! you will see. This time I shall be very nice to him."

° My love (Fr.).

THE STORY OF AN HOUR

⚘

KNOWING THAT MRS. MALLARD was afflicted with a heart trouble, great care was taken to break to her as gently as possible the news of her husband's death.

It was her sister Josephine who told her, in broken sentences; veiled hints that revealed in half concealing. Her husband's friend Richards was there, too, near her. It was he who had been in the newspaper office when intelligence of the railroad disaster* was received, with Brently Mallard's name leading the list of "killed." He had only taken the time to assure himself of its truth by a second telegram, and had hastened to forestall any less careful, less tender friend in bearing the sad message.

She did not hear the story as many women have heard the same, with a paralyzed inability to accept its significance. She wept at once, with sudden, wild abandonment, in her sister's arms. When the storm of grief had spent itself she went away to her room alone. She would have no one follow her.

There stood, facing the open window, a comfortable, roomy armchair. Into this she sank, pressed down by a physical exhaustion that haunted her body and seemed to reach into her soul.

She could see in the open square before her house the tops of trees that were all aquiver with the new spring life. The delicious breath of rain was in the air. In the street below a peddler was crying his wares. The notes of a distant song which some one was singing reached her faintly, and countless sparrows were twittering in the eaves.

There were patches of blue sky showing here and there through the clouds that had met and piled one above the other in the west facing her window.

---

* Chopin's father, Thomas O'Flaherty, died in a train accident when the Gasconade Bridge collapsed as he rode across it .

She sat with her head thrown back upon the cushion of the chair, quite motionless, except when a sob came up into her throat and shook her, as a child who has cried itself to sleep continues to sob in its dreams.

She was young, with a fair, calm face, whose lines bespoke repression and even a certain strength. But now there was a dull stare in her eyes, whose gaze was fixed away off yonder on one of those patches of blue sky. It was not a glance of reflection, but rather indicated a suspension of intelligent thought.

There was something coming to her and she was waiting for it, fearfully. What was it? She did not know; it was too subtle and elusive to name. But she felt it, creeping out of the sky, reaching toward her through the sounds, the scents, the color that filled the air.

Now her bosom rose and fell tumultuously. She was beginning to recognize this thing that was approaching to possess her, and she was striving to beat it back with her will—as powerless as her two white slender hands would have been.

When she abandoned herself a little whispered word escaped her slightly parted lips. She said it over and over under her breath: "free, free, free!" The vacant stare and the look of terror that had followed it went from her eyes. They stayed keen and bright. Her pulses beat fast, and the coursing blood warmed and relaxed every inch of her body.

She did not stop to ask if it were or were not a monstrous joy that held her. A clear and exalted perception enabled her to dismiss the suggestion as trivial.

She knew that she would weep again when she saw the kind, tender hands folded in death; the face that had never looked save with love upon her, fixed and gray and dead. But she saw beyond that bitter moment a long procession of years to come that would belong to her absolutely. And she opened and spread her arms out to them in welcome.

There would be no one to live for her during those coming years; she would live for herself. There would be no powerful will bending hers in that blind persistence with which men and women believe they have a right to impose a private will upon a fellow-creature. A kind intention or a cruel intention made the act seem no less a crime as she looked upon it in that brief moment of illumination.

And yet she had loved him—sometimes. Often she had not. What did it matter! What could love, the unsolved mystery, count for in face of this possession of self-assertion which she suddenly recognized as the strongest impulse of her being!

"Free! Body and soul free!" she kept whispering.

Josephine was kneeling before the closed door with her lips to the key-hole, imploring for admission. "Louise, open the door! I beg; open the door—you will make yourself ill. What are you doing, Louise? For heaven's sake open the door."

"Go away. I am not making myself ill." No; she was drinking in a very elixir of life through that open window.

Her fancy was running riot along those days ahead of her. Spring days, and summer days, and all sorts of days that would be her own. She breathed a quick prayer that life might be long. It was only yesterday she had thought with a shudder that life might be long.

She arose at length and opened the door to her sister's importunities. There was a feverish triumph in her eyes, and she carried herself unwittingly like a goddess of Victory. She clasped her sister's waist, and together they descended the stairs. Richards stood waiting for them at the bottom.

Some one was opening the front door with a latchkey. It was Brently Mallard who entered, a little travel-stained, composedly carrying his grip-sack and umbrella. He had been far from the scene of accident, and did not even know there had been one. He stood amazed at Josephine's piercing cry; at Richards's quick motion to screen him from the view of his wife.

But Richards was too late.

When the doctors came they said she had died of heart disease—of joy that kills.

ATHÉNAÏSE

༄

I

ATHÉNAÏSE WENT AWAY in the morning to make a visit to her parents, ten miles back on *rigolet* de Bon Dieu.* She did not return in the evening, and Cazeau, her husband, fretted not a little. He did not worry much about Athénaïse, who, he suspected, was resting only too content in the bosom of her family; his chief solicitude was manifestly for the pony she had ridden. He felt sure those "lazy pigs," her brothers, were capable of neglecting it seriously. This misgiving Cazeau communicated to his servant, old Félicité, who waited upon him at supper.

His voice was low pitched, and even softer than Félicité's. He was tall, sinewy, swarthy, and altogether severe looking. His thick black hair waved, and it gleamed like the breast of a crow. The sweep of his mustache, which was not so black, outlined the broad contour of the mouth. Beneath the under lip grew a small tuft which he was much given to twisting, and which he permitted to grow, apparently for no other purpose. Cazeau's eyes were dark blue, narrow and overshadowed. His hands were coarse and stiff from close acquaintance with farming tools and implements, and he handled his fork and knife clumsily. But he was distinguished looking, and succeeded in commanding a good deal of respect, and even fear sometimes.

He ate his supper alone, by the light of a single coal-oil lamp that but faintly illuminated the big room, with its bare floor and huge rafters, and its heavy pieces of furniture that loomed dimly in the gloom of the apartment. Félicité, ministering to his wants, hovered about the table like a little, bent, restless shadow.

She served him with a dish of sunfish fried crisp and brown. There was nothing else set before him beside the

---

* A small stream in Natchitoches parish.

bread and butter and the bottle of red wine which she locked carefully in the buffet after he had poured his second glass. She was occupied with her mistress's absence, and kept reverting to it after he had expressed his solicitude about the pony.

"Dat beat me! on'y marry two mont', an' got de head turn' a'ready to go 'broad. *C'est pas Chrétien, tenez!*"*

Cazeau shrugged his shoulders for answer, after he had drained his glass and pushed aside his plate. Félicité's opinion of the unchristianlike behavior of his wife in leaving him thus alone after two months of marriage weighed little with him. He was used to solitude, and did not mind a day or a night or two of it. He had lived alone ten years, since his first wife died, and Félicité might have known better than to suppose that he cared. He told her she was a fool. It sounded like a compliment in his modulated, caressing voice. She grumbled to herself as she set about clearing the table, and Cazeau arose and walked outside on the gallery; his spur, which he had not removed upon entering the house, jangled at every step.

The night was beginning to deepen, and to gather black about the clusters of trees and shrubs that were grouped in the yard. In the beam of light from the open kitchen door a black boy stood feeding a brace of snarling, hungry dogs; further away, on the steps of a cabin, some one was playing the accordion; and in still another direction a little negro baby was crying lustily. Cazeau walked around to the front of the house, which was square, squat and one-story.

A belated wagon was driving in at the gate, and the impatient driver was swearing hoarsely at his jaded oxen. Félicité stepped out on the gallery, glass and polishing towel in hand, to investigate, and to wonder, too, who could be singing out on the river. It was a party of young people paddling around, waiting for the moon to rise, and they were singing "Juanita,"†

---

* Hey, that isn't Christian! (Fr.).

† A traditional Spanish tune with words by Caroline Norton (1808–1877), an aristocratic English woman who fled her own unhappy marriage and led a campaign to change British laws about divorce.

their voices coming tempered and melodious through the distance and the night.

Cazeau's horse was waiting, saddled, ready to be mounted, for Cazeau had many things to attend to before bed-time; so many things that there was not left to him a moment in which to think of Athénaïse. He felt her absence, though, like a dull, insistent pain.

However, before he slept that night he was visited by the thought of her, and by a vision of her fair young face with its drooping lips and sullen and averted eyes. The marriage had been a blunder; he had only to look into her eyes to feel that, to discover her growing aversion. But it was a thing not by any possibility to be undone. He was quite prepared to make the best of it, and expected no less than a like effort on her part. The less she revisited the *rigolet*, the better. He would find means to keep her at home hereafter.

These unpleasant reflections kept Cazeau awake far into the night, notwithstanding the craving of his whole body for rest and sleep. The moon was shining, and its pale effulgence reached dimly into the room, and with it a touch of the cool breath of the spring night. There was an unusual stillness abroad; no sound to be heard save the distant, tireless, plaintive notes of the accordion.

II

ATHÉNAÏSE DID NOT return the following day, even though her husband sent her word to do so by her brother, Montéclin, who passed on his way to the village early in the morning.

On the third day Cazeau saddled his horse and went himself in search of her. She had sent no word, no message, explaining her absence, and he felt that he had good cause to be offended. It was rather awkward to have to leave his work, even though late in the afternoon—Cazeau had always so much to do; but among the many urgent calls upon him, the task of bringing his wife back to a sense of her duty seemed to him for the moment paramount.

The Michés, Athénaïse's parents, lived on the old Gotrain place. It did not belong to them; they were "running" it for a merchant in Alexandria. The house was far too big for their use. One of the lower rooms served for the storing of wood and tools, the person "occupying" the place before Miché having pulled up the flooring in despair of being able to patch it. Upstairs, the rooms were so large, so bare, that they offered a constant temptation to lovers of the dance, whose importunities Madame Miché was accustomed to meet with amiable indulgence. A dance at Miché's and a plate of Madame Miché's gumbo filé* at midnight were pleasures not to be neglected or despised, unless by such serious souls as Cazeau.

Long before Cazeau reached the house his approach had been observed, for there was nothing to obstruct the view of the outer road; vegetation was not yet abundantly advanced, and there was but a patchy, straggling stand of cotton and corn in Miché's field.

Madame Miché, who had been seated on the gallery in a rocking-chair, stood up to greet him as he drew near. She was short and fat, and wore a black skirt and loose muslin sack fastened at the throat with a hair brooch. Her own hair, brown and glossy, showed but a few threads of silver. Her round pink face was cheery, and her eyes were bright and good humored. But she was plainly perturbed and ill at ease as Cazeau advanced.

Montéclin, who was there too, was not ill at ease, and made no attempt to disguise the dislike with which his brother-in-law inspired him. He was a slim, wiry fellow of twenty-five, short of stature like his mother, and resembling her in feature. He was in shirt-sleeves, half leaning, half sitting, on the insecure railing of the gallery, and fanning himself with his broad-rimmed felt hat.

"*Cochon!*" he muttered under his breath as Cazeau mounted the stairs—"*sacré cochon!*"†

---

* A traditional stew of chicken or shrimp thickened with dried sassafras instead of okra.

† Pig! . . . damn pig! (Fr.).

"Cochon" had sufficiently characterized the man who had once on a time declined to lend Montéclin money. But when this same man had had the presumption to propose marriage to his well-beloved sister, Athénaïse, and the honor to be accepted by her, Montéclin felt that a qualifying epithet was needed fully to express his estimate of Cazeau.

Miché and his oldest son were absent. They both esteemed Cazeau highly, and talked much of his qualities of head and heart, and thought much of his excellent standing with city merchants.

Athénaïse had shut herself up in her room. Cazeau had seen her rise and enter the house at perceiving him. He was a good deal mystified, but no one could have guessed it when he shook hands with Madame Miché. He had only nodded to Montéclin, with a muttered *"Comment ça va?"* *

"Tiens! something tole me you were coming to-day!" exclaimed Madame Miché, with a little blustering appearance of being cordial and at ease, as she offered Cazeau a chair.

He ventured a short laugh as he seated himself.

"You know, nothing would do," she went on, with much gesture of her small, plump hands, "nothing would do but Athénaïse mus' stay las' night fo' a li'le dance. The boys wouldn' year to their sister leaving."

Cazeau shrugged his shoulders significantly, telling as plainly as words that he knew nothing about it.

"Comment! Montéclin didn' tell you we were going to keep Athénaïse?" Montéclin had evidently told nothing.

"An' how about the night befo'," questioned Cazeau, "an' las' night? It isn't possible you dance every night out yere on the Bon Dieu!"

Madame Miché laughed, with amiable appreciation of the sarcasm; and turning to her son, "Montéclin, my boy, go tell yo' sister that Monsieur Cazeau is yere."

Montéclin did not stir except to shift his position and settle himself more securely on the railing.

---

* How's it going? (Fr.).

"Did you year me, Montéclin?"

"Oh yes, I yeard you plain enough," responded her son, "but you know as well as me it's no use to tell 'Thénaïse anything. You been talkin' to her yo'se'f since Monday; an' pa's preached himse'f hoa'se on the subject; an' you even had uncle Achille down yere yesterday to reason with her. W'en 'Thénaïse said she wasn' goin' to set her foot back in Cazeau's house, she meant it."

This speech, which Montéclin delivered with thorough unconcern, threw his mother into a condition of painful but dumb embarrassment. It brought two fiery red spots to Cazeau's cheeks, and for the space of a moment he looked wicked.

What Montéclin had spoken was quite true, though his taste in the manner and choice of time and place in saying it were not of the best. Athénaïse, upon the first day of her arrival, had announced that she came to stay, having no intention of returning under Cazeau's roof. The announcement had scattered consternation, as she knew it would. She had been implored, scolded, entreated, stormed at, until she felt herself like a dragging sail that all the winds of heaven had beaten upon. Why in the name of God had she married Cazeau? Her father had lashed her with the question a dozen times. Why indeed? It was difficult now for her to understand why, unless because she supposed it was customary for girls to marry when the right opportunity came. Cazeau, she knew, would make life more comfortable for her; and again, she had liked him, and had even been rather flustered when he pressed her hands and kissed them, and kissed her lips and cheeks and eyes, when she accepted him.

Montéclin himself had taken her aside to talk the thing over. The turn of affairs was delighting him.

"Come, now, 'Thénaïse, you mus' explain to me all about it, so we can settle on a good cause, an' secu' a separation fo' you. Has he been mistreating an' abusing you, the *sacré cochon?*" They were alone together in her room, whither she had taken refuge from the angry domestic elements.

"You please to reserve yo' disgusting expressions, Montéclin. No, he has not abused me in any way that I can think."

"Does he drink? Come 'Thénaïse, think well over it. Does he ever get drunk?"

"Drunk! Oh, mercy, no—Cazeau never gets drunk."

"I see; it's jus' simply you feel like me; you hate him."

"No, I don't hate him," she returned reflectively, adding with a sudden impulse, "It's jus' being married that I detes' an' despise. I hate being Mrs. Cazeau, an' would want to be Athénaïse Miché again. I can't stan' to live with a man; to have him always there; his coats an' pantaloons hanging in my room; his ugly bare feet—washing them in my tub, befo' my very eyes, ugh!" She shuddered with recollections, and resumed, with a sigh that was almost a sob: "*Mon Dieu,*° mon Dieu! Sister Marie Angélique knew w'at she was saying; she knew me better than myse'f w'en she said God had sent me a vocation an' I was turning deaf ears. W'en I think of a blessed life in the convent, at peace! Oh, w'at was I dreaming of!" and then the tears came.

Montéclin felt disconcerted and greatly disappointed at having obtained evidence that would carry no weight with a court of justice. The day had not come when a young woman might ask the court's permission to return to her mamma on the sweeping ground of a constitutional disinclination for marriage. But if there was no way of untying this Gordian knot[†] of marriage, there was surely a way of cutting it.

"Well, 'Thénaïse, I'm mighty durn sorry you got no better groun's 'an w'at you say. But you can count on me to stan' by you w'atever you do. God knows I don' blame you fo' not wantin' to live with Cazeau."

And now there was Cazeau himself, with the red spots flaming in his swarthy cheeks, looking and feeling as if he wanted to thrash Montéclin into some semblance of decency.

° My God! (Fr.).

† An insoluble problem.

He arose abruptly, and approaching the room which he had seen his wife enter, thrust open the door after a hasty preliminary knock. Athénaïse, who was standing erect at a far window, turned at his entrance.

She appeared neither angry nor frightened, but thoroughly unhappy, with an appeal in her soft dark eyes and a tremor on her lips that seemed to him expressions of unjust reproach, that wounded and maddened him at once. But whatever he might feel, Cazeau knew only one way to act toward a woman.

"Athénaïse, you are not ready?" he asked in his quiet tones. "It's getting late; we havn' any time to lose."

She knew that Montéclin had spoken out, and she had hoped for a wordy interview, a stormy scene, in which she might have held her own as she had held it for the past three days against her family, with Montéclin's aid. But she had no weapon with which to combat subtlety. Her husband's looks, his tones, his mere presence, brought to her a sudden sense of hopelessness, an instinctive realization of the futility of rebellion against a social and sacred institution.

Cazeau said nothing further, but stood waiting in the doorway. Madame Miché had walked to the far end of the gallery, and pretended to be occupied with having a chicken driven from her *parterre.*[*] Montéclin stood by, exasperated, fuming, ready to burst out.

Athénaïse went and reached for her riding-skirt that hung against the wall. She was rather tall, with a figure which, though not robust, seemed perfect in its fine proportions. "*La fille de son père,*"[†] she was often called, which was a great compliment to Miché. Her brown hair was brushed all fluffily back from her temples and low forehead, and about her features and expression lurked a softness, a prettiness, a dewiness, that were perhaps too child-like, that savored of immaturity.

---

[*] See *The Awakening,* chap. XXXI, p. 124.

[†] Her father's daughter (Fr.).

She slipped the riding-skirt, which was of black alpaca, over her head, and with impatient fingers hooked it at the waist over her pink linen-lawn. Then she fastened on her white sun-bonnet and reached for her gloves on the mantelpiece.

"If you don' wan' to go, you know w'at you got to do, 'Thénaïse," fumed Montéclin. "You don' set yo' feet back on Cane River,* by God, unless you want to—not w'ile I'm alive."

Cazeau looked at him as if he were a monkey whose antics fell short of being amusing.

Athénaïse still made no reply, said not a word. She walked rapidly past her husband, past her brother, bidding good-by to no one, not even to her mother. She descended the stairs, and without assistance from any one mounted the pony, which Cazeau had ordered to be saddled upon his arrival. In this way she obtained a fair start of her husband, whose departure was far more leisurely, and for the greater part of the way she managed to keep an appreciable gap between them. She rode almost madly at first, with the wind inflating her skirt balloon-like about her knees, and her sun-bonnet falling back between her shoulders.

At no time did Cazeau make an effort to overtake her until traversing an old fallow meadow that was level and hard as a table. The sight of a great solitary oak-tree, with its seemingly immutable outlines, that had been a landmark for ages—or was it the odor of elderberry stealing up from the gully to the south? or what was it that brought vividly back to Cazeau, by some association of ideas, a scene of many years ago? He had passed that old live-oak hundreds of times, but it was only now that the memory of one day came back to him. He was a very small boy that day, seated before his father on horse-back. They were proceeding slowly, and Black Gabe was moving on before them at a little dog-trot. Black Gabe had run away, and

---

* Now a lake, this body of water was once a beautiful river running through Natchitoches and plantation country.

had been discovered back in the Gotrain swamp. They had halted beneath this big oak to enable the negro to take breath; for Cazeau's father was a kind and considerate master, and every one had agreed at the time that Black Gabe was a fool, a great idiot indeed, for wanting to run away from him.

The whole impression was for some reason hideous, and to dispel it Cazeau spurred his horse to a swift gallop. Overtaking his wife, he rode the remainder of the way at her side in silence.

It was late when they reached home. Félicité was standing on the grassy edge of the road, in the moonlight, waiting for them.

Cazeau once more ate his supper alone; for Athénaïse went to her room, and there she was crying again.

III

ATHÉNAÏSE WAS NOT one to accept the inevitable with patient resignation, a talent born in the souls of many women; neither was she the one to accept it with philosophical resignation, like her husband. Her sensibilities were alive and keen and responsive. She met the pleasurable things of life with frank, open appreciation, and against distasteful conditions she rebelled. Dissimulation was as foreign to her nature as guile to the breast of a babe, and her rebellious outbreaks, by no means rare, had hitherto been quite open and aboveboard. People often said that Athénaïse would know her own mind some day, which was equivalent to saying that she was at present unacquainted with it. If she ever came to such knowledge, it would be by no intellectual research, by no subtle analyses or tracing the motives of actions to their source. It would come to her as the song to the bird, the perfume and color to the flower.

Her parents had hoped—not without reason and justice—that marriage would bring the poise, the desirable pose, so glaringly lacking in Athénaïse's character. Marriage they knew to be a wonderful and powerful agent in the development and formation of a woman's character; they had seen its effect too often to doubt it.

"And if this marriage does nothing else," exclaimed Miché in an outburst of sudden exasperaton, "it will rid us of Athénaïse; for I am at the end of my patience with her! You have never had the firmness to manage her"—he was speaking to his wife—"I have not had the time, the leisure, to devote to her training; and what good we might have accomplished, that *maudit** Montéclin—Well, Cazeau is the one! It takes just such a steady hand to guide a disposition like Athénaïse's, a master hand, a strong will that compels obedience."

And now, when they had hoped for so much, here was Athénaïse, with gathered and fierce vehemence, beside which her former outbursts appeared mild, declaring that she would not, and she would not, and she would not continue to enact the role of wife to Cazeau. If she had had a reason! as Madame Miché lamented; but it could not be discovered that she had any sane one. He had never scolded, or called names, or deprived her of comforts, or been guilty of any of the many reprehensible acts commonly attributed to objectionable husbands. He did not slight nor neglect her. Indeed, Cazeau's chief offense seemed to be that he loved her, and Athénaïse was not the woman to be loved against her will. She called marriage a trap set for the feet of unwary and unsuspecting girls, and in round, unmeasured terms reproached her mother with treachery and deceit.

"I told you Cazeau was the man," chuckled Miché, when his wife had related the scene that had accompanied and influenced Athénaïse's departure.

Athénaïse again hoped, in the morning, that Cazeau would scold or make some sort of a scene, but he apparently did not dream of it. It was exasperating that he should take her acquiescence so for granted. It is true he had been up and over the fields and across the river and back long before she

---

* Cursed (Fr.).

was out of bed, and he may have been thinking of something else, which was no excuse, which was even in some sense an aggravation. But he did say to her at breakfast, "That brother of yo's, that Montéclin, is unbearable."

"Montéclin? *Par exemple!*"

Athénaïse, seated opposite to her husband, was attired in a white morning wrapper. She wore a somewhat abused, long face, it is true—an expression of countenance familiar to some husbands—but the expression was not sufficiently pronounced to mar the charm of her youthful freshness. She had little heart to eat, only playing with the food before her, and she felt a pang of resentment at her husband's healthy appetite.

"Yes, Montéclin," he reasserted. "He's developed into a firs'-class nuisance; an' you better tell him, Athénaïse—unless you want me to tell him—to confine his energies after this to matters that concern him. I have no use fo' him or fo' his interference in w'at regards you an' me alone."

This was said with unusual asperity. It was the little breach that Athénaïse had been watching for, and she charged rapidly: "It's strange, if you detes' Montéclin so heartily, that you would desire to marry his sister." She knew it was a silly thing to say, and was not surprised when he told her so. It gave her a little foothold for further attack, however. "I don't see, anyhow, w'at reason you had to marry me, w'en there were so many others," she complained, as if accusing him of persecution and injury. "There was Marianne running after you fo' the las' five years till it was disgraceful; an' any one of the Dortrand girls would have been glad to marry you. But no, nothing would do; you mus' come out on the *rigolet* fo' me." Her complaint was pathetic, and at the same time so amusing that Cazeau was forced to smile.

"I can't see w'at the Dortrand girls or Marianne have to do with it," he rejoined, adding, with no trace of amusement, "I married you because I loved you; because you were the woman I wanted to marry, an' the only one. I reckon I tole you that befo'. I thought—of co'se I was a fool fo' taking things fo' granted—but I did think that I might make you happy in making things easier an' mo' comfortable fo' you. I expected—I was even that big a fool—I believed that yo' coming yere to me would be like the sun shining out of the clouds, an' that our days would be like w'at the story-books promise after the wedding. I was mistaken. But I can't imagine w'at induced you to marry me. W'atever it was, I reckon you foun' out you made a mistake, too. I don' see anything to do but make the best of a bad bargain, an' shake han's over it." He had arisen from the table, and, approaching, held out his hand to her. What he had said was commonplace enough, but it was significant, coming from Cazeau, who was not often so unreserved in expressing himself.

Athénaïse ignored the hand held out to her. She was resting her chin in her palm, and kept her eyes fixed moodily upon the table. He rested his hand, that she would not touch, upon her head for an instant, and walked away out of the room.

She heard him giving orders to workmen who had been waiting for him out on the gallery, and she heard him mount his horse and ride away. A hundred things would distract him and engage his attention during the day. She felt that he had perhaps put her and her grievance from his thoughts when he crossed the threshold; whilst she—

Old Félicité was standing there holding a shining tin pail, asking for flour and lard and eggs from the storeroom, and meal for the chicks.

Athénaïse seized the bunch of keys which hung from her belt and flung them at Félicité's feet.

*"Tiens! tu vas les garder comme tu as jadis fait. Je ne veux plus de ce train là, moi!"**

The old woman stooped and picked up the keys from the floor. It was really all one to her that her mistress returned

---

* Hey! You'll keep them like you used to. I want no more of this business! (Fr.).

them to her keeping, and refused to take further account of the *ménage*.

IV

IT SEEMED NOW TO Athénaïse that Montéclin was the only friend left to her in the world. Her father and mother had turned from her in what appeared to be her hour of need. Her friends laughed at her, and refused to take seriously the hints which she threw out—feeling her way to discover if marriage were as distasteful to other women as to herself. Montéclin alone understood her. He alone had always been ready to act for her and with her, to comfort and solace her with his sympathy and his support. Her only hope for rescue from her hateful surroundings lay in Montéclin. Of herself she felt powerless to plan, to act, even to conceive a way out of this pitfall into which the whole world seemed to have conspired to thrust her.

She had a great desire to see her brother, and wrote asking him to come to her. But it better suited Montéclin's spirit of adventure to appoint a meeting-place at the turn of the lane, where Athénaïse might appear to be walking leisurely for health and recreation, and where he might seem to be riding along, bent on some errand of business or pleasure.

There had been a shower, a sudden downpour, short as it was sudden, that had laid the dust in the road. It had freshened the pointed leaves of the live-oaks, and brightened up the big fields of cotton on either side of the lane till they seemed carpeted with green, glittering gems.

Athénaïse walked along the grassy edge of the road, lifting her crisp skirts with one hand, and with the other twirling a gay sunshade over her bare head. The scent of the fields after the rain was delicious. She inhaled long breaths of their freshness and perfume, that soothed and quieted her for the moment. There were birds splashing and spluttering in the pools, pluming themselves on the fence-rails, and sending out little sharp cries, twitters, and shrill rhapsodies of delight.

She saw Montéclin approaching from a great distance—almost as far away as the turn of the woods. But she could not feel sure it was he; it appeared too tall for Montéclin, but that was because he was riding a large horse. She waved her parasol to him; she was so glad to see him. She had never been so glad to see Montéclin before; not even the day when he had taken her out of the convent, against her parents' wishes, because she had expressed a desire to remain there no longer. He seemed to her, as he drew near, the embodiment of kindness, of bravery, of chivalry, even of wisdom; for she had never known Montéclin at a loss to extricate himself from a disagreeable situation.

He dismounted, and, leading his horse by the bridle, started to walk beside her, after he had kissed her affectionately and asked her what she was crying about. She protested that she was not crying, for she was laughing, though drying her eyes at the same time on her handkerchief, rolled in a soft mop for the purpose.

She took Montéclin's arm, and they strolled slowly down the lane; they could not seat themselves for a comfortable chat, as they would have liked, with the grass all sparkling and bristling wet.

Yes, she was quite as wretched as ever, she told him. The week which had gone by since she saw him had in no wise lightened the burden of her discontent. There had even been some additional provocations laid upon her, and she told Montéclin all about them—about the keys, for instance, which in a fit of temper she had returned to Félicité's keeping; and she told how Cazeau had brought them back to her as if they were something she had accidentally lost, and he had recovered; and how he had said, in that aggravating tone of his, that it was not the custom on Cane River for the negro servants to carry the keys, when there was a mistress at the head of the household.

But Athénaïse could not tell Montéclin anything to increase the disrespect which he already entertained for his brother-in-law; and it was then he unfolded to her a plan

which he had conceived and worked out for her deliverance
from this galling matrimonial yoke.

It was not a plan which met with instant favor, which she
was at once ready to accept, for it involved secrecy and dissimulation, hateful alternatives, both of them. But she was filled
with admiration for Montéclin's resources and wonderful
talent for contrivance. She accepted the plan; not with the
immediate determination to act upon it, rather with the intention to sleep and to dream upon it.

Three days later she wrote to Montéclin that she had abandoned herself to his counsel. Displeasing as it might be to her
sense of honesty, it would yet be less trying than to live on
with a soul full of bitterness and revolt, as she had done for the
past two months.

V

WHEN CAZEAU AWOKE, one morning at his usual very early
hour, it was to find the place at his side vacant. This did not
surprise him until he discovered that Athénaïse was not in the
adjoining room, where he had often found her sleeping in the
morning on the lounge. She had perhaps gone out for an
early stroll, he reflected, for her jacket and hat were not on
the rack where she had hung them the night before. But there
were other things absent—a gown or two from the armoire;
and there was a great gap in the piles of lingerie on the shelf;
and her traveling-bag was missing, and so were her bits of jew-
elry from the toilet tray—and Athénaïse was gone!

But the absurdity of going during the night, as if she had
been a prisoner, and he the keeper of a dungeon! So much secrecy and mystery, to go sojourning out on the Bon Dieu!
Well, the Michés might keep their daughter after this. For the
companionship of no woman on earth would he again undergo the humiliating sensation of baseness that had overtaken him in passing the old oak-tree in the fallow meadow.

But a terrible sense of loss overwhelmed Cazeau. It was

not new or sudden; he had felt it for weeks growing upon him, and it seemed to culminate with Athénaïse's flight from home. He knew that he could again compel her return as he had done once before—compel her to return to the shelter of his roof, compel her cold and unwilling submission to his love and passionate transports; but the loss of self-respect seemed to him too dear a price to pay for a wife.

He could not comprehend why she had seemed to prefer him above others; why she had attracted him with eyes, with voice, with a hundred womanly ways, and finally distracted him with love which she seemed, in her timid, maidenly fashion, to return. The great sense of loss came from the realization of having missed a chance for happiness—a chance that would come his way again only through a miracle. He could not think of himself loving any other woman, and could not think of Athénaïse ever—even at some remote date—caring for him.

He wrote her a letter, in which he disclaimed any further intention of forcing his commands upon her. He did not desire her presence ever again in his home unless she came of her free will, uninfluenced by family or friends; unless she could be the companion he had hoped for in marrying her, and in some measure return affection and respect for the love which he continued and would always continue to feel for her. This letter he sent out to the *rigolet* by a messenger early in the day. But she was not out on the *rigolet*, and had not been there.

The family turned instinctively to Montéclin, and almost literally fell upon him for an explanation; he had been absent from home all night. There was much mystification in his answers, and a plain desire to mislead in his assurances of ignorance and innocence.

But with Cazeau there was no doubt or speculation when he accosted the young fellow. "Montéclin, w'at have you done with Athénaïse?" he questioned bluntly. They had met in the open road on horseback, just as Cazeau ascended the river bank before his house.

"W'at have you done to Athénaïse?" returned Montéclin for answer.

"I don't reckon you've considered yo' conduct by any light of decency an' propriety in encouraging yo' sister to such an action, but let me tell you"—

"*Voyons!*° you can let me alone with yo' decency an' morality an' fiddlesticks. I know you mus' 'a' done Athénaïse pretty mean that she can't live with you; an' fo' my part, I'm mighty durn glad she had the spirit to quit you."

"I ain't in the humor to take any notice of yo' impertinence, Montéclin; but let me remine you that Athénaïse is nothing but a chile in character; besides that, she's my wife, an' I hole you responsible fo' her safety an' welfare. If any harm of any description happens to her, I'll strangle you, by God, like a rat, and fling you in Cane River, if I have to hang fo' it!" He had not lifted his voice. The only sign of anger was a savage gleam in his eyes.

"I reckon you better keep yo' big talk fo' the women, Cazeau," replied Montéclin, riding away.

But he went doubly armed after that, and intimated that the precaution was not needless, in view of the threats and menaces that were abroad touching his personal safety.

VI

ATHÉNAÏSE REACHED HER destination sound of skin and limb, but a good deal flustered, a little frightened, and altogether excited and interested by her unusual experiences.

Her destination was the house of Sylvie, on Dauphine Street,† in New Orleans—a three-story gray brick, standing directly on the banquette, with three broad stone steps leading to the deep front entrance. From the second-story balcony

---

° Go on! (Fr.).

† A street in the French Quarter named after a branch of the Bourbon family.

swung a small sign, conveying to passers-by the intelligence that within were "*chambres garnies*."

It was one morning in the last week of April that Athénaïse presented herself at the Dauphine Street house. Sylvie was expecting her, and introduced her at once to her apartment, which was in the second story of the back ell,* and accessible by an open, outside gallery. There was a yard below, paved with broad stone flagging; many fragrant flowering shrubs and plants grew in a bed along the side of the opposite wall, and others were distributed about in tubs and green boxes.

It was a plain but large enough room into which Athénaïse was ushered, with matting on the floor, green shades and Nottingham-lace curtains at the windows that looked out on the gallery, and furnished with a cheap walnut suit. But everything looked exquisitely clean, and the whole place smelled of cleanliness.

Athénaïse at once fell into the rocking-chair, with the air of exhaustion and intense relief of one who has come to the end of her troubles. Sylvie, entering behind her, laid the big traveling-bag on the floor and deposited the jacket on the bed.

She was a portly quadroon of fifty or there-about, clad in an ample *volante* of the old-fashioned purple calico so much affected by her class. She wore large golden hoop-earrings, and her hair was combed plainly, with every appearance of effort to smooth out the kinks. She had broad, coarse features, with a nose that turned up, exposing the wide nostrils, and that seemed to emphasize the loftiness and command of her bearing—a dignity that in the presence of white people assumed a character of respectfulness, but never of obsequiousness. Sylvie believed firmly in maintaining the color line, and would not suffer a white person, even a child, to call her "Madame Sylvie"—a title which she exacted religiously, however, from those of her own race.

---

* A back extension of the building, at a right angle to the house, in the shape of the letter L.

"I hope you be please' wid yo' room, madame," she observed amiably. "Dat's de same room w'at yo' brother, M'sieur Miché, all time like w'en he come to New Orlean'. He well, M'sieur Miché? I receive' his letter las' week, an' dat same day a gent'man want I give 'im dat room. I say, 'No, dat room already ingage'.' Ev-body like dat room on 'count it so quite (quiet). M'sieur Gouvernail, dere in nax' room, you can't pay 'im! He been stay t'ree year' in dat room; but all fix' up fine wid his own furn'ture an' books, 'tel you can't see! I say to 'im plenty time', 'M'sieur Gouvernail, w'y you don't take dat t'ree-story front, now, long it's empty?' He tells me, 'Leave me 'lone, Sylvie; I know a good room w'en I fine it, me.' "

She had been moving slowly and majestically about the apartment, straightening and smoothing down bed and pillows, peering into ewer and basin, evidently casting an eye around to make sure that everything was as it should be.

"I sen' you some fresh water, madame," she offered upon retiring from the room. "An' w'en you want an't'ing, you jus' go out on de gall'ry an' call Pousette: she year you plain—she right down dere in de kitchen."

Athénaïse was really not so exhausted as she had every reason to be after that interminable and circuitous way by which Montéclin had seen fit to have her conveyed to the city.

Would she ever forget that dark and truly dangerous midnight ride along the "coast" to the mouth of Cane River! There Montéclin had parted with her, after seeing her aboard the St. Louis and Shreveport packet* which he knew would pass there before dawn. She had received instructions to disembark at the mouth of Red River,† and there transfer to the first south-bound steamer for New Orleans; all of which instructions she had followed implicitly, even to making her way at once to Sylvie's upon her arrival in the city. Montéclin had enjoined secrecy and much caution; the clandestine na-

---

* A passenger boat usually carrying mail or cargo.

† A major waterway in northern Louisiana, intersected by the Cane River.

ture of the affair gave it a savor of adventure which was highly pleasing to him. Eloping with his sister was only a little less engaging than eloping with some one else's sister.

But Montéclin did not do the *grand seigneur** by halves. He had paid Sylvie a whole month in advance for Athénaïse's board and lodging. Part of the sum he had been forced to borrow, it is true, but he was not niggardly.[†]

Athénaïse was to take her meals in the house, which none of the other lodgers did, the one exception being that Mr. Gouvernail was served with breakfast on Sunday mornings.

Sylvie's clientèle came chiefly from the southern parishes, for the most part, people spending but a few days in the city. She prided herself upon the quality and highly respectable character of her patrons, who came and went unobtrusively.

The large parlor opening upon the front balcony was seldom used. Her guests were permitted to entertain in this sanctuary of elegance—but they never did. She often rented it for the night to parties of respectable and discreet gentlemen desiring to enjoy a quiet game of cards outside the bosom of their families. The second-story hall also led by a long window out on the balcony. And Sylvie advised Athénaïse, when she grew weary of her back room, to go and sit on the front balcony, which was shady in the afternoon, and where she might find diversion in the sounds and sights of the street below.

Athénaïse refreshed herself with a bath, and was soon unpacking her few belongings, which she ranged neatly away in the bureau drawers and the armoire.

She had revolved certain plans in her mind during the past hour or so. Her present intention was to live on indefinitely in this big, cool, clean back room on Dauphine Street. She had thought seriously, for moments, of the convent, with all readiness to embrace the vows of poverty and chastity; but what about obedience? Later, she intended, in some round-

---

* Play the part of the nobleman (Fr.).

† Stingy.

about way, to give her parents and her husband the assurance of her safety and welfare, reserving the right to remain un-molested and lost to them. To live on at the expense of Montéclin's generosity was wholly out of the question, and Athénaïse meant to look about for some suitable and agree-able employment.

The imperative thing to be done at present, however, was to go out in search of material for an inexpensive gown or two; for she found herself in the painful predicament of a young woman having almost literally nothing to wear. She decided upon pure white for one, and some sort of a sprigged muslin* for the other.

VII

ON SUNDAY MORNING, two days after Athénaïse's arrival in the city, she went in to breakfast somewhat later than usual, to find two covers laid at table instead of the one to which she was accustomed. She had been to mass, and did not remove her hat, but put her fan, parasol, and prayer-book aside. The dining-room was situated just beneath her own apartment, and, like all rooms of the house, was large and airy; the floor was covered with a glistening oil-cloth.

The small, round table, immaculately set, was drawn near the open window. There were some tall plants in boxes on the gallery outside; and Pousette, a little, old, intensely black woman, was splashing and dashing buckets of water on the flagging, and talk-ing loud in her Creole patois to no one in particular.

A dish piled with delicate river-shrimps and crushed ice was on the table; a carafe of crystal-clear water, a few *hors d'oeuvres*,† beside a small golden-brown crusty loaf of French bread at each plate. A half-bottle of wine and the morning pa-per were set at the place opposite Athénaïse.

---

* Lightweight cotton with a small decorative pattern.

† Appetizers (Fr.).

She had almost completed her breakfast when Gouvernail came in and seated himself at table. He felt annoyed at finding his cherished privacy invaded. Sylvie was removing the remains of a mutton-chop from before Athénaïse, and serving her with a cup of café au lait.

"M'sieur Gouvernail," offered Sylvie in her most insinuating and impressive manner, "you please leave me make you acquaint' wid Madame Cazeau. Dat's M'sieur Miché's sister; you meet 'im two t'ree time', you rec'lec', an' been one day to de race wid 'im. Madame Cazeau, you please leave me make you acquaint' wid M'sieur Gouvernail."

Gouvernail expressed himself greatly pleased to meet the sister of Monsieur Miché, of whom he had not the slightest recollection. He inquired after Monsieur Miché's health, and politely offered Athénaïse a part of his newspaper—the part which contained the Woman's Page and the social gossip.

Athénaïse faintly remembered that Sylvie had spoken of a Monsieur Gouvernail occupying the room adjoining hers, living amid luxurious surroundings and a multitude of books. She had not thought of him further than to picture him a stout, middle-aged gentleman, with a bushy beard turning gray, wearing large gold-rimmed spectacles, and stooping somewhat from much bending over books and writing material. She had confused him in her mind with the likeness of some literary celebrity that she had run across in the advertising pages of a magazine.

Gouvernail's appearance was, in truth, in no sense striking. He looked older than thirty and younger than forty, was of medium height and weight, with a quiet, unobtrusive manner which seemed to ask that he be let alone. His hair was light brown, brushed carefully and parted in the middle. His mustache was brown, and so were his eyes, which had a mild, penetrating quality. He was neatly dressed in the fashion of the day; and his hands seemed to Athénaïse remarkably white and soft for a man's.

He had been buried in the contents of his newspaper, when he suddenly realized that some further little attention might be due to Miché's sister. He started to offer her a glass of wine, when he was surprised and relieved to find that she had quietly slipped away while he was absorbed in his own editorial on Corrupt Legislation.

Gouvernail finished his paper and smoked his cigar out on the gallery. He lounged about, gathered a rose for his buttonhole, and had his regular Sunday-morning confab° with Pousette, to whom he paid a weekly stipend for brushing his shoes and clothing. He made a great pretense of haggling over the transaction, only to enjoy her uneasiness and garrulous excitement.

He worked or read in his room for a few hours, and when he quitted the house, at three in the afternoon, it was to return no more till late at night. It was his almost invariable custom to spend Sunday evenings out in the American quarter, among a congenial set of men and women — *des esprits forts*,† all of them, whose lives were irreproachable, yet whose opinions would startle even the traditional *"sapeur,"*‡ for whom "nothing is sacred." But for all his "advanced" opinions, Gouvernail was a liberal-minded fellow; a man or woman lost nothing of his respect by being married.

When he left the house in the afternoon, Athénaïse had already ensconced herself on the front balcony. He could see her through the jalousies§ when he passed on his way to the front entrance. She had not yet grown lonesome or homesick; the newness of her surroundings made them sufficiently entertaining. She found it diverting to sit there on the front balcony watching people pass by, even though there was no one to talk to. And then the comforting, comfortable sense of not being married!

She watched Gouvernail walk down the street, and could find no fault with his bearing. He could hear the sound of her

---

* Short for confabulation, a chat.

† Free spirits (Fr.).

‡ Fearless soldier (Fr.).

§ Windows made of adjustable glass louvers that control ventilation.

rockers for some little distance. He wondered what the "poor little thing" was doing in the city, and meant to ask Sylvie about her when he should happen to think of it.

VIII

THE FOLLOWING MORNING, toward noon, when Gouvernail quitted his room, he was confronted by Athénaïse, exhibiting some confusion and trepidation at being forced to request a favor of him at so early a stage of their acquaintance. She stood in her doorway, and had evidently been sewing, as the thimble on her finger testified, as well as a long-threaded needle thrust in the bosom of her gown. She held a stamped but unaddressed letter in her hand.

And would Mr. Gouvernail be so kind as to address the letter to her brother, Mr. Montéclin Miché? She would hate to detain him with explanations this morning—another time, perhaps—but now she begged that he would give himself the trouble.

He assured her that it made no difference, that it was no trouble whatever; and he drew a fountain pen from his pocket and addressed the letter at her dictation, resting it on the inverted rim of his straw hat. She wondered a little at a man of his supposed erudition stumbling over the spelling of "Montéclin" and "Miché."

She demurred at overwhelming him with the additional trouble of posting it, but he succeeded in convincing her that so simple a task as the posting of a letter would not add an iota to the burden of the day. Moreover, he promised to carry it in his hand, and thus avoid any possible risk of forgetting it in his pocket.

After that, and after a second repetition of the favor, when she had told him that she had had a letter from Montéclin, and looked as if she wanted to tell him more, he felt that he knew her better. He felt that he knew her well enough to join her out on the balcony, one night, when he found her sitting there alone. He was not one who deliberately sought the soci-

ety of women, but he was not wholly a bear.* A little commiseration for Athénaïse's aloneness, perhaps some curiosity to
know further what manner of woman she was, and the natural
influence of her feminine charm were equal unconfessed fac-
tors in turning his steps towards the balcony when he discovered the shimmer of her white gown through the open hall
window.

It was already quite late, but the day had been intensely
hot, and neighboring balconies and doorways were occupied
by chattering groups of humanity, loath to abandon the grateful freshness of the outer air. The voices about her served to
reveal to Athénaïse the feeling of loneliness that was gradually
coming over her. Notwithstanding certain dormant impulses,
she craved human sympathy and companionship.

She shook hands impulsively with Gouvernail, and told
him how glad she was to see him. He was not prepared for
such an admission, but it pleased him immensely, detecting
as he did that the expression was as sincere as it was outspoken. He drew a chair up within comfortable conversational
distance of Athénaïse, though he had no intention of talking
more than was barely necessary to encourage Madame—he
had actually forgotten her name!

He leaned an elbow on the balcony rail, and would have
offered an opening remark about the oppressive heat of the
day, but Athénaïse did not give him the opportunity. How
glad she was to talk to some one, and how she talked!

An hour later she had gone to her room, and Gouvernail
stayed smoking on the balcony. He knew her quite well after
that hour's talk. It was not so much what she had said as what
her half saying had revealed to his quick intelligence. He
knew that she adored Montéclin, and he suspected that she
adored Cazeau without being herself aware of it. He had gathered that she was self-willed, impulsive, innocent, ignorant,
unsatisfied, dissatisfied; for had she not complained that
things seemed all wrongly arranged in this world, and no one

---

* A surly person.

was permitted to be happy in his own way? And he told her he was sorry she had discovered that primordial fact of existence so early in life.

He commiserated her loneliness, and scanned his bookshelves next morning for something to lend her to read, rejecting everything that offered itself to his view. Philosophy was out of the question, and so was poetry; that is, such poetry as he possessed. He had not sounded her literary tastes, and strongly suspected she had none; that she would have rejected The Duchess* as readily as Mrs. Humphry Ward.† He compromised on a magazine.

It had entertained her passably, she admitted, upon returning it. A New England story had puzzled her, it was true, and a Creole tale had offended her, but the pictures had pleased her greatly, especially one which had reminded her so strongly of Montéclin after a hard day's ride that she was loath to give it up. It was one of Remington's cowboys,‡ and Gouvernail insisted upon her keeping it—keeping the magazine.

He spoke to her daily after that, and was always eager to render her some service or to do something toward her entertainment.

One afternoon he took her out to the lake end. She had been there once, some years before, but in winter, so the trip was comparatively new and strange to her. The large expanse of water studded with pleasure-boats, the sight of children playing merrily along the grassy palisades,§ the music, all enchanted her. Gouvernail thought her the most beautiful

---

* A pseudonym for the popular Irish writer Margaret Wolfe Hungerford (?1855–1897), whose novels were considered light reading; in 1893 she published *Lady Verner's Flight*, a work about an abused wife.

† Mrs. Ward was an English writer of serious fiction concerned with social problems.

‡ The reference is to Frederick Remington (1861–1909), a popular magazine artist known for his images of the Wild West.

§ A line of bold cliffs overlooking the water.

woman he had ever seen. Even her gown—the sprigged muslin—appeared to him the most charming one imaginable. Nor could anything be more becoming than the arrangement of her brown hair under the white sailor hat, all rolled back in a soft puff from her radiant face. And she carried her parasol and lifted her skirts and used her fan in ways that seemed quite unique and peculiar to herself, and which he considered almost worthy of study and imitation.

They did not dine out there at the water's edge, as they might have done, but returned early to the city to avoid the crowd. Athénaïse wanted to go home, for she said Sylvie would have dinner prepared and would be expecting her. But it was not difficult to persuade her to dine instead in the quiet little restaurant that he knew and liked, with its sanded floor, its secluded atmosphere, its delicious menu, and its obsequious waiter wanting to know what he might have the honor of serving to "monsieur et madame." No wonder he made the mistake, with Gouvernail assuming such an air of proprietorship! But Athénaïse was very tired after it all; the sparkle went out of her face, and she hung draggingly on his arm in walking home.

He was reluctant to part from her when she bade him good-night at her door and thanked him for the agreeable evening. He had hoped she would sit outside until it was time for him to regain the newspaper office. He knew that she would undress and get into her peignoir and lie upon her bed; and what he wanted to do, what he would have given much to do, was to go and sit beside her, read to her something restful, soothe her, do her bidding, whatever it might be. Of course there was no use in thinking of that. But he was surprised at his growing desire to be serving her. She gave him an opportunity sooner than he looked for.

"Mr. Gouvernail," she called from her room, "will you be so kine as to call Pousette an' tell her she fo'got to bring my ice-water?"

He was indignant at Pousette's negligence, and called severely to her over the banisters. He was sitting before his own door, smoking. He knew that Athénaïse had gone to bed, for her room was dark, and she had opened the slats of the door and windows. Her bed was near a window.

Pousette came flopping up with the ice-water, and with a hundred excuses: "*Mo pa oua vou à tab c'te lanuite, mo cri vou pé gagni déja là-bas; parole! Vou pas cri conté ça* Madame Sylvie?" She had not seen Athénaïse at table, and thought she was gone. She swore to this, and hoped Madame Sylvie would not be informed of her remissness.

A little later Athénaïse lifted her voice again: "Mr. Gouvernail, did you remark that young man sitting on the opposite side from us, coming in, with a gray coat an' a blue ban' aroun' his hat?"

Of course Gouvernail had not noticed any such individual, but he assured Athénaïse that he had observed the young fellow particularly.

"Don't you think he looked something—not very much, of co'se—but don't you think he had a little faux-air of Montéclin?"

"I think he looked strikingly like Montéclin," asserted Gouvernail, with the one idea of prolonging the conversation. "I meant to call your attention to the resemblance, and something drove it out of my head."

"The same with me," returned Athénaïse. "Ah, my dear Montéclin! I wonder w'at he is doing now?"

"Did you receive any news, any letter from him to-day?" asked Gouvernail, determined that if the conversation ceased it should not be through lack of effort on his part to sustain it.

"Not to-day, but yesterday. He tells me that *maman* was so distracted with uneasiness that finally, to pacify her, he was fo'ced to confess that he knew w'ere I was, but that he was boun' by a vow of secrecy to not reveal it. But Cazeau has not noticed him or spoken to him since he threaten' to throw po'

---

* In free indirect discourse, Pousette's patois is translated into English in the sentences that follow, which give a series of excuses for her neglect of Athénaïse.

Montéclin in Cane River. You know Cazeau wrote me a letter the morning I lef', thinking I had gone to the *rigolet*. An' *maman* opened it, an' said it was full of the mos' noble sentiments, an' she wanted Montéclin to sen' it to me; but Montéclin refuse' poin' blank, so he wrote to me."

Gouvernail preferred to talk of Montéclin. He pictured Cazeau as unbearable, and did not like to think of him.

A little later Athénaïse called out, "Good-night, Mr. Gouvernail."

"Good-night," he returned reluctantly. And when he thought that she was sleeping, he got up and went away to the midnight pandemonium of his newspaper office.

IX

ATHÉNAÏSE COULD NOT have held out through the month had it not been for Gouvernail. With the need of caution and secrecy always uppermost in her mind, she made no new acquaintances, and she did not seek out persons already known to her; however, she knew so few, it required little effort to keep out of their way. As for Sylvie, almost every moment of her time was occupied in looking after her house; and, moreover, her deferential attitude toward her lodgers forbade anything like the gossipy chats in which Athénaïse might have condescended sometimes to indulge with her land-lady. The transient lodgers, who came and went, she never had occasion to meet. Hence she was entirely dependent upon Gouvernail for company.

He appreciated the situation fully; and every moment that he could spare from his work he devoted to her entertainment. She liked to be out of doors, and they strolled together in the summer twilight through the mazes of the old French Quarter. They went again to the lake end, and stayed for hours on the water, returning so late that the streets through which they passed were silent and deserted. On Sunday morning he arose at an unconscionable hour to take her to the French market, knowing that the sights and sounds there would interest her. And he did not join the intellectual coterie in the afternoon, as he usually did, but placed himself all day at the disposition and service of Athénaïse.

Notwithstanding all, his manner toward her was tactful, and evinced intelligence and a deep knowledge of her character, surprising upon so brief an acquaintance. For the time he was everything to her that she would have him; he replaced home and friends. Sometimes she wondered if he had ever loved a woman. She could not fancy him loving any one passionately, rudely, offensively, as Cazeau loved her. Once she was so naïve as to ask him outright if he had ever been in love, and he assured her promptly that he had not. She thought it an admirable trait in his character, and esteemed him greatly therefor.

He found her crying one night, not openly or violently. She was leaning over the gallery rail, watching the toads that hopped about in the moonlight, down on the damp flagstones of the courtyard. There was an oppressively sweet odor rising from the cape jessamine. Pousette was down there, mumbling and quarreling with some one, and seeming to be having it all her own way—as well she might, when her companion was only a black cat that had come in from a neighboring yard to keep her company.

Athénaïse did admit feeling heart-sick, body-sick, when he questioned her; she supposed it was nothing but homesick. A letter from Montéclin had stirred her all up. She longed for her mother, for Montéclin; she was sick for a sight of the cotton-fields, the scent of the plowed earth, for the dim, mysterious charm of the woods, and the old tumble-down home on the Bon Dieu.

As Gouvernail listened to her, a wave of pity and tenderness swept through him. He took her hands and pressed them against him. He wondered what would happen if he were to put his arms around her.

He was hardly prepared for what happened, but he stood it courageously. She twined her arms around his neck and wept outright on his shoulder, the hot tears scalding his cheek and neck, and her whole body shaken in his arms. The impulse was powerful to strain her to him; the temptation was fierce to seek her lips; but he did neither.

He understood a thousand times better than she herself understood it that he was acting as substitute for Montéclin. Bitter as the conviction was, he accepted it. He was patient; he could wait. He hoped some day to hold her with a lover's arms. That she was married made no particle of difference to Gouvernail. He could not conceive or dream of it making a difference. When the time came that she wanted him—as he hoped and believed it would come—he felt he would have a right to her. So long as she did not want him, he had no right to her—no more than her husband had. It was very hard to feel her warm breath and tears upon his cheek, and her struggling bosom pressed against him and her soft arms clinging to him and his whole body and soul aching for her, and yet to make no sign.

He tried to think what Montéclin would have said and done, and to act accordingly. He stroked her hair, and held her in a gentle embrace, until the tears dried and the sobs ended. Before releasing herself she kissed him against the neck; she had to love somebody in her own way! Even that he endured like a stoic. But it was well he left her, to plunge into the thick of rapid, breathless, exacting work till nearly dawn.

Athénaïse was greatly soothed, and slept well. The touch of friendly hands and caressing arms had been very grateful. Henceforward she would not be lonely and unhappy, with Gouvernail there to comfort her.

X

THE FOURTH WEEK OF Athénaïse's stay in the city was drawing to a close. Keeping in view the intention which she had of finding some suitable and agreeable employment, she had made a few tentatives in that direction. But with the exception of two little girls who had promised to take piano lessons at a price that would be embarrassing to mention, these attempts had been fruitless. Moreover, the homesickness kept coming back, and Gouvernail was not always there to drive it away.

She spent much of her time weeding and pottering among the flowers down in the courtyard. She tried to take an interest in the black cat, and a mocking-bird that hung in a cage outside the kitchen door, and a disreputable parrot that belonged to the cook next door, and swore hoarsely all day long in bad French.

Beside, she was not well; she was not herself, as she told Sylvie. The climate of New Orleans did not agree with her. Sylvie was distressed to learn this, as she felt in some measure responsible for the health and well-being of Monsieur Miché's sister; and she made it her duty to inquire closely into the nature and character of Athénaïse's malaise.

Sylvie was very wise, and Athénaïse was very ignorant. The extent of her ignorance and the depth of her subsequent enlightenment were bewildering. She stayed a long, long time quite still, quite stunned, after her interview with Sylvie, except for the short, uneven breathing that ruffled her bosom. Her whole being was steeped in a wave of ecstasy. When she finally arose from the chair in which she had been seated, and looked at herself in the mirror, a face met hers which she seemed to see for the first time, so transfigured was it with wonder and rapture.

One mood quickly followed another, in this new turmoil of her senses, and the need of action became uppermost. Her mother must know at once, and her mother must tell Montéclin. And Cazeau must know. As she thought of him, the first purely sensuous tremor of her life swept over her. She half whispered his name, and the sound of it brought red blotches into her cheeks. She spoke it over and over, as if it were some new, sweet sound born out of darkness and confusion, and reaching her for the first time. She was impatient to be with him. Her whole passionate nature was aroused as if by a miracle.

She seated herself to write to her husband. The letter he

would get in the morning, and she would be with him at night. What would he say? How would he act? She knew that he would forgive her, for had he not written a letter?—and a pang of resentment toward Montéclin shot through her. What did he mean by withholding that letter? How dared he not have sent it?

Athénaïse attired herself for the street, and went out to post the letter which she had penned with a single thought, a spontaneous impulse. It would have seemed incoherent to most people, but Cazeau would understand.

She walked along the street as if she had fallen heir to some magnificent inheritance. On her face was a look of pride and satisfaction that passers-by noticed and admired. She wanted to talk to some one, to tell some person; and she stopped at the corner and told the oyster-woman, who was Irish, and who God-blessed her, and wished prosperity to the race of Cazeaus for generations to come. She held the oyster-woman's fat, dirty little baby in her arms and scanned it curiously and observingly, as if a baby were a phenomenon that she encountered for the first time in life. She even kissed it!

Then what a relief it was to Athénaïse to walk the streets without dread of being seen and recognized by some chance acquaintance from Red River! No one could have said now that she did not know her own mind.

She went directly from the oyster-woman's to the office of Harding & Offdean, her husband's merchants; and it was with such an air of partnership, almost proprietorship, that she demanded a sum of money on her husband's account, they gave it to her as unhesitatingly as they would have handed it over to Cazeau himself. When Mr. Harding, who knew her, asked politely after her health, she turned so rosy and looked so conscious, he thought it a great pity for so pretty a woman to be such a little goose.

Athénaïse entered a dry-goods store and bought all manner of things—little presents for nearly everybody she knew. She bought whole bolts of sheerest, softest, downiest white stuff; and when the clerk, in trying to meet her wishes, asked if she intended it for infant's use, she could have sunk through the floor, and wondered how he might have suspected it.

As it was Montéclin who had taken her away from her husband, she wanted it to be Montéclin who should take her back to him. So she wrote him a very curt note — in fact it was a postal card — asking that he meet her at the train on the evening following. She felt convinced that after what had gone before, Cazeau would await her at their own home; and she preferred it so.

Then there was the agreeable excitement of getting ready to leave, of packing up her things. Pousette kept coming and going, coming and going; and each time that she quitted the room it was with something that Athénaïse had given her — a handkerchief, a petticoat, a pair of stockings with two tiny holes at the toes, some broken prayer-beads, and finally a silver dollar.

Next it was Sylvie who came along bearing a gift of what she called "a set of pattern'" — things of complicated design which never could have been obtained in any new-fangled bazaar or pattern-store, that Sylvie had acquired of a foreign lady of distinction whom she had nursed years before at the St. Charles Hotel. Athénaïse accepted and handled them with reverence, fully sensible of the great compliment and favor, and laid them religiously away in the trunk which she had lately acquired.

She was greatly fatigued after the day of unusual exertion, and went early to bed and to sleep. All day long she had not once thought of Gouvernail, and only did think of him when aroused for a brief instant by the sound of his foot-falls on the gallery, as he passed in going to his room. He had hoped to find her up, waiting for him.

But the next morning he knew. Some one must have told him. There was no subject known to her which Sylvie hesitated to discuss in detail with any man of suitable years and discretion.

Athénaïse found Gouvernail waiting with a carriage to convey her to the railway station. A momentary pang visited her for having forgotten him so completely, when he said to her, "Sylvie tells me you are going away this morning."

He was kind, attentive, and amiable, as usual, but respected to the utmost the new dignity and reserve that her manner had developed since yesterday. She kept looking from the carriage window, silent, and embarrassed as Eve after losing her ignorance. He talked of the muddy streets and the murky morning, and of Montéclin. He hoped she would find everything comfortable and pleasant in the country, and trusted she would inform him whenever she came to visit the city again. He talked as if afraid or mistrustful of silence and himself.

At the station she handed him her purse, and he bought her ticket, secured for her a comfortable section, checked her trunk, and got all the bundles and things safely aboard the train. She felt very grateful. He pressed her hand warmly, lifted his hat, and left her. He was a man of intelligence, and took defeat gracefully; that was all. But as he made his way back to the carriage, he was thinking, "By heaven, it hurts, it hurts!"

XI

ATHÉNAÏSE SPENT A day of supreme happiness and expectancy. The fair sight of the country unfolding itself before her was balm to her vision and to her soul. She was charmed with the rather unfamiliar, broad, clean sweep of the sugar plantations, with their monster sugar-houses, their rows of neat cabins like little villages of a single street, and their impressive homes standing apart amid clusters of trees. There were sudden glimpses of a bayou curling between sunny, grassy banks, or creeping sluggishly out from a tangled growth of wood, and brush, and fern, and poison-vines, and palmettos. And passing through the long stretches of monotonous woodlands, she would close her eyes and taste in anticipation the moment of her meeting with Cazeau. She could think of nothing but him.

It was night when she reached her station. There was Montéclin, as she had expected, waiting for her with a two-seated buggy, to which he had hitched his own swift-footed, spirited pony. It was good, he felt, to have her back on any terms; and he had no fault to find since she came of her own choice. He more than suspected the cause of her coming; her eyes and her voice and her foolish little manner went far in revealing the secret that was brimming over in her heart. But after he had deposited her at her own gate, and as he continued his way toward the rigolet, he could not help feeling that the affair had taken a very disappointing, an ordinary, a most commonplace turn, after all. He left her in Cazeau's keeping.

Her husband lifted her out of the buggy, and neither said a word until they stood together within the shelter of the gallery. Even then they did not speak at first. But Athénaïse turned to him with an appealing gesture. As he clasped her in his arms, he felt the yielding of her whole body against him. He felt her lips for the first time respond to the passion of his own.

The country night was dark and warm and still, save for the distant notes of an accordion which some one was playing in a cabin away off. A little negro baby was crying somewhere. As Athénaïse withdrew from her husband's embrace, the sound arrested her.

"Listen, Cazeau! How Juliette's baby is crying! *Pauvre ti chou,*[*] I wonder w'at is the matter with it?"

---

[*] Poor little dear (Fr.).

A PAIR OF SILK STOCKINGS

LITTLE MRS. SOMMERS ONE day found herself the unexpected possessor of fifteen dollars. It seemed to her a very large amount of money, and the way in which it stuffed and bulged her worn old *porte-monnaie** gave her a feeling of importance such as she had not enjoyed for years.

The question of investment was one that occupied her greatly. For a day or two she walked about apparently in a dreamy state, but really absorbed in speculation and calculation. She did not wish to act hastily, to do anything she might afterward regret. But it was during the still hours of the night when she lay awake revolving plans in her mind that she seemed to see her way clearly toward a proper and judicious use of the money.

A dollar or two should be added to the price usually paid for Janie's shoes, which would insure their lasting an appreciable time longer than they usually did. She would buy so and so many yards of percale for new shirt waists for the boys and Janie and Mag. She had intended to make the old ones do by skillful patching. Mag should have another gown. She had seen some beautiful patterns, veritable bargains in the shop windows. And still there would be left enough for new stockings — two pairs apiece — and what darning that would save for a while! She would get caps for the boys and sailor-hats for the girls. The vision of her little brood looking fresh and dainty and new for once in their lives excited her and made her restless and wakeful with anticipation.

The neighbors sometimes talked of certain "better days" that little Mrs. Sommers had known before she had ever thought of being Mrs. Sommers. She herself indulged in no such morbid retrospection. She had no time — no second of time to devote to the past. The needs of the present absorbed

* Wallet (Fr.).

her every faculty. A vision of the future like some dim, gaunt monster sometimes appalled her, but luckily to-morrow never comes.

Mrs. Sommers was one who knew the value of bargains; who could stand for hours making her way inch by inch toward the desired object that was selling below cost. She could elbow her way if need be; she had learned to clutch a piece of goods and hold it and stick to it with persistence and determination till her turn came to be served, no matter when it came.

But that day she was a little faint and tired. She had swallowed a light luncheon—no! when she came to think of it, between getting the children fed and the place righted, and preparing herself for the shopping bout, she had actually forgotten to eat any luncheon at all!

She sat herself upon a revolving stool before a counter that was comparatively deserted, trying to gather strength and courage to charge through an eager multitude that was besieging breast-works of shirting and figured lawn.* An all-gone limp feeling had come over her and she rested her hand aimlessly upon the counter. She wore no gloves. By degrees she grew aware that her hand had encountered something very soothing, very pleasant to touch. She looked down to see that her hand lay upon a pile of silk stockings. A placard near by announced that they had been reduced in price from two dollars and fifty cents to one dollar and ninety-eight cents; and a young girl who stood behind the counter asked her if she wished to examine their line of silk hosiery. She smiled, just as if she had been asked to inspect a tiara of diamonds with the ultimate view of purchasing it. But she went on feeling the soft, sheeny luxurious things—with both hands now, holding them up to see them glisten, and to feel them glide serpent-like through her fingers.

Two hectic blotches came suddenly into her pale cheeks. She looked up at the girl.

---

* Linen or cotton fabrics for making shirts.

"Do you think there are any eights-and-a-half among these?"

There were any number of eights-and-a-half. In fact, there were more of that size than any other. Here was a light-blue pair; there were some lavender, some all black and various shades of tan and gray. Mrs. Sommers selected a black pair and looked at them very long and closely. She pretended to be examining their texture, which the clerk assured her was excellent.

"A dollar and ninety-eight cents," she mused aloud. "Well, I'll take this pair." She handed the girl a five-dollar bill and waited for her change and for her parcel. What a very small parcel it was! It seemed lost in the depths of her shabby old shopping-bag.

Mrs. Sommers after that did not move in the direction of the bargain counter. She took the elevator, which carried her to an upper floor into the region of the ladies' waiting-rooms. Here, in a retired corner, she exchanged her cotton stockings for the new silk ones which she had just bought. She was not going through any acute mental process or reasoning with herself, nor was she striving to explain to her satisfaction the motive of her action. She was not thinking at all. She seemed for the time to be taking a rest from that laborious and fatiguing function and to have abandoned herself to some mechanical impulse that directed her actions and freed her of responsibility.

How good was the touch of the raw silk to her flesh! She felt like lying back in the cushioned chair and reveling for a while in the luxury of it. She did for a little while. Then she replaced her shoes, rolled the cotton stockings together and thrust them into her bag. After doing this she crossed straight over to the shoe department and took her seat to be fitted.

She was fastidious. The clerk could not make her out; he could not reconcile her shoes with her stockings, and she was not too easily pleased. She held back her skirts and turned her feet one way and her head another way as she glanced down at the polished, pointed-tipped boots. Her foot and ankle looked very pretty. She could not realize that they belonged to her and were a part of herself. She wanted an excellent and stylish fit, she told the young fellow who served her, and she did not mind the difference of a dollar or two more in the price so long as she got what she desired.

It was a long time since Mrs. Sommers had been fitted with gloves. On rare occasions when she had bought a pair they were always "bargains," so cheap that it would have been preposterous and unreasonable to have expected them to be fitted to the hand.

Now she rested her elbow on the cushion of the glove counter, and a pretty, pleasant young creature, delicate and deft of touch, drew a long-wristed "kid" over Mrs. Sommer's hand. She smoothed it down over the wrist and buttoned it neatly, and both lost themselves for a second or two in admiring contemplation of the little symmetrical gloved hand. But there were other places where money might be spent.

There were books and magazines piled up in the window of a stall a few paces down the street. Mrs. Sommers bought two high-priced magazines such as she had been accustomed to read in the days when she had been accustomed to other pleasant things. She carried them without wrapping. As well as she could she lifted her skirts at the crossings. Her stockings and boots and well-fitting gloves had worked marvels in her bearing—had given her a feeling of assurance, a sense of belonging to the well-dressed multitude.

She was very hungry. Another time she would have stilled the cravings for food until reaching her own home, where she would have brewed herself a cup of tea and taken a snack of anything that was available. But the impulse that was guiding her would not suffer her to entertain any such thought.

There was a restaurant at the corner. She had never entered its doors; from the outside she had sometimes caught glimpses of spotless damask and shining crystal, and soft-stepping waiters serving people of fashion.

When she entered her appearance created no surprise, no consternation, as she had half feared it might. She seated herself at a small table alone, and an attentive waiter at once approached to take her order. She did not want a profusion; she craved a nice and tasty bite—a half dozen blue-points,* a plump chop with cress, a something sweet—a crème-frappée,† for instance; a glass of Rhine wine, and after all a small cup of black coffee.

While waiting to be served she removed her gloves very leisurely and laid them beside her. Then she picked up a magazine and glanced through it, cutting the pages with a blunt edge of her knife. It was all very agreeable. The damask was even more spotless than it had seemed through the window, and the crystal more sparkling. There were quiet ladies and gentlemen, who did not notice her, lunching at the small tables like her own. A soft, pleasing strain of music could be heard, and a gentle breeze was blowing through the window. She tasted a bite, and she read a word or two, and she sipped the amber wine and wiggled her toes in the silk stockings. The price of it made no difference. She counted the money out to the waiter and left an extra coin on his tray, whereupon he bowed before her as before a princess of royal blood.

There was still money in her purse, and her next temptation presented itself in the shape of a matinée poster.

It was a little later when she entered the theater, the play had begun and the house seemed to her to be packed. But there were vacant seats here and there, and into one of them she was ushered, between brilliantly dressed women who had gone there to kill time and eat candy and display their gaudy attire. There were many others who were there solely for the play and acting. It is safe to say there was no one present who bore quite the attitude which Mrs. Sommers did to her surroundings. She gathered in the whole—stage and players and people in one wide impression, and absorbed it and enjoyed it. She laughed at the comedy and wept—she and the gaudy woman next to her wept over the tragedy. And they talked a

* A type of oyster.

† A whipped-cream drink (Fr.).

little together over it. And the gaudy woman wiped her eyes
and sniffled on a tiny square of filmy, perfumed lace and
passed little Mrs. Sommers her box of candy.

The play was over, the music ceased, the crowd filed out.
It was like a dream ended. People scattered in all directions.
Mrs. Sommers went to the corner and waited for the cable
car.

A man with keen eyes, who sat opposite to her, seemed to
like the study of her small, pale face. It puzzled him to deci-
pher what he saw there. In truth, he saw nothing—unless he
were wizard enough to detect a poignant wish, a powerful
longing that the cable car would never stop anywhere, but go
on and on with her forever.

ELIZABETH STOCK'S ONE STORY

‿✺‿

ELIZABETH STOCK, AN UNMARRIED woman of thirty-eight, died of consumption during the past winter at the St. Louis City Hospital. There were no unusually pathetic features attending her death. The physicians say she showed hope of rallying till placed in the incurable ward, when all courage seemed to leave her, and she relapsed into a silence that remained unbroken till the end.

In Stonelift,* the village where Elizabeth Stock was born and raised, and where I happen to be sojourning this summer, they say she was much given over to scribbling. I was permitted to examine her desk, which was quite filled with scraps and bits of writing in bad prose and impossible verse. In the whole conglomerate mass, I discovered but the following pages which bore any semblance to a connected or consecutive narration.

Since I was a girl I always felt as if I would like to write stories. I never had that ambition to shine or make a name; first place because I knew what time and labor it meant to acquire a literary style. Second place, because whenever I wanted to write a story I never could think of a plot. Once I wrote about old Si' Shepard that got lost in the woods and never came back, and when I showed it to Uncle William he said: "Why, Elizabeth, I reckon you better stick to your dress making: this here ain't no story; everybody knows about old Si' Shepard."

No, the trouble was with plots. Whenever I tried to think of one, it always turned out to be something that some one else had thought about before me. But here back awhile, I heard of great inducements offered for an acceptable story, and I said to myself: "Elizabeth Stock, this is your chance. Now or never!" And I laid awake most a whole week; and

---

* A village in southwest Missouri.

walked about days in a kind of dream, turning and twisting things in my mind just like I often saw old ladies twisting quilt patches around to compose a design. I tried to think of a railroad story with a wreck, but couldn't. No more could I make a tale out of a murder, or money getting stolen, or even mistaken identity; for the story had to be original, entertaining, full of action and Goodness knows what all. It was no use. I gave it up. But now that I got my pen in my hand and sitting here kind of quiet and peaceful at the south window, and the breeze so soft carrying the autumn leaves along, I feel as I'd like to tell how I lost my position, mostly through my own negligence, I'll admit that.

My name is Elizabeth Stock. I'm thirty-eight years old and unmarried, and not afraid or ashamed to say it. Up to a few months ago I been postmistress of this village of Stonelift for six years, through one administration and a half—up to a few months ago.

Often seems like the village was most too small; so small that people were bound to look into each other's lives, just like you see folks in crowded tenements looking into each other's windows. But I was born here in Stonelift and I got no serious complaints. I been pretty comfortable and contented most of my life. There ain't more than a hundred houses all told, if that, counting stores, churches, postoffice, and even Nathan Brightman's palatial mansion up on the hill. Looks like Stonelift wouldn't be anything without that.

He's away a good part of the time, and his family; but he's done a lot for this community, and they always appreciated it, too.

But I leave it to any one—to any woman especially, if it ain't human nature in a little place where everybody knows every one else, for the postmistress to glance at a postal card once in a while. She could hardly help it. And besides, seems like if a person had anything very particular and private to tell, they'd put it under a sealed envelope.

Anyway, the train was late that day. It was the breaking up of winter, or the beginning of spring; kind of betwixt and between; along in March. It was most night when the mail came in that ought have been along at 5:15. The Brightman girls had been down with their pony-cart, but had got tired waiting and had been gone more than an hour.

It was chill and dismal in the office. I had let the stove go out for fear of fire. I was cold and hungry and anxious to get home to my supper. I gave out everybody's mail that was waiting; and for the thousandth time told Vance Wallace there was nothing for him. He'll come and ask as regular as clockwork. I got that mail assorted and put aside in a hurry. There was no dilly dallying with postal cards, and how I ever come to give a second look at Nathan Brightman's postal, Heaven only knows!

It was from St. Louis, written with pencil in large characters and signed, "Collins," nothing else; just "Collins." It read:

"Dear Brightman: Be on hand tomorrow, Tuesday at 10. A.M. promptly. Important meeting of the board. Your own interest demands your presence. Whatever you do, don't fail. In haste, Collins."

I went to the door to see if there was any one left standing around: but the night was so raw and chill, every last one of the loungers had disappeared. Vance Wallace would of been willing enough to hang about to see me home; but that was a thing I'd broken him of long ago. I locked things up and went on home, just ashivering as I went, it was that black and penetrating—worse than a downright freeze, I thought.

After I had had my supper and got comfortably fixed front of the fire, and glanced over the St. Louis paper and was just starting to read my seaside Library novel, I got thinking, somehow, about that postal card of Nath Brightman's. To a person that knew B. from hill's foot, it was just as plain as day that if that card laid on there in the office, Mr. Brightman would miss that important meeting in St. Louis in the morning. It wasn't anything to me, of course, except it made me uncomfortable and I couldn't rest or get my mind fixed on the story I was reading. Along about nine o'clock, I flung aside the book and says to myself:

"Elizabeth Stock, you a fool, and you know it." There ain't much use telling how I put on my rubbers and waterproof, covered the fire with ashes, took my umbrella and left the house.

I carried along the postoffice key and went on down and got out that postal card—in fact, all of the Brightmans' mail—wasn't any use leaving part of it, and started for "the house on the hill" as we mostly call it. I don't believe anything could of induced me to go if I had known before hand what I was undertaking. It was drizzling and the rain kind of turned to ice when it struck the ground. If it hadn't been for the rubbers, I'd of taken more than one fall. As it was, I took one good and hard one on the footbridge. The wind was sweeping down so swiftly from the Northwest, looked like it carried me clean off my feet before I could clutch the handrail. I found out about that time that the stitches had come out of my old rubbers that I'd sewed about a month before, and letting the water in soaking my feet through and through. But I'd got more than good and started and I wouldn't think of turning around.

Nathan Brightman has got kind of steps cut along the side of the hill, going zig-zag. What you would call a gradual ascent, and making it easy to climb. That is to say, in good weather. But Lands! There wasn't anything easy that night, slipping back one step for every two; clutching at the frozen twigs along the path; and having to use my umbrella half the time for a walking stick; like a regular Alpine climber. And my heart would most stand still at the way the cedar trees moaned and whistled like doleful organ tones; and sometimes sighing deep and soft like dying souls in pain.

Then I was a fool for not putting on something warm underneath that mackintosh. I could of put on my knitted wool jacket just as easy as not. But the day had been so mild, it bamboozled us into thinking spring was here for good; especially when we were all looking and longing for it; and the orchards ready to bud, too.

But I forgot all the worry and unpleasantness of the walk when I saw how Nath Brightman took on over me bringing

him that postal card. He made me sit down longside the fire
and dry my feet, and kept saying:

"Why, Miss Elizabeth, it was exceedingly obliging of you;
on such a night, too. Margaret, my dear"—that was his wife—
"mix a good stiff toddy for Miss Elizabeth, and see that she
drinks it."

I never could stand the taste or smell of alcohol. Uncle
William says if I'd of had any sense and swallowed down that
toddy like medicine, it might of saved the day.

Anyhow, Mr. Brightman had the girls scampering around
getting his grip* packed; one bringing his big top coat, another his muffler and umbrella; and at the same time here
they were all three making up a list of a thousand and one
things they wanted him to bring down from St. Louis.

Seems like he was ready in a jiffy, and by that time I was
feeling sort of thawed out and I went along with him. It was a
mighty big comfort to have him, too. He was as polite as could
be, and kept saying:

"Mind out, Miss Elizabeth! Be careful here; slow now.
My! but it's cold! Goodness knows what damage this won't do
to the fruit trees." He walked to my very door with me, help-
ing me along. Then he went on to the station. When the midnight express came tearing around the bend, rumbling like
thunder and shaking the very house, I'd got my clothes
changed and was drinking a hot cup of tea side the fire I'd
started up. There was a lot of comfort knowing that Mr.
Brightman had got aboard that train. Well, we all more or less
selfish creatures in this world! I don't believe I'd of slept a
wink that night if I'd of left that postal card lying in the office.

Uncle William will have it that this heavy cold all came of
that walk; though he got to admit with me that this family
been noted for weak lungs as far back as I ever heard of.

Anyway, I'd been sick on and off all spring; sometimes
hardly able to stand on my feet when I'd drag myself down to
that postoffice. When one morning, just like lightning out of a

---

* Suitcase.

clear sky, here comes an official document from Washington, discharging me from my position as postmistress of Stonelift. I shook all over when I read it, just like I had a chill; and I felt sick at my stomach and my teeth chattered. No one was in the office when I opened that document except Vance Wallace, and I made him read it and I asked him what he made out it meant. Just like when you can't understand a thing because you don't want to. He says:

"You've lost your position, Lizabeth. That what it means; they've passed you up."

I took it away from him kind of dazed, and says:

"We got to see about it. We got to go see Uncle William; see what he says. Maybe it's a mistake."

"Uncle Sam don't make mistakes," said Vance. "We got to get up a petition in this here community; that's what I reckon we better do, and send it to the government."

Well, it don't seem like any use to dwell on this subject. The whole community was indignant, and pronounced it an outrage. They decided, in justice to me, I had to find out what I got that dismissal for. I kind of thought it was for my poor health, for I would of had to send in my resignation sooner or later, with these fevers and cough. But we got information it was for incompetence and negligence in office, through certain accusations of me reading postal cards and permitting people to help themselves to their own mail. Though I don't know as that ever happened except with Nathan Brightman always reaching over and saying:

"Don't disturb yourself, Miss Elizabeth," when I'd be sorting out letters and he could reach his mail in the box just as well as not.

But that's all over and done for. I been out of office two months now, on the 26th. There's a young man named Collins, got the position. He's the son of some wealthy, influential St. Louis man; a kind of delicate, poetical-natured young fellow that can't get along in business, and they used their influence to get him the position when it was vacant. They thinks it's the very place for him. I reckon 'tis. I hope in my soul he'll prosper. He's a quiet, nice-mannered young man. Some of the community thought of boycotting him. It was Vance Wallace started the notion. I told them they must be demented, and I up and told Vance Wallace he was a fool.

"I know I'm a fool, Lizabeth Stock," he said, "I always been a fool for hanging round you for the past twenty years."

The trouble with Vance is, he's got no intellect. I believe in my soul Uncle William's got more. Uncle William advised me to go up to St. Louis and get treated. I been up there. The doctor said, with this cough and short breath, if I know what's good for me I'll spend the winter in the South. But the truth is, I got no more money, or so little it don't count. Putting Danny to school and other things here lately, hasn't left me much to brag of. But I oughtn't be blamed about Danny; he's the only one of sister Martha's boys that seemed to me capable. And full of ambition to study as he was! It would have felt sinful of me, not to. Of course, I've taken him out, now I've lost my position. But I got him in with Filmore Green to learn the grocery trade, and maybe it's all for the best; who knows!

But indeed, indeed, I don't know what to do. Seems like I've come to the end of the rope. O! it's mighty pleasant here at this south window. The breeze is just as soft and warm as May, and the leaves look like birds flying. I'd like to sit right on here and forget every thing and go to sleep and never wake up. Maybe it's sinful to make that wish. After all, what I got to do is leave everything in the hands of Providence, and trust to luck.

THE STORM

A Sequel to "At the 'Cadian Ball"

I

THE LEAVES WERE SO STILL that even Bibi thought it was going to rain. Bobinôt, who was accustomed to converse on terms of perfect equality with his little son, called the child's attention to certain sombre clouds that were rolling with sinister intention from the west, accompanied by a sullen, threatening roar. They were at Friedheimer's store and decided to remain there till the storm had passed. They sat within the door on two empty kegs. Bibi was four years old and looked very wise.

"Mama'll be 'fraid, yes," he suggested with blinking eyes.

"She'll shut the house. Maybe she got Sylvie helpin' her this evenin'," Bobinôt responded reassuringly.

"No; she ent got Sylvie. Sylvie was helpin' her yistiday," piped Bibi.

Bobinôt arose and going across to the counter purchased a can of shrimps, of which Calixta was very fond. Then he returned to his perch on the keg and sat stolidly holding the can of shrimps while the storm burst. It shook the wooden store and seemed to be ripping great furrows in the distant field. Bibi laid his little hand on his father's knee and was not afraid.

II

CALIXTA, AT HOME, felt no uneasiness for their safety. She sat at a side window sewing furiously on a sewing-machine. She was greatly occupied and did not notice the approaching storm. But she felt very warm and often stopped to mop her face on which the perspiration gathered in beads. She unfastened her white sacque* at the throat. It began to grow dark, and suddenly realizing the situation she got up hurriedly and went about closing windows and doors.

Out on the small front gallery she had hung Bobinôt's Sunday clothes to air and she hastened out to gather them before the rain fell. As she stepped outside, Alcée Laballière rode in at the gate. She had not seen him very often since her marriage, and never alone. She stood there with Bobinôt's coat in her hands, and the big rain drops began to fall. Alcée rode his horse under the shelter of a side projection where the chickens had huddled and there were plows and a harrow† piled up in the corner.

"May I come and wait on your gallery till the storm is over, Calixta?" he asked.

"Come 'long in, M'sieur Alcée."

His voice and her own startled her as if from a trance, and she seized Bobinôt's vest. Alcée, mounting to the porch, grabbed the trousers and snatched Bibi's braided jacket that was about to be carried away by a sudden gust of wind. He expressed an intention to remain outside, but it was soon apparent that he might as well have been out in the open: the water beat in upon the boards in driving sheets, and he went inside, closing the door after him. It was even necessary to put something beneath the door to keep the water out.

"My! what a rain! It's good two years since it rain' like that," exclaimed Calixta as she rolled up a piece of bagging and Alcée helped her to thrust it beneath the crack.

She was a little fuller of figure than five years before when she married; but she had lost nothing of her vivacity. Her blue eyes still retained their melting quality; and her yellow hair, disheveled by the wind and rain, kinked more stubbornly than ever about her ears and temples.

The rain beat upon the low, shingled roof with a force and

---

* A loose garment (Fr.).

† An agricultural tool set with spikes, used primarily for pulverizing and smoothing the soil.

clatter that threatened to break an entrance and deluge them there. They were in the dining-room—the sitting-room—the general utility room. Adjoining was her bed-room, with Bibi's couch along side her own. The door stood open, and the room with its white, monumental bed, its closed shutters, looked dim and mysterious.

Alcée flung himself into a rocker and Calixta nervously began to gather up from the floor the lengths of a cotton sheet which she had been sewing.

"If this keeps up, *Dieu sait*° if the levees† goin' to stan' it!" she exclaimed.

"What have you got to do with the levees?"

"I got enough to do! An' there's Bobinôt with Bibi out in that storm—if he only didn' left Friedheimer's!"

"Let us hope, Calixta, that Bobinôt's got sense enough to come in out of a cyclone."

She went and stood at the window with a greatly disturbed look on her face. She wiped the frame that was clouded with moisture. It was stiflingly hot. Alcée got up and joined her at the window, looking over her shoulder. The rain was coming down in sheets obscuring the view of far-off cabins and enveloping the distant wood in a gray mist. The playing of the lightning was incessant. A bolt struck a tall chinaberry tree at the edge of the field. It filled all visible space with a blinding glare and the crash seemed to invade the very boards they stood upon.

Calixta put her hands to her eyes, and with a cry, staggered backward. Alcée's arm encircled her, and for an instant he drew her close and spasmodically to him.

"*Bonté!*"‡ she cried, releasing herself from his encircling arm and retreating from the window, "the house'll go next! If I only knew w'ere Bibi was!" She would not compose herself; she would not be seated. Alcée clasped her shoulders and looked into her face. The contact of her warm, palpitating

---

* God knows (Fr.).

† Embankments for preventing floods.

‡ Goodness! (Fr.).

body when he had unthinkingly drawn her into his arms, had aroused all the old-time infatuation and desire for her flesh.

"Calixta," he said, "don't be frightened. Nothing can happen. The house is too low to be struck, with so many tall trees standing about. There! aren't you going to be quiet? say, aren't you?" He pushed her hair back from her face that was warm and steaming. Her lips were as red and moist as pomegranate seed. Her white neck and a glimpse of her full, firm bosom disturbed him powerfully. As she glanced up at him the fear in her liquid blue eyes had given place to a drowsy gleam that unconsciously betrayed a sensuous desire. He looked down into her eyes and there was nothing for him to do but to gather her lips in a kiss. It reminded him of Assumption.

"Do you remember—in Assumption, Calixta?" he asked in a low voice broken by passion. Oh! she remembered; for in Assumption he had kissed her and kissed and kissed her; until his senses would well nigh fail, and to save her he would resort to a desperate flight. If she was not an immaculate dove in those days, she was still inviolate; a passionate creature whose very defenselessness had made her defense, against which his honor forbade him to prevail. Now—well, now—her lips seemed in a manner free to be tasted, as well as her round, white throat and her whiter breasts.

They did not heed the crashing torrents, and the roar of the elements made her laugh as she lay in his arms. She was a revelation in that dim, mysterious chamber; as white as the couch she lay upon. Her firm, elastic flesh that was knowing for the first time its birthright, was like a creamy lily that the sun invites to contribute its breath and perfume to the undying life of the world.

The generous abundance of her passion, without guile or trickery, was like a white flame which penetrated and found response in depths of his own sensuous nature that had never yet been reached.

When he touched her breasts they gave themselves up in quivering ecstasy, inviting his lips. Her mouth was a fountain of delight. And when he possessed her, they seemed to swoon together at the very borderland of life's mystery.

He stayed cushioned upon her, breathless, dazed, enervated, with his heart beating like a hammer upon her. With one hand she clasped his head, her lips lightly touching his forehead. The other hand stroked with a soothing rhythm his muscular shoulders.

The growl of the thunder was distant and passing away. The rain beat softly upon the shingles, inviting them to drowsiness and sleep. But they dared not yield.

The rain was over; and the sun was turning the glistening green world into a palace of gems. Calixta, on the gallery, watched Alcée ride away. He turned and smiled at her with a beaming face; and she lifted her pretty chin in the air and laughed aloud.

III

BOBINÔT AND BIBI, trudging home, stopped without at the cistern to make themselves presentable.

"My! Bibi, w'at will yo' mama say! You ought to be ashame'. You oughtn' put on those good pants. Look at 'em! An' that mud on yo' collar! How you got that mud on yo' collar, Bibi? I never saw such a boy!" Bibi was the picture of pathetic resignation. Bobinôt was the embodiment of serious solicitude as he strove to remove from his own person and his son's the signs of their tramp over heavy roads and through wet fields. He scraped the mud off Bibi's bare legs and feet with a stick and carefully removed all traces from his heavy brogans. Then, prepared for the worst—the meeting with an over-scrupulous housewife, they entered cautiously at the back door.

Calixta was preparing supper. She had set the table and was dripping coffee at the hearth. She sprang up as they came in.

"Oh, Bobinôt! You back! My! but I was uneasy. W'ere you been during the rain? An' Bibi? he ain't wet? he ain't hurt?" She had clasped Bibi and was kissing him effusively. Bobinôt's explanations and apologies which he had been composing all along the way, died on his lips as Calixta felt him to see if he were dry, and seemed to express nothing but satisfaction at their safe return.

"I brought you some shrimps, Calixta," offered Bobinôt, hauling the can from his ample side pocket and laying it on the table.

"Shrimps! Oh, Bobinôt! you too good fo' anything!" and she gave him a smacking kiss on the cheek that resounded. "*J'vous réponds,*° we'll have a feas' to night! umph-umph!"

Bobinôt and Bibi began to relax and enjoy themselves, and when the three seated themselves at table they laughed much and so loud that anyone might have heard them as far away as Laballière's.

IV

ALCÉE LABALLIÈRE wrote to his wife, Clarisse, that night. It was a loving letter, full of tender solicitude. He told her not to hurry back, but if she and the babies liked it at Biloxi,† to stay a month longer. He was getting on nicely; and though he missed them, he was willing to bear the separation a while longer—realizing that their health and pleasure were the first things to be considered.

V

AS FOR CLARISSE, she was charmed upon receiving her husband's letter. She and the babies were doing well. The society was agreeable; many of her old friends and acquaintances were at the bay. And the first free breath since her marriage seemed to restore the pleasant liberty of her maiden days. Devoted as she was to her husband, their intimate conjugal life was something which she was more than willing to forego for a while.

So the storm passed and every one was happy.

---

* I'm telling you (Fr.).

† A coastal resort in Mississippi.

THE GODMOTHER

಄

I

TANTE ELODIE ATTRACTED YOUTH in some incomprehensible way. It was seldom there was not a group of young people gathered about her fire in winter or sitting with her in summer, in the pleasant shade of the live-oaks that screened the gallery.

There were several persons forming a half circle around her generous chimney early one evening in February. There were Madame Nicolas' two tiny little girls who sat on the floor and played with a cat the whole time; Madame Nicolas herself, who only came for the little girls and insisted on hurrying away because it was time to put the children to bed, and who, moreover, was expecting a caller. There was a fair, blonde girl, one of the younger teachers at the Normal School.* Gabriel Lucaze offered to escort her home when she got up to go, after Madame Nicolas' departure. But she had already accepted the company of a silent, studious-looking youth who had come there in the hope of meeting her. So they all went away but young Gabriel Lucaze, Tante Elodie's godson, who stayed and played cribbage† with her. They played at a small table on which were a shaded lamp, a few magazines and a dish of *pralines* which the lady took great pleasure in nibbling during the reflective pauses of the game. They had played one game and were nearing the end of the second. He laid a queen upon the table.

"Fifteen-two," she said, playing a five.

"Twenty, and a pair."

"Twenty-five. Six points for me."

---

* A college for training teachers.

† A two-person card game in which each player tries to form various counting combinations of cards.

"Its a 'go.'"

"Thirty-one and out. That is the second game I've won. Will you play another rubber,* Gabriel?"

"Not much, Tante Elodie, when you are playing in such luck. Besides, I've got to get out, it's half-past eight." He had played recklessly, often glancing at the bronze clock which reposed majestically beneath its crystal globe on the mantelpiece. He prepared at once to leave, going before the gilt-framed, oval mirror to fold and arrange a silk muffler beneath his great coat.

He was rather good looking. That is, he was healthy looking; his face a little florid, and hair almost black. It was short and curly and parted on one side. His eyes were fine when they were not bloodshot, as they sometimes were. His mouth might have been better. It was not disagreeable or unpleasant, but it was unsatisfactory and drooped a little at the corners. However, he was good to look at as he crossed the muffler over his chest. His face was unusually alert. Tante Elodie looked at him in the glass.

"Will you be warm enough, my boy? It has turned very cold since six o'clock."

"Plenty warm. Too warm."

"Where are you going?"

"Now, Tante Elodie," he said, turning, and laying a hand on her shoulder; he was holding his soft felt hat in the other. "It is always 'where are you going?' 'Where have you been?' I have spoiled you. I have told you too much. You expect me to tell you everything; consequently, I must sometimes tell you fibs. I am going to confession. There! are you satisfied?" and he bent down and gave her a hearty kiss.

"I am satisfied, provided you go to the right priests to confession; not up the hill, mind you!"

"Up the hill" meant up at the Normal School with Tante Elodie. She was a very conservative person. "The Normal" seemed to her an unpardonable innovation, with its teachers

---

* An odd game played to determine the winner of a tie.

from Minnesota, from Iowa, from God-knows-where, bringing strange ways and manners to the old town. She was one, also, who considered the emancipation of slaves a great mistake. She had many reasons for thinking so and was often called upon to enumerate this in her wordy arguments with her many opponents.

II

TANTE ELODIE distinctly heard the doctor leave the Widow Nicolas' at a quarter past ten. He visited the handsome and attractive young woman two evenings in the week and always left at the same hour. Tante Elodie's double glass doors opened upon the wide upper gallery. Around the angle of the gallery were the apartments of Madame Nicolas. Any one visiting the widow was obliged to pass Tante Elodie's door. Beneath was a store occasionally occupied by some merchant or other, but oftener vacant. A stairway led down from the porch to the yard where two enormous live-oaks grew and cast a dense shade upon the gallery above, making it an agreeable retreat and resting place on hot summer afternoons. The high, wooden yard-gate opened directly upon the street.

A half hour went by after the doctor passed her door. Tante Elodie played "solitaire." Another half hour followed and still Tante Elodie was not sleepy nor did she think of going to bed. It was very near midnight when she began to prepare her night toilet and to cover the fire.

The room was very large, with heavy rafters across the ceiling. There was an enormous bed over in the corner; a four-posted mahogany covered with a lace spread which was religiously folded every night and laid on a chair. There were some old ambrotypes* and photographs about the room; a few comfortable but simple rocking chairs and a broad fire place in which a big log sizzled. It was an attractive room for any

---

* An ambrotype is a positive picture made of a photographic negative on glass backed by a dark surface.

one, not because of anything that was in it except Tante
Elodie herself. She was far past fifty. Her hair was still soft and
brown and her eyes bright and vivacious. Her figure was slender and nervous. There were many lines in her face, but it did
not look care-worn. Had she her youthful flesh, she would
have looked very young.

Tante Elodie had spent the evening in munching *pralines*
and reading by lamp-light some old magazines that Gabriel
Lucaze had brought her from the club.

There was a romance connected with her early days.
Romances serve but to feed the imagination of the young; they
add nothing to the sum of truth. No one realized this fact more
strongly than Tante Elodie herself. While she tacitly condoned
the romance, perhaps for the sake of the sympathy it bred, she
never thought of Justin Lucaze but with a feeling of gratitude
toward the memory of her parents who had prevented her marrying him thirty-five years before. She could have no connection between her deep and powerful affection for young Gabriel
Lucaze and her old-time, brief passion for his father. She loved
the boy above everything on earth. There was none so attractive
to her as he; none so thoughtful of her pleasures and pains. In
his devotion there was no trace of a duty-sense; it was the spontaneous expression of affection and seeming dependence.

After Tante Elodie had turned down her bed and undressed, she drew a gray flannel *peignoir* over her nightgown
and knelt down to say her prayers; kneeling before a rocker
with her bare feet turned to the fire. Prayers were no trifling
matter with her. Besides those which she knew by heart, she
read litanies and invocations from a book and also a chapter
of "The Following of Christ." She had said her *Notre Père*, her
Salve Marie and *Je crois en Dieu* and was deep in the litany* of
the Blessed Virgin when she fancied she heard footsteps on
the stairs. The night was breathlessly still; it was very late.

---

* A catalogue of Catholic devotions intended to show that Tante
Elodie is a faithful believer—an ironic detail, given her subsequent
actions.

"*Vierge des Vierges: Priez pour nous. Mère de Dieu: Priez—*"[*]

Surely there was a stealthy step upon the gallery, and now a hand at her door, striving to lift the latch. Tante Elodie was not afraid. She felt the utmost security in her home and had no dread of mischievous intruders in the peaceful old town. She simply realized that there was some one at her door and that she must find out who it was and what they wanted. She got up from her knees, thrust her feet into her slippers that were near the fire and, lowering the lamp by which she had been reading her litanies, approached the door. There was the very softest rap upon the pane. Tante Elodie unbolted and opened the door the least bit.

"*Qui est là?*"[†] she asked.

"Gabriel." He forced himself into the room before she had time to fully open the door to him.

III

GABRIEL STRODE PAST her toward the fire, mechanically taking off his hat, and sat down in the rocker before which she had been kneeling. He sat on the prayer books she had left there. He removed them and laid them upon the table. Seeming to realize in a dazed way that it was not their accustomed place, he threw the two books on a nearby chair.

Tante Elodie raised the lamp and looked at him. His eyes were bloodshot, as they were when he drank or experienced any unusual emotion or excitement. But he was pale and his mouth drooped excessively, and twitched with the effort he made to control it. The top button was wrenched from his coat and his muffler was disarranged. Tante Elodie was grieved to the soul, seeing him thus. She thought he had been drinking.

"Gabriel, w'at is the matter?" she asked imploringly. "Oh,

---

* Virgin of Virgins, pray for us. Mother of God, pray (Fr.).
† Who's there? (Fr.).

my poor child, w'at is the matter?" He looked at her in a fixed way and passed a hand over his head. He tried to speak, but his voice failed, as with one who experiences stage fright. Then he articulated, hoarsely, swallowing nervously between the slow words:

"I—killed a man—about an hour ago—yonder in the old Nigger-Luke Cabin." Tante Elodie's two hands went suddenly down to the table and she leaned heavily upon them for support.

"You did not; you did not," she panted. "You are drinking. You do not know w'at you are saying. Tell me, Gabriel, who 'as been making you drink? Ah! they will answer to me! You do not know w'at you are saying. *Boute!*° how can you know!" She clutched him and the torn button that hung in the button-hole fell to the floor.

"I don't know why it happened," he went on, gazing into the fire with unseeing eyes, or rather with eyes that saw what was pictured in his mind and not what was before them.

"I've been in cutting scrapes and shooting scrapes that never amounted to anything, when I was just as crazy mad as I was to-night. But I tell you, Tante Elodie, he's dead. I've got to get away. But how are you going to get out of a place like this, when every dog and cat"—His effort had spent itself, and he began to tremble with a nervous chill; his teeth chattered and his lips could not form an utterance.

Tante Elodie, stumbling rather than walking, went over to a small buffet and pouring some brandy into a glass, gave it to him. She took a little herself. She looked much older in the *peignoir* and the handkerchief tied around her head. She sat down beside Gabriel and took his hand. It was cold and clammy.

"Tell me everything," she said with determination, "everything; without delay; and do not speak so loud. We shall see what must be done. Was it a negro? Tell me everything."

° The bottle! (Fr.).

"No, it was a white man, you don't know, from Conshotta,*
named Everson. He was half drunk; a hulking bully as strong
as an ox, or I could have licked him. He tortured me until I
was frantic. Did you ever see a cat torment a mouse? The
mouse can't do anything but lose its head. I lost my head, but
I had my knife; that big hornhandled knife."

"Where is it?" she asked sharply. He felt his back pocket.

"I don't know." He did not seem to care, or to realize the
importance of the loss.

"Go on; make haste; tell me the whole story. You went
from here—you went—go on."

"I went down the river a piece," he said, throwing himself
back in the chair and keeping his eyes fixed upon one burning ember on the hearth, "down to Symund's store where
there was a game of cards. A lot of the fellows were there. I
played a little and didn't drink anything, and stopped at ten. I
was going"—He leaned forward with his elbows on his knees
and his hands hanging between. "I was going to see a woman
at eleven o'clock; it was the only time I could see her. I came
along and when I got by the old Nigger-Luke Cabin I lit a
match and looked at my watch. It was too early and it
wouldn't do to hang around. I went into the cabin and started
a blaze in the chimney with some fine wood I found there.
My feet were cold and I sat on an empty soap-box before the
fire to dry them. I remember I kept looking at my watch. It
was twenty-five minutes to eleven when Everson came into
the cabin. He was half drunk and his face was red and looked
like a beast. He had left the game and had followed me. I
hadn't spoken of where I was going. But he said he knew I was
off for a lark and he wanted to go along. I said he couldn't go
where I was going, and there was no use talking. He kept it
up. At a quarter to eleven I wanted to go, and he went and
stood in the doorway.

" 'If I don't go, you don't go,' he said, and he kept it up.

---

* A variant of Coushatta, a town on the east bank of the Red River
and seat of Red River parish.

When I tried to pass him he pushed me back like I was a feather. He didn't get mad. He laughed all the time and drank whiskey out of a bottle he had in his pocket. If I hadn't got mad and lost my head, I might have fooled him or played some trick on him—if I had used my wits. But I didn't know any more what I was doing than the day I threw the inkstand at old Dainean's head when he switched me and made fun of me before the whole school."

"I stooped by the fire and looked at my watch; he was talking all kinds of foolishness I can't repeat. It was eleven o'clock. I was in a killing rage and made a dash for the door. His big body and his big arm were there like an iron bar, and he laughed. I took out my knife and stuck it into him. I don't believe he knew at first that I had touched him, for he kept on laughing; then he fell over like a pig, and the old cabin shook."

Gabriel had raised his clinched hand with an intensely dramatic movement when he said, "I stuck it into him." Then he let his head fall back against the chair and finished the concluding sentences of his story with closed eyes.

"How do you know he is dead?" asked Tante Elodie, whose voice sounded hard and monotonous.

"I only walked ten steps away and went back to see. He was dead. Then I came here. The best thing is to go give myself up, I reckon, and tell the whole story like I've told you. That's about the best thing I can do if I want any peace of mind."

"Are you crazy, Gabriel! You have not yet regained your senses. Listen to me. Listen to me and try to understand what I say."

Her face was full of a hard intelligence he had not seen there before; all the soft womanliness had for the moment faded out of it.

"You 'ave not killed the man Everson," she said deliberately. "You know nothing about 'im. You do not know that he left Symund's or that he followed you. You left at ten o'clock. You came straight in town, not feeling well. You saw a light in my window, came here; rapped on the door; I let you in and gave you something for cramps in the stomach and made you warm yourself and lie down on the sofa. Wait a moment. Stay still there."

She got up and went shuffling out the door, around the angle of the gallery and tapped on Madame Nicolas' door. She could hear the young woman jump out of bed bewildered, asking, "Who is there? Wait! What is it?"

"It is Tante Elodie." The door was unbolted at once.

"Oh! how I hate to trouble you, *chérie*. Poor Gabriel 'as been at my room for hours with the most severe cramps. Nothing I can do seems to relieve 'im. Will you let me 'ave the morphine which doctor left with you for old Betsy's rheumatism? Ah! thank you. I think a quarter of a grain* will relieve 'im. Poor boy! Such suffering! I am so sorry dear, to disturb you. Do not stand by the door, you will take cold. Good night."

Tante Elodie persuaded Gabriel, if the club were still open, to look in there on his way home. He had a room in a relative's house. His mother was dead and his father lived on a plantation several miles from town. Gabriel feared that his nerve would fail him. But Tante Elodie had him up again with a glass of brandy. She said that he must get the fact lodged in his mind that he was innocent. She inspected the young man carefully before he went away, brushing and arranging his toilet. She sewed the missing button on his coat. She had noticed some blood upon his right hand. He himself had not seen it. With a wet towel she washed his face and hands as though he were a little child. She brushed his hair and sent him away with a thousand reiterated precautions.

IV

TANTE ELODIE WAS not overcome in any way after Gabriel left her. She did not indulge in a hysterical moment, but set about accomplishing some purpose which she had evidently had in

---

* A minute portion.

her mind. She dressed herself again; quickly, nervously, but with much precision. A shawl over her head and a long, black cape across her shoulders made her look like a nun. She quitted her room. It was very dark and very still out of doors. There was only a whispering wail among the live-oak leaves.

Tante Elodie stole noiselessly down the steps and out the gate. If she had met anyone, she intended to say she was suffering with toothache and was going to the doctor or druggist for relief.

But she met not a soul. She knew every plank, every uneven brick of the side walk; every rut of the way, and might have walked with her eyes closed. Strangely enough she had forgotten to pray. Prayer seemed to belong to her moments of contemplation, while now she was all action; prompt, quick, decisive action.

It must have been near upon two o'clock. She did not meet a cat or a dog on her way to the Nigger-Luke Cabin. The hut was well out of town and isolated from a group of tumbled-down shanties some distance off, in which a lazy set of negroes lived. There was not the slightest feeling of fear or horror in her breast. There might have been, had she not already been dominated and possessed by the determination that Gabriel must be shielded from ignominy—maybe, worse.

She glided into the low cabin like a shadow, hugging the side of the open door. She would have stumbled over the dead man's feet if she had not stepped so cautiously. The embers were burning so low that they gave but a faint glow in the sinister cabin with its obscure corners, its black, hanging cobwebs and the dead man lying twisted as he had fallen with his face on his arm.

Once in the cabin the woman crept toward the body on her hands and knees. She was looking for something in the dusky light; something she could not find. Crawling toward the fire over the uneven, creaking boards, she stirred the embers the least bit with a burnt stick that had fallen to one side. She dared not make a blaze. Then she dragged herself once

more toward the lifeless body. She pictured how the knife had
been thrust in; how it had fallen from Gabriel's hand; how the
man had come down like a felled ox. Yes, the knife could not
be far off, but she could not discover a trace of it. She slipped
her fingers beneath the body and felt all along. The knife lay
up under his arm pit. Her hand scraped his chin as she withdrew it. She did not mind. She was exultant at getting the
knife. She felt like some other being, possessed by Satan.
Some fiend in human shape, some spirit of murder. A cricket
began to sing on the hearth.

Tante Elodie noticed the golden gleam of the murdered
man's watch chain, and a sudden thought invaded her. With
deft, though unsteady fingers, she unhooked the watch and
chain. There was money in his pockets. She emptied them,
turning the pockets inside out. It was difficult to reach his left-
hand pockets, but she did so. The money, a few bank notes
and some silver coins, together with the watch and knife she
tied in her handkerchief. Then she hurried away, taking a
long stride across the man's body in order to reach the door.

The stars were like shining pieces of gold upon dark velvet.
So Tante Elodie thought as she looked up at them an instant.

There was the sound of disorderly voices away off in the
negro shanties. Clasping the parcel close to her breast she began to run. She ran, ran, as fast as some fleet four-footed creature, ran, panting. She never stopped till she reached the gate
that let her in under the live-oaks. The most intent listener
could not have heard her as she mounted the stairs; as she let
herself in at the door; as she bolted it. Once in the room she
began to totter. She was sick to her stomach and her head
swam. Instinctively she reached out toward the bed, and fell
fainting upon it, face downward.

The gray light of dawn was coming in at her windows. The
lamp on the table had burned out. Tante Elodie groaned as
she tried to move. And again she groaned with mental anguish, this time as the events of the past night came back to
her, one by one, in all their horrifying details. Her labor of
love, begun the night before, was not yet ended. The parcel

containing the watch and money were there beneath her, pressing into her bosom. When she managed to regain her feet the first thing which she did was to rekindle the fire with splinters of pine and pieces of hickory that were at hand in her wood box. When the fire was burning briskly, Tante Elodie took the paper money from the little bundle and burned it. She did not notice the denomination of the bills, there were five or six, she thrust them into the blaze with the poker and watched them burn. The few loose pieces of silver she put in her purse, apart from her own money; there was sixty-five cents in small coin. The watch she placed between her mattresses; then, seized with misgiving, took it out. She gazed around the room, seeking a safe hiding place and finally put the watch into a large, strong stocking which she pinned securely around her waist beneath her clothing. The knife she washed carefully, drying it with pieces of newspaper which she burned. The water in which she had washed it she also threw in a corner of the large fire place upon a heap of ashes. Then she put the knife into the pocket of one of Gabriel's coats which she had cleaned and mended for him; it was hanging in her closet.

She did all this slowly and with great effort, for she felt very sick. When the unpleasant work was over it was all she could do to undress and get beneath the covers of her bed.

She knew that when she did not appear at breakfast Madame Nicolas would send to investigate the cause of her absence. She took her meals with the young widow around the corner of the gallery. Tante Elodie was not rich. She received a small income from the remains of what had once been a magnificent plantation adjoining the lands which Justin Lucaze owned and cultivated. But she lived frugally, with a hundred small cares and economies and rarely felt the want of extra money except when the generosity of her nature prompted her to help an afflicted neighbor, or to bestow a gift upon some one of whom she was fond. It often seemed to Tante Elodie that all the affection of her heart was centered upon her young protégé, Gabriel; that what she felt for others was simply an emanation—rays, as it were, from this central sun of love that shone for him alone.

In the midst of twinges, of nervous tremors, her thoughts were with him. It was impossible for her to think of anything else. She was filled with unspeakable dread that he might betray himself. She wondered what he had done after he left her: what he was doing at that moment? She wanted to see him again alone, to insist anew upon the necessity of his self-assertion of innocence.

As she expected, Mrs. Wm. Nicolas came around at the breakfast hour to see what was the matter. She was an active woman, very pretty and fresh looking, with willing, deft hands and the kindest voice and eyes. She was distressed at the spectacle of poor Tante Elodie extended in bed with her head tied up, and looking pale and suffering.

"Ah! I suspected it!" she exclaimed, "coming out in the cold on the gallery last night to get morphine for Gabriel; *ma foi!* as if he could not go to the drug store for his morphine! Where have you pain? Have you any fever, Tante Elodie?"

"It is nothing, *chérie*. I believe I am only tired and want to rest for a day in bed."

"Then you must rest as long as you want. I will look after your fire and see that you have what you need. I will bring your coffee at once. It is a beautiful day; like spring. When the sun gets very warm I will open the window."

V

ALL DAY LONG Gabriel did not appear, and she dared not make inquiries about him. Several persons came in to see her, learning that she was sick. The midnight murder in the Nigger-Luke Cabin seemed to be the favorite subject of conversation among her visitors. They were not greatly excited over it as they might have been were the man other than a comparative stranger. But the subject seemed full of interest, enhanced by the mystery surrounding it. Madame Nicolas did not risk to speak of it.

"That is not a fit conversation for a sick-room. Any doctor—anybody with sense will tell you. For Mercy's sake! change the subject."

But Fifine Delonce could not be silenced.

"And now it appears," she went on with renewed animation, "it appears he was playing cards down at Symund's store. That shows how they pass their time—those boys! It's a scandal! But nobody can remember when he left. Some say at nine, some say it was past eleven. He sort of went away like he didn't want them to notice."

"Well, we didn't know the man. My patience! there are murders every day. If we had to keep up with them, *ma foi!* Who is going to Lucie's card party to-morrow? I hear she did not invite her cousin Claire. They have fallen out again it seems." And Madame Nicolas, after speaking, went to give Tante Elodie a drink of *tisane.*

"Mr. Ben's got about twenty darkeys from Niggerville, holding them on suspicion," continued Fifine, dancing on the edge of her chair. "Without doubt the man was enticed to the cabin and murdered and robbed there. Not a picayune left in his pockets! only his pistol—that they didn't take, all loaded, in his back pocket, that he might have used, and his watch gone! Mr. Ben thinks his brother in Conshotta, that's very well off, is going to offer a big reward."

"What relation was the man to you, Fifine?" asked Madame Nicolas, sarcastically.

"He was a human being, Amelia; you have no heart, no feeling. If it makes a woman that hard to associate with a doctor, then thank God—well—as I was saying, if they can catch those two strange section hands that left town last night—but you better bet they're not such fools to keep that watch. But old Uncle Marte said he saw little foot prints like a woman's, early this morning, but no one wanted to listen to him or pay any attention, and the crowd tramped them out in little or no

---

* An infusion made from herbs, believed to have medicinal properties (Fr.).

time. None of the boys want to let on; they don't want us to know which ones were playing cards at Symund's. Was Gabriel at Symund's, Tante Elodie?"

Tante Elodie coughed painfully and looked blankly as though she had only heard her name and had been inattentive to what was said.

"For pity sake leave Tante Elodie out of this! it's bad enough she has to listen, suffering as she is. Gabriel spent the evening here, on Tante Elodie's sofa, very sick with cramps. You will have to pursue your detective work in some other quarter, my dear."

A little girl came in with a huge bunch of blossoms. There was some bustle attending the arrangement of the flowers in vases, and in the midst of it, two or three ladies took their leave.

"I wonder if they're going to send the body off to-night, or if they're going to keep it for the morning train," Fifine was heard to speculate, before the door closed upon her.

Tante Elodie could not sleep that night. The following day she had some fever and Madame Nicolas insisted upon her seeing the doctor. He gave her a sleeping draught and some fever drops and said she would be all right in a few days; for he could find nothing alarming in her condition.

By a supreme effort of the will she got up on the third day hoping in the accustomed routine of her daily life to get rid, in part, of the uneasiness and unhappiness that possessed her.

The sun shone warm in the afternoon and she went and stood on the gallery watching for Gabriel to pass. He had not been near her. She was wounded, alarmed, miserable at his silence and absence; but determined to see him. He came down the street, presently, never looking up, with his hat drawn over his eyes.

"Gabriel!" she called. He gave a start and glanced around.

"Come up; I want to see you a moment."

"I haven't time now, Tante Elodie."

"Come in!" she said sharply.

"All right, you'll have to fix it up with Morrison," and he

opened the gate and went in. She was back in her room by the time he reached it, and in her chair, trembling a little and feeling sick again.

"Gabriel, if you 'ave no heart, it seems to me you would 'ave some intelligence; a moment's reflection would show you the folly of altering your 'abits so suddenly. Did you not know I was sick? did you not guess my uneasiness?"

"I haven't guessed anything or known anything but a taste of hell," he said, not looking at her. Her heart bled afresh for him and went out to him in full forgiveness. "You were right," he went on, "it would have been horrible to saying anything. There is no suspicion. I'll never say anything unless some one should be falsely accused."

"There will be no possible evidence to accuse anyone," she assured him. "Forget it, forget it. Keep on as though it was something you had dreamed. Not only for the outside, but within yourself. Do not accuse yourself of that act, but the actions, the conduct, the ungovernable temper that made it possible. Promise me it will be a lesson to you, Gabriel; and God, who reads men's hearts, will not call it a crime, but an accident which your unbridled nature invited. I will forget it. You must forget it. 'Ave you been to the office?"

"To-day; not yesterday. I don't know what I did yesterday, but look for the knife—after they—I couldn't go while he was there—and I thought every minute some one was coming to accuse me. And when I realized they weren't—I don't know—I drank too much, I think. Reading law! I might as well have been reading Hebrew. If Morrison thinks—See here Tante Elodie, are there any spots on this coat? Can you see anything here in the light?"

"There are no spots anywhere. Stop thinking of it, I implore you." But he pulled off the coat and flung it across a chair. He went to the closet to get his other coat which he knew hung there. Tante Elodie, still feeble and suffering, in the depths of her chair, was not quick enough, could think of no way to prevent it. She had at first put the knife in his pocket with the intention of returning it to him. But now she dreaded to have him find it, and thus discover the part she had played in the sickening dream.

He buttoned up his coat briskly and started away.

"Please burn it," he said, looking at the garment on the chair, "I never want to see it again."

VI

WHEN IT BECAME distinctly evident that no slightest suspicion would be attached to him for the killing of Everson; when he plainly realized that there was no one upon whom the guilt could be fastened, Gabriel thought he would regain his lost equilibrium. If in no other way, he fancied he could reason himself back into it. He was suffering, but he some way had no fear that his present condition of mind would last. He thought it would pass away like a malignant fever. It would have to pass away or it would have to kill him.

From Tante Elodie's he went over to Morrison's office where he was reading law. Morrison and his partner were out of town and he had the office to himself. He had been there all morning. There was nothing for him to do now but to see anyone who called on business, and to go on with his reading. He seated himself and spread his book before him, but he looked into the street through the open door. Then he got up and shut the door. He again fastened his eyes upon the pages before him, but his mind was traveling other ways. For the hundredth time he was going over every detail of the fatal night, and trying to justify himself in his own heart.

If it had been an open and fair fight there would have been no trouble in squaring himself with his conscience; if the man had shown the slightest disposition to do him bodily harm, but he had not. On the other hand, he asked himself, what constituted a murder? Why, there was Morrison himself who had once fired at Judge Filips on that very street. His ball had gone wide of the mark, and subsequently he and Filips had adjusted their difficulties and become friends. Was

Morrison any less a murderer because his weapon had missed?

Suppose the knife had swerved, had penetrated the arm, had inflicted a harmless scratch or flesh wound, would he be sitting there now, calling himself names? But he would try to think it all out later. He could not bear to be there alone, he never liked to be alone, and now he could not endure it. He closed the book without the slightest recollection of a line his eyes had followed. He went and gazed up and down the street, then he locked the office and walked away.

The fact of Everson having been robbed was very puzzling to Gabriel. He thought about it as he walked along the street.

The complete change that had taken place in his emotions, his sentiments, did not astonish him in the least: we accept such phenomena without question. A week ago—not so long as that—he was in love with the fair-haired girl up at the Normal. He was undeniably in love with her. He knew the symptoms. He wanted to marry her and meant to ask her whenever his position justified him in doing so.

Now, where had that love gone? He thought of her with indifference. Still, he was seeking her at that moment, through habit, without any special motive. He had no positive desire to see her; to see any one; and yet he could not endure to be alone. He had no desire to see Tante Elodie. She wanted him to forget and her presence made him remember.

The girl was walking under the beautiful trees, and she stood and waited for him, when she saw him mounting the hill. As he looked at her, his fondness for her and his intentions toward her, appeared now, like child's play. Life was something terrible of which she had no conception. She seemed to him as harmless, as innocent, as insignificant as a little bird.

"Oh! Gabriel," she exclaimed. "I had just written you a note. Why haven't you been here? It was foolish to get offended. I wanted to explain: I couldn't get out of it the other night, at Tante Elodie's, when he asked me. You know I couldn't, and that I would rather have come with you." Was it possible he would have taken this seriously a week ago?

"Delonce is a good fellow; he's a decent fellow. I don't blame you. That's all right." She was hurt at his easy complaisance. She did not wish to offend him, and here she was grieved because he was not offended.

"Will you come indoors to the fire?" she asked.

"No; I just strolled up for a minute." He leaned against a tree and looked bored, or rather, preoccupied with other things than herself. It was not a week ago that he wanted to see her every day; when he said the hours were like minutes that he passed beside her. "I just strolled up to tell you that I am going away."

"Oh! going away?" and the pink deepened in her cheeks, and she tried to look indifferent and to clasp her glove tighter. He had not the slightest intention of going away when he mounted the hill. It came to him like an inspiration.

"Where are you going?"

"Going to look for work in the city."

"And what about your law studies?"

"I have no talent for the law; it's about time I acknowledged it. I want to get into something that will make me hustle. I wouldn't mind—I'd like to get something to do on a railroad that would go tearing through the country night and day. What's the matter?" he asked, perceiving the tears that she could not conceal.

"Nothing's the matter," she answered with dignity, and a sense of seeming proud.

He took her word for it and, instead of seeking to console her, went rambling on about the various occupations in which he should like to engage for a while.

"When are you going?"

"Just as soon as I can."

"Shall I see you again?"

"Of course. Good-by. Don't stay out here too long; you might take cold." He listlessly shook hands with her and descended the hill with long rapid strides.

He would not intentionally have hurt her. He did not realize that he was wounding her. It would have been as difficult for him to revive his passion for her as to bring Everson back to life. Gabriel knew there could be fresh horror added to the situation. Discovery would have added to it; a false accusation would have deepened it. But he never dreamed of the new horror coming as it did, through Tante Elodie, when he found the knife in his pocket. It took a long time to realize what it meant; and then he felt as if he never wanted to see her again. In his mind, her action identified itself with his crime, and made itself a hateful, hideous part of it, which he could not endure to think of, and of which he could not help thinking.

It was the one thing which had saved him, and yet he felt no gratitude. The great love which had prompted the deed did not soften him. He could not believe that any man was worth loving to such length, or worth saving at such a price. She seemed, to his imagination, less a woman than a monster, capable of committing, in cold-blood, deeds which he himself could only accomplish in blind rage. For the first time, Gabriel wept. He threw himself down upon the ground in the deepening twilight and wept as he never had before in his life. A terrible sense of loss overpowered him; as if someone dearer than a mother had been taken out of the reach of his heart; as if a refuge had gone from him. The last spark of human affection was dead within him. He knew it as he was losing it. He wept at the loss which left him alone with his thoughts.

VII

TANTE ELODIE was always chilly. It was warm for the last of April, and the women at Madame Nicolas' wedding were all in airy summer attire. All but Tante Elodie, who wore her black silk, her old silk with a white lace fichu,* and she held an embroidered handkerchief and a fan in her hand.

Fifine Delonce had been over in the morning to take up

---

* A triangular piece of lace or fine fabric worn around the neck or shoulders (Fr.).

the seams in the dress, for, as she expressed herself, it was miles too loose for Tante Elodie's figure. She appeared to be shriveling away to nothing. She had not again been sick in bed since that little spell in February; but she was plainly wasting and was very feeble. Her eyes, though, were as bright as ever; sometimes they looked as hard as flint. The doctor, whom Madame Nicolas insisted upon her seeing occasionally, gave a name to her disease; it was a Greek name and sounded convincing. She was taking a tonic especially prepared for her, from a large bottle, three times a day.

Fifine was a great gossip. When and how she gathered her news nobody could tell. It was always said she knew ten times more than the weekly paper would dare to print. She often visited Tante Elodie, and she told her news of everyone; among others of Gabriel.

It was she who told that he had abandoned the study of the law. She told Tante Elodie when he started for the city to look for work and when he came back from the fruitless search.

"Did you know that Gabriel is working on the railroad, now? Fireman! Think of it! What a comedown from reading law in Morrison's office. If I were a man, I'd try to have more strength of character than to go to the dogs on account of a girl; an insignificant somebody from Kansas! Even if she is going to marry my brother, I must say it was no way to treat a boy—leading him on, especially a boy like Gabriel, that any girl would have been glad—Well, it's none of my business; only I'm sorry he took it like he did. Drinking himself to death, they say."

That morning, as she was taking up the seams of the silk dress, there was fresh news of Gabriel. He was tired of the railroad, it seemed. He was down on his father's place herding cattle, breaking in colts, drinking like a fish.

"I wouldn't have such a thing on my conscience! Goodness me! I couldn't sleep at nights if I was that girl."

Tante Elodie always listened with a sad, resigned smile. It did not seem to make any difference whether she had Gabriel or not. He had broken her heart and he was killing her. It was not his crime that had broken her heart; it was his indifference to her love and his turning away from her.

It was whispered about that Tante Elodie had grown indifferent to her religion. There was no truth in it. She had not been to confession for two months; but otherwise she followed closely the demands made upon her; redoubling her zeal in church work and attending mass each morning.

At the wedding she was holding quite a little reception of her own in the corner of the gallery. The air was mild and pleasant. Young people flocked about her and occasionally the radiant bride came out to see if she were comfortable and if there was anything she wanted to eat or drink.

A young girl leaning over the railing suddenly exclaimed *"Tiens!* some one is dead. I didn't know any one was sick." She was watching the approach of a man who was coming down the street, distributing, according to the custom of the country, a death notice from door to door.

He wore a long black coat and walked with a measured tread. He was as expressionless as an automaton; handing the little slips of paper at every door; not missing one. The girl, leaning over the railing, went to the head of the stairs to receive the notice when he entered Tante Elodie's gate.

The small, single sheet, which he gave her, was bordered in black and decorated with an old-fashioned wood cut of a weeping willow beside a grave. It was an announcement on the part of Monsieur Justin Lucaze of the death of his only son, Gabriel, who had been instantly killed, the night before, by a fall from his horse.

If the automaton had had any sense of decency, he might have skipped the house of joy, in which there was a wedding feast, in which there was the sound of laughter, the click of glasses, the hum of merry voices, and a vision of sweet women with their thoughts upon love and marriage and earthly bliss. But he had no sense of decency. He was as indifferent and relentless as Death, whose messenger he was.

The sad news, passed from lip to lip, cast a shadow as if a cloud had flitted across the sky. Tante Elodie alone stayed in its shadow. She sank deeper down into the rocker, more shriveled than ever. They all remembered Tante Elodie's romance and respected her grief.

She did not speak any more, or even smile, but wiped her forehead with the old lace handkerchief and sometimes closed her eyes. When she closed her eyes she pictured Gabriel dead, down there on the plantation, with his father watching beside him. He might have betrayed himself had he lived. There was nothing now to betray him. Even the shining gold watch lay deep in a gorged ravine where she had flung it when she once walked through the country alone at dusk.

She thought of her own place down there beside Justin's, all dismantled, with bats beating about the eaves and negroes living under the falling roof.

Tante Elodie did not seem to want to go in doors again. The bride and groom went away. The guests went away, one by one, and all the little children. She stayed there alone in the corner, under the deep shadow of the oaks while the stars came out to keep her company.

A LITTLE COUNTRY GIRL

◈

Ninette was scouring the tin milk-pail with sand and lye-soap, and bringing it to a high polish. She used for that purpose the native scrubbrush, the fibrous root of the palmetto,* which she called *latanier*. The long table on which the tins were ranged, stood out in the yard under a mulberry tree. It was there that the pots and kettles were washed, the chickens, the meats and vegetables cut up and prepared for cooking.

Occasionally a drop of water fell with a faint splash on the shining surface of the tin; whereupon Ninette would wipe it away and carrying the corner of her checked apron up to her eyes, she would wipe them and proceed with her task. For the drops were falling from Ninette's eyes; trickling down her cheeks and sometimes dropping from the end of her nose.

It was all because two disagreeable old people, who had long outlived their youth, no longer believed in the circus as a means of cheering the human heart; nor could they see the use of it.

Ninette had not even mentioned the subject to them. Why should she? She might as well have said: "Grandfather and Grandmother, with your permission and a small advance of fifty cents, I should like, after my work is done, to make a visit to one of the distant planets this afternoon."

It was very warm and Ninette's face was red with heat and ill-humor. Her hair was black and straight and kept falling over her face. It was an untidy length; her grandmother having decided to let it grow, about six months before. She was barefooted and her calico skirt reached a little above her thick, brown ankles.

Even the negroes were all going to the circus. Suzan's daughter, who was known as Black-Gal, had lingered beside the table a moment on her way through the yard.

---

* A low-growing fan-leaved palm.

"You ain't gwine to de suckus?" she inquired with conde-
scension.

"No," and bread-pan went bang on the table.

"We all's goin'. Pap an' Mammy an' all us is goin'," with a
complacent air and a restful pose against the table.

"Where you all goin' to get the money, I like to know."

"Oh, Mr. Ben advance' Mammy a dollar on de crap;* an'
Joe, he got six bits lef' f'om las' pickin'; an' pap sole a ole
no'count plow to Dennis. We all's goin'."

"Joe say he seed 'em pass yonder back Mr. Ben's lane. Dey
a elephant mos' as big as dat corn-crib,† walkin' long des like
he somebody. An' a whole pa'cel wild critters shet up in a
cage. An' all kind o' dogs an' hosses; an' de ladies rarin' an'
pitchin' in red skirts all fill' up wid gole an' diamonds."

"We all's goin'. Did you ax yo' gran'ma? How come you
don't ax yo' gran'pap?"

"That's my business; 'tain't none o' yo's, Black-Gal. You
better be gettin' yonder home, tendin' to yo' work, I think."

"I ain't got no work, 'cep' iron out my pink flounce' dress
fo' de suckus." But she took herself off with an air of lofty contempt, swinging her tattered skirts. It was after that that
Ninette's tears began to drop and spatter.

Resentment rose and rose within her like a leaven,‡ causing her to ferment with wickedness and to make all manner of
diabolical wishes in regard to the circus. The worst of these
was that she wished it would rain.

"I hope to goodness it'll po' down rain; po' down rain; po'
down rain!" She uttered the wish with the air of a young
Medusa pronouncing a blighting curse.

"I like to see 'em all drippin' wet. Black-Gal with her pink
flounces, all drippin' wet." She spoke these wishes in the very
presence of her grandfather and grandmother, for they under-

---

* A gambling game played with two dice.

† A building for storing corn.

‡ A rising agent, such as yeast.

stood not a word of English; and she used that language to express her individual opinion on many occasions.

"What do you say, Ninette?" asked her grandmother. Ninette had brought in the last of the tin pails and was ranging them on a shelf in the kitchen.

"I said I hoped it would rain," she answered, wiping her face and fanning herself with a pie pan as though the oppressive heat had suggested the desire for a change of weather.

"You are a wicked girl," said her grandmother, turning on her, "when you know your grandfather has acres and acres of cotton ready to fall, that the rain would ruin. He's angry enough, too, with every man, woman and child leaving the fields to-day to take themselves off to the village. There ought to be a law to compel them to pick their cotton; those trifling creatures! Ah! it was different in the good old days."

Ninette possessed a sensitive soul, and she believed in miracles. For instance, if she were to go to the circus that afternoon she would consider it a miracle. Hope follows on the heels of Faith. And the white-winged goddess—which is Hope—did not leave her, but prompted her to many little surreptitious acts of preparation in the event of the miracle coming to pass.

She peeped into the clothes-press to see that her gingham dress was where she had folded and left it the Sunday before, after mass. She inspected her shoes and got out a clean pair of stockings which she hid beneath the pillow. In the tin basin behind the house, she scrubbed her face and neck till they were red as a boiled crawfish. And her hair, which was too short to plait, she plastered and tied back with a green ribbon; it stood out in a little bristling, stiff tail.

The noon hour had hardly passed, than an unusual agitation began to be visible throughout the surrounding country. The fields were deserted. People, black and white, began passing along the road in squads and detachments. Ponies were galloping on both sides of the river, carrying two and as many as three, on their backs. Blue and green carts with rampant mules; top-buggies and no-top buggies; family carriages that groaned with age and decrepitude; heavy wagons filled with piccaninnies* made a passing procession that nothing short of a circus in town could have accounted for.

Grandfather Bézeau was too angry to look at it. He retired to the hall, where he sat gloomily reading a two-weeks-old paper. He looked about ninety years old; he was in reality, not more than seventy.

Grandmother Bézeau stayed out on the gallery, apparently to cast ridicule and contempt upon the heedless and extravagant multitude; in reality, to satisfy a womanly curiosity and a natural interest in the affairs of her neighbors.

As for Ninette, she found it difficult to keep her attention fixed upon her task of shelling peas and her inward supplications that something might happen.

Something *did* happen. Jules Perrault, with a family load in his big farm-wagon, stopped before their gate. He handed the reins to one of the children and he, himself, got down and came up to the gallery where Ninette and her grandmother were sitting.

"What's this! what's this!" he cried out in French, "Ninette not going to the circus? not even ready to go?"

"*Par exemple!*" exclaimed the old lady, looking daggers over her spectacles. She was binding the leg of a wounded chicken that squawked and fluttered with terror.

" '*Par exemple*' or no '*par exemple*' she's going and she's going with me; and her grandfather will give her the money. Run in, little one; get ready; make haste, we shall be late." She looked appealingly at her grandmother who said nothing, being ashamed to say what she felt in the face of her neighbor, Perrault, of whom she stood a little in awe. Ninette, taking silence for consent, darted into the house to get ready.

And when she came out, wonder of wonders! There was her grandfather taking his purse from his pocket. He was drawing it out slowly and painfully, with a hideous grimace, as though it were some vital organ that he was extracting. What

---

* Pejorative slang meaning small black children.

arguments could Mons. Perrault have used! They were surely
convincing. Ninette had heard them in wordy discussion as
she nervously laced her shoes; dabbed her face with flour;
hooked the gingham dress; and balanced upon her head a
straw "flat"* whose roses looked as though they had stayed out
over night in a frost.

But no triumphant queen on her throne could have presented a more beaming and joyful countenance than did
Ninette when she ascended and seated herself in the big
wagon in the midst of the Perrault family. She at once took
the baby from Mme. Perrault and held it and felt supremely
happy.

The more the wagon jolted and bounced, the more did it
convey to her a sense of reality; and less did it seem like a
dream. They passed Black-Gal and her family in the road,
trudging ankle-deep in dust. Fortunately the girl was barefooted; though the pink flounces were all there, and she carried a green parasol. Her mother was *semi-décolletée*† and her
father wore a heavy winter coat; while Joe had secured piece-
meal, a species of cake-walk‡ costume for the occasion. It was
with a feeling of lofty disdain that Ninette passed and left the
Black-Gal family in a cloud of dust.

Even after they reached the circus grounds, which were
just outside the the village, Ninette continued to carry the
baby. She would willingly have carried three babies, had such
a thing been possible. The infant took a wild and noisy interest in the merry-go-round with its hurdy-gurdy§ accompaniment. Oh! that she had had more money! that she might have

---

* A flat hat.

† Wearing a somewhat low-cut dress.

‡ Gaudy, brightly colored clothing, an allusion to an African-
American tradition in which lavishly dressed couples promenade in
competition for a cake.

§ A musical instrument that makes a droning sound, played by turning a handle with one hand while pressing keys with the other.

mounted one of those flying horses and gone spinning round in a whirl of ecstasy!

There were side-shows, too. She would have liked to see the lady who weighed six hundred pounds and the gentleman who tipped the scales at fifty. She would have wanted to peep in at the curious monster, captured after a desperate struggle in the wilds of Africa. Its picture, in red and green on the flapping canvas, was surely not like anything she had ever seen or even heard of.

The lemonade was tempting: the pop-corn, the peanuts, the oranges were delights that she might only gaze upon and sigh for. Mons. Perrault took them straight to the big tent, bought the tickets and entered.

Ninette's pulses were thumping with excitement. She sniffed the air, heavy with the smell of saw-dust and animals, and it lingered in her nostrils like some delicious odor. Sure enough! There was the elephant which Black-Gal had described. A chain was about his ponderous leg and he kept reaching out his trunk for tempting morsels. The wild creatures were all there in cages, and the people walked solemnly around, looking at them; awed by the unfamiliarity of the scene.

Ninette never forgot that she had the baby in her arms. She talked to it, and it listened and looked with round, staring eyes. Later on she felt as if she were a person of distinction assisting at some royal pageant when the be-spangled Knights and Ladies in plumes and flowing robes went prancing round on their beautiful horses.

The people all sat on the circus benches and Ninette's feet hung down, because an irritable old lady objected to having them thrust into the small of her back. Mme. Perrault offered to take the baby, but Ninette clung to it. It was something to which she might communicate her excitement. She squeezed it spasmodically when her emotions became uncontrollable.

"Oh! *bébé*! I believe I'm goin' to split my sides! Oh, la! la! if gran'ma could see that, I know she'd laugh herse'f sick." It was none other than the clown who was producing this agreeable impression upon Ninette. She had only to look at his chalky face to go into contortions of mirth.

No one had noticed a gathering obscurity, and the ominous growl of thunder made every one start with disappointment or apprehension. A flash and a second clap, that was like a crash, followed. It came just as the ring-master was cracking his whip with a "hip-la! hip-la!" at the bare-back rider, and the clown was standing on his head. There was a sinister roar; a terrific stroke of the wind; the center pole swayed and snapped; the great canvas swelled and beat the air with bellowing resistance.

Pandemonium reigned. In the confusion Ninette found herself down beneath piled-up benches. Still clutching the baby, she proceeded to crawl out of an opening in the canvas. She stayed huddled up against the fallen tent, thinking her end had come, while the baby shrieked lustily.

The rain poured in sheets. The cries and howls of the frightened animals were like unearthly sounds. Men called and shouted; children screamed; women went into hysterics and the negroes were having fits.

Ninette got on her knees and prayed God to keep her and the baby and everyone from injury and to take them safely home. It was thus that Mons. Perrault discovered her and the baby, half covered by the fallen tent.

She did not seem to recover from the shock. Days afterward, Ninette was going about in a most unhappy frame of mind, with a wretched look upon her face. She was often discovered in tears.

When her condition began to grow monotonous and depressing, her grandmother insisted upon knowing the cause of it. Then it was that she confessed her wickedness and claimed the guilt of having caused the terrible catastrophe at the circus.

It was her fault that a horse had been killed; it was her fault if an old gentleman had had a collar-bone broken and a lady an arm dislocated. She was the cause of several persons hav-

ing been thrown into fits and hysterics. All her fault! She it
was who had called the rain down upon their heads and thus
had she been punished!

It was a very delicate matter for Grandmother Bézeau to
pronounce upon—far too delicate. So the next day she went
and explained it all to the priest and got him to come over and
talk to Ninette.

The girl was at the table under the mulberry tree peeling
potatoes when the priest arrived. He was a jolly little man who
did not like to take things too seriously. So he advanced over
the short, tufted grass, bowing low to the ground and making
deep salutations with his hat.

"I am overwhelmed," he said, "at finding myself in the
presence of the wonderful Magician! who has but to call
upon the rain and down it comes. She whistles for the wind
and—there it is! Pray, what weather will you give us this afternoon, fair Sorceress?"

Then he became serious and frowning, straightened himself and rapped his stick upon the table.

"What foolishness is this I hear? look at me; look at me!"
for she was covering her face, "and who are you, I should like
to know, that you dare think you can control the elements!"

Well, they made a great deal of fuss of Ninette and she felt
ashamed.

But Mons. Perrault came over; he understood best of all.
He took grandmother and grandfather aside and told them
the girl was morbid from staying so much with old people,
and never associating with those of her own age. He was
very impressive and convincing. He frightened them, for he
hinted vaguely at terrible consequences to the child's intellect.

He must have touched their hearts, for they both consented to let her go to a birthday party over at his house the
following day. Grandfather Bézeau even declared that *if it
was necessary* he would contribute toward providing her with
a suitable toilet for the occasion.

INSPIRED BY *THE AWAKENING*

❧

KATE CHOPIN LIVED AND thought well ahead of her time. Known initially as a "local colorist" and a writer of short stories in the style of Maupassant, she eventually amassed a significant body of work and left a legacy that has only recently been realized. Chopin's many stories display her natural craft as a writer, but it is *The Awakening* (1899) that dramatically presents her modern views about an individual woman's need for fulfillment and the role of women in society. Widely and viciously panned by critics, the novel found a sparse audience when it was first published. After being reprinted once in 1906, it went out of print for more than five decades.

Then, in the latter half of the twentieth century, Chopin's work was resurrected as the world finally caught up to her. *The Awakening* resurfaced in the 1960s and 1970s during the revival of the women's movement, as women's writing began to enjoy wider exposure and acclaim. The novel's fiercely independent heroine, Edna Pontellier, inspired a new generation of readers to herald Chopin as a premiere, even prescient, voice of feminism. In *The Awakening*, Edna breaks with the spiritual and intellectual mores to which women in her society are traditionally bound, eventually going so far as to free herself from the physical bonds of life itself.

Edna boldly betrays the social contract, which dictates strict familial commitment, marital fidelity, and sexual passivity for women. Despite the fact that Chopin did not consider herself a feminist or a suffragist, finding such labels inhibiting and contradictory to the larger freedom she sought, in this character Chopin delivered a model for strong women to emulate. Additionally, she foreshadowed a sexual liberation that was nearly unthinkable in her own time, but one that would help shape the lives of women for years to come.

Chopin's writing is also remarkable for its humanity. All of her characters—men and women, white and black—are made vivid through speech and action; she simultaneously strives to reproduce authentic dialect and to reveal the soul of a character through his or her actions. Chopin's treatment of African-American characters in particular reveals a sensitivity no writer could express who was not attuned to the individuality and dignity of her characters.

Chopin's focus on strong characters and their humanity may be what has given her work such endurance. The latter half of the twentieth century saw a resurgence of interest in all of it—more than 100 novels, short stories, and poems—and *The Awakening* has become a paradigm of feminist literature that now appears on the required reading lists of college courses across the country.

COMMENTS & QUESTIONS

❦

In this section, we aim to provide the reader with an array of perspectives on the text, as well as questions that challenge those perspectives. The commentary has been culled from sources as diverse as reviews contemporaneous with the work, letters written by the author, literary criticism of later generations, and appreciations written throughout history. Following the commentary, a series of questions seeks to filter Kate Chopin's The Awakening *through a variety of points of view and bring about a richer understanding of this enduring work.*

Comments

ST. LOUIS GLOBE-DEMOCRAT

[*The Awakening*] is not a healthy book; if it points any particular moral or teaches any lesson, the fact is not apparent. But there is no denying the fact that it deals with existent conditions, and without attempting a solution, handles a problem that obtrudes itself only too frequently in the social life of people with whom the question of food and clothing is not the all absorbing one. . . . It is a morbid book, and the thought suggests itself that the author herself would probably like nothing better than to "tear it to pieces" by criticism if only some other person had written it.

—May 13, 1899

TIMES-HERALD

Kate Chopin, author of those delightful sketches, "A Night in Acadie," has made a new departure in her long story, "The Awakening." The many admirers whom she has won by her earlier work will be surprised—perhaps disagreeably—by this latest venture. That the book is strong and that Miss Chopin has a keen knowledge of certain phases of feminine character will not be denied. But it was not necessary for a writer of so great refinement and poetic grace to enter the overworked field of sex fiction.

—Chicago (June 1, 1899)

WILLA CATHER

A Creole *Bovary* is this little novel of Miss Chopin's. Not that the heroine is a Creole exactly, or that Miss Chopin is a Flaubert—save the mark!—but the theme is similar to that which occupied Flaubert. There was, indeed, no need that a second *Madame Bovary* should be written, but an author's choice of themes is frequently as inexplicable as his choice of a wife. It is governed by some innate temperamental bias that cannot be diagrammed. This is particularly so in women who write, and I shall not attempt to say why Miss Chopin has devoted so exquisite and sensitive, well-governed a style to so trite and sordid a theme. . . . Edna Pontellier and Emma Bovary are studies in the same feminine type; one a finished and complete portrayal, the other a hasty sketch, but the theme is essentially the same. Both women belong to a class, not large, but forever clamoring in our ears, that demands more romance out of life than God put into it. Mr. G. Bernard Shaw would say that they are the victims of the over-idealization of love. They are the spoil of the poets, the Iphigenias of sentiment. The unfortunate feature of their disease is that it attacks only women of brains, at least of rudimentary brains, but whose development is one-sided; women of strong and fine intuitions, but without the faculty of observation, comparison, reasoning about things. Probably, for emotional people, the most convenient thing about being able to think is that it occasionally gives them a rest from feeling. Now with women of the Bovary type, this relaxation and recreation is impossible. They are not critics of life, but, in the most personal sense, partakers of life. They receive impressions through the fancy. With them everything begins with fancy, and passions rise in the brain rather than in the blood, the poor, neglected, limited one-sided brain that might do so much better things than badgering itself into frantic endeavors to love. For these are the people who pay with their blood for the fine ideals of the poets, as Marie Delclasse paid for Dumas's great creation, Marguerite Gauthier. These people really expect the passion of love to fill and gratify every need of life, whereas nature only intended that it should meet one of many demands. They insist upon making it stand for all the emotional pleasures of life and art; expecting an individual and self-limited passion to yield infinite variety, pleasure, and distraction, to contribute to their lives what the arts and the pleasurable exercise of the intellect gives to less limited and less intense idealists. So this passion, when set up against Shakespeare, Balzac, Wagner, Raphael, fails them. They have staked everything on one hand, and they lose. They have driven the blood until it will drive no further, they have played their nerves up to the point where any relaxation short of absolute annihilation is impossible. Every idealist abuses his nerves, and every sentimentalist brutally abuses them. And in the end, the nerves get even. Nobody ever cheats them, really. Then "the awakening" comes. Sometimes it comes in the form of arsenic, as it came to Emma Bovary, sometimes it is carbolic acid taken covertly in the police station, a goal to which unbalanced idealism not infrequently leads. Edna Pontellier, fanciful and romantic to the last, chose the sea on a summer night and went down with the sound of her first lover's spurs in her ears, and the scent of pinks about her. And next time I hope that Miss Chopin will devote that flexible iridescent style of hers to a better cause.

—from the Pittsburgh *Leader* (July 8, 1899)

Questions

1. Are the *Globe-Democrat* and the *Times-Herald* reacting against Chopin's treatment of her subject or the subject matter itself?

2. The critics above assert that a writer of Chopin's talent should have chosen a more appropriate subject matter. Are

talent as a writer and choice of subject matter so easily separable?

3. Willa Cather says that Edna Pontellier, like Emma Bovary, is one of those people who "really expect the passion of love to fill and gratify every need of life" and that she is a victim "of the over-idealization of love." Does the text of *The Awakening* justify that description of Edna Pontellier?

4. Are Edna Pontellier's dissatisfactions the product of (a) her individual personality—that is, she's spoiled; (b) her particular circumstances—that is, her husband is a drag; (c) the situation of middle-class women of the time—that is, she is given comfort in exchange for self-determination and freedom; or (d) human nature and the human condition, which generate longings they cannot satisfy?

5. Even her detractors praise Kate Chopin's style. Describe its characteristics. Is it dated? Chopin does not fill up her scenes with inventories of concrete detail. Does she lack interest in material actuality? Or is she simply a poor observer?

FOR FURTHER READING

❦

Biography

Rankin, Daniel S. *Kate Chopin and Her Creole Stories.* Philadelphia: University of Pennsylvania Press, 1932.

Seyersted, Per. *Kate Chopin: A Critical Biography.* Baton Rouge: Louisiana State University Press, 1969.

Toth, Emily Rines. *Unveiling Kate Chopin.* Jackson: University Press of Mississippi, 1999.

Walker, Nancy. *Kate Chopin: A Literary Life.* New York: Palgrave, 2001.

Critical Works

Barrish, Phillip. *"The Awakening's* Signifying 'Mexicanist' Presence." *Studies in American Fiction* 28:1 (Spring 2000), pp. 65–76.

Beer, Janet. *Kate Chopin, Edith Wharton, and Charlotte Perkins Gilman: Studies in Short Fiction.* New York: St. Martin's Press, 1997.

Bimbaum, Michelle A. " 'Alien Hands': Kate Chopin and the Colonization of Race." *American Literature* 66:2 (1994), pp. 301–323.

Culley, Margo. *The Awakening: An Authoritative Text, Contexts, Criticism.* New York: W. W. Norton, 1994.

Delbanco, Andrew. "The Half-Life of Edna Pontellier." In *New Essays on* The Awakening, edited by Wendy Martin. Cambridge and New York: Cambridge University Press, 1988, pp. 89–108.

Dimock, Wai-Chee. "Kate Chopin." In *Modern American Women Writers*, edited by Elaine Showalter, Leah Baechler, and A. Walton Litz. New York: Collier Books, 1993.

DeKoven, Marianne. "Gendered Doubleness and the 'Origins of Modernist Form." *Tulsa Studies in Women's Literature* 8 (1989), pp. 19–42.

Fox-Genovese, Elizabeth. "Kate Chopin's Awakening." *Southern Studies* (1979), pp. 261–290.

Gilbert, Sandra. "The Second Coming of Aphrodite: Kate Chopin's Fantasy of Desire." *Kenyon Review* 5:3 (1983), pp. 42–66.

Gilmore, Michael T. "Revolt Against Nature: The Problematic Modernism of *The Awakening.*" In *New Essays on* The Awakening, pp. 59–88.

McCullough, Ken. *Regions of Identity: The Construction of America in Women's Fiction, 1885–1914.* Stanford: Stanford University Press, 1999.

Petry, Alice Hall, ed. *Critical Essays on Kate Chopin.* New York: G. K. Hall/Simon and Schuster, 1996.

Pizer, Donald. "A Note on Kate Chopin's *The Awakening* as Naturalist Fiction." *Southern Literary Journal* 33:2 (Spring 2001), pp. 5–13.

Rowe, John Carlos. "The Economics of the Body in Kate Chopin's *The Awakening.*" In *Kate Chopin Reconsidered: Beyond the Bayou,* edited by Lynda S. Boren and Sara deSaussure Davis. Baton Rouge: Louisiana State University Press, 1992.

Showalter, Elaine. "Tradition and the Female Talent: *The Awakening* as a Solitary Book." In *New Essays on* The Awakening, pp. 33–58.

Walker, Nancy. The Awakening: *A Case Study in Contemporary Criticism.* Second edition. New York: Bedford / St. Martin's, 2000.

Works Cited in the Introduction:
Reviews of *The Awakening*

"*The Awakening*." *The Nation* 69 (August 3, 1899), p. 96.

Deyo, Charles L. Review of *The Awakening*. *St. Louis Post-Dispatch* (May 20, 1899), p. 4.

Review of *The Awakening* from "100 Books for Summer." *New York Times Saturday Review of Books and Art* (June 24, 1899), p. 408.

Review of *The Awakening*. *Public Opinion* 26 (June 22, 1899), p. 794.

"Mrs. Chopin's 'Night in Acadie.'" *The Critic* 29 (April 16, 1898), p. 266.

"A *Night in Acadie*." *St. Louis Post-Dispatch* (December 11, 1897), p. 4.